Born in Tonawanda New York, grew up in a small little village called Wilson, New York right on Lake Ontario. I have always loved to read and writing is a passion. In ninth grade my love of writing exploded and I was placed in charge of the school's literary magazine, which for a freshman is a huge deal. I have many different jobs but none as amazing as becoming an author, except for the one I carry every day which of course is being a mother of five amazing kids and a grandmother to two going on three granddaughters.

The Story of Faline

Nicholette De'Lac

The Story of Faline

Vanguard Press

VANGUARD PAPERBACK

© Copyright 2024
Nicholette De'Lac

The right of Nicholette De'Lac to be identified as author of
this work has been asserted by her in accordance with the
Copyright, Designs and Patents Act 1988.

All Rights Reserved

No reproduction, copy or transmission of this publication
may be made without written permission.
No paragraph of this publication may be reproduced,
copied or transmitted save with the written permission of the publisher, or
in accordance with the provisions
of the Copyright Act 1956 (as amended).

Any person who commits any unauthorised act in relation to
this publication may be liable to criminal
prosecution and civil claims for damages.

A CIP catalogue record for this title is
available from the British Library.

ISBN 978-1-80016-573-1

This is a work of fiction. Names, characters, businesses, places, events and incidents are either the products of the author's imagination or used in a fictitious manner. Any resemblance to actual persons, living or dead, or actual events is purely coincidental.

*Vanguard Press is an imprint of
Pegasus Elliot Mackenzie Publishers Ltd.*
www.pegasuspublishers.com

First Published in 2024

**Vanguard Press
Sheraton House Castle Park
Cambridge England**

Printed & Bound in Great Britain

My book is dedicated to my family and friends who never gave up on me or let me give up on myself.

Prologue

Centuries ago when kings ruled the lands, various gods and goddesses were worshipped, dragons were said to take to the skies and one ever knew what to expect when traveling through the woods. There could be anything lying among the trees: fairies, sprites, witches, trolls, and if you were lucky, you may even see a unicorn prancing through the lush parts of the forest. Or so it was said in the stories that were told to the small children. The unicorns protected pieces of the forest, and you knew they were there because everything was so beautiful, the wild life was plentiful, and no harm befell that part of the land. This was also a time when the kings that ruled wanted to make sure that they were the "only" king. They had no interest in sharing their claims to the world with anyone else, especially not another self-proclaimed king.

So, great battles often happened throughout the lands, destroying everything in their path with their fires and great armies, driving everything and everyone away. There were a lot of mangled and scarred remnants of what was after they finished their pillaging and warmongering through the great wilderness and valleys. The people living in most of these areas didn't have the means or the provisions to be able to protect themselves very well. They weren't knights or trained to fight the way the warriors that came stomping through their quaint villages were. So they either were killed amid the battles or they fled to try and find another safe place to call home.

The way things were with the random burning of villages, slaughtering of men women and children, and the mass destruction going on everywhere, there weren't very many places left that were safe. Every part of the world it seemed was being governed and abused by one king or another. Currently, there were three kings. There was Balthazar in the west, Silas in the north and Martin in the east. There was no king in the south, and frankly, the people preferred it that way. The claim was that the south was guarded by some unknown force, and not even Balthazar, as nasty and powerful as he was, wanted to try and tackle something he knew nothing about. Spirits were a force to be reckoned with, no matter how powerful you thought you were.

That's the way it's been since anyone can remember, and no one could ever imagine it changing. Three kings to challenge the world and the only safe place to dwell unscathed by their wars was in the south, with whatever the unknown thing was there guarding it. Even though travelling into an unknown section of the world, with an unknown entity was a frightening thought, you took your chances knowing there was a freedom to be had. It was far less frightening than going to tuck your babies into bed and not knowing if that would be the night some travelling band of knights was going to come and kill you all.

Our story begins in a lush valley surrounded by great forests, bisected by wide fresh running streams, cattle and sheep grazing the grasslands among the quiet and peaceful village built of wooden huts. The folk who lived there loved their valley home. On any given day you could walk out of your front door and smell the sweet scent of the wild flowers floating across the breeze through the belly of the valley. Everyone got along except for a few silly spats over trifles, like a chicken having gone missing without explanation. No one wanted to make claims to whatever beasts may be in the forest. It was too scary a thought for them, some random beast eating their animals, so they blamed someone in the village instead. Simple problems among people, all just trying to live their lives the best they knew how. Everyone in the village had his or her own job, whether it was sewing, crafting, making bows and arrows for hunting, etc. Most everyone had migrated from somewhere else and each was able to do many different things. This came in handy when someone else became ill or was tending to their newborn child. For a long while this peaceful little valley was just that, peaceful. The wars of the kings didn't seem to want to come there and they all felt safe. Like anywhere else however, nothing ever stayed that way, they would eventually come to learn.

Chapter 1

The Child is Born

One sunny afternoon the people were out tending the fields and feeding their animals. It was a gorgeous day. The sun was shining brightly and a soft warm breeze blew through the trees and the long grasses, filling the air with the sweet smells of summer. Everyone was in a great mood. There was one couple who were expecting to have their first baby any time now. Drake and his wife Lacey had been some of the first people to start their lives living in the valley.

Lacey, a raven-haired, green-eyed woman with a soft complexion and medium build, had been brought to the valley by her father Jonas when she was thirteen after her village had been burned to the ground by King Balthazar's army. Her mother had been killed before they could get safely out, leaving Jonas to tend to her on his own and he felt he had done a grand job of raising her. He taught her everything he knew about everything from crafting and wielding different types of weapons, to farming and raising animals, and naturally to be an honest, hard working young lady.

At fifteen, Drake was, a blonde haired, blue eyed, strapping young man who had already been living in the valley with his mother and father and he fell in love with the dark haired beauty the instant he laid eyes on her. It didn't take long for the boy to convince Jonas that he was the perfect match for his Lacey. He was a hard working honest young man with a ton of potential. They were married as soon as Lacey turned sixteen, and while they waited the pair were inseparable. It was a match meant to be.

They had tried for a long time to have a child and were finally successful after five years of hardship and disappointment. They were so overwhelmed with excitement they could hardly contain themselves. It was a long wait to get to the end, and as the day drew near when they knew their pride and joy was going to be in the world with them, it was all they could do just to get through each passing day with the anticipation that he or she would be here.

"Lacey," Jonas said as calm as he could walking to the side of the house where Lacey was feeding the chickens, "you need to be inside resting, not out here working."

"I know, I know" she said anxiously "but I can't seem to stop. I am so nervous and excited and…."

"It isn't good for you or the baby to be out and about on your feet working all day," Jonas said plainly.

"Your father is right, my love." as he lovingly placed a hand on her belly. "You really ought to go inside and rest." Lacey tossed the rest of the chicken feed onto the ground and huffed off towards the house, stopping only for a second to whip her head around and give a small glare at both her father and her husband. She then made her way into the house and smacked the little makeshift wooden door shut.

"Ouch." Drake grimaced.

"Drake, she has been hard headed since the day she was born, you ought to know that by now." chuckled Jonas. "She'll be fine after she takes a good nap." He smiled at Drake and turned to go and make sure that she was in fact lying down and not attempting house chores, mumbling about her stubbornness along the way. Drake sighed and went back to finish splitting the firewood so he could gather some produce from the fields.

Inside Jonas found his daughter washing dishes, mumbling under her breath about how she didn't feel tired and she couldn't see how the task of feeding chickens was too stressful. Jonas walked over to her and gently laid a hand on her shoulder.

"Lacey." Jonas said softly, "we are only trying to look out for the best interests of you and the baby." Lacey turned around without hiding the looks of frustration and anxiety in her eyes.

"Father, I am not a small child, I don't care to be told what to do, and if you and Drake feel like you could have done this any better than I have…" she trailed off tears coming to her eyes and buried her head into her father's shoulder. "I'm just so scared," she sobbed. "I have waited so long and been through so much to get here, I just don't know how to relax."

Jonas sighed and smiled gently. "I know, we all know. It's going to be all right, but you really need to take it easy." Jonas pulled his daughter's face away from the crook in his arm where it was buried and looked her in the eyes, his face soft and his eyes bright. "Everything is going to be okay. It's almost time and we will be right here with you." Giving his daughter one last all-knowing fatherly look, he gave her a big hug and scooted her to the back of the little wooden hut to her bed. "Now just rest for a little while that's all. You are not being confined in here," he chuckled, "just rest a little."

Lacey wiped the remaining tears from her eyes and agreed that she might need to lie down for just a few minutes. "Want me to tuck you in?" Jonas asked half joking.

"Very funny," Lacey said smiling up at her father. Once Jonas was sure she wasn't going to get back up, he gave her one last smile and "sweet dreams", before turning and leaving the room.

Jonas sat inside quietly thinking to himself of all the good times he and Lacey had shared while she was growing up. Raising a daughter alone hadn't been easy. He had only had brothers, so a girl was out of his range of knowledge. He remembered the fire, the screaming of people and animals alike when King Balthazar's army marched on their village. He saw visions of his beloved wife Aggie trying to get away, but one of the soldiers in their black armour with the golden dragon embossed on it, shot an arrow and it found his poor Aggie's heart. He knew there was nothing he could do and trying to go back would surely have got him and his daughter killed. So he took Lacey and ran for the forest on the edge of the village. The two had found a dense thicket in which to hide, that the soldiers didn't find them. Lacey had told him then that everything was going to be all right, and now he would get to make sure that for her, everything WAS all right.

"How blessed are we, Aggie?" Jonas began saying softly to himself "to have a daughter as wonderful and intelligent as our Lacey. I'd have never lasted this long without her." Jonas sat in the little chair quietly for a few minutes more, reflecting on his life and how he felt so fortunate before Drake came in with a few baskets of fruit and vegetables.

"How's she doing?" Drake asked Jonas with a concerned look on his face as he set the baskets down on the floor.

"Well..." replied Jonas, "she's resting now, after a little pushing on my end to get her to do it. I came in to find her muttering to herself and attempting to clean." He laughed gently and shook his head before looking at Drake and telling him that all would be fine.

"I hope so." said Drake quietly. "She would be devastated if something happened now that we have come so far. And I wouldn't blame her at all." Drake turned his head away to hide the tears that had begun to well up in his eyes, took a deep breath and began organising the produce he had brought in.

Once he had finished Drake sat across from Jonas and they submerged themselves in a quiet conversation about farming, animals, the weather, and anything else they could talk about to pass the time while Lacey slept. Suddenly, there was a scream from where Lacey had been resting. Both men leapt up and ran to Lacey. They found her doubled over in the bed sweating and writhing in pain.

"Lacey! Lacey! What's happening?" said Drake half shouting and half crying.

"It's ... Coming..." Lacey was barely able to say through clenched teeth.

Jonas who had taken a seat on the edge of the bed next to his daughter held her hand. He looked up at Drake and told him to hurry and get Margo. Drake nodded and hastily ran for the door not stopping to close it on his way through. He hurried up the dirt path as fast as his shaking legs could take him until he made it to Margo's door. He tried not to beat on the door when knocking, but his nerves were getting the better of him and he slammed his fist on the door until she answered. Margo, a short, round, older woman with streaks of grey running through her brown hair, opened the door to find a shaking, sweating, panicked Drake on the other side.

"It's time!" he stammered looking down at the woman.

Margo's brown eyes lit up and she went back into the little hut and grabbed a small bag before following Drake back down the dirt path. When they reached the wooden hut of the expecting parents, Margo instructed Drake to start a fire and get some water boiling immediately. She then walked into the bedroom and looked at the poor woman on the bed trying not to panic.

"Jonas," Margo said calmly "get me a bunch of fresh linens." Jonas nodded and did as she asked. Margo looked down at Lacey and put a hand to her forehead.

"You're starting to run a fever, child, you need to try and control your breathing, and as much as I know it hurts, try and relax a little."

Lacey with no sense of time or space was breathing heavily but gave a quick nod to the woman who she knew was there to deliver the baby. Her teeth clenched, sobbing and trying to do as the woman asked, she rolled onto her back and drew up her knees trying in vain to control her breathing.

"Margo…it's so hard… I am in so much pain!" Lacey panted.

"I know, child. I am here, and you are going to be fine if you do as I say." The little woman smiled down at Lacey despite knowing that if she didn't calm herself, Lacey could put herself and the baby in distress. After what felt like an eternity to Lacey, Drake and Jonas came running back into the room with the items that Margo had requested.

"Good," said Margo. "Put the linens on the table here and the pot of water by the side of the bed."

They did as they were instructed and stepped back to give Margo room to work. She started immediately to put linens into the pot and retrieving items from her bag. She turned and looked at the two shaking men standing behind her and told them they needed to leave. Lacey who was gasping for air tried to deny Margo's request, but Margo insisted.

"She is hyperventilating, feverish and it's affecting the delivery. I'm sorry but you both need to leave and let me do my job." Hesitantly, they took one last look at the now shaking, sweating woman in the bed, then left the room and took seats as close to the door as they could.

After what seemed like an eternity to both men, who were by now white knuckling the arms of their chairs listening to the screams of their beloved Lacey coming from beyond the door, they heard Margo scream over the top of Lacey.

"PUSH LACEY! PUSH NOW!"

There was a loud screaming groan, then silence. The two men glanced at one another, sweating bullets, eyes wide, before jumping up and staring at the door. A few seconds later, they heard two small smacks and the most beautiful sound they had ever heard…a baby began to cry. They turned to one another and began to cry before they hugged one another, sighing with relief. Drake put his face into his hands and dropped to his knees thanking the gods that their wishes had finally been granted.

Jonas looked at his son-in-law and said as calmly as he could, "We aren't out of the woods yet. We must wait and see how mother and child are doing before we believe that all is well."

Drake stood back up and nodded. He paced the floor while he waited, glancing at the door where he knew his wife and new baby were, trying not to tremble all over. Several minutes later Margo opened the door. She was wiping her hands on one of the linens from the water. She was red in the face and had sweat across her brow. Looking at the men, she slowly let out a gentle smile.

"Lacey is going to be all right. She needs a lot of bed rest right now due to her fever and panic attacks during delivery which caused her a great deal of added stress. Quite frankly, it was a little iffy towards the end, but she is a strong girl and made it through just fine."

"Oh, thank the gods!" Drake cried out. "What about the baby? Is it a boy? Girl? All fingers and toes?"

"The baby is going to be fine." Margo grinned. "She was stuck in the canal for a little bit, so she was without oxygen, but not enough to cause any kind of fatal or permanent damage."

Jonas and Drake looked at one another and a grin spread across each man's face like a wildfire taking over the dry grass in the fields. They were beyond containing themselves, as Margo had just informed them that it was a girl.

"It's a girl!" Jonas shouted. "I am a grandfather of a healthy baby girl!" He threw his arms in the air and spun in a small circle, thanking the gods for his luck.

"Can I go see them Margo? I mean… can we see them?" Drake said quickly, making a move for the door but stopping to make sure it was safe and all right with the little woman standing before him.

"Give her a little time to rest first, and let me explain something to you both," Margo said with an air of pride and concern in her voice.

Reluctantly, they agreed. Drake snatched another chair and offered it to Margo. who spent a few minutes cleaning up a little more of the sweat and blood from her hands, arms, and face; birthing babies is not a clean job. Jonas offered her something to drink and eat, which she readily accepted.

Taking a glass of water and biting into an apple, she sat and organised her thoughts for a moment. She then turned to Drake with a concerned motherly like look on her face.

"Drake, do you remember when you were younger, the stories your parents would tell you before you slept?" she asked.

Drake sat for a moment and searched the archives of his mind. "Sort of," he began. "I remember the stories of the unicorns protecting the forests, the fairies that helped the lands stay fertile, witches looming in the dark places in the world." He ran a hand through his hair and looked between Jonas and Margo. "Are those what you are referring to?"

Jonas had heard these stories as well since they came to live in the small village in the valley. He had also heard a plethora more and looked confused for a moment before the look on Margo's face almost gave away where she intended to take this discussion.

"Well, yes and no," she sad. "As much as I believe all of those things to be true, even though I myself have never seen them, I want to know if you remember the story of the prophecy."

After saying the words aloud Margo looked as if she had swallowed a large lump in her throat. Drake and Jonas's eyes became very wide, and they sat there staring at her with a look of disbelief on their faces.

"Okay," said Margo with a sense of urgency and almost seeming elated at the same time. "The prophecy speaks of a child born into nothing that will take everything, either in the name of peace or destruction. This child will bear a birth mark like the shape of a lion's head, which will be the meaning of strength, courage and the ability to communicate with animals. The child will be born with the hair as dark as a raven and eyes as blue as the ocean and will either be loved or feared by all depending on the path he or she chooses to take. This child is either our saviour finally reuniting all the lands or the one who will put all the lands into darkness."

Margo paused for a moment looking between the two men who had let their mouths hang open in awe as she spoke. They had been sitting there listening intently to the woman's story, not sure if she was trying to tell them that Lacey had just birthed the champion of the world.

She cleared her throat after sipping her water and very matter of fact said, "With what I have seen of your new child, I believe her to be the one from the prophecy and you must do everything in your power to keep her in the light."

"So, you are saying that my new born baby daughter already has a destiny? One that could potentially get her killed, and I am supposed to sit back and say, OH YES! Please let my daughter go out and try not to die while saving the world from itself..." Drake said almost mocking the woman. "My parents used to tell me tons of crazy stories when I was a boy. I have never seen a witch or a fairy or a... a... unicorn ever in my whole life! This is crazy!"

He slumped forward a little and put a hand to his forehead trying not to over react. Jonas reached out and put a hand on his shoulder.

"Margo, as interesting as that sounds, and as much as I am sure everyone everywhere would love to see this prophecy fulfilled, isn't it possible that it's just a story?" Jonas said his voice shaking a little.

"Of course." said Margo seeming displeased with the lack of respect she felt this tale deserved. "Of course it could be just a story. And if it's not?" she asked Jonas.

"Well..." Jonas began "I suppose we will just have to wait and see what happens. No sense rushing into getting all sorts of people's hopes up for nothing."

Margo nodded her head and extended a small polite apology to Drake before getting up to go back and check on her patient one more time. Drake smiled telling her he meant no offence, he was just not convinced that any of these things were real. He was a 'need to see it to believe it' kind of guy. She smiled at him and patted his head, then turned around and went to look in on Lacey. After she had closed the door, Drake turned and looked to Jonas who had sat down with a nice plump red apple and a glass of milk.

"Do you believe all that stuff Jonas? I mean really believe it?" Drake questioned.

Jonas swallowed his bite of apple and looked at Drake with a soft smile. "I do and I don't. As you said it is hard to believe in things that you cannot see, but in the same token, hope is not something to be left in the background of your mind either."

Drake sighed and sat back in his chair. "I don't know." he said. "I just want Lacey and I to raise and love our daughter. I guess we should let the fates do as they please."

"That is exactly what you should do." Jonas replied with a smile. "Raise her, love her, and teach her everything you know about everything. Lacey and I will teach her all we know as well. She will grow up knowing she is loved and will have the knowledge she needs to survive like we do. That's all you can offer a child as a father. Trust me, I know."

He gave a wink and motioned his head towards the door where Lacey was. Both men laughed and waited until Margo said it was time for the two of them to go and see their family. A few minutes later she returned to the door with a bright smile on her face and motioned for them to enter.

"Both of them still need plenty of rest, so don't linger too long." she told them sternly. "For now I will take my leave. I will come back again tomorrow to check on them and make sure everything is going smoothly."

Drake shook the woman's hand and thanked her for all that she had done. Jonas followed suit and both said farewell and turned to enter Lacey's room. Drake pulled two chairs up to the side of the bed for Jonas and himself to sit on. He sat down and took Lacey's free hand into his and smiled at her.

"Lacey, I'm here with you," Drake said lovingly to his wife. "You did so great. Your father and I are so proud of you."

"The baby is beautiful, my sweet girl," Jonas said quietly. "I am indeed very proud."

Lacey stirred in her bed and turned her head, slowly opening her eyes and looking upon the two men sitting by her side. She briefly managed a gentle smile and sighed. She was tired beyond compare and both men knew it. Every inch of her showed the trials she had just undergone having birthed the baby. After a few minutes of sitting in silence and simply looking upon one another Lacey began to speak. She was so quiet because of her exhaustion that it made both men lean in to hear her properly.

"Drake, my love, I am so tired." Lacey began.

"I know," he replied. "It's all right though, you've had a rough day and it will soon get better." He leaned over and gently kissed her forehead.

"We have a little girl." she said softly smiling down at the baby cradled in her arms.

"Yes love, and she's beautiful," he whispered gently to her. "What are we to name this fair beauty?"

"Faline." She smiled again at the baby sleeping soundly wrapped in the fresh linens on her chest. "Her name will be Faline."

Jonas, still sitting quietly next to his family smiled. "Faline, a beautiful name, for a beautiful girl." His eyes beamed with pride as he sat and stared down at the tiny baby on his daughter's chest. He couldn't be happier than he was at that moment.

The two men each stood and gave small soft kisses to the foreheads of mum and baby before retreating from the room. They walked out with a dance in their step and beaming with pride. That night Drake slept away from the two of them to ensure Lacey and the baby got a proper night's rest, and Jonas returned home to his little hut next door.

Over the next week, Margo came and checked in on Lacey and Faline quite often to make sure that both were doing all right. Lacey's fever broke after a short time, and she was able to feed the baby on her own. In Margo's opinion it was always better to be able to feed your own baby rather than call upon a nursemaid, "It builds the bonding experience" she said.

Drake and Jonas couldn't be happier with the progress that the two were making. Lacey was getting stronger every day and beginning to get up and move around, and Faline was starting to show the power in her lungs and grabbing onto fingers. Margo insisted that Lacey should still take the time to rest up, instructing her to wait a few weeks before trying to resume her normal activities as her labour was hard. Lacey nodded in agreement and promised to take it easy.

Several weeks went on without any problems. After that Lacey would join her husband and father in the fields with the baby in a sling against her chest. She'd go out and feed the chickens, do some light housework, and occasionally she could be found in one of the orchards retrieving some fresh fruits. They would then finish out their day with a nice meal and sit by the fire at night singing songs to the baby girl they all adored.

This is what the four of them did every day without fail. They stored food, planted and harvested, cut wood, tended animals, made repairs to the huts, and slowly days turned to weeks, and weeks to months. Faline was growing at what seemed a rapid rate and they all got a kick out of every new thing that she did. Her first tooth was a beast. They didn't know how to handle it at all. Upon inquiring, Margo told them to rub some wine on it or give her a cool rag to suck on and it would help ease the pain. She had begun eating fruits and vegetables that Lacey would mash up for her, carrots being one of her favourite foods along with apples. She was not fond of broccoli however, it made her small face curl up in a most disgusted look that made the three adults laugh every time they would feed it to her.

    Their world as far as they were concerned, was perfect. They had everything they had ever dreamed of and nothing could bring them down off the cloud they floated on. This in turn made them completely oblivious to what was happening outside their little sanctuary in the valley.

Chapter 2

The Prophecy Revealed

A few years had gone by with no troubles except for the ones that Faline always seemed to find herself in. She was going to be five years old in a couple of days and her parents and grandfather, along with their everyday tasks, had the job of watching her as well. Ever since she could walk and talk on her own, she was constantly running around pointing at various things asking, "What's that?" After a time of playing the "what's that" game, Faline knew what everything was and then it became "Why?" It made things around the little gardens and animal pens difficult on too many occasions. Trying to keep up with a toddler, gather food and plant new seeds, it was ultimately exhausting.

To everyone's amazement, Faline was not only getting bigger and stronger with each year that passed, but the child's intelligence was seemingly higher than any child they had ever encountered. For a while they all chalked it up to her being so "into" everything as well as the numerous questions Faline had, but as time went on they knew they would have to sit down and discuss some very important matters.

Jonas and Drake, sitting back watching what was unfolding had been dreading the time that Lacey came to ask the both why they didn't seem as amazed as she was at all the things their baby girl could do. She walked and talked at an early age and cut all her teeth by the time she was a year and a half. By the time she was two she was having conversations with them that no child her age should be having. Lacey wondered how her little girl could do such astonishing things for her age, like pushing a coffee table across the floor when she was barely able to walk. It was perplexing, and eventually there would have to be an explanation.

For the time being, at the end of each day, wiping the sweat from their brows and making dinner, they all laughed and commented on how they survived another day. Then they would sit back and relax for a little while after dinner, tell Faline a nice little story before tucking her soundly into bed. This is how it went until Faline and her curiosity got bigger.

Faline decided that she had learned the how's and why's of pretty much everything, so she needed something else to occupy herself. She knew she wasn't big enough to pick fruit as the trees were far too tall, or work the horse to plough, or anything that the grown-ups could do. So what could she do? She sat there for a bit one sunny morning watching her parents do all their normal household and farming chores, noticing that they kept looking over at her to make sure she wasn't causing any mischief. Even her grandfather kept peering over at her. She just sighed and kicked at the little pebbles on the ground.

"I don't understand why I have to just sit around all day." she mumbled quietly to herself still kicking the little pebbles in the dirt. "I am almost five, I am big enough to do something."

As she sat and looked around she saw the chicken pen, and that gave her an idea. She was big enough to feed chickens and gather eggs. Her little face lit up with a big beaming smile and she leapt to her feet and tore off for the chickens. This caught Lacey off guard and she dropped the basket of apples she had been picking and went off after her daughter.

"Faline! Wait! Please don't go in there!" Lacey panted running through the little orchard.

Faline ignored her mother's pleas to stop and proceeded to lift the latch on the little pen holding the chickens and stepped in. The chickens were all lazily scratching at the dirt and stopped for a moment when they heard the latch click. They looked up at the little person standing there with them only for a moment before strutting their way over before her feet. They stood there and simply waited. Lacey having made it to the little chicken pen, almost completely out of breath, stood there staring at the sight before her eyes not sure what she was witnessing. The sight of the chickens all standing before her daughter in one neat row was unbelievable, and no one would believe it if they didn't see it for themselves.

She turned and called over her shoulder. "Drake, Father, you must come here! Quickly!"

Not sure what to make of the situation, the two men immediately stopped what they were doing and ran to where Lacey stood. She pointed into the pen, and both turned white in the face. Drake and Jonas looked at one another not needing to speak, each of them already knew that the other was remembering the things that Margo had said the day Faline was born.

"Um," Drake choked a little "Did she say or do anything to make them act that way?"

"I haven't heard her say one word to those birds," said Lacey. "She has just been standing there and so have the chickens. It's like they are waiting for her to tell them to do something."

Jonas spoke calmly to his beloved granddaughter. "Faline, why don't you feed those hens while you are in there? No sense in just standing there and staring at one another."

"Okay, grandfather," Faline said happily. She walked over to grab the feed with the chickens right behind her. She dropped the feed on the ground for the chickens to eat, and they just stood there.

"Why won't they eat it?" she frowned.

"Did you tell the chickens it was time to eat?" Jonas asked. He then turned and looked at Drake with a look on his face that Drake had never seen before, before turning back to watch what happened.

"Well, no." she shook her head. "I didn't know you had to. Mother never does."

"You are not mother, sweetheart." replied Drake calmly. "Take another small bit and tell the hens it is time to eat."

"Okay, Papa." Faline then grabbed another tiny handful of chicken feed and before tossing it to the ground looked at the chickens and said, "Okay, little chickens, it is time for you to eat now." With that she sprinkled the feed onto the ground, and the chickens merrily clucked and began eating.

"They did it! I did it! I fed the chickens like a big girl!" Her face beamed with pride.

"Yes love, you did. Now it is time to leave the chickens to eat and come on out of there." Lacey told her.

Standing with her little head held high, Faline marched out of the chicken pen and hugged her parents, thanking them for letting her feed the hens. For the remainder of the day, Lacey had her help pick apples. She got to decide whether they went into the basket for eating, or for storing as sauce. Faline seemed satisfied with that job and Lacey was happy to have her so close.

When the work was done for the day and they were all back inside preparing dinner for the evening, Lacey began to interrogate her father and her husband. She had noticed the exchanged looks of fear and awe between the two of them earlier and she was going to know why.

"So" she said in a somewhat motherly tone "who's going to tell me what today was all about?" She began eyeing up both men at the table as they helped her prepare dinner.

"I'm not sure what you are referring to Lacey," Drake half mumbled before looking to Jonas for help.

"I'm sure you do," she said glaring at him now.

"Oh, come now," said Jonas. "No reason to get everyone all wound up. It was a long day for all. Can't we just have some dinner and be grateful today went so well and without incident?"

"NO!" Lacey half shouted under her breath taking care that Faline did not hear. "Because it didn't go without incident, did it? What was all that between you two today at the chicken pen? And don't tell me nothing because I saw it and it was something!"

She was getting angry, and they knew it. It was not something that either of them enjoyed or wished to happen often. Last time she was angry she brooded in the house for a week cleaning everything repeatedly and forcing the two of them to cook and take care of the outdoor stuff by themselves. Not to mention that she didn't speak to them at all.

"Okay," whimpered Drake not wanting an argument. "We will tell you about it after Faline goes to bed."

"Fine." She chopped the tops off the carrots she was cutting so hard that she splintered a bit of the cutting board. Drake winced a little. Jonas just chuckled.

Dinner was eaten almost in complete silence except for the small rustlings of clothes across the little chairs at the table, or the clanking of the knives and forks upon the plates. Lacey was noticeably becoming more irritated with the situation as the evening drew on, making Jonas and Drake shift uncomfortably. The only thing that was able to brighten the mood of the room at all was when Faline began gleefully chirping about her experience in the chicken pen, still so proud of her accomplishment.

"Wasn't it great, Papa?" she said smiling at Drake.

"Yes, sweetheart." he cooed at her "It was the best feeding of the chickens I have ever seen."

Faline looked around the table at each person sitting there with her, donning the most prideful expression they had ever seen come across the small girl's face. She was simply beaming and positioned herself to sit in her chair with her back erect and shoulders square, head held high. There was nothing that could make her feel sour at this moment.

They finished up the remainder of their dishes quickly, Faline still beaming, and began clearing the table. Faline offered to help her mother to tend to the dishes, and with her current state of mind, Lacey couldn't say no and allowed her to dry and stack them once they were washed. They made it a normal night so that Faline didn't get concerned or upset and began asking questions. The whole family gathered by the fire for their evening bedtime story, which usually consisted of some dancing fairies, or unicorns running across rainbows. It was always a beautiful story to send her off to sleep properly.

Once she was all tucked into bed and goodnight kisses and hugs had been given, they closed her door and went back to the chairs surrounding the little fire. Lacey promptly took her seat, crossed her legs and folded her arms across her chest looking at the two men standing before her as if to say "Well?"

Drake and Jonas exchanged a brief anxious look between one another before taking their seats across from her. Neither of them wanted to begin the conversation and sat instead staring at the floor picking dirt from under their fingernails. Lacey, not wishing to prolong the conversation any longer, knowing that whatever it was they had kept it from her long enough, shifted in her chair for a brief second and cleared her throat.

"I believe that the two of you have something that you want to explain?" she said matter- of- factly.

"Oh," said Drake beginning to sweat a little. "Yes we do. I do want to say that I, I mean we, only did it to protect the two of you."

Jonas sitting back a little in his chair and contemplating how he wanted to approach the subject without alarming his daughter, who he treasured more than anything in the world next to his granddaughter, finally decided he was just going to do it.

"Lacey," he began softly, "when you had finally brought our beautiful angel into the world, and were in the back room resting, Margo came out and had a little talk with us."

Lacey sat there staring at her father waiting for him to go on while he paused briefly to get his pipe lit. To her it seemed to take him longer than usually to tap it out, and get it freshened up.

"She started to tell us about a prophecy that has been lingering around for centuries I gather." He lit a small match and puffed his pipe a bit to get it going before continuing. "From what she told us, and to kind of put it neatly for you, there was to be a child born from nothing and grow to control everything. The child would have the ability to control and talk with animals. It would have black hair and blue eyes, and a birth mark resembling a lion's head. This child is supposed to be either the ultimate good or evil in a nutshell. Either it will bring peace or dominate the lands far worse than any king in the history of the world."

Lacey, still sitting in her seat, was pale in the face by this time and unable to speak or move. She could not believe the words that were coming out of her father's mouth. It had to be wrong, it couldn't be true. She began trembling a little as she searched her mind for what to say. Nothing was coming. She just sat there looking at her father in some hopes that he would read her mind and just say what she wanted him to. By this time Drake had stopped sweating as Jonas had done all the hard work, and he finally managed to find his own voice.

"We didn't know what to say to her really." Drake said with a hint of a tremble in his voice. "I didn't believe that it was possible. How could I really? I mean, to have finally been blessed with a child, only to have someone tell you that she is going to take on the world someday. It seemed ridiculous."

Lacey, half sobbing, looked at her two men. "Why?" she asked. "Why didn't you just tell me this to begin with? Why did you let me sit around for the last five years scratching my head, wondering how it was possible that she was able to do everything that she could well before any other child her age?!"

"We both agreed that it wouldn't do anyone any good if you were traumatised after having had such a tough time having her. After a little while, we both put it out of our minds and frankly didn't think about it again until the incident with the chickens today," Drake said making an effort to defend his and Jonas's actions.

"Now that it is out in the open," Jonas interrupted before he watched an argument unfold, "what we need to do is watch her carefully. She doesn't need us to make her feel like less of a person as she is obviously capable of doing a great many things, even at her age."

"You're saying we shouldn't hinder her wanting to help, and allow her to do whatever she wants?" Lacey blurted out jumping to her feet.

"Not at all," he said gesturing for her to sit back down and relax. "What I am saying is that if she asks to help, we let her. We control it of course and make sure she does everything properly, but we let her do it just the same."

"Your father is right," Drake said quietly. "If what Margo said is true, then we don't want her to get frustrated all the time. She needs to feel proud and accomplished. She needs to be led in the 'right' direction. Letting Faline feel down on herself all the time is only going to make her angry. That will lead to bad intentions."

"Well, I suppose if this is what we have to do from now on, then it's what we have to do," Lacey said begrudgingly. "I certainly don't want my daughter to turn into the destroyer of the world."

"None of us want that my dear." Jonas chuckled at the thought of that sweet girl turning into a tyrant. "We have only ever wanted what was best, and we will continue to do so. Our best bet is to keep everything the same so as not to throw Faline off. She is a very smart girl, and if she begins to think that something is wrong, she is going to start asking questions."

Lacey sighed and got to her feet, a look of concern spread across her face. "Well, I suppose there isn't much we can do about what is happening. All we can do is pray to the gods that nothing leads her down a road of destruction."

She kissed her father's forehead and gave Drake a quick kiss before excusing herself to the bedroom for the night. The two men still sitting by the fire remained silent for quite some time before either of them spoke.

"I think that went all right all things considered," Drake commented almost rolling his eyes.

Jonas puffed his pipe and nodded his head in agreement. "She'll be okay. It's a lot to take in, and maybe she's right. Maybe we should have told her right from the moment we knew."

"Are you nuts?" She'd have gone off the deep end and wrung our necks," said a wide-eyed Drake.

"Maybe, maybe not. She's even angrier about it now. Either way she knows now, and nothing is going to stop her from hawking Faline every moment of every day. Honestly, that isn't going to do either of them any good. It will frustrate both," said Jonas.

Drake knew as well as anyone that Lacey was stubborn and severely over protective of their daughter as it was. This was going to make it so much worse. He was fearful of what could result if she didn't let go some. He and Jonas both knew the consequences of an angry Faline, and neither of them wanted to have that happen. If the prophecy was indeed true, they wanted her to be the saviour of the world, not the one who would be the end of them all. He stood and stretched, extended a hand to his father-in-law, and bade him good night. Both knew that they had a lot of work to do, and things were potentially going to become very stressful. Jonas said he was getting ready to retire himself and that he would see Drake in the morning.

"Try to get some sleep, son," Jonas said patting him on the back. "Lacey will come around, she always does."

Drake faked a smile and showed him out before walking toward the bedroom. He was secretly hoping that Lacey had fallen asleep already and opening the door slowly he let out a relieved breath seeing that she was. He changed into his bed clothes and quietly slipped into bed, closing his eyes and trying to let the day be done. For the first time that he could ever remember he didn't fall immediately asleep and so he lay there in the dark thinking about all that had happened. Eventually the visions faded and his eyes grew too heavy to keep open. He listened to Lacey's soft breathing and his mind drifted away into the quiet darkness finally allowing him to sleep.

Chapter 3

The Birthday Gift

As the sun came streaming in through the windows as it did every day in the valley they called home, Drake and Lacey were woken by a jumping, singing five-year-old girl. It was Faline's fifth birthday and she was too excited to contain herself. She came bounding into their room just as the little bluebirds began singing outside their house, and the rooster didn't even have the chance to crow before she was in there leaping onto their bed.

"Mom and dad, it's my birthday! I am five whole years today! I am such a big girl!" she sang all the way into their bed until she was snuggled up in between the two.

"Yes my love, you most certainly are a lovely, big, five-year-old girl." Lacey smiled and hugged her little girl.

"Oh? Five years? I thought you were twenty." Drake said jokingly prompting Faline to smack his arm playfully.

"No Papa, I am only five, but I am still a very big girl." She beamed a big, toothy smile at him.

"That's right, and five is the perfect age for my beautiful young lady." Drake smiled back at her. "So my very big girl, what would you like to have for birthday breakfast?"

"Let's see, I would like eggs, bacon, and some bread with jam. I love jam!" Her mouth was watering at the thought of her mother's home made jam.

"That is quite the hardy breakfast pumpkin, hungry this morning?" Lacey asked looking her over a little shocked at the size of her appetite.

"Oh yes, mama. I am starving today. Big girls need lots to eat to stay strong." Faline hopped out of the bed. "I'll go set the table for you, mama."

"Okay, just be careful placing the knives out please," she called after her.

This was the first day they were going to have to really pay attention to the happenings with their girl. Lacey was already having a hard time, her daughter after all was only turning five, and she felt as though she was being forced to almost let her go. She didn't want to see it that way of course, but she had waited so long to have a baby, and now it was like she only had this baby to give her to the world. She didn't want to share her baby with the world. She wanted to keep her to herself like any normal parent.

It was going to be a struggle for her, she knew it. Lacey also knew she was going to do everything possible to be the best mother she could so that her baby grew up to do great things.

Drake and Lacey resigned to get out of the bed and assist their very ambitious daughter. Drake got dressed and went next door to get Jonas, while Lacey got up and started to prepare breakfast. There were a lot of things to be discussed: How many different crops needed to be seeded; fruit trees that needed to be pruned; a chicken that had stopped laying eggs that needed to be slaughtered for the meat and feathers; the one cow that was getting ready to calf, and of course what Faline wanted for her birthday. Topics were rolling around just like marbles spilling out of a bag, and before they knew it Lacey announced that breakfast was ready for serving.

"Hooray! I am soooo hungry!" Faline said smacking her lips together eyeing the food being served on her plate.

"Everything looks wonderful, dear," said Jonas politely as Lacey spooned him some eggs and bacon.

"I agree with your dad, another beautiful meal made by a beautiful woman. I am a lucky man." Drake kissed his wife's cheek and sat in his chair.

Lacey smiled at all of them. "Thank you for your compliments. I suppose I will continue to cook for all of you." She winked.

After she had dished out some food, for herself, she sat down with the rest of them and they all ate quietly. Every few bites one or the other would say something about how great the food was, or there would be a short sigh of delight coming from Faline while she inhaled her bread and jam. Birthday breakfast was a smashing success. By the time everyone was using bits of bread to clean the last remnants of egg and bacon off their plates, finishing the last bits of their milk, and wiping any left overs off their face, there was a knock at the door which startled them all.

Lacey sat and stared at Drake eyes wide in her chair "Who on earth could that be?"

"I don't know." he said.

As Drake got up and went for the door Lacey, Jonas, and Faline all positioned themselves in their chairs so that they could see through the crack in the door when Drake began to open it. Faline, catching the smallest notion of who was there, leapt out of her chair like a bolt of lightning.

"GRAMPA!" she shouted running for the door, arms stretched out before her.

Drake jumped out of the way so he didn't get run down or smacked by the door. Upon hearing the shout of his granddaughter coming his way the door burst open. On the other side was a very large man. He had long brown curly hair with whitish grey streaks running through it that he kept tied back with a bit of twine. He had a bushy brown beard that also had white, grey streaks in it, his skin was very tanned and leathery from spending most of his time outdoors and everything he wore was made up of some sort of animal hide.

"There's my little wolf cub!" he bellowed in his big booming voice.

"Grampa, I have missed you so!" Faline cried as she leapt up into his arms. "Where have you been?"

"I have missed you too." he said cradling her in his arms. She looked a lot smaller than she was in the giant man's arms. "I have been off hunting and gathering furs for the cool seasons. That is what grampa is best at, so that is what I do." He smiled at her.

"I know grampa, but do you always have to be gone so long?" she asked making her eyes all big and sad to try and make him stay longer this time.

"Unfortunately, yes. Trapping and gathering furs is a long hard process. It takes me a while to get all that I need, and all that will be worth my trip back here," he said to her, wincing a little at his granddaughter's perfect pouty face.

"Okay, grampa." She sniffled a fake sniffle, squiggled to the floor and stood in front of him staring up at him with her huge blue eyes. It was as if she was waiting for him to give her something from his trip.

He simply looked down at her and smiled giving her a small wink and asked, "Oh? Am I forgetting something today?"

Moving her hands sternly to her hips, she wrinkled her small brow and replied, "Yes grampa, it is my birthday today and I am five whole years."

"Oh goodness!" he laughed looking around the room at the others, who were also laughing at seeing Faline scold him. "Has it been a whole year already? I do suppose that you do look bigger than last I saw you. Turn around and let me see all ya."

Faline twirled in her little grey dress with a huge smile pasted across her face. When she came back around to face him she stood as straight as an arrow to make sure she looked as big as possible.

"Yep, I see it now." he said. "You are a very big girl and being that it is your fifth birthday and all, grampa has a very big girl birthday present for you."

Faline about jumped out of her skin leaping off the floor in excitement clapping her hands. Jonas, Drake, and Lacey who had all been seated watching the conversation between the two looked between themselves. What could he have brought for her? Quite frankly, Lacey seemed a little nervous. Knowing her father-in-law was a good man all around really, but ever since his wife had passed he had taken to a life of travelling out deep into the southern woods to trap animals for fur and meat, only to return for special occasions and get more provisions. No one travelled that far into the southern woods, the valley they lived in was as far as anyone would dare to go, except Zeke.

"Um, Dad?" Drake finally said getting up from his place at the table. "What exactly did you bring her for her birthday?"

Zeke laughed and gave his son a big bear hug. "Well son, let's all go outside and see shall we?"

Faline again jumped for joy and shot like a bolt for the door before anyone could blink an eye. The four adults laughed, shrugged their shoulders and got up to follow her outside. Once out the front door they saw that as per usual, Zeke's hunting sled was packed to the point of overflowing over with all sorts of different animal fur. Generally when he would come back he would give some of the furs to his family and trade the rest to the villagers for provisions for the time he would be away hunting. This would include jarred food, medicines, bandages, arrows; whatever they had to offer really. Zeke didn't mind what it was, he usually could find a use for everything. The only thing that was missing this time around was Zeke's companion, his husky named Sasha. Faline had been the first to notice and immediately had questions.

"Grampa? Where is Sasha? She is always here to lick my face," she asked him with concern.

"Well my dear, poor Sasha has passed away," Zeke responded. "She was old and her time had come to be with the other dogs in the other world."

"Oh, that is sad, grampa. I'm sorry she has gone." Faline said as little tears welled up in her eyes.

"It's okay. She was a very good friend, and she loved us all as much as we loved her," he told her wiping the tears from her eyes.

"Yes grampa, she was a wonderful dog. I will still miss her very much though," she whimpered.

"I'm sorry, Zeke," Lacey said placing a hand on his shoulder. "How did it happen? Hopefully, she didn't suffer."

"Funny you should ask." He laughed.

This made all of them look at each other. In their opinion, when a member of the family passed it generally was not found to be humorous. Now they were all curious as to what was going on since Zeke's behaviour was so strange.

"Well Faline, it's your birthday, so you get to pick anything you want off my sled," Zeke said.

"Okay, grampa. I will look now," she said taking the extra few steps towards the sled.

"What I want you to keep in mind as you look and are choosing your piece, is that Sasha, who loved you and I most of all, left us a gift. Let's see if you figure out what it is." He turned and winked at Lacey and Drake, both standing there hoping it wasn't poor Sasha's pelt. It was after all Zeke's specialty.

"Really? She left me a present!" Faline stammered excitedly running her hands along the furs on the top of the huge pile.

"Yes, love. She did." He smiled at her.

Jonas who had otherwise been quiet up to that point, and was not afraid to speak plainly, turned and whispered something to Zeke that made him look shocked at first. Then he had smiled and responded. "I would never have done that." Jonas nodded and stood back to watch Faline rummage through the mountain of furs on the sled.

After several minutes of watching Faline pick furs out, inspect them thoroughly running her hands along them and carefully setting them aside, she had come close to meeting the centre of the pile. This made Zeke stand a little taller, waiting with anticipation for her to find what was stowed away in there. He had made sure that just before he had reached the house, to carefully place the gift in there so it would be well concealed. It took some since there was a lot to be rearranged and moved. This was it though, only a few more furs and she would notice. He could barely contain himself.

"Grampa, why didn't you pack these the way you normally do? You left a big hole in the middle," she said raising an eyebrow at him.

"I thought I might try something different this time, you know, see if it travelled better." he said as calmly as he could.

"WAIT! There is something in there. It's…. it's…. MOVING!" she jumped back a bit staring at the sled.

Her little blue eyes were as wide as anyone had ever seen them. She stood there, eyes fixed on the sled not knowing what was there or why for the first time ever, her grampa had brought back an animal skin that was able to move. This was a very scary moment for someone who is only five years old, even when you feel like you are a very big girl.

"Don't be afraid," said Jonas who at that moment had figured out what was on the sled. "Go back Faline, go back and see what's down there. You are a very big girl, a very brave girl at that, and we are all right here."

She turned and looked at them all, glancing from one person to the next before slowly walking back to the sled. Lacey who had all but ran to grab her up in her arms to shield her frightened baby, stopped when her father said it was all right. He would never steer Faline into harm's way, so she stepped back and waited like the rest. Faline edged up to the side of the sled and the still towering mound of animal pelts and peered down into the dark hole in the centre. Something was moving in there, she just couldn't tell what.

"Reach your hand in, Faline," Zeke told her.

She looked at him for a minute, not quite sure she wanted to do. This was not something she was used to. Surprises, yes she loved surprises, reaching her hand into a dark hole for an unknown moving object, never.

Finally Drake walked over and stood by his daughter's side. He peered down into the hole for a second and smiled. Being much taller than Faline, the light from the sun hit the opening of the hole a little better and he could see what was in there. He bent down on one knee and looked at his daughter with a big smile.

"It's okay, Faline. No one here is ever going to try to hurt you, not ever. If Grampa says that it is okay to do it, then you are going to be just fine." The smile on his face got a little bigger and there was a sparkle in his eye.

Smiling back and straightening up she replied, "Okay, daddy. I should know that. It is just scary to put your hand into a dark space, especially when that dark space moves."

"I know, but you are a very big girl and we all love you. It is time to find out what is in there, you can't leave your present waiting all day now can you? It might get sad." Drake again smiled at her and patted her slightly on the head before walking back to join the rest.

Faline forced a small smile "Okay, I'm gonna do it now. I'm not scared any more."

They all laughed and responded okay while waiting for her to do it. Drake went back and told Lacey what was there which made her instantly more comfortable with the whole situation. Jonas laughed at her and said she was a severe worry wart, making Lacey give him one of her notorious glares.

Faline got up on the edge of the sled so that she could reach her hand most of the way to the bottom of the hole if necessary. She was hoping that after all of this, she didn't have to ask for help to get it out of there. She took a deep breath and began slowly putting her hand into the hole. The further down she got, the closer her ear became to it and she whooped her hand out quick.

"There are TWO somethings in there!" she yelped.

"Well? Don't you want to know what the something is yet?" Zeke asked. "I know you are a very curious girl, you have to want to know by now."

"I do but..." she said nervously. "Oh, all right."

She again started sliding her hand slowly down the inside of the fur hole. She figured if she ran her hand along the furs themselves very slowly, she wouldn't startle whatever was down there. She didn't want it to bite her if it was in fact the biting type. She pushed her arm in as far as it would go, her ear resting on top of the furs, her face pointing in the direction of her smiling family and waited. It took all of ten seconds for the things in the hole to find her small hand and slime it, making her nose wrinkle and the people watching to burst out laughing at the sight.

"Well?" chuckled Zeke "What happened?"

"Um, it slimed my hand, Grampa." she said. "And now they are sniffing my hand and sliming me more."

She wrinkled her nose up just a bit more.

"Oh? It slimed you, huh," laughed Drake. "Is that what we call it now?"

"You are all terrible picking fun at her." Lacey began chuckling herself now. "What else baby, what else do you feel?"

"Well, sometimes I feel little cold wet things touch me, then slimy warm things, and…" she stopped short, her eyes growing wide. She threw up her other hand and waved it a little to tell the grown people to be quiet so she could hear better what was there. After several seconds Faline's eyes began to sparkle and a big smile spread across her face.

"Whining, I hear them whining! Get them out, grampa! Get them out!" she shouted.

Zeke took a few big steps and was there with her. He reached his hands down the hole and each one came back out grasping a small wriggling puppy.

"PUPPIES!" Faline cried with excitement. "Is this what you meant Grampa? Sasha left us puppies?"

"Yes. This was the last thing she needed to do before she left us." he smiled at her as she played with the two small balls of fur on the ground.

"They are wonderful, Grampa." she said smiling.

"They sure are," he told her.

"Zeke," Jonas said, "those don't really look like they are all husky, they look, well bigger."

"You would be correct, sir." Zeke grinned. "Seems that my Sasha didn't want just any ordinary babes, she went and found herself a wolf."

"Oh my," Lacey gasped. "Is this going to be safe for her to have?"

"She is going to be just fine. Wolves are as loyal as any dog, and with Sasha's blood running through their veins Faline will have the best dog ever," Zeke said reassuringly.

"I get to have whichever I choose Grampa?" Faline asked smiling up at him.

"Yes my dear, whichever one catches your fancy." he replied. "I will take the other one back with me when I go. I need to make sure I always have a sound hunting dog with me."

Faline spent quite a bit of time studying and playing with the two pups, watching their every move. She wanted to make sure that she chose the one that suited her and her needs best, even though she was not certain what her needs were exactly. While she was out playing with the pups, Lacey had shown Zeke inside to get him something proper to eat as she called it. None of that root and berry breakfast would do for him that morning. Jonas motioned for Drake to head on inside as well to spend time with his father while he was around and said he would stay out and watch the three young uns. Drake couldn't resist a small chuckle at the comment, nodded and went inside the little wood house.

Jonas took a seat atop the small wooden chopping block to the side of the small house and took out his pipe. He sat in silence smiling to himself as he watched his precious granddaughter play with the two little balls of fluff scampering around her feet. Neither of the pups strayed too far from her, and they always came to her every time she let out a little call. He kept thinking back to what Margo had said the night she was born, how she would be able to control all animals and that no matter what kind it was, it would basically be loyal to the death. It didn't matter which pup she chose, either one would be as faithful to her as the other. Either one would gladly give its life for hers if it needed to and was going to be a snap for her to train.

"Grampa Jonas, I think I have made my decision," she said.

"Oh?" Jonas said smiling. "Which of these lucky pups has found a place by your bed?"

"This one." Faline smiled picking up the small black and white female.

"She's a beautiful little girl, for a beautiful little girl." he winked.

"Yes. She is going to be a fabulous friend, Grampa. She is very special." Faline looked over at him and raised her eyebrows. "Do you know why?"

Jonas, a little perplexed by her expression, simply shook his head and replied, "No, my dear, I don't. Is it because she is yours?"

"Well that could be a reason, but the real reason is because she has one blue eye and one brown one." she said turning the little pup's face towards her own.

"I see," said Jonas. "I would have to say that does make her a very special pup."

"I'm going to go in and tell mom, dad, and Grampa Zeke!" she said getting to her feet and skipping to the house.

Jonas nodded his head and watched as she skipped merrily past him. He knew it wouldn't be long before she came back out with the rest of the family to show them which pup she had chosen, and not long after that Zeke would take the other and his wares and depart. He never stayed long. He had things to do to make sure that when he returned to the far reaches of the south, he had enough provisions to survive until he returned. He didn't like making "unnecessary trips" as he called them. I guess from where Jonas sat, he couldn't blame him in the least. It was a long hike and Zeke was not getting any younger.

A few minutes later after a little commotion and shouts of excitement, everyone had exited the little wooden house and filed into the yard to look at the pups still happily playing there. The little black and white female was toying with the reddish coloured male, nipping at his ears and feet as she hopped around him in circles. At one point she snapped his tail and he let out a sharp little cry, tucking his wounded little tail between his back legs that made them all laugh and feel sorry for the little guy.

"The time has come for the big reveal," Lacey said. "Our Faline has chosen her companion, and it is time for her to name it as well."

"I agree," Zeke nodded. "A dog must be named in order to train it properly. Also, you cannot talk to someone without addressing them by name, that's just rude." he chuckled.

They all sat on logs waiting to be chopped and waited for Faline to make her announcement. She felt like a star standing in front of all of them. She smiled the biggest of smiles, her little blue eyes twinkling in the late morning sun and turned around to snatch up the little female pup.

"I have chosen the little female with the different coloured eyes. I felt she was perfect for me, and since the little boy was red in his colourings, he reminded me of Sasha and I felt it was only fair that Grampa Zeke took him," she said smiling at her grandfather.

"I believe that you have made the perfect choice for yourself, Faline." Zeke said smiling back at her. "I appreciate you having kept me in your thoughts as you chose. I am honoured."

"I am impressed, Faline." Drake winked. "That was a very noble decision for you to have made. You always find new ways to make us all so proud."

"Thank you, dad." Again, she smiled. "I wanted to make sure I had the right one, but I also knew I had to be sure it was the right one for both of us."

Jonas looked at her with pride written all over his face. "You are wise beyond your years Faline. You are what you say you are, a very big girl."

They all sat and nodded in agreement, smiling at one another and at her. Everyone was so proud of their little Faline who at only five could make some tough decisions already but was able to do it keeping others feelings in mind as well as her own.

Faline broke the silence by raising the little pup over her head into the rays of sun and the soft blowing breeze with a stern but loving declaration. "This girl pup is now my friend and loyal companion until the gods deem it fit to take one from the other. Let it be known by all that her name from now until that time is Cairo."

She let the pup down slowly and gave her a small kiss on the forehead and placed her back on the ground to resume playing with her brother. The adults sitting on their logs were awestruck. They had no idea that she knew to do that or that what she did was even a "thing" to do. Lacey grew a little pale at the exhibition even though she had tried not to. Drake sat with his mouth hanging open, Jonas and Zeke both had their eyebrows raised, and all four had to hurry up and straighten their faces before Faline had finished turning to look at them.

She had taken one look at her mother and immediately asked, "Mama, are you okay? Is it getting too hot out?"

"My dear, I am fine. I think I just need a glass of water." she replied with a forced smile.

Faline walked over and gave her a hug. "Okay mama, I will go and get one for you." She took off like a dart towards the house so her mother didn't have to wait.

"What in the name of the gods was that?" Zeke said once she passed through the door.

Drake let his body relax and looked at his father. "I will explain before you go. I can only tell you what we know and what we have witnessed."

Zeke stroked his beard as he often did when he was stressed or upset by something. "Well I certainly hope so because I have never seen anything of the sort, nor have I ever done that with any dog I have ever owned in my entire life."

Lacey folded her hands gently into her lap as she sat trying better to compose herself. "Don't worry, Zeke," she said softly, "we will make sure you know what we do. I don't know what to make of it, none of us do really, but we were going to tell you anyway. We wanted to wait until Faline couldn't hear."

Zeke nodded understandingly as Faline rushed back out of the house with the glass of water for her mother. She was trying to hurry and not spill it at the same time, which is no small task. Lacey thanked her for the water and begin sipping at it while Faline gave her another quick hug and went back to playing with the puppies.

It was obvious that they loved her as much as she loved them. As she sat on the ground to play with them they both raced up jumping in and out of her lap and racing circles around her. She managed to get little pets in here and there as they raced around playfully nipping at and pouncing on one another. Being that they were small yet it didn't take long before they tired themselves out and crawled into Faline's lap curling up into one huge fluffy ball and falling asleep. She thought this was great and happily sat there stroking their fur as they slept.

It was determined while they sat outside that Zeke's pup would be named Duke. Faline thought that was a funny, but a good name for him and made sure that just as she did with Cairo, she called him by it every chance she got to familiarise him with it. She knew this to be one step in proper puppy training according to her grandfather. Among a slew of other things that she knew were going to make her new friend the very best of dogs, she had to teach her to sit, lay, shake, and come on command. This was going to be a lot of work, but she knew that she was more than capable of doing this and she was going to have a lifelong friend as a result.

The day was coming into the late afternoon hours, the bright blue sky was lit with a bright orange sun, with a few fluffy clouds passing slowly by, and a soft sweet breeze filled the air. The commotion from the puppies had settled down and the family had all gathered in the house for lunch, which had consisted of smoked pork sandwiches, sweet strawberry jam on bread, and some corn on the cob. There were little bits of conversation about Zeke's travels and all his hunting excursions, which always had Faline on the edge of her seat eyes closed imagining herself in his place going on all his adventures. Something inside of her longed for those adventures and she could feel it tugging at her soul every time he came and told her about more of his journeys. She would often find herself daydreaming about them and others of her own making after he departed.

Faline decided while listening to his stories today that some day she would go on a journey. It would be her own, and it would make a fabulous story just like her grampa's. She now had her travelling companion and as soon as she was big enough to go, and Cairo was nice and trained they would make her dreams a reality. She smiled to herself at the thought of going out into the world, travelling further down into the south to see what was down there. Were there really unicorns, fairies and witches? She had to know, and she was determined now more than ever to do it.

The meal having ended and his last story finished, Zeke wiped the last of the jam from his beard and got to his feet.

"Thank you all for your hospitality as always. It warms my heart to see that my family is here safe and doing well," he smiled.

"Zeke, you know you are always welcome here, and you also know that you don't have to go," Lacey replied getting to her feet.

Zeke patted his belly "I am grateful to visit, but you know I am not a person that enjoys living in civilised communities for long, dear. I enjoy the quiet and being able to trek out whenever my bones say we need to go."

Lacey nodded and sighed. "I know you enjoy your space, but I always feel inclined to offer you to stay. I don't want you to think anything has changed."

Drake got up and moved towards the door. "Come on dad, I'll help you bundle your furs back up before you go. Lacey, Jonas, you two don't mind helping do you?" He looked between them and raised his eyebrow.

Jonas and Lacey knew that the time had now come to tell Zeke the story that Margo had told them the night Faline was born. They both nodded and made their way outside.

"Faline, why don't you take Cairo out for a walk through the orchard? You know show her around our little farm." Jonas winked at her.

"Okay, Grampa. It is probably best for her to get used to the place as soon as possible anyway," she said.

Faline ran over to Zeke and wrapped her small arms about his waist as far as she could. She told him that she loved him a ton and thanked him again for her gift. She then wished him well on his journey and that she would miss him until he returned. He kissed her on her forehead, returned her love and promised he would return at the beginning of the following summer. At that she took Cairo and skipped out the door towards the orchard.

As soon as Faline was out of earshot, Lacey, Drake and Jonas explained the story that Margo had told them the best they could. They then went on in detail about all the different happenings since she was a baby until now, her rapid growth, her intelligence, the chicken incident and whatever other odd thing that they could remember having happened. Zeke having sat on the corner of his sled full of furs, Duke quietly sleeping in his lap, sat there wide eyed and constantly looking as if someone had hit him in the face with a gauntlet. Once they had finished telling him all they could, they too sat upon some unsplit logs and waited for a comment from Zeke.

"So if I am correct, what you are saying is that my granddaughter is some sort of saint? Saviour? God? What?" he shouted, getting to his feet so fast it startled poor Duke who was still sleeping in his lap.

"We aren't sure what exactly she is going to do or be as of yet," said Jonas calmly. "We only know that in order for her to do the right thing, we have to make sure that we teach her the right things to do."

"Jonas is exactly right." Drake nodded. "We cannot let her become the thing that destroys, we want her if nothing else to be the one who saves, loves and cherishes the world and all who inhabit it."

"Okay," Zeke sighed. "Is there anything I can do to help her?"

Lacey stood and walked over to him gently placing a hand on his shoulder. "I believe that you already have." She smiled. "You gave her a gift that will not only become her very best friend, but one that I foresee keeping her safe when the time comes for her to go out and start her journey."

"The pup?" he asked quietly. "She is so young, and so is the pup, who's to say that the pup will live that long? Dogs don't live forever ya know."

"We know that and so does Faline, but if she is who Margo believes that she is then who knows how long that pup will live for?" Lacey said unhesitatingly.

"All right. With all this astounding information that you all have bestowed upon me, it is best that I should be going. I have too many people to visit, and a lot of things to acquire in order to maintain my solitude down south." Zeke smiled slightly and finished checking the knots that tied his furs to the sled.

Drake stepped over and gave his father a hug. "I'm sorry we had to tell you this all at once, and I know it's a lot to take in, but you only come once a year and the thing with the chickens made it apparent to us that Margo's story may not be just a story. It was time to tell you."

"I appreciate your honesty as always and I will take the time away to ponder over everything. Maybe there are more ways in which I can help her other than just giving her a companion. I am a handy man after all." he smiled and gave a small wink.

"We love you, dad." a small tear forming in Drake's eye. "I wish you would reconsider staying with us one of these times. We would really enjoy having you around more."

"I know son, I miss all of you while I'm away as well. I really must get going though before it gets too late and I can't see the path," Zeke said choking back his own sad feelings.

They all exchanged their last hugs, handshakes and farewells before watching the big burly man take hold of the ropes to his sled and pull it away down the dirt road. Duke was merrily sleeping atop the big pile of furs and paid no mind to any of the goings on. The three of them stood and watched until they could no longer see him before returning inside to clean up after lunch and return to their usual duties.

The rest of the day went on without a hitch. Chores outside were much easier now that Faline had something of her own to be responsible for, which is something that she had been longing for. They would watch her every now and then as she praised or scolded Cairo depending on what she was doing.

By the end of the day everyone was all tuckered out and ready to retire. Dinner had been made, served, and eaten. Songs had been sung around the fire, and a small cake had been made to honour Faline's birthday, which to her was simply amazing. Lacey took Faline into the back to tuck her into bed and with a lot of persuading and a little arguing, Faline convinced her mother to let Cairo sleep in the bed with her. She gave her sweet daughter a kiss goodnight, one last wish of a happy birthday, scratched Cairo on her head and blew the candle out next to the bed.

The rest of the family said their goodnights to one another and headed off to bed themselves. It had been a long day, and each of them went to bed knowing that this was officially the beginning of whatever grand thing that was to befall their Faline. All they could do was sit back and wait hoping for the best, and that was not going to be a very easy thing to do.

Chapter 4

The Armoured Man

As time passed in the quiet beautiful valley the only thing that ever seemed different was the slight change in the seasons. The valley was not like most places in the world, it didn't snow and the leaves never died and fell from the trees. The temperatures would only get slightly cooler towards what would be the autumn and winter months, therefore making it a time for planting and harvesting different types of crops. The people grew right along with the plants and changed with the seasons. It was a harmonious existence for all.

Not unlike everyone and everything else, Faline had been growing as well as time went on. She was nearing ten now and just as rambunctious and carefree as ever. Often you could find her tearing around the farm lands with Cairo, her black hair flowing wildly behind her without a care in the world. Cairo was huge as they expected she would be, and due to Faline's constant training was as loyal and obedient a dog as they had ever seen. The two of them were inseparable and if one became ill, the other lay with the other until they were better. Cairo was never more than a few feet away from Faline, it didn't matter where she was or what she was doing. You always knew where she was just by where Cairo was. It was almost funny to watch and some people did give a little laugh when they watched the two of them stroll by. It wasn't to be mean, just out of joy and amusement to see such devotion.

Lacey, Drake and Jonas naturally could not be happier that she had someone to watch over her as much as Cairo did. It made them feel more at ease while they tended to their normal duties. There was a time they recalled when Faline was seven and trying her hand at climbing all the trees in the orchard. Naturally, she fell out and broke a leg. Cairo came and dragged

Drake to where she was to help her. Had it not been for her, only the gods know how long it would have been before they had found their sweet daughter writhing in pain on the ground..

"Faline! Cairo! Dinner!" Lacey shouted.

"That might bring them in," Jonas chuckled. "I wouldn't hold my breath though."

"That girl may be the death of me yet," Lacey grimaced.

"Oh honey, she is the light of your life and you know it." Drake kissed her cheek.

"Yes I know, but I sure wish she would be around when it was time to eat and sleep at least," Lacey said sharply. "I think she deliberately tests my patience."

Lacey began setting plates out on the table while Drake and Jonas sat by the fire playing a game of checkers as they waited for their meals. Both men just shook their heads a little knowing that Lacey was frustrated with their nonchalant little Faline, and there was nothing that either of them could do about it. Moments later there was a loud smack against the door as Cairo's shoulder hit it to allow herself entry into the house.

"Aw, you beat me again!" Faline panted coming in seconds behind her four-legged friend.

Cairo let out a small yip and licked her hand as she sat by her feet waiting to be coddled. Faline knelt on the floor beside her and stroked her coat gently while telling her how much she loved her and what a good dog she was. Cairo's glazed-over eyes and tongue lolling out of the side of her mouth told Faline that she loved her too and was enjoying her rubdown.

Lacey looked at her with a hand on her hip. "I should say that it is about time the two of you got in, and I assume you are going to go and get cleaned up for dinner now?" she said with a small scowl on her face and her eyebrow raised.

"Of course, mother. We didn't mean to come so late, but we didn't miss anything," Faline said softly.

"No you didn't, but I could have used a hand. You know those two are of no help to me in the kitchen." She pointed at her father and Drake sitting by the fire playing checkers.

Drake turned abruptly and looked at her. "Hey now, that's not fair! You know I have tried to help you."

Jonas just laughed in his chair shaking his head. "It's no use son, this is a battle better left untouched. I tried having conversations like this with Aggie from time to time, I always lost. Men are better at tending fields, chopping wood and the like. We are not made for lady things, we are made for bull work." Again, he laughed.

Lacey rolled her eyes at her father's comment. She knew as well as he did that she was more than capable of doing anything that they were. "Bull work... bull crap is more like it," she mumbled under her breath. Faline heard her and looked a little shocked as her mother didn't have anything negative to say very often.

She then turned to Faline. "Now that we have established that men apparently are not suited to cook, mind helping me put dinner on the table?"

Faline got to her feet brushing some dog hair from her dress. "Of course no, mother. Just let me get washed up real quick."

Lacey nodded her head and began getting the dishes off the shelves. As Faline was washing her hands Cairo came and nudged the back of her knee as a gesture that she too would enjoy some water. Faline grabbed a bowl and filled it up before the pump stopped pushing the water through and set it down for her eagerly waiting pal. She then set to work helping her mother get the dishes and food out onto the table for dinner.

Jonas sat in his chair by the fire with Drake still playing checkers while they waited patiently for dinner to be done and began grumbling under his breath.

"What's that Jonas? I can't quite hear you," Drake laughed.

Jonas looked up at him unamused. "I said," he began, "that I don't understand how with all my years of playing this confounded game, I have never beaten you. It's impossible!" His face twisted into a grimace.

"I can't explain my luck. That's all it is though, luck." Drake again laughed.

"Sure," retorted Jonas. "Luck."

"Come on now you two. Put away your silly game and come eat dinner," Lacey called to them over their bickering.

"Okay love, we're coming." Drake smiled at her.

"Gladly," said Jonas half tempted to stuff his pieces into the fireplace and forget the game existed.

As Drake got up he made sure to take his last move laughing a bit and jumping a few more of Jonas's pieces before making his way to the table and taking the win. Jonas merely grumbled under his breath which in turn made Drake laugh even harder than he was already. They took their seats at the table and looked over the dinner before them. Jonas eyed up the beef roast Lacey had prepared and had almost immediately forgotten how miserable the game had made him.

"Lacey my dear, that roast looks spectacular," his mouth watering as he spoke.

"Thank you dad, I hope it is as good as it looks," she replied smiling.

"I agree," said Drake. "Nothing beats a roast with carrots and potatoes. I can't wait to eat it."

Faline had finished setting the little cloths they used for napkins under the silverware and began pouring each of them a glass of fresh milk. She ran over and got Cairo her dinner so she wasn't left out of the family meal and then took her own seat at the table. Once everyone was seated each dish was passed around, along with a plate of freshly baked bread and butter in the middle of the table. Lacey always knew when everyone really enjoyed the food she had made because they ate it slowly. They said it was so they could enjoy every bite. They also used the bread and butter to soak and scoop up every bit on their plates. This is exactly what she was watching them do with dinner tonight. It was making her enjoy her dinner just that much more. As they were nearing the end of dinner and contemplating a possible dessert there was a rapid knock at the door which gave them all a start.

Lacey grew instantly uncomfortable. "Who on earth is calling this late in the day?"

"I haven't a clue," responded Drake his curiosity peaked as he got up from his chair. "But I will go and see who it is."

Drake took his napkin and gave another wipe to his mouth and hands but before he had reached the door there was another more loud and vigorous knocking..

"All right, all right, I'm coming," he said.

Once he had opened the door part way a very frantic sweating Margo pushed it the rest of the way for him. Her eyes were wide and panicked looking. Her face was pale and flushed and sweat was beading across her forehead. If he hadn't known any better he'd have thought she may have been frightened.

"Margo! What on earth is the matter!" he said reaching out to grab hold of the woman's trembling arm.

Margo, her chest heaving as she struggled for breath, slowly panted. "One of the boys who watch out for our village from the tree tops. He came to me saying there was an armoured rider coming this way."

Drake didn't quite know how to react to this. It wasn't something any of them had ever dreamed would happen here. "What do you propose we do, Margo?"

Margo grew a little more calm having had a minute to collect herself and her breathing starting to become less stressful. She responded shakily. "I don't know really. I told the boy to go back to the trees. I came right here to you folks. This isn't something I had ever planned for. Soldiers don't come here they are too afraid of what lies beyond the valley. Besides it's not just any soldier."

Jonas, now walking over, asked, "What do you mean by that? What kind is he?"

Margo hesitated and again went a little pale. "The boy said he wore black armour with a gold dragon on the chest." She replied.

Lacey instantly went rigid and dropped the plate she had been drying on the floor not flinching as it splintered around her feet. She knew that armour, it was something she would never forget. That was the same armour the knights wore who raided and burned her village to the ground when she was a small girl. It was also the same knights who killed her mother. She was sick to her stomach now and ever so angry, but she stayed there with her dishes cleaning up the broken one never speaking a word while the others talked. Jonas, hearing the plate crash, had turned and watched her for a moment to make sure she was okay. He gave her a smile but let her be once he caught the look on her face.

"I suppose we should all go outside and wait for this stranger to come in. I see no sense in letting him travel too far into the village and start riling folks," Jonas said as he got ready to go out.

Margo nodded. "I guess that would be best. We should stop and interrogate him and his intentions. Who knows how many more are following behind somewhere hiding, waiting for some sort of signal?"

"Let's not be too hasty here," Drake said holding up a hand to try to quieten things down. "There is nothing to say. This man isn't just fleeing, maybe he's a scout. We cannot be too quick to judge, no matter what they are wearing." He turned and quietly looked to Lacey who was trying desperately to busy herself and not look annoyed or afraid.

Drake motioned for Lacey, Jonas and Margo to follow him outside to await their visitor. Faline had wanted to come along, but Lacey insisted she remain inside. She stomped off to her room with Cairo hot on her heels and flopped onto her bed to wait. Fortunately, they didn't have to wait long for the man to come riding up. Once he had made it past the opening in the trees he slowed his horse having caught sight of the four people standing there waiting for him. He allowed himself to get close enough to make out the look on their faces before pulling his horse to a halt and waiting.

The four of them stood there arms folded across their chests studying the man on the white horse in the armour. He was handsome, well groomed, blond hair, greenish looking eyes. His armour was well cared for, a long broadsword with a gold hilt hanging from his side and a bow with a quiver of arrows draped across his back over his black riding cloak. The thing that caught most of their attention was the stirring mass hiding under a charcoal grey travelling cloak now buried against the man's chest.

Jonas broke the silence first. "Who are you and what on earth do you want here?" he asked gruffly.

The rider hesitated and his horse stamped its hoof anxiously. "I mean you no harm," he replied.

"Well if that's the case why don't you come closer, weapons on the ground, so we may get a better look at you?" Jonas shouted.

The hooded figure who had briefly peeked through the corner of its shroud, leaned in again causing the man to bend in his saddle a bit. After a moment, the man nodded and gave a tiny nudge to his horse with his heels to make it move forward slowly. He made it within a hundred feet of the four strangers before Drake threw his hand up and made him stop.

"That will be far enough, please. You are still armed," motioning to the rest of the group and then to himself, "we are obviously not. We are also not sure you and your companion are alone."

Again the man leaned into the hooded figure and nodded. He got down from the horse and began removing all his arms laying them gently on the ground.

"Please, we aren't here to hurt anyone and if you want us to leave I understand," he said quietly.

Lacey tossed her hair back and placed a hand on her hip. "Your armour, sir. I am aware of what comes with that armour and the price it has. I lost my home and my mother to it. What makes you think you can waltz in here with no name, in that armour and expect me or anyone else to just say Oh, yes please come here and eat my food, live on my land or anything of the sort!" Her face had grown redder than any apple Drake had ever seen by the time she had finished her rant.

"I agree with her," Margo frowned. "That armour has cost a lot of people a great deal and frankly unless you can prove otherwise, people will not trust you."

The man sighed and hung his head knowing that if he was to do what he set out to do, he needed to do it right. No lies, no false beginnings, and these people were going to have to know the whole truth. He also knew there wasn't anywhere else he could go, not anywhere that was safe anyway.

"I understand you're being hesitant if I were you I would be also. If you don't mind would it be all right if we all had a seat? If I am to be totally up front and honest telling you everything you may need or want to know, it will take a bit," the rider said calmly.

Drake looked to his family and friends for their approval. They all nodded and motioned to the logs strewn across the ground. Lacey jumped when the man turned back to the horse thinking he was going for his weapons, but she calmed down when she saw him reach to collect the small, cloaked figure leaving the weapons where they lay before sitting with the rest of them.

Jonas looked him over again and now that he was closer to him the man's face looked so familiar. "Now, son. You must tell us who you are, why you are here, and what you are expecting to gain from it. Do you understand?"

The rider nodded. "Yes, sir. I do."

Drake took Lacey's hand into his own to help calm her. "Well for a start at least he has some manners. So with that let's get started, shall we?"

The rider took a deep breath before turning and looking them over one last time before beginning to tell his tale.

"My name is Tobias Drakona. I am the only son of Balthazar and the late Elizabeth Drakona. My father found out that I had fallen in love with a pig farmer's daughter after trying for several years to marry me off to some princess in the east in order to merge our kingdoms and take control of more land. He was enraged and started questioning people about the two of us, threatening their lives if they didn't offer some information regarding our situation. He eventually was informed that the two of us had been seeing each other for many years and that she had bore a son, my son." He reached over and removed the cloak hiding the shuddering person's face to reveal a small red haired boy with bright green eyes.

Margo took a deep breath and frowned. "This is your son I assume?"

"Yes," Tobias replied. "His name is Nolan and he is eleven-years-old."

"I guess it is safe to say that's why you are here then," Jonas grumbled. "You took the boy to hide him?"

Tobias tilted his head to the side and raised an eyebrow. "Yes and no. I came here to hide us both really. After my father found out that I had a son with Dania he immediately had her hunted and slaughtered.

He would have killed Nolan too but I had already got to him and ran. I was already banished, or so my father said as he screamed at me for defying him and tainting the blood lines of our family with the blood of a commoner, and he swore to kill them both. She was out in the fields when they got her and he was out riding when I snatched him from his pony and bolted. I couldn't help her." He winced recalling having seen her being stabbed to death before they cut her throat in the potato field. "I would have helped her had I got there sooner, but it was all I could do to get my boy out alive."

Drake scratched his head before placing his hands firmly on his knees staring into the eyes of the man across from him. "There will be soldiers looking for you and your boy and you know that if you stay here we are all at risk."

"I understand your concern, sir," Tobias said. "I assure you that no one followed me, and I have lived my whole life out there with them and there isn't a single man, woman or child that I know that would dare come this far. I only did this for the life of my son. As a parent yourself," motioning to the window of the house where Faline sat watching, "I am sure you understand how important he is to me. I would go to the ends of the earth to keep him safe if it came to that."

Lacey looked toward the house where her precious child sat waiting for them to return and knew how he felt. All her anxiety seemed to melt away thinking about how he must have felt watching the mother of his child be murdered and leave everything he knew behind. She knew how that felt, she had already gone through it and now this man and his boy had too. She stood up and brushed off the skirt of her dress and motioned for the house.

Quietly, she said to Tobias, "Why don't the two of you stay here tonight? We don't have any extra beds to offer, but we have a few extra pillows and blankets with a little left over dinner you can eat as I am sure you are both hungry."

Drake, Margo and especially Jonas were shocked. Lacey was the last person they expected to offer a place at her table, but she did and it was done. All they could do now was hope things didn't go wrong.

Tobias smiled at her. "I am honoured to be welcomed into your home, Miss. The floor will be better than trying to sleep under a tree with a saddle bag as a pillow, roots and rocks jabbing your ribs and your cloak as a blanket. Fleeing from imminent death is not something you take time to pack for I'm afraid."

Drake stood and extended his hand which Tobias promptly readily accepted. "Well if my wife says it is happening then it is happening." "I'm Drake Blackwell, my wife Lacey, that's Jonas Durant and lastly our fine Miss Margo Kelper. Oh yes, the little lady peeking from the window there is our pride and joy, Faline."

Tobias placed a hand to his heart and bowed slightly "It's a pleasure to make your acquaintance. I just want to say thank you again for giving me the opportunity to explain and be granted admittance into your beautiful valley."

Lacey smiled a little for the first time since having heard there was a rider and started walking into the house.

"It is getting late so let's got the two of you cleaned up and fed so maybe we can all get some sleep," she said.

"I agree," Jonas said yawning. "It's time for a nice fresh pipe and warm seat by the fire to relax my old bones before turning in for the night."

Faline wasted no time coming out of her room once everyone had made it in and struck up a conversation with Nolan. He was a shy boy and it took her some prodding to get him to speak, but she seemed to manage all right. By the time she had finished needling him about where he had come from, what he did to pass his time, if he had any pets, his favourite colour and anything else she could think of to interrogate the poor boy, everyone had got themselves ready for bed. Lacey had several blankets and pillows stretched out on the floor for their guests as makeshift beds prompting Tobias to thank her again for her hospitality. Drake, Lacey and Jonas said their good nights, and Lacey shuffled Faline and Cairo back to their room for bed as well.

The next morning everyone woke and gathered in the kitchen area to begin their daily ritual of making breakfast. Lacey was humming softly to herself as she whipped up eggs while Faline peeled some potatoes to fry in the pan. Drake went out to the chicken pen and gathered up some more eggs to accommodate their guests. Jonas was busy setting the table and gathering a couple more seats along with slicing bread and placing it in the basket in the centre of the table next to the butter and jam.

Tobias standing there stretching asked Lacey politely, "Is there anything Nolan and I can do to help you? I don't want to stand around being useless."

"Not at the moment. We are all accustomed to having our little duties for breakfast." Lacey smiled.

"If you change your mind we will be happy to help in any way we can," he said as he took a seat at the table.

Wiping her hands on a small plaid rag she smiled and thanked him again before beginning to lay food out on the plates Jonas had set on the table. Everything was piping hot and smelled great. Cairo lay on the floor next to Faline's chair in the hopes that she would drop her some bits of her breakfast as she so often did when no one was looking. She got caught once and was promptly scolded by her mother being told that Cairo had her own food and did not need to be eating theirs. Breakfast was enjoyed by all until every bit of egg had been scooped up off their plates with some mild discussion about the day and its upcoming events. Generally this involved what needed to be harvested, weeded, trimmed or potentially slaughtered. Tobias and Nolan had nothing to offer this conversation and being that Tobias had been feeling a little low since he and his son were given sanctuary here, he felt it necessary to contribute somehow.

"If you will pardon my intrusion on your conversation for a moment," he began quietly, "I am not much of a farming man due to my upbringing, I do however feel it necessary to contribute in some way in the village and I do have a certain skill set that may come in very handy if you all would like to learn." A wide white grin spread across his face as the thought of being able to do something useful made him feel much better about being taken in.

Jonas sat perplexed for a moment trying to figure out what it could be before agreeing to an unknown thing, then decided it would just be best to ask. "I suppose before we agreed to anything it would be best to know what it is that you are offering to teach us, son?"

Tobias sat back in his chair and folded his hands in his lap. "I can manipulate steel," he said proudly.

Drake's face had twisted a little trying to figure out what that meant exactly. "What do you mean?"

Tobias chuckled a little. "Sorry," he said. "I can do blacksmithing. You know, forge weapons and things like that. Swords, arrow tips, knives, anything that you can make out of steel really. I have tried my hand at armour a few times. That gets a little tricky and I haven't quite mastered that yet," he said rubbing his chin thinking about how he could better make the suits.

"So what is it that we can do?" Lacey asked.

"Well it's quite simple really," Tobias replied. "I just get a little house built for my son and I, and beside it I will make a half house with a big oven type fire place in it. I craft myself some basic moulds out of some nice hard woods and stone and voila! a blacksmith has been born in the village. You all can help me by, well by just helping me get the stuff built. It would take me forever if it was just Nolan and I putting it together, and once it is done I can teach you how to chisel out the stone, melt the metals and create the weapons. It takes time to do all those things. The more people the better really," he grinned.

Jonas looked between Drake and Lacey to gauge their impressions, but neither one looked like they had anything negative to say about it. "Well I can't see why this venture would hurt us at all, in fact the only thing I can see it doing is aiding us and the village in the future," he said leaning back in his chair.

"I agree with that," Drake said getting up to help Lacey clear the table. "Besides, what happens if soldiers do come looking for Tobias and Nolan? We can't stop them with wooden pitchforks and torches when they are all carrying around what Tobias rode in with now, can we?"

Lacey sighed pumping water into the little tub they used for washing dishes. "I suppose we haven't got much of a choice now really."

"I'm not trying to pressure anyone into doing anything they don't want to do, it was just a suggestion." He shrugged trying not to look a little hurt.

Jonas leant forward resting his elbows on his knees and looked at him. "It was a very good suggestion. We have been safe here for quite some time, but nothing ever stays that way forever. You were able to find us here, who is to say that there won't be others? Who is to say that those others will be as kind as you are? We cannot guarantee our safety any more and that needs to come first. We have spent too many years making this valley what it is and I intend to see it stay that way," he said smacking his fist on that table.

They all decided that this was the best decision and finished cleaning up after breakfast. Then they promptly set tasks for each person so that everyone was doing something different and there weren't three people collecting wood, and no one harvesting food or tending animals. They all knew this wasn't going to be an easy process, it took a long time just to build a house and now they were talking about building a shop of sorts to go along with it. Not one of them knew how to build any of the things Tobias had talked about, so that would take longer since he would have to guide them all through it. Everyone was so determined though and they almost saw it as a long awaited adventure.

Chapter 5

Hard Work Pays Off

After almost three years of toiling away, Tobias had everything he needed to survive in the valley with his son. During the first year the group spent time getting supplies together to make him a sturdy house to dwell in. While it was being built Jonas told him he and Nolan could come and stay in his house in the spare room instead of on Lacey's floor. It was still not a palace, but at least it had a bed, and Jonas, being as handy as he was, made a hammock in the corner for Nolan to sleep in. They would all get up and go next door to see Drake, Lacey and Faline every day for breakfast, lunch and dinner like normal, and the daily activities ran without a hitch. With the kids getting older, Faline took the time to show Nolan around the valley and introduce him to others as well as around the farm. Nolan, being a farm boy, came in useful, and while the adults were busy tending to the affairs of Tobias and his living arrangements, Faline and Nolan took care of Drake and Lacey's farm. It was almost a perfect situation.

Once the house had been finished, Drake did a little fancy woodworking and carved out some nice beds for Tobias and Nolan, while Lacey sewed some down into fabric to make large pillow type mattresses, and a few smaller ones for them to rest their heads upon. Margo pitched in and crocheted them some beautiful angora blankets as a housewarming gift. She had also gone down the lane to visit Lilly Tuttle, the village seamstress, and had her fix them up some decent clothes to wear out of some of the hides that Zeke had left behind.

Most of the people in the village made clothes, jackets, boots and gloves from the hides as they lasted longer than a fabric did. The only fabric to be worn really were undershirts, underpants, socks if you chose to wear them, stockings and garments to sleep in. Plus in order to get fabric, you had to send a scout on a very long secret journey in order to get it and it was very costly. They found it easier to just keep things the way they were. Tobias told them not to worry about helping them make other furnishings for a while as they were always over there eating anyway. He was just grateful not to impose on them all day now, and that he and his son could retire in their own home at night. Drake agreed and they left it at that for now.

The next task they took on was the blacksmith's hut, and that proved to be a little more difficult than they had imagined it would be. Tobias said that it would be best to build the very large oven for heating the metals first, after that they could build the structure around it.

"If you build the structure first," he began scratching his head looking around a bit, "trying to bring all the stone inside and tearing a hole in the roof will just cause problems. Besides, if the oven needs to be bigger once you begin laying the stone, you can move it. If the building is already there, you are stuck with it."

"I see what you are saying and feel that you have saved us a lot of very difficult work," said a very pleased looking Jonas stretching his arms above his head.

Tobias nodded. "I'm happy to do so really. I am not looking to make this take any longer than it needs to."

They all nodded in agreement and set about gathering the stone and making mortar to set it. It took about a week to build the large oven properly, making sure it had a chimney stack to filter the smoke out of the roof and a lip on the front to set the plates. When they had finished Tobias was very pleased with their hard work and patted his fellow workers on their backs.

"This is as fine a steel working oven as ever I've seen one!" he shouted merrily. "You two should go into business making them," he laughed.

Drake laughed a bit as he wiped the dirt and sweat from his brow. "I am truly flattered but having built one of these giant things in my life is plenty."

Jonas nodded brushing some dirt from his pants. "I think we did a fine job, too. I also believe that I am too old to go running around building these monstrosities for a living."

Drake and Tobias looked at one another and began to laugh. They poked fun at Jonas for a few minutes asking him if he needed a nap, or if he wanted them to woodwork him a cane now before heading in for dinner. Jonas simply shook his head and gave them each a good punch in the shoulder to let them know he was still in fairly good shape and not to be trifled with.

They spent the next several months building an open faced house type structure around the giant oven. They took great care in making sure that the walls remained several feet away from any of the externals of the oven so it didn't catch fire. Drake had fashioned several hooks and pegs for the walls so that Tobias could hang his finished wares or his tools, he also made him two sturdy tables that he could work on.

Faline and Nolan had been wandering about one day after tending to their duties returning to the workshop, heads held high as they dragged a giant metal block they had found all the way there. Neither of them was completely sure what it was, they just knew it was something that Tobias had to have.

"Where on earth did you find that?" Jonas gasped.

Faline's smile faded slightly. "It was out behind the big horse barn down the road. It never gets used," she stammered.

"Did you think to ask for it by chance?" Jonas asked.

"Well," Faline was now looking at her feet not able to meet her grandfather's eyes. "I didn't think I had to since it was just sitting there and no one uses it. It has a purpose here."

Drake chuckled a little. "Jonas, don't be too hard on her. She's right. That thing has been sitting out behind that barn as a bird stoop for as long as I can remember."

Jonas gave Faline a knowing look and turned to go back to work. Drake gave his daughter a pat on the head and started sanding down the top of the second table. Faline and Nolan looked around at what their parents had built in awe. This was an exciting time at all that had been accomplished over the last several years. They took one last look around as the others were putting finishing touches here and there. Tobias nodded his head with a smile and moved his new anvil towards the base of the oven. Faline and Nolan smiled back happy that someone appreciated their efforts and took their leave. Once outside and nearing the chicken pen to gather eggs before heading to the orchards Faline stopped and turned to Nolan.

"Do you think your dad will teach me how to do all of that?" she asked.

"I don't know, maybe." he shrugged. "Why would you want to know anyway?"

"Why?!" she yelled at him angrily. "What do you mean WHY?! Oh, I get it because I'm a girl right? And girls aren't supposed to know what boys do. Is that it?"

Nolan was beside himself. "I'm sorry Faline. I didn't mean to make you mad. That's not what I meant at all," he said, his cheeks getting red.

"Well then, what?" Faline hollered throwing her hands in the air.

By this time Nolan's whole face was red from embarrassment. He looked toward the ground, kicked a few pebbles and then slowly looked back up to meet her angry glare.

"I only meant that I didn't think that girls were interested in things like that. At least I have never met one before." He tried to smile but it immediately disappeared once he noticed that her expression had not changed.

She continued to glare at him for a few more seconds before she let herself relax a little. "I guess I shouldn't jump to conclusions." She put her hands firmly on her hips and said, "And you should be aware that I am NOT your typical girl. I enjoy all that life has to offer, not just things meant for girls."

Nolan's smile returned to his face. "I will do my best to keep that in mind."

"Good," she said as she turned and walked into the chicken pen. "Don't ever forget."

"Trust me," he began as he followed her into the pen. "I will really try not to."

Faline and Nolan often had little spats from time to time. Lacey reminded them that all good friends had their ups and downs, it was part of life and growing up. Her favourite thing to tell them was that "If you two always got along there would nothing for you to work towards. Friendship like everything else takes work." Faline would generally mimic her mother by saying this quietly to herself as she spoke as she had heard it so many times, Nolan thought it to be funny and did his best not to laugh out loud.

After today's little bout, it was not surprising that Faline caught herself thinking about her mother and what she would say.

She turned and looked at Nolan "Come on, we've got to get the eggs and then pick some fruit from the orchard before lunch. Mother will be upset if we don't."

Nolan nodded in agreement and set to work on chasing chickens out of their nests so that Faline could snatch their eggs. She always got a good laugh out of watching him flap his arms and try to make angry chicken noises at them as he ran about the pen. Anyone that had been walking by would have really, if they chose to come that far down the road that is. She hurried and gathered all the eggs she could stuff into the basket before the chickens came back around and got angry noticing what she was doing. Then the pair left the pen and went to the orchard.

"What did Lacey say to pick today, Faline?" Nolan asked.

She stopped briefly and thought for a moment. "Oh uh, well she said she wanted some red apples, pears and peaches I believe."

Nolan shook his head. "I don't think a guessed fruit is going to cut it. Are you sure it was peaches?"

"Pretty sure," she replied.

He shrugged and started picking the items she said Lacey had requested. It took them a little bit, but between the two of them they got it finished and were merrily heading back to the house with their goods. Cairo who had been sleeping under one of the big shade trees heard the two coming and got up with a moan and a stretch before following behind them to the house.

"Cairo, I don't understand how you can be so lazy sometimes." Faline laughed as she stopped to scratch her faithful friend behind the ears. Cairo gave a small sigh and licked her hand.

Nolan, Faline, and Cairo all entered the house to find that everyone else had made it in already and were patiently waiting for them to get there. Lacey went over to help them with their baskets while Cairo took her spot on the rug near the fireplace.

"You got everything I asked for today." Lacey said smiling at the two nervous kids.

Slowly the colour returned to Nolan's face as he said, "Happy to oblige Miss Lacey."

She laughed. "Nolan, I have told you before that you don't have to refer to me as Miss. Just Lacey is fine with me. I appreciate your courtesy though," as she patted his head as she walked to the tub of water waiting to clean the fruit.

"What's for lunch today, mama?" Faline cooed.

Lacey smiled. She loved hearing her daughter so happy and adored being called mama from time to time. "Well today, we are going to have a lighter lunch. It will be some strawberry jam on some fresh bread, a nice salad, and some fresh red apple slices on the side."

"It sounds delicious, mama," Faline grinned. "Why a light lunch though? I am sure the men are starving after all their man building." She laughed as she flexed her arms into tiny little muscles.

The men sitting at the table were doubled over in hysterics watching her display. Faline always had a way of entertaining and she could make a joke out of pretty much anything.

Lacey getting a good laugh watching her daughter as well responded, "The lunch is light because the dinner is going to be large." She winked at her.

"Are we celebrating something? Did I miss a birthday somewhere?" Her face was reddening at the thought of having forgotten someone.

"No love, you haven't forgotten anyone. We are celebrating though," Drake said from his seat at the table.

Faline brightened right up. "Really! Hooray! What are we celebrating?"

Tobias stood and raised his arms in the air. "The completion of my homestead!" he bellowed merrily.

"Really father? You mean it? We can finally be all moved in and start building furniture!" Nolan said excitedly.

Tobias laughed. "Yes, my dear boy. We have an official home. Yes, we can build furniture and yes, before you even ask, we will have plenty of animals and such for you to tend to."

Nolan ran across the room and held his arms tightly around his father's chest. Tobias had never been happier in his whole life than he was right at this moment and thought he may even cry, if of course that was a thing men did. He quickly wiped the tear from his eye before anyone saw it was there.

"Thank you, father." Nolan wept into his father's shirt.

Tobias hugged him a little harder and then held him at arm's length by the shoulders. "You are more than welcome, son," his eyes beaming with pride as he looked upon his boy.

"Well, all right!" Jonas chirped. "Let's have some celebratory lunch so we can go get some supplies from the villagers and get some animals over there, shall we." He winked at Nolan who was drying his eyes on his shirt sleeve.

"Oh thank you, Jonas," Nolan said.

"Anytime my boy. Anyone who tends animals the way you do should always have them." Jonas smiled.

"Agreed," said Drake. "That's why we all sat down and had a nice conversation about how to get you some."

"Really? You did that for me?" Nolan asked shocked he was thought of so fondly.

"Yes," laughed Drake. "We decided to give you one of our roosters and three hens to start you on your way. We are waiting for the piglets to be born, so we figured it best to go see the Platters down the road a bit and see if you could have a piglet of theirs. I'm sure they wouldn't mind."

"Then we thought," Jonas piped in, "since we lost one of our rams and we need a new one to keep the lines fresh, we would go see the Fritz's about one of those too."

Nolan was beside himself. He had already taken a seat to try and not pass out once Drake offered him a breeding set of chickens. Now he was being offered a piglet and a ram too. This was the most amazing day of his life. Tobias stood tall beaming with pride as he watched his only son glow with excitement and anticipation of having his own stock of breeding animals to tend to. He looked around the room at all the people sitting there with him, all of whom were also smiling, and cleared his throat.

"I just wanted to thank all of you for everything that you have done for Nolan and me in the last few years," he began as a tear welled in his eye. "You took us in knowing who we were and where we came from and then you helped us to build our future here. I don't think we will ever be able to repay you for all you have done." He took the seat next to his son and wrapped his arms around his shoulders.

"Just because you are who you are doesn't mean you are like the rest, and you have shown us over the last several years that you are in fact quite the opposite," Jonas said calmly. "We were happy to help you along your way, and if you can do what you say you can, well then you are going to be more useful to us here than somewhere else."

"I will most assuredly hold up my end of the bargain," Tobias replied. "I can and will teach you to forge and build some of the strongest weapons this village has ever dreamed of. I swear it by the gods."

Lacey began circling the table and dishing out food onto all the plates. "We shall see how things go, but for the time being let's focus on eating lunch, shall we?"

Drake looked up at her making her pause for a moment at his plate long enough to kiss her hand. "I agree. Let's eat our lunch and focus on work later. We have done enough toiling for the time being."

With that being said and the food having been distributed, Lacey took her place at the table next to her husband and they all began enjoying their wonderful lunch. They sat and discussed some of the furniture that Drake would help them to build due to them only having beds to furnish their home at the moment, and then they decided it would be best if Drake taught Tobias and Nolan how to work the wood in exchange for being taught metalworking. Tobias found this fair since he didn't want to impose on Drake's time any more than he already had and this way he would be able to build his own furniture.

Drake told him not to worry about the first few pieces coming out a bit "rough", over time he would eventually get better at it and he would be able to fashion himself some grand pieces. They all finished up their food and set to clearing the table. Faline and Nolan were excused to go out and gather firewood and some potatoes from the field for dinner. Drake took his leave with Tobias to go down the lane to Graham Braxton's place to acquire the necessary materials to make furniture.

"So this Mr Braxton, he's a woodsman?" Tobias asked.

"Yes he is," Drake replied. "A mighty fine one at that. He is also our village master carpenter, so any woodworking items that you may need you can get from him."

Tobias smiled. "I hope I can do with wood what I can with metals," he laughed.

"I am sure you are going to find that working wood is much easier and more than likely takes less time depending on what you are fashioning." Drake chuckled.

After a little while Tobias found himself standing in front of a small, but ornate little house surrounded by fallen logs, sawdust, saws of many shapes and sizes, and a bunch of other odd looking tools. Behind the beautiful little house was a larger wooden structure built on four large posts with a roof and no walls. He supposed that this was a work area after looking around briefly at the tables inside. They were covered in bits of wood, more tools, buckets of sawdust and drawings hanging on nails from the posts. Drake watching him laughed a little at his awe-inspired curiosity, walked to the front door and gave the knocker three solid raps. Not long after a burly man in his mid-forties with longer brown curly hair, amber eyes, and a brown beard beginning to show signs of age, opened the door and peered out at the two visitors. His face softened some when he moved his eyes from Tobias to Drake and promptly extended his hand to which Drake readily accepted.

"Drake my boy, how the hell are ya?" he bellowed.

"Graham!" Drake boomed back. "I am just fine thanks, and yourself?"

Graham folded his arms across his chest and took a deep breath. "Well I'm gettin' along just fine, thanks. What brings my little prodigy all the way down here?"

Drake smiled and looked over at Tobias. "I am going to teach this fellow right here how to work wood."

Graham studied Tobias for a minute wrinkling his brow before leaning in to whisper "Are you sure this pretty fellow can use tools?"

Drake was beside himself and it was all he could do to keep himself from falling over because he was laughing so hard. After catching the look on his companion's face he pulled himself together and choked out a "Yes, I am sure he will catch on." wiping a tear from his eye and taking a nice deep breath to calm himself a little more.

"Excuse me for interrupting, sir," Tobias said politely, "but I can work metal with the finest of blacksmiths, and I have offered to trade my knowledge for his."

Graham raised his eyebrow and replied, "Well then, if that's the case, what can I do to aid you in your learning?"

Drake now completely calmed down said, "We will need some wood to make some furniture and naturally he hasn't any tools to craft, so we will need some of them as well."

"Hmm." Graham ran his hand along his beard thinking. "I understand that these things are necessary, but what am I to get in exchange for my goods? I can't go running around giving everything away for free ya know."

"I understand," Drake replied casually. "I am prepared to offer one or two piglets from the next birthing of my finest sow. She is due to give birth within the next few weeks and it should be a nice sized litter."

Graham smiled. "I am very fond of pigs. They are fun to watch grow and get all fat before they are proper for some very fine meals." He sat smiling at the thought of watching some little pigs rolling in the mud behind his house.

"Depending on all we get from you should allow you to determine how many piglets you require as payment," Drake said breaking up his little daydream.

"Fair enough," Graham said. "I will pull a cart out from the back so you can load all you need on it. Just make sure to bring my cart back if you please. I'd hate to have to build another one."

He once again looked over Tobias with a more than curious gaze and started walking out, the two men following behind. Graham pulled a cloth off a large wooden cart and rolled it out in front of his company.

"All right gents, go ahead and find whatever it is you need and put it onto the cart. I will assess what you have taken once you are finished and determine my payment." He nodded at Drake and went back into the house.

Tobias shook his head a little "He doesn't like me much, does he?" he asked quietly.

Drake just smiled. "He is a little rough around the edges at first, give him time and he'll warm up to ya."

"I hope so." Tobias mumbled. "I feel as though after this visit I am to be coming here without you."

Drake nodded. "I can't hold your hand forever," he smirked and went about looking at the different logs Graham had strewn about.

Tobias followed along trying to determine which wood was good for what. He was not at all keen on selecting woods and couldn't quite get a feel for how Drake was analysing them. He watched as Drake looked them all over stooping to run his hands along some pieces, flipping around others, leaning some on end and eyeing them straight down to the ground.

"What is it that you are doing there?" he questioned.

"Well," Drake replied, "I am eyeing this one to see if it is straight. If you hold one end to your face and look straight down its body to the ground you can generally tell if it is."

Tobias looked confused. "You can't tell if it's just lying on the ground?"

Drake waved a finger before answering. "Not really. The ground is generally more uneven than the wood."

"I would have never thought of that." Tobias shrugged before testing this trick for himself.

Drake set the log back onto the ground. "Picking out wood is like picking out produce in a way," he told him. "You must check for flaws, smells, and how it looks. If it is flawed you may not want that for certain pieces. If it has an odour not common to the wood you are choosing, there may be rot setting in and it will be of no use. Lastly, you want to make sure that you choose a wood that 'makes' your furniture meaning if you are to build a nice bedside table you want a nice mahogany for its colour and texture, and not a pine as it is too grainy, knotty and plain."

Tobias scratched his head a little. "I see I have a lot to learn about different woods and their own unique capabilities."

Drake shrugged. "It will all come to you over time. There are tons of different wood, and only a few types of metal. Working both are generally the same I assume. You want the best kind for the piece you are creating."

"Now that I understand completely," he smiled.

"Excellent!" Drake rubbed his hands together. "Now let's fill up this cart, go home and get some work done, shall we?"

They spent the next couple of hours examining woods of all types briefly stopping from time to time for Drake to explain the kind of wood and what it was best suited for. After they gathered all the necessary lumber Drake took him over to the tools and began telling him about each one in a short summary before loading them onto the cart as well. Before they knew it they had a full cart and went back to the house to get Graham. Graham came out and took a brief inventory of the wares on their cart before determining what his payment would be.

"It appears you have loaded a lot of oak, some mahogany, a little cherry and a bit of cedar. You have also taken at least one of every tool I own," he said laughing. "So I figure that'll cost you two maybe three piglets depending on the size of the litter your sow creates."

Drake sighed a little. "I suppose that considering all the tools and better woods we have taken that's more than fair. Thank you my friend." He reached out his hand to seal the deal.

Graham shook Drake's hand and then reluctantly did the same with Tobias. He bid them farewell before watching the two men grab hold of the arms of the cart and begin hauling it away slowly. The task of pulling the cart was hard as the cart was very heavy and the road was uneven and rocky. They found themselves stuck on several occasions and had to carefully rock the cart free without rolling any supplies off it. Once they had finally reached Tobias's little farm they were sweating, tired and relieved dropping the cart handles and themselves on the ground.

"I have never pulled something so heavy, for that long in my entire life!" Tobias gasped.

Drake managed a little laugh wiping the sweat from his brow. "Next time maybe we should ask to borrow a mule."

Tobias's eyes went wide. "Are you kidding me!" he yelped. "We could have borrowed a mule to have hauled that confounded thing here!"

Drake clasped his hands together resting his elbows on his knees and merely nodded, a little smirk spreading across his face. Tobias groaned and flopped back onto the ground arms and legs spread out in defeat and exhaustion. His whole body felt like a wiggly, shuddering mass as he lay there.

"We will rest for a minute and then we have to unload it and get the cart back to Graham," Drake mused.

Tobias slowly shifted his gaze towards Drake looking at him from the corner of his eye. He was not at all impressed nor did he act as though he was going to get up from his sprawled position on the ground. Drake got up from his seated position after a few minutes and dusted himself off. He then stooped down and offered a hand to a still unmoving Tobias.

"Come on champ, got to keep moving or your body will not cooperate with you before long," he said again offering to help him up.

Tobias moaned and slowly took Drake's hand allowing him to help heave him off the ground. "Aargh!" he groaned. "This is not at all what I was expecting to happen to me today." He griped under his breath while brushing the debris off his clothes.

"You'll get used to it," said a laughing Drake.

It took them less time to unload the cart than it did to get it all on there. They chose a good spot in Tobias's workshop to lay out all the wood into their own separate piles and hung all the tools on the walls. Drake labelled them as they hung them so that Tobias would know which was which until he grew used to them. Tobias sighed as he watched him do it mumbling something about dummy labels, but Drake convinced him it was for the best and that Graham had done it for him when he was first learning. Once they had finished unloading and organising the two men grabbed hold of the cart once more and began walking it back to Graham's place. This time however it was a breeze to haul the wooden cart and they didn't get stuck at all, allowing them to get to Graham's place in no time.

"At this rate we will make it home just in time for dinner," Drake said happily.

Tobias grinned. "I will be happy to have finished with this wood run to be honest. It has humbled me in a way I never thought possible."

Drake smiled. "Every man has his limits, you have just begun to test yours really. I only laugh when you gripe because you come from a life of privilege. You have never known hard labour like we all do. This will become easier as you do it more often. You are going to be all right my friend." He gave Tobias a pat on the shoulder and went to go rap Graham's door knocker. Tobias stood a little more proudly knowing that he had passed his first test in Drake's eyes as truly being part of their village. It made him feel good and his smile widened as a result.

Graham opened the door with a big grin on his face. "Ah, my prodigy has returned, and with my cart and his new student still standing! Well done! Well done indeed!" he hollered as he clapped his hands looking at Tobias.

"Thank you, sir," Tobias replied smiling even wider now.

Drake extended his hand to Graham who readily took it and gave it a hardy shake. Graham waved to Tobias who then walked up to the two men and Graham offered him his hand as well. Tobias was honoured. Graham gave him a very firm handshake with a big smile on his face.

"To be honest, son I really didn't think you had the stones to do what you just did." He winked.

"With all due respect, sir, neither did I," Tobias said politely.

All three men stood there for a moment looking at one another before they all began laughing hysterically. Once everyone had calmed down, Drake and Tobias thanked Graham for the use of his cart to haul their goods and bade him farewell. Graham told Tobias to stop by anytime as he was more than welcome now that he knew he wasn't a feather weight. Tobias laughed and thanked him for his hospitality. Drake and Tobias took their leave heading back down the road towards home.

Lacey and the others were finishing up dinner when Drake and Tobias came strolling through the door sweating, dirty and laughing. The family just stopped and stared at them and waited to see if there was something they needed to say, but they just walked over to the wash tub to get cleaned up for dinner.

Drake threw his head back and smelled the air around him taking a nice deep breath. "Ahhh! My love it seems you have truly outdone yourself tonight. It smells terrific." He walked over and gave her a huge hug and a big kiss to go along with it.

Lacey's face reddened. "It's nothing really," she said softly slightly embarrassed. "Not anything in comparison to the things that you men have accomplished over the last few years." She smiled at all of them.

Jonas smiled up at her from his seat at the table. "It was what any good man would have done, my dear. Any man can build, not any woman can make delicious food."

Again, she grew red in the face. "Well then I guess we should get ready to serve the dinner then shouldn't we?"

"I will help you, mama!" Faline shouted as she came running out from her room. "What can I get ready this time?"

"Why don't you put the potatoes into one of the nice dishes, and the bread and butter can be placed on the table?" Lacey motioned to the items she spoke of sitting on the counter top.

Faline rushed right over to the pot on the counter and began scooping the potatoes into the nicest dish they owned and set it onto the table followed by the bread and butter. Next she grabbed the green beans with mushroom sauce that she had helped her mother prepare and laid that out on the table. She then turned and went about setting plates, napkins, knives and forks. Lacey looked at Drake and told him that the main course was inside the oven and it was his job to get it out and prepare it for serving. He did as he was asked simply because he couldn't wait to see what it was. When he opened the oven door his mouth began to salivate. It was none other than a rack of lamb with apple cinnamon dressing. He pulled it out, set it on the counter and began slicing the rack into portions and placing it as neatly as he could on the plate Lacey had set out for it. Once he had finished he brought it over and set the arranged plate of steaming meat into the centre of the table. He and Lacey then took their seats next to one another and all of them sat in silence for a while staring at the grand feast Lacey had prepared.

"This is the most amazing meal I have ever seen in my life!" Nolan exclaimed excitedly licking his lips.

"I have to agree," Jonas nodded smiling. "Lacey, my dear, you have surely outdone yourself."

The others nodded their heads, mouths watering, forks in hand waiting for their cue to dig in. Lacey sighed and smiled with contentment as she looked upon her family and friends all waiting to eat her food. She had never been so proud to have cooked a meal before this moment.

"All right, everyone," Lacey began softly, "feel free to help yourself, but please be polite about it." She laughed knowing they wanted nothing more than to just start scooping mountains of food onto their plates and start shoving it into their mouths.

Each one of them nodded in compliance and started passing plates and bowls around, pausing briefly with each person long enough to take what they wanted from the dish before passing it to the next one in line. It was quite the production line but it didn't take long before each person had some of everything and they all began to eat. There was no dinner time discussions of any sort as no one stopped inhaling their food long enough to be able to have one. This told Lacey that this was the ultimate dinner ever as there was always some topic of discussion over every meal. Before long, all the food had been finished and everyone's bellies were full and round forcing them to lean back in their chairs and give them a little pat. Lacey laughed watching them all get so fat on food that none of them could make the effort to get up from the table for quite some time.

Still chuckling, she said softly, "You all are too fat to help me clean up the dinner I slaved over now."

Wiping his face with his napkin, Drake replied, "I'm sorry dear, just give me a few more minutes and I would love to do it for you."

"We will all clean up for you Lacey. You can go and have a nice seat by the fire and relax." Tobias said rubbing his belly.

Lacey shrugged and got up from her seat. "As you wish." Again, she chuckled as she walked over to the rocking chair by the fire.

The rest of them slowly got up with their round little bellies and started clearing the table. Faline oversaw the washing, Nolan dried, Jonas put away, Tobias brought them the things to be washed and Drake cleaned the table and the oven. Even though they were all overstuffed and very sluggish, the kitchen was cleaned thoroughly and everything was finished allowing them to take seats along with Lacey by the fire.

"Well done everyone." Lacey grinned. "I am impressed that you got it done as quickly as you did, and so coordinated at that."

"We learned from the best, my love." Drake leaned over and kissed her cheek.

Jonas leaned back in his chair and readied his pipe as he did every night after dinner. "Well now that we are all fat and happy," he laughed, "we have some things to work out. We have a lot of work ahead of us it seems."

"That we do, my friend." replied Tobias. "It's not anything that we must work out really. It's going to be relatively simple once we get going."

"Be that as it may," Jonas said puffing his pipe, "everyone needs to know what they are doing and how it will be done."

Drake nodded. "Agreed. I suggest we do it in one week intervals. One week spent woodworking, one metal crafting, one farming, and one fighting. Then we just keep rotating like that. This way it keeps everything fresh, no one will get too frustrated over anything or worn out and the teachers have a chance in between to be the student."

"I think that sounds like the best way to do it," Tobias agreed. "I am in for that plan."

"Father, am I going to be allowed to learn what Tobias knows?" Faline asked looking up at him making the puppy eyes and batting her eyelashes.

Drake sighed. He could never say no to her when she made that face at him no matter what it was she was asking for. "Of course you can learn to do those things my little love." he smiled.

She jumped up and gave him a huge hug. "Oh thank you, father! Thank you!"

He laughed. "All right all right, don't get all worked up now. It is getting late and you should head off to bed. We all are going to need a good night's sleep to begin our day of learning tomorrow."

"Yes, father." She smiled her biggest smile at him and gave him another huge hug. She ran around the room hugging everyone goodnight and danced her way into her room with Cairo trotting behind her.

Once Faline was in her room and the door was closed Lacey immediately spoke up. "I cannot believe you agreed to let our daughter learn to create and use weapons!" she hissed at Drake.

"You and I both know that this is in her best interests, Lacey," Drake said in his defence.

"He's right my dear," Jonas said casually puffing his pipe. "She is going to have to learn. Besides, do you really want her wandering around in the world unable to defend herself?" Raising his eyebrow he turned and looked at his daughter waiting for her retort, but she had nothing to offer. She merely hung her head and frowned.

"I promise that no harm will come to your little girl, Lacey. I will train her to be the best of the best. She will not be defeated easily once I am through with her," Tobias said proudly.

She looked up at him with tears in her eyes. "I hope you're right Tobias. If what I've been told about her is true, she is going to need all the help she can get."

Tobias looked confused, and Lacey realised that she may have said more than she had wanted to. Drake shifted in his chair knowing that Tobias was going to start asking questions. Knowing that he was not a threat he figured it best to just tell him what they knew on the condition that Nolan was sent home first. Tobias agreed and sent Nolan on his way after he thanked them for the wonderful meal once more and wishing them a good night. Over the next hour they filled Tobias in on the story Margo had told them the night of Faline's birth, leaving him sitting in his chair mouth agape just as Zeke had been previously. The story having been finished, Tobias readily agreed to help them in whatever way possible. He vowed to make Faline the best fighter he could as well as a great blacksmith so she could fashion her own weapons no matter where she was and out of whatever she could find.

"By the time I am through with her she'll be taking down men as large as any of us, and she'll be able to make any kind of weapon you can imagine as long as she can find a stone, a stick or any combination of things. You won't need to worry about her at all." Tobias said placing a hand over his heart to swear his intentions to be true.

"We thank you for everything that you are about to do Tobias," Drake said extending his hand to Tobias. "I know now that you have come to us as a gift from the gods to help our Faline on her quest, whatever that may turn out to be."

Tobias took Drake's hand and gave it a firm shake. "I don't know about being any kind of gift for anyone if anything you all have been a gift for me and my son. Maybe we were meant to have each other for the greater good." He smiled at all of them.

"I will accept that to be true," Lacey said nodding. "We are all meant to be here helping one another. Without one another we cannot learn all we need to learn."

Jonas smiled. "This has been a grand day indeed. A glorious new homestead has been finished for Tobias and Nolan, a fantastic meal, and a superb new friendship that comes with new skills to acquire from all. Who could ask for more than that?"

"Not anyone that I can think of," laughed Drake. "However it is getting very late and we all have a lot to do tomorrow. We really ought to get to bed ourselves. Our children are going to be up and raring to go and we will be half awake."

Lacey stood up from her rocker and stretched. "I agree. All that cooking and chatting has left me rather tired. We do have a lot coming towards us and we should be rested properly every day."

Jonas, Drake and Tobias all stood as well. Each one took turns shaking hands and saying their goodnights before taking their leave. Drake escorted the two to the door and shut the latch behind them once they had left leaving him and Lacey alone.

She walked over and wrapped her arms around his chest and rested her head on his shoulder. "I hope we are right about all of this," she sighed into his shoulder.

He closed his arms tightly about her shoulders with his chin on top of her head. "Don't fret my love, everything is going to be just fine. For now we need to get some rest." He bent his head down and kissed the top of her head as they turned arm in arm and went into the bedroom and shut the door.

Chapter 6

All in a Day's Work

The next morning Faline was up and out of the bed as soon as the sun had crept over the top of her window sill. She couldn't wait to get started and there wasn't a soul that was going to be able to stop her. She hurried into her clothes, washed her face and brushed her teeth before tying her hair back with a piece of white ribbon. She whistled to Cairo who jumped to her feet and followed her out the door and into the main room. She knew that there was not going to be anyone awake, but she still groaned at the sight of the empty room. She bent down and gave Cairo a scratch behind the ears and tried sitting by the unlit fire in the fireplace, got restless and began pacing back and forth. Cairo was following her for a bit but grew weary of going nowhere and decided to lay on the rug instead. Faline looked out of the window and watched the birds and chickens all flitting around pecking at the ground.

"This is absolutely ridiculous!" she shouted throwing her hands in the air. "Why in the name of the gods am I the only bloody person awake in this house?"

"Calm down, Faline," Lacey moaned as she finished tying her housecoat string around her waist. "Honestly. Are you trying to wake the whole village, or just half of it?"

Faline glared at her mother for a moment before catching sight of her father coming out of the bedroom at last. "Father! It is morning and time to get ready to learn all the great things that Tobias can teach us." Her eyes were growing wide with anticipation of what the day was going to bring her.

Drake was still trying to pull himself together and shake the sleep off, smiled at her. "Yes, Faline I understand it is morning, but it is also still so early. The roosters have not even crowed yet. Patience my dear is something that you must acquire in order to be fully successful in your learning."

Faline slumped into the rocking chair and hung her head. She sat there for a time staring at her hands wondering if they were going to be able to do everything that Tobias needed them to do. She thought about the upcoming days and what they might hold for her. She was excited and scared at the thought of all the things she knew she had to learn, and she knew her father was right and she needed patience to learn everything.

"Patience," she mumbled to herself. "I have patience."

Drake and Lacey fumbled around the kitchen space preparing a small breakfast of eggs, bacon and some bread and jam. They were still both pretty tired from having stayed up to fill Tobias in on their daughter and hoped they would get through the day without forgetting something. They looked at one another and laughed a little at seeing the little purple circles under each other's eyes and finished up making breakfast.

"Maybe a good meal in our bellies will help us get this day started." Lacey yawned.

"I hope you're right, love," Drake mumbled as he stirred the eggs.

Once breakfast had finished cooking they moved it all onto plates and set them on the table motioning to Faline to join them. She reluctantly got up from the rocker scuffing her feet as she walked over to the table and sat down. Picking up her fork she started plunging it into her eggs flipping them around her plate and mushing them between the tines.

"Faline, please don't play with your food," Lacey grumbled. "You are going to need a full stomach to begin your lessons today."

Faline merely looked at her mother and set her fork down to rest on the side of the dish, eggs still clinging to it as they had been thoroughly mashed into it.

"Your mother is right I'm afraid," Drake said calmly. "You aren't going to get very far if you are feeling weak and hungry. Your muscles will tire out very quickly and you will lose focus."

"Ugh. Fine," she groaned as she picked the fork back up and slowly started eating her food.

Lacey looked at Drake and rolled her eyes. She knew that as her daughter got older she would encounter the normal teenage girl type mood swings, but this was ridiculous. It was only breakfast and already she was acting as if the world were ending just because things were not going how she wanted them to. All she could do was hope that things got better as the day went on. She was far too tired to deal with this attitude all day long.

The remainder of breakfast continued in silence. Everyone was either too tired or in Faline's case, too irritated to talk to one another. Drake sat there figuring that this was best for everyone and would guarantee that no fights broke out at the table, leaving him somewhat relieved. They finished eating and each one got up and cleaned their dishes and put them away. Just as they were about finished there was a knock at the door which sent Faline running to answer it with a sparkle in her eye. She whipped the door open and to her delight it was Tobias and Nolan standing on the other side, taken back a little by Faline having opened the door so forcefully.

"Good morning, Faline," Tobias smiled. "May we come in?"

She slid over some to allow entrance and nodded, her eyes wide and her smile wider, and the two visitors entered. Nolan nodded a hello as he passed and Tobias patted the top of her head before making their way to the table to join the others and discuss what was to occur that day.

"So where do we begin?" Tobias asked Drake folding his hands on the table.

Drake cleared his throat and took a seat across the table from him. "I guess it would be best if we started with you teaching us how to work the metals as that is probably going to be the most labour intensive."

Before the conversation went into any detail, Cairo raised her head and perked her ears right before there was another rap on the door. Lacey having been washing the last of the breakfast dishes went to get it. Jonas gave her a big hug after the door was opened far enough for him to get hold of her.

"It would seem you are just in time, dad," she said hugging him back.

"I'm glad I made it," Jonas smiled. "I'd hate to miss anything important." He walked over and took a seat next to Drake nodding a good morning to everyone there.

"As I was saying," Drake began, "metal working seems the best way to start, we just need to know exactly what we have to do to get started."

Tobias sat back in his chair. "On our ride here Nolan and I passed by a nice little mountain range with a good water system that had a lot of potential for mining iron ore. I saw a lot of red and black rock there which tells me that is where we start."

Jonas nodded. "All right then let's get some things together and get going. I assume we need a few horses, a cart and a pick or two?"

"Yes. We will need all those things and a few pairs of gloves. You will want to protect your hands," Tobias added.

Drake got up and made for the door stopping long enough to kiss Lacey on the way by. "Well let's get a move on then. I want to be back before dinner."

Jonas laughed. "Always thinking about your stomach."

"On the contrary," Drake commented, "I want to try and get some decent sleep tonight."

"Agreed," Tobias replied. "We are all going to be very tired men once we return."

The three men headed outside and started gathering their items when Faline raced out to them and tugged on Drake's arm.

"I'm afraid that this is something that you are going to have to stay here for. This is not the type of work for you my love," he told her kissing her forehead.

She put on her best pout face and batted her eyes for a moment before realising that for the first time ever it wasn't going to work. "Aw, come on dad! I can do it!" she cried.

Drake finished packing the saddle bag on the side of his horse. "I'm sorry but you're going to have to stay here and help your mother around the farm."

She stomped her foot and spun around to walk back into the house. "FINE!"

Tobias and Jonas stood there trying to conceal their laughter as they too finished packing their bags and fixed them to the sides of their horses. Drake sighed and hooked the cart he had to the back of his horse before mounting while the other two hopped into their own saddles.

"She'll calm down soon enough and realise that it was for the best," Jonas said reassuringly.

Drake frowned looking back toward the house and sighed. "I hope you're right."

Tobias nudged his heels gently into the sides of his horse and started moving with the other following behind. After a short time Faline who had been watching them ride away from the window could no longer see them any more and sat down in the chair with a huff.

"Don't be like that Faline," Lacey scolded softly. "They will be back before you know it and besides, you don't want to end up with cuts and blisters all over your hands. You are going to need them to be in tip top shape in order to craft and wield weapons."

Still slumped in the chair Faline smiled a little thinking about eventually swinging a real sword not just a stick she pretended was one or shooting a bow and arrow. She was going to make every effort to be the best at everything Tobias taught her no matter what it was.

She sat up in the chair and looked at her mother finally smiling her normal bright and cheerful smile. "All right, mother. I will wait for them to come home and help you and Nolan the best I can like always. I know that you, father and grandfather are only looking out for me. I'm sorry to have got upset."

"My dear, you are a wonderful young lady and we are proud to call you ours." She walked over and gave her a hug and a kiss on the cheek. "Now, let's get going out there as there is much to be done today and we have lost half our crew."

Nolan and Faline nodded following Lacey outside. They had a very full day ahead but between the three of them they were sure they would get it done somehow. They spent the rest of the morning hours pulling weeds and picking some of the ripened vegetables before the sun got too high making it unbearable to be in the middle of the field with no shade. They managed to pick a basket each of tomatoes, cucumbers, green peppers, corn, and squash all while pulling weeds as they went to hasten the process.

Once the field was tended they took a break for lunch which consisted of tomato sandwiches and cucumber salad, a lunch often enjoyed on the hotter days. After that they went back out and into the chicken pen. Lacey pulled the feed out which distracted the fowl long enough for Nolan and Faline to gather up all but a few of the eggs. They had designated nests that they always left to be hatched into new chicks. Faline peered into one of them and came back to report to her mother about them immediately as they were close to hatching.

"The eggs in the last nest are starting to crack, mama, she told her mother excitedly.

"Wonderful!" Lacey exclaimed. "That means that our friend Nolan here might get a couple chicks to go onto his farm sooner than later." She smiled at him and his face instantly grew as bright and cheerful as she had ever seen it.

"Thank you so much, Lacey," he said grinning from ear to ear. "I cannot believe I am going to have my own animals to take care of."

Lacey gently placed a hand on his shoulder. "Well believe it because it is happening soon."

He smiled and gave a small nod and continued to tend to his duties in the pen. Once they had finished there they went out back to the barn area to milk and feed the cow, let the sheep out into the side pen to graze and unfortunately shovel the manure out of the barn. This was not a task anyone enjoyed yet it needed to be done. Faline was proud of herself as she had only gagged once and fought off the urge to punch Nolan in the arm for laughing at her for it.

The three of them finally finished with the barn duties, let the cow out to graze as well before going to the small orchard to pick some of the fruit from the trees. They managed to get a half basket of peaches, a basket of red apples, almost a full basket of pears and a half basket of green apples as well. They walked back into the house and set them on the floor beside the kitchen counter before sitting at the table.

"Wow mother, we managed to do an awful lot today," Faline said wiping some sweat from her brow. "I can't believe how late it has got."

Lacey looked around the room at all the baskets of produce they had hauled in and smiled. "We did do a lot didn't we? And you are right, it is getting to be that time when I should start thinking about preparing dinner."

"Don't worry, mama, we will help you make dinner, won't we Nolan?" She turned and looked at the boy leaning back in his chair trying not to fall asleep.

He sat up a little, nodded his head and gave her a thumbs up.

Lacey laughed. "I know, I know. We are all tired but imagine how tired the three men that left us this morning are. So let's just keep dinner simple and painless."

Faline looked around at all the food they had brought in and what was already there to begin with. "Well even though we had some for lunch we could have some cucumber salad, but this time we could add some tomato to it."

"Okay, that's a start," Lacey said. "Um, we could also have some fried potatoes."

"How about some more of your delicious strawberry jam, too," Nolan added licking his lips.

Lacey winked at him and then her eyes lit up. "I've got it!"

She ran over and lifted the little door in the floor that let you into the root cellar beneath the house. She came back up a few minutes later with a handful of smoked sausage. Faline clapped her hands and Nolan about fell over.

"I forgot that Margo brought these to me a day or two ago. I put them down there to keep them cool and now I am so happy that I have them still." she was putting them into an iron skillet on top of the wood burning oven singing softly to herself, all while thanking the gods that she had such wonderful friends.

"Fantastic mama!" Faline merrily shouted. "We have a great painless dinner to make now. We will help you get everything cut up and dished out."

Faline took out the cucumbers and tomatoes and began cutting them into bite size pieces while placing them into a large bowl. Once she had them all chopped up she mixed in some olive oil, salt, pepper and a little vinegar as a nice dressing for her veggie salad before leaving the dish on the table. Nolan took the potatoes and washed them before chopping them up along with some onion. He took the liberty to cut some extra onion for Lacey and her sausages, before placing the potatoes, onions, a little ground pepper and some butter inside another skillet on the oven next to the sausages. While Lacey cooked on the oven, Nolan and Faline went about setting the table with plates, utensils, napkins, and glasses for the fresh milk Lacey had acquired that afternoon.

"Oh mama, this is going to be another marvellous dinner." Faline swooned.

"Thank you, my love. I am happy to oblige." Lacey laughed. "Thank you both very much for helping me prepare tonight's feast."

"It was our pleasure," Nolan replied with a little bow.

The three of them began to laugh as Nolan stood back to admire his little display. As the food was about ready to be set upon the table they could hear the cartwheels and the horse hooves on the dirt road outside the window. Faline raced over and peered outside quickly before throwing the door open and making her way to her father. She ran up just as he was dismounting and managed to get her arms about his waist before he had fully hit the ground.

"Well, a big hello to you too!" he laughed.

"I've missed you, dad!" she said squeezing him tightly.

"I missed you too, sweetie," he replied kissing her head. "I do have to get the cart unhitched and the horses tended then we can come inside."

She smiled and ran back inside only to come back out moments later with Nolan in tow.

"Nolan and I will help put the horses away, father, then you, grampa and Tobias can put the cart away and get washed for dinner." She smiled.

"That is the finest idea I have heard all day," Jonas rasped as he got down from his horse.

"I also agree that's a fine idea. I am starving and not at all suitable for a meal in Lacey's kitchen," Tobias said handing his reins to Nolan.

Jonas handed his reins to Faline who followed behind Nolan to the barn with his father's horse. Tobias took Drake and his horse with the cart over to his workhouse. They unhitched the cart from the horse near the side wall and put a few big rocks under the wheels to keep it from rolling anywhere. They all agreed that after putting in such long hard hours that day, they would unload it as needed for now and head back to Drake's barn with his horse.

Faline and Nolan had just about finished brushing out and watering the other two and told them to leave Drake's with them and go get washed. With nods and thank you's they left the barn and headed back to the house. Lacey laughed at seeing her men all dirty covered in rock dust and bits of pebble falling from their boots when they took them off. She promptly moved out of the way of the wash tub as the men filed their way over to wash, each one sighing in relief at the refreshing feel of the cool clean water on their faces and hands.

"You are all just in time," she smiled walking over to the table to put the bowl of potatoes down. "I have just finished the last of dinner so have a seat when you are done."

"Excellent!" Jonas exclaimed. "I am famished."

Nolan and Faline returned from the barn and joined the men at the wash tub to clean up. They wiped off the last bits of water and went to take their seats at the table. Everything smelled so wonderful for dinner again tonight that the dishes immediately began getting passed around until everyone had some. Although everybody sitting at the table that night had been through one of the hardest days they had experienced in quite some time, dinner conversation went on as per usual.

Faline was more than entertained listening to her father, Jonas and Tobias talk of their trip to the mountain to gather the iron ore. She figured since she wasn't allowed to go she would press them for as much information as she could: How many swings of the pick axe it took to break pieces off; if they found some in the water or just in the rock faces; how heavy the chunks were and if they were all large or some broke too small; did they have to wash them before loading them on the cart? She was brimming with questions and the more she asked the more Jonas laughed.

"You should have just taken her, Drake," he chuckled. "Then we wouldn't be getting blasted with so many questions."

Drake shook his head. "Next time she can go."

"You mean it? Really!" she shouted almost jumping from her seat.

"Yes." Drake sighed. "Only if you quit interrogating us now and tell us about your day instead."

She quickly quietened down and started filling them in on what she, Nolan and her mother had spent the day doing. Their day may not have held as much hard labour as her fathers and the others, but they still worked just as long making sure that the farm had been properly taken care of while they were gone. The grand finale in her eyes was that there were baby chicks just about ready to hatch.

"That's excellent news" Drake said swallowing a, big bite of potatoes. "That means our boy Nolan here will soon have some chicks of his own to tend to." He looked over at Nolan who was already smiling at the thought.

Tobias leaned over and patted his son's back in congratulations before continuing to eat his dinner. Nolan looked over at him and smiled then over at Drake and nodded a thank you as his mouth was full of food and he didn't want to be rude talking with his mouth full. His mother would have disapproved of such things and he was sure Lacey would have felt the same way.

By the time everybody had finished their food it had become dark and being that the day had already been filled with so much work and exerted energy, they all figured it best to turn in a little early. They all pitched in tonight to help clean up the dishes and put everything in order before bidding each other a fond good night and the promise of seeing one another in the morning.

Tobias and Nolan were the first to leave thanking Lacey once again for her excellent cooking and Drake for his help mining the ore. Jonas did not stay to light a fire or smoke his pipe. He said his old bones had been through enough that day and they needed to find their way into bed. He too made his way around the house giving hugs and kisses to Lacey and Faline, a hearty handshake along with a good evening to Drake, and of course a nice ear scratch for Cairo who wouldn't have let him leave otherwise. After he had gone Lacey told Faline that she and Drake were going to call it a night and that she and Cairo should rest as well.

"Mother," Faline said quietly. "Now that there are going to be weapons here, do you think it is going to scare folks?"

Lacey thought for a moment before she replied. "I'm not sure really. We have never thought about having weapons in the valley before. There has never been a reason to have them. I don't know how people will handle it."

Faline furrowed her brow some. "That's just it. If Tobias decided to ignore his reservations and come all the way down here no matter what, then who's to say that others won't follow? Who's to say that someone more dangerous won't follow?"

Drake put a hand up to stop her from saying any more. "Faline, I hear your concern, and we all felt the same way when Tobias came riding up, but we must try to put things like that out of our heads for now. We must keep the faith that we are safe here and stick to the plan of working with Tobias regularly to make as many weapons as we can, and train with them as often as we can."

She cocked her head to the side like a curious puppy. "So you are saying that we are going to be as prepared as possible as quickly as we can and pray to the gods that nothing happens?"

"Exactly." Drake forced a tired smile. "Now let's go get some sleep, shall we?"

"I suppose that makes some sense," she replied shaking her head. She walked over to give her mother and father a hug and kiss goodnight before taking Cairo to her room and shutting the door.

Lacey looked at Drake with concern written all over her face. "She is getting too smart for her own good. Pretty soon there isn't going to be anything that she can't figure out for herself. Her desire to want to do everything is getting stronger and she is becoming less satisfied with all, well this."

"I know," Drake said taking her hand. "For now we will just keep hoping for the best. She is going to venture out into the world at some point, and we need to feel as though we have done everything we could to make sure she does the right thing. Letting Tobias and his son stay here knowing where he came from showed mercy and love for humanity, that is something she needs to know and hold onto. Letting her learn how to build and wield weapons is going to be another useful bit of knowledge for her and may potentially keep her alive at some point. We cannot hold her back, all we can do is guide her in the right direction now."

Lacey buried her head into his shoulder and tried not to cry. "That's our baby, Drake. Our baby is not supposed to be so big." Her body started to tremble and Drake wrapped his arms around her to comfort her.

"You are a wonderful mother, and if I may be so bold I haven't been a terrible father," Drake whispered in her ear. "Jonas has been a truly wonderful part of her life as well. She has had nothing but love, support and encouragement her whole life. We have done nothing wrong and have raised a strong, loving, courageous, brilliant young lady. She is going to do some great things. I can feel it."

"My love," Lacey said calmly wiping the last tear from her eye. "How did I get so lucky to have such a wonderful family?"

He laughed a little putting his hand under her chin and lifting her face to look into her eyes. "I got just as lucky as you did." He smiled and kissed her. "Now let's go get some much deserved rest as we have both earned it."

"Agreed." She smiled back as she took his arm and went with him into the bedroom.

Chapter 7

Learning a Trade

The next morning as predicted everyone had slept in a little since the day before had been so laborious for everyone. There hadn't been a day where there weren't enough people to help with all the necessary tasks in a long time, and no one was used to being shorthanded. So once the rooster crowed to let them all know it was in fact morning and time to get up, they all moaned in their beds and lay there a few extra minutes before rising.

Faline and Cairo as per usual were the first ones to enter the main room that morning. They sat down and waited patiently for her parents to emerge to begin making breakfast. Drake and Lacey appeared a few minutes later both stretching at the door before greeting their daughter with a good morning smile. They prepared a simple breakfast of eggs, potatoes and bread with jam making sure to have enough for the inevitable visitors that would be knocking soon. Just as breakfast was being finished as expected Jonas came walking in, followed by Tobias and Nolan who was still trying to rub the sleep from his eyes.

"Hope you don't mind," Jonas began, "but I found these two stragglers outside on the road and thought they might want some breakfast."

Drake smiled. "The more the merrier. Besides, we can't all go running around on empty stomachs."

"One of these days we are going to be sitting here when you get up with breakfast already prepared or something like that," Tobias said. "As much as we appreciate you always feeding us, I have some guilt about it as well."

Lacey walked to the table with a couple of prepared plates and set them in front of Tobias and Nolan. "We don't mind at all," she said patting him on the shoulder. "Some day you will have a full running farm and we will take turns with dinner if it eases your mind some. As for now, we have plenty of food to fill your bellies."

Nolan and Tobias nodded and thanked her for breakfast before picking up their forks to begin enjoying their food. Lacey and Faline finished passing out plates and took their seats at the table as well.

"Let's not get ahead of ourselves here," Drake grimaced. "How are we to know that our friend here can cook?"

Seeing a look of concern spread across Drake's face over the thought of bad food was the funniest thing they had all seen in days. Immediately the entire room burst into laughter which left him sitting there looking completely confused and made them laugh even harder. It took them all a few minutes to collect themselves with an unimpressed Drake still not understanding why they had all laughed at him so hard, but eventually the laughter died down and they were able to resume eating.

They talked for a while through breakfast and after about how they were going to handle the activities that day. It was decided that Faline and Drake be brought to Tobias's every day for the first week to see how the ore they had mined was turned into a weapon. Jonas, Lacey and Nolan could handle the farm for a week and the others were just down the way a bit if they needed them to return. Faline's training on the craft was far more important than Drake's, so if help was needed it was determined that he would go and she would stay with Tobias. Faline was getting anxious to get going so they finished cleaning up and she, Cairo, Tobias and Drake all said goodbye and took their leave.

"Well my dear," Jonas said smiling at Lacey, "it's not getting any earlier, best we get started."

She smiled back at her father and nodded. "Okay, dad, let's get going. I'll help you two boys until lunch time. I'm going to come back here and prepare an apple pie with some of the apples we picked yesterday."

"That sounds like a great plan to me," he said rubbing his belly envisioning a steaming apple pie emerging from the oven. He turned and winked at Nolan who also looked like he was dreaming of a fresh apple pie.

The three of them laughed and went outside making their way towards the fields, animals and orchard. Lacey said she would go and tend to all the animals first and meet up with the other two after. Jonas said that was fine and took Nolan to go and pull weeds and gather more produce.

Meanwhile over at Tobias's workshop Drake and Faline had already learned how to break down the ore and get it ready for melting. Breaking the ore down and putting it into the cast iron pot was hard work and Faline was growing tired already. She kept at it though viciously pounding away at the rock to break it up into smaller pieces so that you could fit more in and so that it would melt faster. Tobias had got a blazing fire going inside the oven so that when the pot was ready it could be placed inside and the ore could be melted down.

Tobias looked at Faline and Drake very seriously. "When you are melting ores of any kind you must make sure that your fire stays hot. If the ores don't stay hot and begin to cool you are just going to get frustrated. The hotter the better or they won't melt."

Faline watched Tobias intently as he worked the fire while she tried to keep pounding away at the rocks before her. Her brow was covered in sweat and the dirt her hands left behind when she tried to wipe the sweat away. Cairo watched her as she worked but stayed a little further away than normal to avoid the spray of the debris that came from the rock when she hit it with the hammer. She was not far enough it seemed as her nice shiny black and white coat was still collecting little bits of reddish and black coloured rock fragments making her stand and shake herself off every so often. Faline just looked over and laughed apologising for getting her friend dirty and promising that it was unintentional. She and Drake spent about an hour hammering on rocks before Tobias told them they had enough to get started and let them set the hammers to the ground offering them both tall glasses of water he had retrieved from the well.

"This has got to be the best glass of water I have ever had," Drake said finishing his with a loud sigh and wiping some sweat from his forehead.

Tobias laughed. "I'm glad you are enjoying it. You and your daughter have worked very hard for it."

He bent down and grabbed the big handle on the oversized pot and set it on top of the roaring fire inside the wide mouthed open oven. He grabbed two small shovels and handed one to Drake instructing him to start scooping up the crushed rock and placing it into the pot. He handed Faline the poker for the fire and told her to shift some of the wood around under the grate holding the pot above the embers so they could put more wood in and keep the fire as hot as possible. Once this had been finished Tobias stepped back and smiled looking at what they had now achieved.

"Okay crew, now all we have to do is keep that fire going and wait for that ore to melt." He grinned.

Faline, now finishing the last of her water and having a seat on one of the logs inside the workshop, peered up at him with a questioning look. "How do we know when it's ready Tobias?"

"When you look inside the pot and the ore is glowing as red as the embers beneath, it is finished and ready to begin working with.", he replied.

She cocked her head to the side "What happens when it is red like that? And what do you mean by work with it?"

Tobias laughed. "You are a curious sort, aren't you?"

He pulled another log over and sat down across from her, Drake followed suit so he could listen to what Tobias had to say and figured he may as well be sitting while he did. Tobias took a sip of his own water and put his hands on his knees before proceeding.

"The purpose of heating the ore is to burn off the unnecessary rock sediment, leaving mostly the good metal behind and melting it. In order to melt an ore it must be heated for a long period of time over extreme heat which is why the fire must be always maintained." He paused briefly to turn and check the fire and add another piece of wood.

"Working the metal starts when the ore is at its hottest point and able to be poured into a mould. The ore will begin to cool and harden very quickly once it comes out of the pot and fills the mould as the air is much colder than an iron pot soaked in fire. You pour as much in as the mould requires and leave the rest in the pot to heat another time. The metal will have to be beaten into shape, reheated several times, beat some more, soaked in a big pot of cold water at times to cool it quickly and lots of other things that will be best for you to learn once we make it that far."

"I see. There is a lot to this metal crafting, a lot more than working wood like my father does. So are we going to have to go and get a lot more firewood today?" Faline asked.

"I would say that is going to be a necessary evil if we are going to make sure we have proper weapons," Tobias responded politely.

Faline smiled and her eyes grew big and bright. "Do I get to go out into the woods with you both to get it?"

Drake shook his head. "How did I know you were going to ask that? I suppose that if you are going to be a part of this, you may as well be a part of the whole thing."

She leapt from her seat and lunged at her father giving him a huge hug. "Thank you, father! I promise to be careful and stay close to you both."

"I certainly hope so because your mother would kill me if anything happened to you out there." Drake rubbed the back of his neck as the hair on it stood on end thinking about what Lacey was going to say knowing her beloved daughter had travelled into the woods. It was frightening to say the least.

Tobias grabbed a piece of the oak wood, a chisel and a hammer and began chiselling out the middle of the wood into an elongated pointed shape. Faline and Drake watched as he worked and kept putting pieces of wood into the fire when he would instruct them to do so. Before t long Tobias had sculpted a somewhat narrow long pointed shape in the centre of the wood that when he held it properly, showed them that it was in fact the blade of a sword.

Drake was impressed to say the least and didn't hesitate to reach over and shake Tobias's hand. "That was some mighty fine work there, and fast too if I do say so myself."

"Thank you," Tobias grinned. "I spent a lot of time around the blacksmiths as a boy studying what they did. I didn't have much else to do really but wander around the castle grounds and watch what the other people were doing. Well, unless you count in all the lessons and training my father had me doing."

"I should say that it has paid off quite nicely," Drake said picking up the carved out piece and looking it over.

Tobias ran his fingers through his thick blond hair and sighed. "It isn't done yet I'm afraid. I must make the iron mould over top. So what we need now is a big tub of water so that after I get the iron poured in I can cool it off immediately before it burns through the wood."

"I guess that makes sense," Drake replied.

Tobias took the bellows off the hook and blew air into the fire making it roar even higher than it was before throwing a few more pieces of wood onto the burning coals. He peered into the large iron pot and grabbed the pair of oversized tongs from beside the oven bringing them over and setting them onto the table next to his carved-out wood.

"Okay, let's go get some water and one of the spare horse troughs from behind the barn while the fire is still going really good," Tobias instructed.

Drake and Faline each grabbed a bucket along with Tobias and headed for the well where they left the buckets before going towards the barn. Faline stayed and started filling water buckets and carrying them to the workshop while the two men retrieved the trough and took it back as well. Once it was there Faline started emptying the buckets she'd brought into it and they all went and grabbed more buckets of water bringing them back in turn until the trough had successfully been filled.. Tobias again took the bellows and blew air onto the coals to heat them up throwing more wood onto the fire. Looking into the pot he turned and smiled at his two helpers.

"We are almost ready to begin" he announced. "It, has to be fast this time, so be ready to do what I say when I say to do it."

Drake and Faline nodded and stood at the ready. Neither one knew exactly what to expect, they just knew they didn't want to let Tobias down after they had got this far. Tobias slid a smaller table in front of the big pot and set the carved wood on it. He handed the tongs to Drake and told him to pinch the end of the wood that he had left whole with the tongs as tightly as he could so it didn't slip out. He told Faline to get some rags and dunk them into the water and drape them over the side of the trough next to the table in case someone got burned. He then gave the fire one last shot of air from the bellows before slipping on a very thick pair of gloves that went all the way up to his elbows he had retrieved from the saddle bag he brought when he first arrived in the little village.

"Drake, when I tip the melted ore into the wood I am not trying to fill it, so when I stop you need to take it and dip it into the water. Make sure it stays flat or it may slip off and be no good," he said firmly.

"Okay, keep the wood and my arm straight. Got it?" Drake replied.

"Faline, you need to be at the ready with those towels in case of any splashes. The spout on the front should keep it from happening but you never know," he told her calmly.

All she could do was nod. For the first time in her life Faline had no words. She felt like a statue and she knew she had to shake it off, but this was so important it was almost scary to be a part of. She was sweating and her body was trembling from nerves and anticipation. How was she supposed to go on grand adventures if she couldn't handle this?

"Pull yourself together, dummy." she whispered to herself.

Tobias looked again to the pot that had been sitting atop an inferno for the last several hours, turned and looked at Drake and Faline. "Ready?"

"Yes," both replied in unison.

"GO!" Tobias shouted as he slowly started tipping the pot of smouldering liquid metal into the carved out wooden sword blade. As soon as it had slowly coated the entire thing he raised the pot back and Drake did as he was told and spun to his left and with a loud hiss and a huge mass of steam filling the air around them, the metal hit the water draining the red colour from its body. Drake pulled it back out once all the red had disappeared and handed it to Tobias. Tobias grabbed a small hammer and the chisel, removing the metal from the wood he set it on the table. Using the tongs to hold it as it was still too hot to hold on its own, Tobias started hammering the inside to flatten it in and bring back more of the original mould shape. He would beat it in the middle then flip it on one if its sides and beat it there to raise the sides up more. Faline was now starting to understand what he meant by working the metal. They both watched him for about an hour before he stopped pounding on it and set it down.

"Well?" said Faline. "Is it any good?"

Tobias shrugged. "It's a little rough but it's just a mould so you aren't going to use a mould blade, only a finished one. This will be more than enough to get the job done. It will just take a little more time to finish a blade."

"I guess we could have done better then, huh?" Drake asked a little disheartened.

"No my friend, you did everything exactly the way I asked. I said I knew how to do it, but what I failed to mention is that I always had a mould to start with. This is the first mould I have ever built." He smiled between the two hoping to ease their concern.

"Okay," Drake said casually. "I suppose for now that's all we can do until it gets good and hard. Right?"

"That's right," Tobias nodded.

"Well since that's it then and it's well past noon we best be getting to my place for some lunch. Lacey is probably waiting on us." Drake motioned for them to follow him home.

"Good idea, father. I'm very hungry," Faline said grabbing at her now viciously rumbling stomach.

The three of them made their way back to the house to find that no one was there. Lacey did them the courtesy of leaving plates of food on the table for when they arrived and they all sat and greedily dug in without stopping to wash up first. Cairo nudged Faline's side with her nose wanting her lunch too, so she excused herself from the table for a minute to get her canine something to eat as well.

"Mama sure would be mad if she found out we all ate without having washed up first." Faline groaned seeing her filthy hands as she dished Cairo's food into her bowl.

Drake, looking at his own hands, winked at her. "We won't tell her if you won't."

"Oh, I'm not telling her anything," she said shaking her head. "She'd whip me for sure and she's never whipped me in my life."

Tobias and Drake both laughed and continued stuffing their mouths full of food almost faster than they could swallow it. Faline shrugged, sat back down and ate her lunch as well. Once finished they took a few minutes to clean up figuring it was the least they could do since they didn't have to make it and went back outside.

"Okay, so do you think that the woods around here will let the horse and cart through to gather, or are we taking the sled and dragging it back?" Tobias asked Drake.

"The horse should have no problem pulling the cart through the woods," Drake smiled. "My father has forged a pretty healthy trail line through one part of it, so we will just stay on that."

"Sounds good to me," Tobias grinned.

The group went out back to the barn and hooked the cart up to the horse as quickly as they could as they only had a few hours before they would have to turn around and come home before it began to get dark. Drake said that being in the woods while it was dark was something that only his father was brave enough to endure. He told Tobias that when you walked to the edge of the woods sometimes when the day was slowly fading into night, you could hear strange noises coming from within and that was enough to keep the people in the valley from wandering in.

Once the cart was secure they took the leads for the horse and led him down the road towards the big line of trees that surrounded their beloved valley and paused for a moment at the entrance. Drake pulled the reins a little and the horse followed behind him and Tobias. Faline, taking a deep breath, crossed the line between her safety and the unknown, her whole body quivering with fear and excitement as she took in as much of her surroundings as she could. She had never been allowed into the forest. It was forbidden and even the scouts that sat in the trees to watch for anyone coming didn't dare venture in more than about fifty feet.

Drake stopped the horse and pointed to the ground just inside the trees. "There are plenty of fallen trees in here," he told them. "It is best to collect them from the ground and not stray too far from the path. You don't want to get lost in here."

Tobias started making his way through a thick patch of bushy plants and thorny bushes towards the logs nearest him. "I hope we don't have to fight our way through plant life to collect all the wood." he mused while pulling at a thorn-covered branch that had caught on his pants leg.

"No, we won't," Drake said laughing while Tobias fought with the bramble bush. "Some of the areas are cleaner."

"That's a relief," he said pulling the last thorn out. "I'd hate to be bloodied and bruised when we go home for dinner. I'd be embarrassed to say I was defeated by a thorn bush."

Faline and Drake got a good chuckle out of his comment and moved on to find more fallen wood. Faline however was not paying attention to the ground so much as she was watching the crow she felt had been following her since she entered the forest. She managed to trip over a branch that was partly buried in the dirt from the last rainfall and would have fallen on her face had Cairo not grabbed the back of her dress to steady her.

"Thank you. my friend." She patted Cairo on the head as the dog's tongue lolled out the side of her mouth. "If I didn't know any better I'd say that bird is following us, Cairo," she whispered.

Cairo looked up towards the crow sitting high on a branch and peering down on them with a steady watchful gaze. She looked to Faline and let out a tiny whine before stuffing her nose into her back to keep her moving along with the others, who had by now moved on down the road. She took the hint and trotted a little bit to catch up to her father who was emerging from the bushes with an armload of wood.

"There's more there than I have seen anywhere so far. Go in and grab some please," Drake instructed.

"Okay, father." She went through the patch of bushes and saw a bunch of dead fallen trees that had split apart over time and began collecting what she could carry.

Tobias came to help her as Drake told him this would probably be the last stop they had to make with all the wood on the ground. He was happy to oblige especially since it meant there weren't any more thorns. The three of them spent the next hour tramping back and forth through the brush with arms filled with wood to the cart. They filled it up right there just as Drake had predicted which meant they could now head home for dinner. It also meant they could get out of the forest before it became dark out. They didn't want to be hanging around in there when the light of the sun had vanished. Drake and Tobias made sure the wood stayed secure in the cart by tying it down with twine before heading out.

"There we have it." Drake grinned cinching the last knot tight. "We shouldn't have to worry about anything of importance falling off now."

"That's excellent news, now can we get out of here," Tobias said glancing around uneasily. "This place is starting to give me the creeps."

Drake looked up at the sky which was now turning different shades of red and orange. "Yeah, we should definitely start making our way back now."

He grabbed hold of the horse's reins and began steering him around to face home then continued forward down the dirt road. Tobias stayed at the rear of the cart in case there was a problem and Faline along with Cairo walked alongside her father. As they walked he noticed that she kept looking up at the trees here and there. Curiosity began to get the better of him when she almost walked right off the side of the path and into a bush.

Grabbing her arm and pulling her back into reality he quietly asked, "Is there something that you want to talk about?"

She looked at him before turning her attention again to the trees. "No, not really."

Drake wasn't satisfied with this answer pushed a little more. "Are you sure, because I just saved you from having a nasty run in with a nice sized bramble bush while you are what? Daydreaming? Looking for something?"

"Father, do you think it is possible that an animal can show interest in what people do?" she asked.

"I suppose they could at times if their curiosity was peaked. Some animals are naturally curious." Drake tried to figure out why she had asked but couldn't read her face at all.

"That makes sense I guess." Her gaze was still fixed above her head scanning the trees for something that she expected to be there.

"Faline," Drake said sternly slowing down the movement of their caravan. "You need to tell me what's going on here. You aren't paying attention and you're going to get hurt."

His voice was very stern at that point and it forced Faline to turn and look at him eyes wide as she had never heard him be so aggressive towards her before. If she had been younger then she was she may have cried a little, but she told herself that crying was for babies and a baby she was not.

"I'm sorry, father." she began quietly. "I will pay attention to where I am going. I didn't mean to upset you." She hung her head and clasped her hands in front of her.

Drake rolled his eyes and about kicked himself for being so angry, but the last thing he wanted was his daughter to get hurt and to have to explain the who, what, why, where, when and how's to Lacey. For several minutes they walked along in silence. The edge of the forest was slowly coming back into view, which given the fading light was all but perfect timing. Then from behind them like it was waiting for her to stop looking came the caw of the crow. Faline stopped dead in her tracks and whipped around looking for it. Her father stopped because she did and felt the need to look for it too.

"That's it! That's what I have been watching for!" she hollered.

"Hush, Faline," Drake whispered. "It's getting too late and who knows what you will draw out of the shadows hollering like that."

She nodded and said, "Father, that crow has been following us since we came in here, I just know it."

He looked up at the shining black bird peering down at them with what Drake could swear were purple eyes. He convinced himself that it was the light playing tricks and no animal could have purple eyes.

"Drake, the light," Tobias moaned. "We need to get the hell out of here!"

Drake did not hesitate. He grabbed Faline's hand and pulled her along with the horse towards the opening of the forest. They were so close to home and he was not about to get trapped, eaten, maimed or anything else when they were a mere fifty feet from the exit. Everyone was moving at a hastened pace and before they knew it the forest was behind them and the house was right there.

"Please don't ever do that again!" he shouted at Faline.

"But father, the crow," she started but was instantly silenced when Drake held up a hand.

"If you ever intend on making another trip with me into those woods you will do as you are instructed and nothing more. Is that clear?" he grumbled through clenched teeth.

Again Faline hung her head this time not able to stop the tears from falling. "Yes, father," she whined before turning and running into the house. She did not stop until she had reached her room and shut the door.

Faline lay in her bed stroking Cairo who had curled up next to her trying to comfort her distressed master. She could hear the soft mumbling of the conversation in the main room as dinner was being prepared, yet she had no interest in going out there to be any part of it. Having her father become so angry with her was almost embarrassing and she didn't want to have to face her mother on top of it. She was sure that Drake was out there informing her mother what had happened and was waiting for her to come bursting through her door wanting to know what she was thinking lingering in the woods. It was more than she could bear so she felt it best to stay put.

As she lay there staring out of her little window, she thought about the crow with its purple eyes having followed them all around the forest. She couldn't figure out what it had wanted but she was certain that it had wanted something. Her mother's voice was calling her to come to dinner but she was so caught up in thinking about the crow she tuned it out. She wasn't in the mood to eat any dinner that night, every part of her being was consumed with trying to work out what the bird had wanted.

The noise of the voices in the other room slowly became faint, and the only sounds left to be heard were that of Cairo's breathing as Faline began drifting off to sleep. The soft glow of the bird's purple eyes began to show more clearly in her mind the further she drifted into sleep. It was almost like the bird was trying to communicate with her from inside her mind as she slept making it hard at first for her to fall into a deep sleep. Eventually the eyes staring at her and Cairo's slow breathing became a mesmerising duo and she was sleeping heavily and everything else had faded away.

Chapter 8

The Dream Becomes Reality

Time went by without any major incidents. Had it not been for the rotation of the crops and the growth of all the baby animals, you would have never known that much time had passed. Most of their days were filled with lessons and teachings of metal crafting, farming, woodworking and weaponry. Everyone had gained a lot of knowledge about all these things and as far as they could tell, each person was earning high marks in all their lessons. Tobias was especially happy with the natural ability Faline had shown with all the weapons he had been teaching her to use and create. He hadn't taught her that many yet because he wanted her to have a good feel for the most recent one before moving her on to the next.

Faline had learned how to craft her own bow and arrows with or without metal tips, and she had been recently studying the use of the short sword. He would only have her use the actual sword when practising on her own, if she was sparring with Drake, Nolan, Jonas or Tobias himself, who had learned from Drake how to fashion wooden ones so no one got seriously hurt. Faline was having the time of her life learning how to build and use these things, especially the archery.

On the other hand while Faline was out and about enjoying her days fencing, practising archery, crafting new weapons and still managing to help her parents around the farm, her nights were something completely different. Ever since they spent the first day in the forest outside their little village, Faline had had her dreams haunted by the purple-eyed crow. It still never spoke, it merely watched her with its glowing purple eyes. She went to sleep every night waiting for the bird. She even tried talking to it a few times asking it who it was, what it wanted, if it was in trouble, but still it said nothing. Her sleep was not as restful as a result of the uneasy feeling she was getting not knowing why the crow kept coming. If only she knew why maybe she could accept it being there.

Lacey was out in the kitchen area one morning preparing breakfast as per usual when an overtired Faline came stumbling out of her room. The giant dark circles under her eyes told Lacey everything she needed to know.

"Dearest, you have not been sleeping well for months now," she said softly. "Tell me what is going on."

Faline looked sheepishly up at her mother folding her hands in her lap. "I don't know really. I try to go to sleep, but it just doesn't come."

Lacey sat next to her daughter and began stroking her hair. "Do I need to start making you teas before bed? You are fifteen after all and one cup of herbal tea before bed might help you."

"Maybe tonight I will try a cup." Faline yawned. "Thank you very much, mother."

"I still wish you would tell me what is bothering you, and don't tell me there isn't anything because I can read it on your face," Lacey said as she walked back over to tend to breakfast.

"If it becomes a more serious problem I promise I will tell you. Other than that, I think it is just something I need to work out." Faline smiled at her hoping it would make her drop it.

Lacey furrowed her brow. "If it becomes any more serious Faline you are not going to sleep at all."

"Mother, I said I would tell you if it got worse," she said getting to her feet. "Can we please drop it now?"

Lacey shook her head. "All right all right, no sense in both of us getting all worked up this early in the morning. Let's just finish making breakfast and enjoy this beautiful day."

Faline sighed. "That sounds like a great idea." She stretched a little and went over to help her mother finish preparing the food and setting it out on the table just as everyone else started walking in the room.

Drake stuffed his nose in the air and took a deep breath in. "Oh boy, does something smell awful good this morning, ladies." He looked at the two of them grinning.

Jonas, Tobias and Nolan came strolling in through the front door at just the right time just like always and took their seats at the table. There was nothing like starting your day with a big family breakfast complete with quiet conversation and occasionally a few laughs.

"So what's the game plan today, son?" Jonas asked Drake in between bites of eggs and sausage.

Drake swallowed his oversized bite before replying. "I suppose we should probably pick the rest of the peaches before they rot on the trees. Lacey can jar some up and get them down in the root cellar, and we can take some out into the village for a few extra goods we need."

"Sounds good enough to me," Tobias nodded. "I could use a day of farming instead of being beaten up by your daughter." He turned and winked at Faline who smiled at him.

"I agree that a light day is what everyone is in desperate need of," Lacey commented. "We have all been pushing ourselves so hard to get as much done as possible, that we all need a break."

Nolan, cleaning his plate with a slice of bread before stuffing it in his mouth, nodded his approval. "I have barely had time to raise my animals properly since I've gotten them. Do you mind if I go and tend to them today? I will take some time out to catch some fresh fish for dinner too."

Tobias patted his son's shoulder. "How about you help us pick for an hour or two, then you can have the rest of the day to do as you please?"

Nolan was ecstatic. "Yes, sir. That sounds more than fair to me."

Lacey looked over at Faline who was barely keeping her eyes open and frowned. "Faline, I want you to take the day to rest. You are far too tired to be doing anything today."

Faline looked up from her half eaten plate of food and gave her mother a quick smile and a nod. She lay her fork upon the table and asked to be excused before going and placing some food in Cairo's dish. Once Cairo had been fed she wished everyone a pleasant day, went back to her room and flopped onto the bed. She listened to the conversation outside her door, some of which was about her and the concern her parents were showing at her exhaustion, and some had to do with the harvesting of the peaches and tending the animals.

She was tired; this she knew for certain, but how could she sleep when every time she shut her eyes she had that bird staring at her. She lay there with her eyes closed listening to the fading voices of her family and friends as they left the house until the only ones left inside were her and Cairo.

After what seemed an eternity the exhaustion took over and she fell asleep, once again the purple eyes peering out at her from the darkness she lay in. She tossed and shifted around in her bed until her subconscious could stand it no more. She began shouting at the bird inside her mind.

"WHAT IS IT THAT YOU WANT!" she screamed, hearing her own voice echoing in her mind. "TELL ME!"

The eyes simply stared, but for the first time since she began seeing them they blinked. It was like a small notion of the bird saying I hear you.

"Please." Faline began more calmly this time so as not to offend the bird. "Please tell me why you are here."

A low soft voice of a woman came out of nowhere and startled Faline. "I'm here for you," she said.

"What do you mean by that?" Faline asked the voice behind the eyes.

"You are who I have been waiting for. Now I have found you," the soft voice answered.

She was perplexed and had no idea what to say or do but managed to keep questioning the voice. "Why have you been waiting for me? Who are you?"

"All in good time. Come back to the forest," the voice told her.

"I can't go back there, it's forbidden for me to go alone," Faline gasped.

"You must come back, it's the only way," the voice said with some urgency.

Faline was now trying to wake herself up. She was not interested in going to the forest alone to see about some nameless creature which kept staring at her while she slept.

"Please!" the voice begged. "Please come to the forest. You will find me there and I mean you no harm. I promise."

"You are a bird! How can you possibly hurt me anyway?" Faline grumbled. "The only thing you are doing is preventing me from sleeping and I don't even know why."

The purple eyes began to fade away slowly. "If you promise to come to the forest, I promise to leave you alone while you sleep." The voice giggled.

"Promise?" Faline asked with some scepticism in her voice.

"I swear it." the voice said calmly.

"Ugh. Fine, if it will get you to let me sleep." Faline moaned throwing her hands up in defeat.

"Excellent. Thank you so much, Faline," said the voice. "I will be seeing you soon." And with that the purple eyes flickered out and disappeared.

Faline lay in her bed for a little while longer before opening her eyes and looking about her room. She was unsure if what she just saw was a dream or not as she had been so tired. It could have just been a manifestation of some sort that she made up to try and set her mind at ease. She knew that there was only one true way to find out. She was going to have to go to the forest and see what, if anything, was there.

"Great!" she mumbled under her breath. "Not only am I going to be wandering around today with no sleep, but now I get the privilege of going into the forest chasing phantom eyes and voices." She shook her head and slipped on her boots.

"Come on, Cairo," she said leaning down to stroke her furry friend. "We are going on a small adventure."

Cairo looked up at her and left a meaty paw on her knee almost as if she understood what she had just been told. Faline scratched her head for a minute and stood up from the side of the bed. With a big stretch upon rising she made for the door briefly pausing to grab a pouch filled with water and one of the knives she had crafted with Tobias, just in case. She took a quick peek around to make sure nobody was watching and ran to the end of the road towards the opening of the forest. Once she was there she stopped and listened to the sounds coming from within. Every bird seemed to be singing; there were sounds of wolves in the distance, and of course the sound of a crow somewhere inside. She turned and looked over her shoulder once more to make sure she hadn't been followed and continued into the trees.

"Cairo, there sure is a lot more activity in here today than there has ever been when we have come with father and Tobias," Faline whispered to her furry friend.

Cairo looked up at her and whined moving closer to her side to make her feel more at ease. The two of them walked down the dirt road trying not to disturb anything or make any noise. The plus side was that there was so much noise in the forest today that you couldn't hear their footsteps, the downside you couldn't hear what was coming either. At one point while she was avidly searching for signs of the crow, Faline had stepped on a small branch that cracked under the weight of her foot which made both jump about a foot in the air.

"I don't know about this any more," she whispered. "The whole thing is making me feel really uncomfortable."

They had made it about a quarter mile into the woods when finally the crow appeared before them having flown onto a low sitting branch of a tree a few feet away. Faline and Cairo stopped dead in their tracks staring up at the bird which in turn stared back with its purple eyes. For several minutes nobody moved or blinked; she wasn't sure if it was more fear or curiosity now that held her where she stood, but she knew for certain that she was in it now and could not turn back. Relaxing just a little but not letting her guard down as she placed a hand on the hilt of the knife stowed in the tie of her dress, she began to speak to the bird that had haunted her dreams.

"Well. I came all this way," she began, her voice quivering a little "I don't intend to just stand here staring at one another all day."

The crow stared at her intently and before she knew it the voice was back in her head.

"Please do not be afraid," the woman's voice told her.

"I promise to try," Faline said aloud. "This is very new to me. I've never had an animal talk to me before, nor have I had one get into my head like you do."

The crow tipped its head to the side. "I'm sorry to have been such a pest. I generally don't go out of my way to bother people. Usually it's the other way around."

"Why me then?" Faline said getting a little annoyed. "And if I might ask, why like this? Why didn't you just do or say something while I have been in the woods before?"

"It wasn't safe for me to do it then," the bird answered. "I am willing to stop being in your brain, but you must promise not to be afraid, and not come after me with the knife you have with you."

Faline grew a little pale and let go of the handle of the knife she had been hiding. How did the bird know she had it? "All right, I will not attack you," she said calmly. "I gather you aren't here to hurt me then."

"No," the bird replied. "I want to help you. Are you prepared to meet me now?"

Faline raised an eyebrow looking confused. "Meet you? Haven't I done that just now?"

The bird laughed. "Not quite. I don't generally really meet people until I am sure they are ready."

"Okay then, I guess I'm as ready as I'll ever be. I didn't come all this way for nothing," Faline half mumbled under her breath.

Again the bird laughed then took a flapping leap off the branch it was perched on towards the ground. There was a bright flash of purple light that was so bright it made Faline throw a hand up to shield her eyes. Once the light had gone standing before her was not a crow, but to her amazement a woman. She was a beautiful woman at that with bright red hair, purple eyes, pale skin, wearing a forest green crushed velvet dress with gold trim that came into the shape of wings spreading across the breast, and a hooded cloak made entirely of black feathers. She was speechless. What do you say in that situation? What do you do? Cairo sat next to her growling at the woman waiting for her master to tell her what to do.

"Please, Faline, do not be afraid, as I said I am not here to hurt you or your furry friend. I merely want to help you." The woman casually took a step forward.

Faline took a small step back. "I don't mean any offence but this is just, oh I don't know, bizarre."

The woman nodded. "I understand that the unknown is a bit scary and will take some time to get used to, but I am begging you to stay and listen."

Faline cleared her throat and tried to grab hold of her lost courage. "Can you at least tell me your name? Maybe that would help me out some."

The woman threw her hands up in the air causing Cairo to jump in front of Faline, its teeth bared and a low growl coming from the pit of her stomach. "Of course!" she laughed. "How could I be so rude? My name is Hildy."

"Okay, Hildy, who or what are you exactly?" Faline asked placing a hand on top of Cairo's head to calm her down.

"I am a witch," she exclaimed proudly. "And if I do say so, a mighty fine one at that as I am the high priestess of my coven."

"A witch! And there are more of you? I thought witches were stories told to little kids to scare them from going into the woods." Faline gasped, her eyes growing wide. "Are they going to get into my head now, too?"

"Ha-ha! No, no, no. I have set strict limits on who can do what and when. They all must come to me before doing anything." Hildy smiled. "Otherwise they are removed from my coven, boundaries you know. To answer your question, yes there are many more, we are all quite real and most of us are very friendly."

Faline sighed. "I suppose in a way that's a relief. So what exactly are you here to help me do? I was unaware that I was doing anything that fantastic to make someone like you come out of their way to find me."

Hildy motioned for Faline to follow her into the forest and off the road. Once inside the safety of the trees Hildy waved her hand over some little red polka dot mushrooms, which sprouted up out from the ground with a small rumble into little mushroom shaped chairs. Faline's eyes grew wide watching the little show and it made Hildy laugh.

"Please take a seat." Hildy pointed to the mushroom chair as she sat on her own.

Faline looked at it for a moment, even poked it first to see if it was real, then did as she was told when she was sure it was there and not a figment of her imagination. Hildy crossed her legs and folded her hands neatly in her lap and looked at Faline with a big smile spreading across her face. It made her feel a little uneasy, but she figured that if this woman had wanted to hurt her she'd have done it already.

"So now that we are comfy," Hildy began, "let's get some things out of the way."

"Such as?" Faline asked.

"Well for starters I know you are still sceptical of all that is happening and why it is happening to you." Hildy simply said. "That is easy to answer. You are the chosen one as it appears."

Faline twisted her face in confusion. "Chosen for what exactly?"

Hildy chuckled. "See now that is where the second half of the answer comes in and gets harder to answer precisely."

"Well, why don't you try?" Faline said, a tinge of sarcasm in her voice.

Hildy took a deep breath and smiled. "Okay, bear with me while I do my best. You my dear were born with a destiny, one so great that it has taken hundreds of years for the person meant to carry it out to be born. Because of this, you have been watched by beings like me since the day you took your first breath, although you and your family never knew. We have watched you so that no harm befell you as your life is far more important than any of our own. We needed to make sure that you grew up to carry out what you were born to do. After all our waiting here you are, on the verge of sixteen and almost ready to begin your adventure."

Faline's mouth had slowly begun to hang open not even realising that she was sitting there catching bugs as her mother would say. This was absurd. No way was she someone who was that important. She was just a simple farm girl doing simple farm things.

"No way. I think you have the wrong girl," she said shaking her head as she got up from her mushroom.

"I think not my friend." Hildy was more serious than she had been since their conversation began. "You are she who is meant to save the world. We have waited hundreds of years to fight by your side and aid you in all your quests and adventures. There is no way we are wrong as the prophecy told us it was you."

"Prophecy? What prophecy? Why am I always the last to hear about everything? I mean seriously." Faline shouted throwing her hands all about and kicking the log next to her on the ground.

"Calm down, Faline," Hildy urged. "You possess the gifts, you just need to harness their power."

"What gifts?" Faline turned and stared at her.

"Haven't you noticed that animals follow you? Gift number one, you can control animals. You can talk to them with your mind which is how you could talk to me as a crow. All will listen to you no matter what kind it is."

"So you're saying if I happened upon let's say, oh a dragon, it would do what I say?" Faline crossed her arms across her chest in disbelief.

"Yes, that is exactly what I am saying," Hildy said calmly. "You will also be someone who will master the art of weaponry without challenge. You will have no rivals really. Can you get hurt? Oh, yes. Will you die? Not very likely, especially when we are all around to help you."

"So you are saying that I am to go on some epic quest to save the world with all sorts of animals and all of you by my side, and that I am going to slay my way to the top?" Faline asked still not sure this was happening.

"That is exactly what I am telling you," Hildy said smiling.

Faline sat back down on her mushroom and put her head in her hands. Cairo came and licked the backs of her hands trying to comfort her master but got nowhere. Faline was in shock and had nothing left to say. She sat there silently for quite some time pondering all the things that Hildy had just told her, trying to make sense of it all but she couldn't. How was this happening?

Faline looked up at Hildy, her face filled with concern. "What am I saving the world from if I may be so bold as to ask?"

Hildy laughed. "Of course you can ask, silly girl. In a nutshell there are three kings all fighting to take control of everything that there is on this beautiful earth. None of them have ever been successful, they have only destroyed more and more land, people and animals as they have tried. Their wars have marred and mangled so much that we need you to finally put an end to it all, uniting all the kingdoms into one big happy family once more."

Faline sat there staring at her wanting to speak but no words would come.

"I understand that this is a lot to take in and I am terribly sorry that I dumped it all on you like this," Hildy said softly. "I never meant to alarm you or make you upset, but I was running out of time and I had to tell you now."

Faline looked up at her with tears in her eyes. "I just don't understand how I was the one to get chosen for something like this. I'm not anyone special. How am I supposed to save the world when I don't know anything but farming? I'll get everyone killed."

Hildy walked over and knelt by her feet placing one hand on her knees and the other took one of her hands. "My dear, since the day you were born you have never been alone, there has always been someone with you whether it be your family, friends, or us. We would never let you do this alone which is why I had to communicate with you. I needed you to know we were here. You will always have help when you need it, and sometimes when you don't. Someone or something is always going to be by your side."

She reached over slowly and gave Cairo a scratch behind the ears. For the first time Cairo didn't growl at the purple-eyed woman and this gave Faline hope. Cairo was an instant judge of character, and if she liked her then Faline would accept her as well. Faline sat up straight in her little mushroom chair and wiped the tears from her eyes as Hildy stood up.

"Okay, Hildy I believe you now," she said sniffling a little. "Tell me what I have to do."

Hildy once again let the huge smile envelope her face. "For now all you need to focus on is your studies with Tobias and getting some rest. The quests will begin to unfold when you are ready. You will know when it is time, trust me. Until then we will keep in touch. I will visit when it is necessary and you can come here and find me anytime."

Faline stood up and looked towards the sky noticing it was getting late. "Thank you, Hildy. I best be getting home before they start looking for me."

Hildy lurched forward and squeezed her so tightly Faline thought she might pop. "You have made me so very happy today! Thank you so much, Faline!"

"You're welcome," Faline gasped.

"Oh, before I forget." Hildy reached into the pocket of her cloak and pulled out a shining red stoned amulet and handed it to Faline. "This amulet is going to protect you in some ways, guide you in others and when the times are right it will let you know when something of great value is near."

Faline smiled for the first time since stepping into the woods and let Hildy put the amulet around her neck. "Thank you, Hildy, that's very thoughtful of you."

"Don't thank me," said Hildy. "Thank the gods as they are the ones that left it here for you hundreds of years ago."

Faline was dumbfounded as she held the stone in her hand and thought about the gods having intentionally left something here just for her knowing that she would have it some day. After everything that she had just been through, this shouldn't have surprised her and she was almost ashamed that it did.

"Okay, Hildy, I will make sure to thank them tonight before I go to sleep." She smiled.

"Make sure you do, they'll be expecting it." Hildy laughed. "Now go home before you are found out. We will talk again soon."

"Okay, see you around, Hildy," Faline said as she turned to walk away.

Hildy gave one last wave before a big blast of purple light flooded the place where they'd been sitting. The mushrooms had shrunk back to their normal size and Hildy was cheerfully cawing as she flew away. Faline knew it was almost time for dinner back home and she needed to hurry if she was to make it there before they all returned from the fields. She ran as fast as her legs would carry her almost wishing that she could ride Cairo back as her furry friend was much faster. Cairo did not go speeding off down the path like any other dog would have done. Instead she stayed right by Faline's side as she ran, almost as if she didn't want to get ahead of her in case something happened. She was always happy to have Cairo with her, but today being in the forest Faline was especially glad she was there.

When the two of them reached the entrance to the forest they stopped and looked around making sure that no one was able to see them coming out of there. When she was sure no eyes were upon them Faline took off like a shot down the road towards the house and bolted in through the door not stopping until she reached the safety of her bedroom. She sat down on the side of the bed breathing heavily, Cairo panting by her feet, and shook her head.

"Cairo, we could have been in big trouble." she gasped.

Cairo looked up at her, her tongue hanging out of the side of her mouth, and if Faline hadn't known any better winked at her. She blinked a few times staring at her furry companion wondering if she just saw her dog wink at her, then decided that it was in fact possible and scratched behind her ears as a thank you for being so loving and loyal. Then they both sat and relaxed waiting for the others to come inside and get ready for dinner.

The door to the house opened a short while later and the rest of the family, tired, dirty and hungry came in from their work outside. Faline having had ample time to catch her breath and regain the colour in her face went out to greet them. She offered to assist her mother in preparing dinner while the men got washed and had a chance to relax, which Lacey graciously accepted.

"Are you feeling a little better then?" Lacey asked taking hold of her daughter's chin and looking her face closely. "You seem to have a little more colour than last I saw you."

"I feel a little better now, thank you." Faline smiled at her. "I guess I have just been doing too much and not sleeping enough."

"Well tonight I will make you a nice chamomile tea and that should help you get a proper night's sleep." Lacey winked.

"Thank you, mother," Faline said peeling some carrots. "I am sure it will do wonders for me tonight and tomorrow I will be back to my old self."

"I sure hope so," Jonas piped in. "I don't like seeing you all down and out, my dear. It makes your poor old grampa sad."

"Don't worry grampa, I'll be okay," she said smiling at him.

"Good to hear. We gotta get you back on the crew. Wasn't the same without you there today." Jonas grinned.

"I missed you today as well grampa," Faline said and gave him a hug as he walked by.

"Come on, old man," Drake mused. "Time to get beat at least once before dinner."

"Sorry my dear, your father thinks his horseshoe is standing strong." he winked. "Maybe tonight I will show him what's for."

"Maybe, grampa," Faline laughed. "Good luck."

Jonas took a seat across from Drake to play a game of checkers while dinner was being made. Tobias and Nolan offered their assistance with dinner as well, Lacey not wanting to say no to any help she was offered had them set the table and start the fire. She and Faline made a large salad, peeled some potatoes for frying, and finished cleaning the fish Nolan had caught earlier. While they were cooking Jonas was again griping in the background about Drake being a cheater, which made Tobias laugh.

"Maybe you need to play against someone else, Jonas," Tobias smirked. "Then you might win."

"You just hush up over there!" Jonas growled.

Drake laughed so hard he almost fell out of his chair. "There's no need to get so angry."

"I've said it before and I'll say it again, you sir are insanely lucky or a cheater," Jonas said angrily as he got up from the checker board and went to take his place at the dinner table.

"I give up," said Drake throwing his hands in the air. "I guess I'll just have to find a new opponent."

Lacey and Faline were finishing setting the food out while Drake and Jonas took their seats along with Tobias and Nolan. Lacey then sat followed by Faline after she fed Cairo her food too so she wasn't left out of the group.

"I believe you should have found someone else to play a long time ago," Lacey said flatly.

"Oh sure, take his side," Jonas mumbled.

"Father, I am not taking any sides," she said passing him the bowl of salad. "I am simply saying that it is time you two stopped bickering over a silly game."

Taking the bowl of salad and scooping some onto his plate before passing it on, Jonas grimaced. "Maybe I am just too old to play games."

"You are not too old, grampa," Faline said smiling at him. "You are just right."

He smiled and patted her head. "Thank you my lovely little girl. You always make me feel so much better."

"Good," she replied. "Now let's forget all this nonsense and eat some of this food before it gets cold."

"Great idea," Tobias agreed. "I for one am starving as I am sure everyone is after a long day of work."

They all nodded and finished passing around the plates of food. The regular clacking of cutlery on plates filled the room along with simple dinner conversation. Faline was happy to hear about everyone's day as it allowed her to push her own thoughts out of her mind for a while. She especially enjoyed Nolan's tale of how his new piglets spent a good part of their free time rolling away in the mud so he had to give them a bath. Envisioning having to give fat little pigs a bath was just the sort of happy thought she needed now. Dinner finished up with everyone pitching in to help clean everything up and allowing Lacey, along with Faline, to go and sit by the fire first since they cooked. Jonas came to sit lighting his pipe not long after, then Tobias, Nolan and finally Drake who put the dishes away before joining them.

They spent a little while longer chatting by the fire allowing their food to digest before Jonas, Tobias and Nolan bade everyone a good night and took their leave for the night. Lacey got up and made Faline a nice hot cup of chamomile tea and they sat by the fire a little while longer. Lacey had begun to prod Faline a little more about what might be troubling her, but Faline said that it was just having been doing too much in a small amount of time and Lacey let it go. Drake gave Faline a good night hug and went to bed as she was just finishing her tea. Lacey hugged her good night as well telling her to leave her cup in the wash tub and she would take care of it in the morning. Faline thanked her again and made her way to her own room for the night.

As she lay in her bed she couldn't help but wonder if everything that had happened earlier in the day had happened. Faline peered over the side of her bed and looked at Cairo who was lying on her side fast asleep already.

"Lucky dog," she whispered.

Faline reached up and felt around where the red stoned amulet lay resting on her chest and she knew that the events of the day had happened. She still didn't know how she was selected to be such an important person or why for that matter, all she knew now was that she had a lot more work to do than she thought. On a lighter note she did have a guarantee that Hildy would not be invading her dreams preventing her from sleeping unless it was important and she had to get hold of her immediately.

So this is it. This is the beginning of my first adventure. This is something I have thought about doing since I was a little girl listening to grampa Zeke tell me of his adventures, only I didn't think mine was going to be so challenging. she thought to herself. *I only hope I can make everyone proud.*

She smiled thinking about being able to communicate with animals, maybe pull a few pranks on Nolan while she was learning to harness the ability. That would be fun and he wouldn't know she did it. She clutched the amulet tightly in her hand wondering if that was going to make sure she succeeded at acquiring all her abilities. Faline figured she would let time tell the tale as Hildy told her it would.

Still clutching the amulet she said softly, "Thank you great gods for giving me this gift. I hope I can use it to achieve the goals you have set for me."

She rolled over onto her side draping her arm over the bed so she could rest her hand in Cairo's fur. Within a few short minutes, her other hand still holding tight to the amulet, she had fallen fast asleep.

Chapter 9

Hildy Pays a Visit

More than a year passed by in what seemed like a few weeks. Every day Faline spent training as hard and as long as she could to master everything made available to her. Tobias couldn't be happier with her progress and often told her she was far better than any man he had ever trained. She generally laughed when he said things like that thinking he was only poking fun at her to make her work harder, but one day she realised he was telling the truth.

Faline could hit the bull's eye on the archery target more often than all of them combined, she had beaten them all at knife throwing, and she had bested all of them but Tobias with the short sword. He knew it wouldn't be long before she took him.

"My dear, you are one of the most astonishing people I have ever met." Tobias panted trying not to let her beat him.

She swung her sword a few times barely missing his arm twice. "I have a great teacher," she smiled.

They scrambled around in the grass, swords clanking together with a loud ringing and a few sparks, both getting tired and neither wanting to admit defeat. Finally, Faline made one last broad swing and knocked the sword out of Tobias's hand, then quickly manoeuvred into place putting the tip of her sword to his Adam's apple.

"Do you give up?" Faline said breathing heavily.

Tobias stood with his arms up eyes wide and locked on hers. "I do believe our training is finished."

Faline lowered her sword and took a step back. She smiled at him while the two caught their breath. He shook his head then bent down to retrieve the weapon that had been smashed so relentlessly out of his hand. Upon picking it up he noticed that there was a crack in the blade. He turned and looked at her, she was still smiling from her victory. Tobias could not believe that not only had she finally bested him, but she almost cracked his sword in two.

"Come on great warrior," he chuckled. "Let's get inside for dinner."

"Okay, Tobias," she nodded. "Oh, can I be the one to tell them I beat you? Please."

He laughed and shook his head. "As much as it will embarrass me, be my guest. You've certainly earned it."

"YES!" she shouted happily and raced for the house.

Moments later Faline she had burst through the door with a loud thud. Everyone jumped at the commotion and turned to look at the heavily breathing young girl that obviously had something important to tell them.

"You will never guess what happened today," she said with a huge smile on her face.

Lacey smiled at her knowing the look of pride on her face meant she had finally bested Tobias. "You are probably right Faline, so why don't you spare us all the suspense and tell us what happened?"

Tobias came walking in at that time and made his way to the wash tub. Jonas winked at him knowing full well that he had been beaten today. Tobias merely held his hands up, shook his head and got washed for dinner.

"Okay, I'll tell you," said Faline excitedly. "I finally beat Tobias with the short sword."

The whole room lit up with excitement. There was applause, cheering and some small bangs of their fists on the table, all of which made Faline feel even better about her accomplishment. In her eyes it took forever to have made it that far, in their eyes she graduated too soon.

"Congratulations, Faline," Nolan said politely.

"Thank you, Nolan," she replied nodding her head.

"Well done love, now will you please take your place at the table for dinner." Drake chuckled.

Tobias helped Lacey set out the food out before taking his own seat followed by Lacey. Dinner was filled with excited chatter about all the happenings from the day. Nolan told how his chickens had been successfully laying some beautiful eggs now that they were full grown, Faline went on about her fight with Tobias making him hang his head some, and Drake told them that the new calf that was born last spring was coming along nicely, and he would make a fine working bull in time.

Lacey however remained moderately quiet. The thought of her baby having grown up so fast, now a champion fighter, made her a little uneasy. Faline was just about sixteen and with everything that had occurred, all that she has learned, Lacey knew it was only a matter of time now before she went out on some adventure. Faline was going to go somewhere that she couldn't be around to protect her, and she didn't like it at all.

Dinner had finished, dishes were washed, and everyone had their time to relax by the fire before bidding one another a good night. Jonas, Tobias and Nolan all left leaving Drake, Lacey and Faline to finish out their evening in peace. Faline didn't last much longer and decided it was time for her and Cairo to go and get some sleep. She wished her mother and father goodnight, giving hugs and kisses before excusing herself from the room. Drake looked at Lacey who appeared frustrated and sad.

"What's the matter, love?" Drake asked as he reached out to take her hand.

"Our baby is all grown up, Drake," she replied quietly.

"Yes, she most certainly is." Drake smiled. "She'll be sixteen tomorrow and she has accomplished so much." He leaned back in his chair thinking about all her victories.

"Drake, don't you get it?" Lacey squeezed her lips closed trying to hide the fact that they were quivering. "She's going to leave."

"We don't know that for sure. Margo told that tale but who's to know what's going to happen?" Drake said trying to console his distraught wife.

She leaned over and buried her head in his chest and began to sob. "I don't want this to happen. I don't want her to go and be a saviour." she wept. "I want her to stay here with us so we can protect her like normal parents."

Drake rubbed her back and gently stroked her hair. "If it is truly her destiny, then we cannot stop it."

They sat by the fire for a little while longer allowing Lacey to cry some more in the comforts of his loving arms. Drake did his best to calm her down so they could go get some sleep themselves. Eventually she had stopped crying and began collecting herself. He stood up reached out his hand to help her out of her seat and enveloped her in a tight loving hug.

"Come on, my love. Let's go get some sleep." He gently kissed her forehead and led her to their room.

That night as Faline slept she couldn't shake the feeling that something was coming. After a few hours, the feeling proved true as the luminescent purple eyes of Hildy returned to her mind. Faline lay there for a few minutes while the purple eyes watched her and decided that she should find out what Hildy wanted.

"Hello Hildy." Faline said imagining that she had waved to her. "It has been a long time, so I assume that you came for a reason."

Hildy laughed. "Of course I did, silly. I told you I wouldn't come unless it was warranted."

"Okay then, what is it?" Faline asked.

"You have done and grown so much since last we talked Faline," Hildy told her. "It's time you went out and tried a few of your new found skills."

Faline thought for a moment before saying anything. She wanted to make sure she understood; she didn't fully get what Hildy meant. She shifted a little in her bed and finally came to the conclusion that maybe it was her weapons training Hildy was talking about, and kind of hoped it wasn't a task to send her out for battle. Faline felt that she had studied hard and learned to fight very well, but she knew she wasn't ready for something like that.

"Hildy. you aren't sending me to war are you?" she asked anxiously.

Hildy began to laugh. "No, no, no, I wouldn't send you off to do something like that right away," she chuckled. "It is a beginner's task, a scavenger hunt if you will."

Faline sighed in relief. "That's good because I am not ready for any type of huge battles, Hildy."

"I know that, dear," Hildy said sincerely. "What you are going to do is travel the woods towards the west until you come across a cave in front of a giant mountain called Mt. Diamanti. You can't miss it."

"What am I doing going into some cave in the mountains?" Faline asked curiously.

"Well, if I told you it wouldn't be as exciting now would it?" Hildy again started laughing. "You will know what you are looking for once you find it. For now just know that your job is to travel through the woods towards the west until you reach the mountain cave. Once there you obviously must go into the cave, yes it will be dark so I suggest taking some torches. You will find what you need inside."

There was more sincerity in Hildy's voice as she told Faline what she needed to do than there was joking. This was something that Faline was not accustomed to when talking with Hildy as she was generally very playful. The task she was being sent on had to be important.

"All right, Hildy, I will go and seek out this cave in the mountains." Faline finally agreed. "What happens if I get lost?"

"You can't get lost really. The mountain stands tall above the trees and will act as your guide," Hildy responded quickly.

"Well, what about the way home? There isn't a mountain here," Faline said, a hint of sarcasm in her voice.

Hildy sighed. "Faline, you are destined for great things and have many more secrets hiding within yourself to unlock. You will not and I repeat, not get lost. Trust me." Hildy's one purple eye closed as she winked at Faline.

"Okay, if you say so," Faline replied. "When am I to leave?"

"When you have gathered all of your supplies and are ready to go," she answered.

"Can I take Cairo?" Faline knew she would take her regardless, but she figured she had better ask to be courteous.

"Of course you can," Hildy giggled. "You can take anyone who is willing to go really."

"Okay, then I will start preparing in the morning. It will be interesting to see what everyone says about it. They don't even let me into the woods near the house alone, and now I am going so much further."

Hildy did not seem concerned and replied calmly. "Leaving is never easy, letting a loved one go is even harder I imagine. Your family will have to get used to it."

Faline groaned. "Guess this is it then. I better get some sleep, Hildy, I have a lot to do to make all this happen."

"Correct, you are my dear." Hildy's voice told Faline she was smiling. "Thank you again for being patient with me. I wish you all the best on your journey and remember there is always help when you need it. All you must do is ask."

"Thank you, Hildy, I will remember that." Faline smiled at her. "I will talk to you later then?"

"Absolutely!" Hildy partly shouted. "Sorry, didn't mean to yell. I'm just so excited for you. I will be in touch."

Faline said goodbye to Hildy and tried to sleep. She knew that she was somewhat sleeping through their conversation as it was always in Faline's mind, but she needed some real sleep. The upcoming days were going to be long and potentially lonely. She needed to make sure she had all the supplies she needed to go, and she honestly wasn't sure what that entailed. Faline figured she would ask her father, he'd know what she needed to bring.

This was a huge moment in her life, tomorrow she would be sixteen and now she was embarking on a journey to find, she didn't know what yet, she just knew it needed finding. She needed rest now though, so after forcing everything out of her head she finally drifted back off to sleep.

The following morning it was business as usual in the house, breakfast being cooked, chores being handed out and all the usual commotion of people coming inside to join them. Drake and Lacey were preparing eggs, sausage, and bread with peach jam for breakfast. Faline loved the smell of sausage cooking. It made her mouth water making her want it more than she already did.

"Good morning, mom and dad," she said smiling at them both. "The food smells great."

"I'm glad you think so birthday girl," Lacey cooed running over to hug her daughter.

Faline was almost shocked that she had forgotten it was her own birthday. "I almost forgot it was my birthday," she laughed.

"How on earth could you forget that?" Drake was astounded and looked at her to make sure she was feeling all right.

"I'm fine, dad, just a little less sleep than I'd have liked," Faline said putting her parents at ease. "When breakfast is over I need to talk to you both before we go out and work."

Lacey's eyes widened, fearful of what she had to say, but managed to fake a smile on her daughter's behalf. "We will not go until we have had the chance to have our chat." She leaned over and kissed Faline's forehead.

"Thank you mom, I appreciate it." Faline grinned and went to take a seat at the table with the others.

Breakfast time at the house like always was a joyful time filled with high hopes for the day to come. Faline was especially excited that morning knowing that she was about to start preparing for her first official adventure. This was a monumental occasion in her eyes and nothing was going to get in her way.

As they all finished up and helped get things cleaned and put away, the house slowly cleared out as everyone set about their chores. Lacey and Drake stayed behind with Faline so that she could tell them what was on her mind.

"So, my dear, what's on your mind?" Drake asked as he took his seat back at the table, followed by Lacey who gently folded her hands in her lap and smiled at her.

Faline looked down at her feet. Now that the time had come to tell them she had about lost her nerve. She snapped herself out of it after a moment, telling herself that this was bound to be the easiest part, and if she couldn't do this she'd never make it to the mountain. She took a deep breath and looked up at her parents.

"Okay, here goes nothing." Faline began softly. "About a year ago or so I began having visions of big purple eyes staring at me while I slept. No voice, no face, just eyes. It took a bit of time and a lot of sleepless nights before I finally made the eyes tell me who it was. I was instructed to go to the forest to meet the person they belonged to and I did."

Lacey jumped up from her seat at the table cutting off her story "What do you mean you went to the forest?" she hollered.

Drake grabbed her arm and held her where she stood trying to get her to sit down. Faline simply sat there waiting for her to calm down so she could finish.

"Mother, this was a long time ago and I haven't been since, so if you wouldn't mind letting me finish I'd appreciate it," Faline said calmly.

"I'm sorry. I just don't like that you went alone, and you know how we feel about the forest, Faline." Lacey grumbled taking her seat and folding her arms across her chest.

"I wasn't alone, I had Cairo with me." she responded matter of factly. "Now where was I? Oh yes, when I got to the forest to see who had been pestering me all those weeks it turned out to be a woman named Hildy. She was very beautiful with magnificent red hair and bright purple eyes that almost glowed. She is not just any woman though, she is a witch and apparently she has been watching me as I have been growing."

Drake and Lacey stared at her, their faces growing a little ashen from what they were hearing. "A witch you say?" Drake asked as calmly as he could. "And she has been watching you? You don't find that odd or creepy or nuts?" he stammered.

"Ugh! Dad seriously, if you and mother have questions wait until I am done. I am sure most of them are going to be answered while I tell you what I have to say anyway." Faline groaned.

"Sorry I can't even describe how I am feeling really." Drake muttered.

"Think about how I felt or am feeling then. How would you like having a set of eyes staring at you while you were trying to sleep?" Faline shouted.

Drake and Lacey hung their heads and both promised to be quiet until she had finished. They had instantly felt bad for getting upset or questioning her at all at this point. They were unsure as to why, they just knew they did and that they didn't want to continue making her mad.

"Good," Faline mumbled under her breath. "After talking with Hildy, she and a bunch of other magi as she called them, have been waiting for me to grow up and be the saviour of the world. I didn't really believe her at first, but she convinced me otherwise. She said I had special gifts. Some of them I already knew I had such as my mastery in weapons and crafting, and others I had to find. She said I was going to have a very special way with animals too." Faline smiled deviously. "She said I was going to be able to talk to and control all animals, even dragons!"

"Oh how exciting!" Lacey clasped her hands together trying to be happy for her daughter. Inside she was terrified.

"I know it is, isn't it?" Faline chirped. "Anyway, Hildy said that after some time I was going to be all trained up in weapons and it would be time for me to go on a special quest. She told me that I would know when the time was getting near, and I did as soon as I beat Tobias. She came to me last night and told me what I had to do."

Drake cleared his throat and held his hand up a little asking permission to speak. Faline rolled her eyes and nodded.

"I assume this is the part when you are going to tell us you are departing?" Drake asked with a small tear coming to his eye.

"Don't get all squishy, father and yes I will be leaving but not for a few days. I need some supplies before I go." Faline laughed.

"I can't help it," Drake moaned. "I love you and the thought of you leaving for somewhere makes my heart ache a little."

"It will be all right father, I promise." Faline grinned.

"So the supplies you need to have, are they obtainable here or are we to get them from around the village?" Lacey asked her eyes watering as well.

"I suppose most of them I can just gather around the farm, but we will see." Faline shrugged.

"Where exactly are you going?" Drake asked. "You never made it to that."

"Oh right!" Faline slapped a hand on her forehead. "How stupid of me. I am headed for Mt. Diamanti in the western forest. There is a cave there that I must go in. I guess there is something inside I need to find that is going to help me in the future."

Lacey teetered on her feet and about fainted. Drake had to throw an arm about her waist to help steady her. His face said everything both were thinking, his eyes wide and his mouth agape.

"All the way to the mountains in the western forest?" he stammered. "But that's so far."

"It really is going to be all right, father," Faline said placing her hand on his.

"Do you have to go alone?" Lacey asked a little frantic.

Faline smiled. "No, mother. Hildy said I could take someone with me if I chose to."

Drake and Lacey let out a relieved breath and sat down before they fell. It was a lot to take in first thing in the morning and this was just the beginning. They both knew that this task was a simple one in comparison to some that Faline would probably have in the future.

"Have you decided whether or not you will be taking anyone?" Drake fought back the urge to make her take him or Tobias and waited to see what she would say instead.

"Yes, I have." Faline smiled at them. "I have decided that I am going to take Cairo of course and I figured I would see if Nolan wanted to go. All that boy does is play with his animals and he's familiar with some of the woods anyway, so I figure he'd be helpful to me."

Drake seemed a little unsettled by her answer but he let it go. It was her choice not his and he knew there was nothing he could do about it. He got up from the table and went into his bedroom instead coming back out a few moments later with a large bag. He put it on the table and began emptying its contents for Faline to examine. Inside were candles, flint, linens for torch making, a small flask of oil, a small rolled up wool blanket and fishing line.

"Wow, this is great!" Faline exclaimed picking up each item and inspecting them carefully.

"I figured you would need this more than I do now," he said smiling at her. "There is plenty of room still for more things to be added, just make sure you can carry it comfortably."

"I will. father, thank you so much." She leaned over and gave him a huge hug.

Lacey got up from her seat and hugged her from the other side trying not to cry. She left them to go into the root cellar. Faline and Drake reassembled the bag of goodies when she came back up with more things to add to the bag. Lacey had in her arms a jar of jam, a loaf of bread, some smoked salmon, smoked sausages, and a half dozen apples, all which Faline stuffed into the bag.

"I am sure this will not provide for you on the entire journey, but it will make do for when you cannot acquire anything for yourself," Lacey said forcing a smile.

"Thank you, mother," Faline said hugging her again. "I will do my best to make it last."

"Now Faline, make sure that you and Nolan hunt, fish and gather as much food as you can while you are gone. We can provide some things that won't spoil too quickly like the smoked meats and the jar of jam, but the bread will go stale and the apples will rot. You must be smart out there," Drake urged.

"I know, father. Hildy told me that no matter what I was never going to be alone and not to be fearful on my journey," she said simply. "She also told me that if I needed help all I had to do was ask. So I am confident that I am going to be just fine."

Lacey placed a hand on Faline's shoulder. "I am grateful for your new friend, darling, and I hope you have the chance to acquire many more in the future," she said softly. "I feel that you are going to need them more than we all know."

Drake nodded in agreement and helped her place her bag by the door taking Cairo all but three seconds to go over and sniff it all up to make sure it was safe.

"I guess you had better go and find Nolan and see about getting him to go with you. Mother and I have things to tend to around here," Drake said heading towards the door. "We love you, Faline. Please know that no matter what, we will support you."

"That means a great deal to me, father," she said, a small tear coming to her eye. "I will go find him. See you all later." She blew them both kisses before taking off out the door, Cairo hot on her heels.

She ran down the little dirt road a bit to Tobias's house and out towards the back where Nolan usually was tending his animals. There she found him sitting in the middle of the small chicken pen he had built himself letting the chicks peck the feed out of his hands.

"Hey Nolan!" Faline shouted as she made her way across the grass towards where he was sitting.

He turned and waved for her to come inside the pen. She walked in slowly so she didn't interrupt what he had going on and sat on the ground near him.

"Hi, Faline," he said with a smile. "What can I do for ya?"

"I have sort of a question slash proposition for you," she replied with a coy grin.

He cocked his head to the side and raised an eyebrow. "Oh, and what might that be exactly?"

Faline's smile widened. "I am going on a quest and was wondering if you wanted to come along."

The expression that came across his face at that moment was priceless. He looked scared, excited and perplexed all at the same time. His brow furrowed and his nose wrinkled some. "A quest, huh? What kind of quest could you possibly be going on?" he jested.

Faline stood up with her hands on her hips. "You don't have to get all snide about it Nolan. If you don't want to go then just stay here and play with your animals. I don't care." She turned and began stomping away.

Nolan brushed the rest of the chicken feed from his hands onto the ground and went after her. "Wait, Faline! Please wait!" he called out.

She turned abruptly glaring at him as she usually did when he made her mad. "Why?" she said angrily. "I was all excited to come and talk to you about this and YOU ruined it."

Nolan bowed his head. "I'm sorry, Faline, I didn't mean to. I was just joking around a little. You need to lighten up a bit."

"Ugh!" She got red in the face and turned to start walking again.

Nolan kept pace and prodded her a bit. "What kind of quest are you going on? Is it dangerous?"

"Why should I tell you now?" she asked bitterly.

"Come on, Faline. I really am sorry and would enjoy knowing about your upcoming adventure." He grabbed her arm to make her stop walking. "Please. Please tell me," he said smiling.

She rolled her eyes knowing he wasn't going to let her be until she told him. "Fine, I'll tell you, but no more stupid comments."

"No problem." He put his fingers to his lips and made it look like he was locking them shut and tossing the key away.

Faline took a deep breath and told him all about Hildy and the other magi, the mountain she needed to find with the big cave in it, and how there was something hidden inside the cave for her to find. She also told him about the neat things she was supposed to learn and the powers she was supposed to discover within herself. Nolan stood there listening to her tale not sure what to make of it, but it was far too interesting to stop her from telling it. He waited patiently for her to finish before he tried making any comments so he was sure to get the whole story.

"So what you are saying is that you get to choose a companion to go travelling through the forest to the west, locate a giant mountain that you cannot miss with a cave in it, travel around in the darkness of the cave to find some random object or objects that you are supposed to know when you find them, and then you are supposed miraculously to find your way back home. Have I got that straight?" he asked curiously.

"Exactly," she replied, the smile returning to her face.

"Well, all right, when do we leave?" He grinned.

"You'll go?" Faline asked almost shocked that he wanted to leave his pets.

"Sure, why not? I could use a little excitement." Nolan shrugged. "Besides, who else are you going to take?"

Faline laughed. "I could take anyone really. I chose you because of your knowledge and compassion for animals and the fact that you have some base knowledge about wooded areas."

"Well that being said, I'm your guy." He extended his hand which she took and they shook on their new journey together.

"We will be leaving tomorrow, so I suggest packing all the things you feel we might need," she told him. "I have a few candles, some flint, linens and oil for torches, apples, bread, jam, a blanket, a little sausage and salmon, and a bit of fishing line. I will of course be bringing my sword, a dagger and my bow and arrows." She turned to begin walking back towards home.

"Okay I will make sure to pack my bag accordingly," he assured her. "Oh, Faline. Just a suggestion if you don't mind of course."

"Sure, Nolan. What is it?" She glanced back at him.

"You may want to think about trading in your dress for some pants." He looked towards the ground briefly. "I only say that because we will be doing a lot of climbing, hiking and lots of other things. A dress could slow you down or get caught on stuff." He was almost embarrassed talking about it.

She thought for a moment and nodded. "You are probably right. I will talk to my parents about it when I get home. Thank you, Nolan." She smiled at him before waving goodbye. "See you in the morning."

"Okay, Faline. Thank you for inviting me!" he shouted to her as she left.

"You're welcome!" she hollered back and ran the rest of the way home.

When she arrived she spoke with her mother about the pants Nolan said she should probably have, and even though Lacey thought that pants were unbecoming a lady, she agreed that he was probably right and took her to see Lilly. Lilly took Faline's measurements and told her to come back later that evening to collect her new clothes.

After returning home Faline spent the rest of the day collecting the things she thought she might need on her quest. She sharpened her sword and knife, fashioned herself plenty of arrows for her bow, went through the bag her father gave her once more and added a few extra candles, another small blanket and some dry tinder, just in case. She was very curious as to what Nolan was packing in his own bag and thought about going over there to see but figured she would talk to him about it in the morning. They could gather the last little bits of supplies then and leave.

Drake and Lacey came in from the fields as the daylight began to fade to start dinner. Lacey insisted that Drake take Faline to Lilly's so that he wasn't left to make the dinner. He figured that was probably their best bet considering he was not a world class chef.

Once down the road at Lilly's little house Faline got to try on her new pants. They felt strange on her legs as she was accustomed to wearing her little plain grey dresses. Those didn't squeeze anything or require much work to get on really. These you had to get your legs in, pull them up, and then you had to tie them to make sure they didn't fall off. The pants weren't as soft as a dress either really, but she knew this was for the best. She thanked Lilly for her hard work as she and Drake left to go home for dinner.

"Did you get what you needed?" Lacey asked as they came in through the door.

"Sure did, mother." Faline grinned.

Lacey began setting food on the table. "What do you think of them?"

Faline shrugged. "Well they aren't a dress that's for sure. They are a lot of work to get on, but I'm sure I'll get used to them quickly enough."

Drake laughed. "I'm sure you'll be fine. The important thing is that you have something protecting your legs while you are travelling the forest. A dress would have got in the way, or possibly got you hurt the way you will be travelling."

"I agree. That's why I traded in my dress for the time being." Faline giggled.

Lacey frowned. "Hopefully, you will be back quickly and unscathed. Then you can get back into your normal routine, dress and all."

"I can hope," said Faline smiling at her mother.

As per usual the rest of the dinner guests showed up just in time to eat and took their seats at the table. Faline helped Lacey get the rest of the food set out along with plates, silverware and glasses. Dinner at the house was a little slower tonight as everyone wanted to enjoy the time they had left with the two kids before they departed in the morning.

There was plenty of discussion about safety topics like don't sit or sleep too close to the fire, and don't run after the food you are hoping to kill with your knife lest you slip and fall on it, gut the animals and fish with the blade pointing away from your body. Faline and Nolan sat there politely and smiled while their folks drilled them with bits of information. Occasionally they would look at one another and snicker a little because they thought this was a little much, but they took it in their stride knowing their parents were just concerned.

Once dinner finished they all sat around the fire a while before taking their leave for the night. Tobias and Nolan were the first to leave. Nolan smiled as he waved to Faline saying he'd see her bright and early. Jonas finished his after dinner pipe, got up and hugged everyone goodbye with an extra long squeeze for Faline before leaving. This left Lacey, Drake and Faline together. They got up and hugged one another before sending Faline to bed to get some much needed rest before her journey.

"I hope she'll be all right," Lacey said watching Faline and Cairo go to their room.

"She'll be just fine, my love," Drake reassured her.

"I hope you're right," Lacey replied taking his arm to walk with him to their room.

"I know I'm right." He smiled as he kissed her forehead and turned to close the bedroom door.

Chapter 10

Faline's Quest Begins

The next morning everyone was awake and moving around before the rooster crowed. The bustle inside the house could be heard a mile away. Breakfast was being made in grand fashion as Lacey didn't want Nolan and Faline leaving on an empty stomach, not to mention that she was unsure as to when they would have a proper meal again. Faline was once again going through her bag making sure she had everything she needed with Drake peering over her shoulder smiling. Jonas, Tobias and Nolan came in shortly after breakfast was being set on the table as if they knew breakfast was going to be early that morning. Nolan came in with a large bag and sat on the floor next to Faline and the two began comparing their contents.

"Okay," began Faline. "I have plenty of candles, flint, oil, linens, and tinder. I am bringing my sword, bow and arrows, fishing line, a knife and two small blankets. I also have a little bit of food packed in here. What have you got?" She finished peering at the contents of his bag now placed neatly on the floor by his feet.

"Well I have a fishing line, flint, oil, candles, two blankets, gloves, a hatchet, a bow and arrows, a hunting knife, my sword, some dry tinder, a bit of food, and a rope," he replied.

"A rope! Great idea, Nolan," she smiled. "I also wouldn't have thought of the hatchet, so I appreciate that too."

He smiled back at her. "I'm glad I could be useful already."

The pair repacked their bags and joined the others for breakfast. Faline paused briefly to give Cairo a big helping of food of her own before taking her place at the table. Unlike dinner the night before, breakfast was eaten relatively quickly that morning as there was a lot to be done and the kids needed to get going. Daylight was something she needed to utilise wisely if she was to make good time to the mountain. Tobias had already interrogated Nolan on the contents of his bag before leaving the house and seemed confident that his son would be all right. Drake and Jonas dug through Faline's bag to make sure she had all she needed and decided that she had done a thorough job of obtaining all the things she would require.

"I guess this is it," Faline said moving her fork back on the table and going to grab her bag. "We don't want to waste daylight so we really need to get started."

Drake got up and went to the little cabinet next to the wash tub. He pulled out a little parcel and handed it to Faline. She took it from him with a quizzical look and held it in her hands for a moment.

"It's from your grandfather," Drake told her. "He left it for you the last time he was here and told me to give it to you when you went on your first adventure."

She smiled. "Grandfather left it, huh?" She began to unwrap the little linen lined package and inside she found a pair of bearskin gloves. "Wow! My very own pair of gloves!" she shrieked joyfully.

"He said they were bearskin and would be very light, durable and warm. He wanted to give you something that you would need and use often," Drake replied softly.

"Too bad I won't be here to thank him when he comes home next week," Faline sighed. "I would wait, but Hildy made it seem like I needed to get a move on."

"I'm sure he'll understand my dear," Jonas said. "He's not the type to get upset about such things."

"Yes, I suppose you are right, grampa." She smiled at him.

Lacey walked across the room and squeezed Faline so tightly she thought her mother might squash her. She let out a little groan and Lacey let up some, apologising and trying not to cry while she held her baby girl one last time before she left.

"I will be back, mother. Don't you worry," Faline said trying to console her mother.

"I know, love. I just want to hold you a little bit longer before you go," Lacey said still squeezing her tightly.

Faline returned the embrace as best she could with her arms pinned at her sides. "Oh, mother," she chuckled.

Drake casually walked over to the pair and joined in. "Me, too!" he exclaimed.

"Group hug!" shouted Jonas as he ran over to join in.

Tobias hugged his son on his own and shook Faline's hand wishing her well on her journey. Nolan and Faline grabbed their bags and made for the door taking one last look around the house before stepping outside and making their way towards the forest.

"Are you scared at all, Faline?" Nolan asked quietly.

"Not really," she replied. "I was when Hildy first came and talked to me about it. Now that I have had time to think about it I think I'm fine. Why, are you?"

"A little," he replied somewhat embarrassed.

"It's going to be all right, Nolan," she said patting his shoulder. "We have each other and Cairo. Plus Hildy said all I must do is ask if I need help."

He laughed a little. "I guess that makes me feel a little better about it. Still a little embarrassed that I'm scared and you're not, but I'm sure I'll get used to that."

They made their way down the little dirt road until they reached the edge of the forest. There they stopped and stared ahead of them into the sun-streaked trees the wind gently rustling the leaves inside. Animals of all kinds could be heard within and it made them hesitate for a moment before crossing the line between the safety of their home and the unknown of the forest.

"Come on!" Faline said after a moment. "We can't just stand here staring at it."

Faline began walking into the forest with Cairo and with a deep breath Nolan began to follow. They walked for quite some time listening to all the sounds the forest made. The trees would rustle and creak with the wind, bushes would jump and twitch with little animals scurrying in and out, birds chirping high in the branches of the trees, wolves howling in the distance, and some owls hooting from their hollows.

Faline and Nolan absorbed it all as they made their way down the path making every effort not to miss a thing. Eventually the path made a sharp decline and at the bottom it seemed to split in three directions. The paths to the north and the east seemed well trod, but the path to the west was partly covered and seemed far less travelled.

"I guess that is the way we go," laughed Nolan. "Figures we get to go down the path that has over grown bushes and roots all over it."

"It wouldn't be a proper quest if it was easy, Nolan," Faline said sternly. "Since it is about lunch time, shall we eat something quickly before we start tackling that path?"

Nolan nodded and sat down to start rummaging through his bag while Faline took a seat across from him on a fallen log. They each took out a nice apple and decided those would be fine to eat for the time being along with a drink of water. Neither of them wanted to waste food since the day had just begun and they were by no means starving. They figured it was best to eat a light lunch and see what else they could find for dinner. They finished up their apples and got to their feet throwing the cores far into the opposite direction from which they intended to walk.

"All right, let's see how far we can make it before we need to stop and make camp," Faline said smiling.

"Agreed," Nolan said beginning to make his way through the tall brush. "Faline, this stuff is full of thorns so be careful."

"Mmm," she mumbled pushing low hanging branches aside and stepping over high roots. "I guess you were right about the pants."

Nolan laughed. "To be honest, I didn't want to have to keep stopping and releasing the skirt of your dress from whatever it got caught on. It would have been embarrassing for both of us," his face turning red as he spoke.

She merely smiled and nodded politely. "I could see how that might be a little embarrassing. When we get to the next clear spot we should probably get our gloves out. It will make it easier to move all this stuff out of our way."

"I hear you on that," he said grimacing as he got caught by another branch of thorns. "I think we have shed enough blood for one day."

They walked for about an hour or so before they could finally see a beautiful sunlit clearing up ahead. It was something that both after walking through all the bramble, thorns, jutting roots, low hanging branches and jagged hidden rocks in their path had been waiting to see. They wanted to run for it but knew if they did they would trip and fall for sure, and the quest would probably be over already due to some broken bone or lacerated appendage. So they slowly picked and twisted their way through the last of the dilapidated path they had been following before arriving in the open fresh air of the clearing.

It was beautiful! The sun was pouring in from every direction, wild flowers of all types were growing all over, berry bushes scattered around, and there was a fresh pool of water fed by a lovely stream right in the centre. Faline ran over to it and gazed in looking at her reflection in the water before reaching her hands in and taking a drink. It was clean, cool and refreshing. It felt great to have been there at that moment being able to drink that water. Nolan came and knelt beside her and enjoyed some of the fresh water himself, smiling as he did. He had never tasted water so wonderful in all his life.

"Isn't it beautiful here?" Faline asked as she lay on her back in the grass staring up at the sky.

Nolan sat cross-legged in the grass beside her. "Yes, it really is."

"Too bad we can't stay here, huh?" she said turning to look at him.

He looked back at her briefly. "I guess so. It would get lonely out here."

She lay there for a few more minutes allowing her time to take it all in before getting back to her feet. "Well, I guess we should fill our water pouches up while we are here and get a move on. We probably only have a couple more hours before we must stop for the night."

Nolan looked again towards the sky noticing that the sun was on its way toward the east which meant it was starting to set. "Yes, we should probably go. We don't want to get caught in the bramble in the dark. Who knows where we would end up."

Faline laughed. "Are you suggesting that we would get lost in the woods?"

"As a matter of fact, I am," Nolan chuckled.

"Well then sir, let's get going." Faline bowed and pointed in the direction they needed to go. "Come on, Cairo."

Cairo came bounding away from the pool, little drops of water slopping out of the sides of her mouth as she ran. She stopped at Faline's feet waiting for her to start moving. Faline bent down and gave her loyal friend a good scratch behind the ears before reaching into her bag and giving her one of her sausages. Nolan gave her a curious look and decided it was best not to say anything at all.

Noticing his look, Faline shrugged and merely said, "What? She must eat, too." Then she began to make her way across the clearing to the path on the other side.

Nolan simply laughed and followed behind her and Cairo back into the tangled mess of the forest. The day was going well as far as they were concerned. There hadn't been any major hang-ups really except for the extra time it took to walk due to the obstacles on the path. Neither of them saw any animals of note, just a few small things like birds, chipmunks and squirrels.

Eventually the daylight was beginning to grow dim and they both knew they were going to have to think about calling it a night soon. As soon as they came across a space on the path that was somewhat clear of debris, Nolan and Faline began to make their camp. Nolan went to collect some firewood while Faline took her bow and went to find some dinner with Cairo.

Cairo was sniffing around the ground for a moment before catching the scent of some poor creature that was about to be made into dinner. Her pace quickened as she searched for it sniffing the air wildly. Finally after several minutes Cairo slowed a bit before coming to a halt beside a large bush. Faline squatted down and readied her bow. Her canine companion took slow steps toward the large shrub, each one making it rustle a little more. Cairo took one more step growling at the bush before a large rabbit came bouncing out chattering wildly. Faline took her chance and fired an arrow hitting it square in the side of the neck as it took its second leap through the air trying to escape the large dog that was creeping up on it. The rabbit squealed once before falling to the ground with a thud allowing Faline to get up and proudly retrieve it.

"Well done, Cairo," she said patting her large dog's head. "We are going to have a fine meal tonight thanks to you."

Cairo wagged her tail as she licked Faline's hand. The hunting duo walked tall back to the camp site where Nolan had been busy building and starting a fine fire. Faline came walking back into their little clearing holding the rabbit up by its ears with a huge smile on her face.

Nolan looked up at her as she neared and grinned. "Wow! That is a huge rabbit," he said taking it from her. "I will get it ready to eat as quickly as I can. Don't know about you, but I'm starving!"

"I'm glad I could be of service," Faline said proudly taking a seat on the ground by the fire.

Cairo lay by her side as she watched Nolan skin and gut the rabbit for cooking. He had sharpened a stick and skewered it length wise through the centre of the rabbit so he could roast it over the fire. Faline was impressed, she had never really seen anyone do what he had just done before.

"Good job, Nolan. Some day you will have to teach me how to do that on my own," Faline said nudging him in the arm.

"Sure, Faline," he replied. "It's not that hard really once you have done it a few times."

Faline's stomach began to gurgle. "Will it take long to cook?" she asked.

Nolan chuckled. "Not too long. Are we having anything else with it?"

"I suppose we could have a little of the bread and jam my mother sent along," she said reaching into her bag..

"Sounds great!" he exclaimed rubbing his stomach.

Faline began slicing a few pieces of bread and covering them with the jam as Nolan finished cooking the rabbit. Cairo was especially excited about the cooking meat. All she did was sit and stare at it as Nolan turned it slowly over the fire. He pulled a very small piece off and tasted it to see if it was done, sighing with relief when the meat chewed nicely in his mouth and didn't taste raw.

"It's finished and ready to eat," he said proudly.

Faline began eating her slice of bread while Nolan cut the rabbit in half on a flat rock he had set next to him on the ground. He put her rabbit on a piece of bark and took his own piece of bread. Faline pulled pieces of her rabbit off bit by bit taking turns with Cairo eating the bits of cooked meat. Cairo couldn't be happier as she gulped each piece down barely chewing it at all before waiting for her next one.

"Some day my friend you are going to choke if you don't learn to chew," she laughed at her drooling dog.

When they had finished both Nolan and Faline gave the rest of the rabbit carcass to Cairo to fill her belly a little more and decided that it was time to try and get some sleep. They had another big day ahead of them tomorrow and the huge mountain was still far away.

Lying by the fire and looking up at the darkened sky, Faline thought about home and what everyone was probably doing. She imagined her mom, dad and Jonas out tending the fields and animals, while Tobias made weapons and other metal objects in his workshop. She thought about their family meals and how wonderful it would be to sit down with them at the table and talk about the day and its events. She knew that it was going to be a little while before she was going to be able to do that again and sighed gently.

Before long she had begun to fall asleep listening to the sounds of the soft breeze flowing through the tops of the trees and the owls hooting in the distance. Cairo had finished her rabbit and had come back to snuggle up against her side for the night. Nolan was a safe distance from the fire but still close enough to keep warm and was already sound asleep. Faline giggled a little to herself seeing him lying there mouth hanging partly open, before rolling onto her side and draping an arm over Cairo. She curled up tightly to her furry friend and with the comfort of Cairo's rhythmic breathing was soon fast asleep.

Chapter 11

The Watcher in the Woods

Next morning Faline and Nolan woke as daylight broke through the trees. It had been an uncomfortable night as the ground, having been so uneven and full of debris, didn't do them any favours. The only one of them that didn't seem to have a problem was Cairo who still lay there waiting for their day to start. They had a quick breakfast with some of the sausage, bread and jam that Faline had in her bag, snuffed the remaining coals out in the small fire Nolan had built the night before and started making their way down through the tangled overgrown path once more.

The group of travelling companions only veered off the path for short periods making their way to the small stream that ran off the clear pool they had stopped at the day before, filling their water pouches and allowing Cairo to fill her belly with water. They found it to be very convenient that the stream was nearby for the most part and they didn't have to stray too far from the path they could barely make out when they were on it.

Several hours had gone by since they had woken, Faline and Nolan growing weary of thorned branches clinging to their clothes, rocks jutting out of the dirt that they could not see, tree roots arching up just enough to snag the tips of their boots making it impossible not to fall at least once, finally got some reprieve. The path ahead was beginning to clear up which made them look at one another and smile.

"Time for a break," Faline said wiping some sweat and dirt from her brow. "We need to stop and get some water and eat a little before we pass out."

Nolan had all but forgotten his growling stomach while fighting with the plant life in the forest and quickly agreed. Walking a bit further Faline found a suitable log on the ground to sit on and rummaged through her bag taking out two apples and handing one to Nolan. The pair sat on their little log bench eating their apples while Cairo took her chance to lay by Faline's feet and relax.

"After we finish these we should go and fill our water bags and get moving," she whispered eyeing the trees around them.

Nolan looked at her curiously. "Something the matter?" he asked.

She turned and put a finger to her lips to quieten him. "Shh," she murmured. "I think I hear something."

Nolan looked all about straining his ears to hear what she was talking about but heard nothing. Cairo sat up straight ears going in all directions making Faline nervous. The three of them sat there in silence for several minutes before Faline got up and quietly made her way to the stream, making carefully placed steps so she didn't make unnecessary noise. She motioned for Nolan to follow.

"We are going to get our water quickly and get out of here," she turned and whispered to Nolan.

"How do you know it isn't some little forest animal?" Nolan whispered back.

"I don't," she said, "but I am also not hanging around to find out what it is."

They filled their bags as quickly as they could and ran back in the direction they needed to go. Faline and Cairo didn't stop running until they were about a quarter of a mile away from where they sensed the presence in the forest. Only then did they pause for a minute to catch their breath before moving on.

"Was it necessary to run?" Nolan asked out of breath after trying to keep up with the two of them.

"Honestly, I'm not sure," Faline panted. "I am only sure of one thing. There was something there and I wasn't taking any chances."

Nolan who had been bent over with his hands on his knees catching his breath, stood up. "Fair enough I suppose," he replied quietly.

They stood there for a minute to collect themselves and having a quick drink of water before beginning to move on. Cairo walked close to Faline now more than she had since the beginning of their journey. Her ears were still scanning the area periodically making sure there wasn't any danger. Faline and Nolan were both very happy to have her along.

They were also very happy that the path they had originally begun walking on had opened quite a bit. It was wider now with far less obstacles to overcome, and more sunlight came pouring in through the canopy overhead making it much easier to see where they were going. Up ahead looming in the distance the great mountain could be seen, clouds ringing its peak like a fluffy crown.

"We will probably make it to the mountain in another day or two if we have a good road to walk on like this one," Nolan said cheerfully.

Faline smiled at him knowing he was trying to take her mind off their previous situation. "I am hoping that it stays somewhat smooth going like this," she laughed. "I don't know if I can sleep on roots again tonight."

"Cairo didn't seem to mind." He gestured to her furry companion.

"She is accustomed to sleeping just about wherever. One of her favourite spots was in the orchard back home." Faline giggled as she patted Cairo's head.

"Dogs are pretty resilient I suppose," he said.

"Yes, they are." Faline smiled.

"Well we have a few hours before the sun decides it wants to start its descent, so let's keep an eye open for a good spot to sleep for the night while we are walking," Nolan said happily.

Faline laughed. "Do you ever think about things other than your stomach, animals or sleep?" she jested.

He shot her a look out of the corner of his eye that could have melted snow before smiling. "I think of lots of other things, but while we are out here sleep, food, and warmth are my main priorities."

"Fair enough I suppose," Faline said giggling softly to herself.

Faline stopped for a minute looking this way and that, straining her ears to hear if something was following them. This caught Nolan by surprise draining some of the colour from his face as he watched her. Cairo had picked up on what Faline was looking for, her furry ears twitching madly in every direction. Faline remembered what Hildy had said about her gift with animals along with hidden ones she had yet to discover. She looked down at her canine and stared at her intently, trying to focus hard enough to talk to Cairo with her mind and see if Cairo would talk back.

"I know you hear it, Cairo," she whispered in her head. Cairo looked up into Faline's eyes as if she was telling her she understood before going back to scanning their surrounding area.

"What is out there Cairo?" she asked her furry friend. To her surprise a woman's voice she had never heard answered back.

"It's an animal of sorts. Smells funny. Not normal," Cairo answered as she sniffed the air all around.

Faline's eyes grew wide with excitement when she figured out she was really communicating with her beloved dog. "Is it dangerous?"

Cairo looked up at her and tilted her head to the side. "Not sure, but it's bigger than I am."

"How do you know that?" Faline asked abruptly, then immediately felt bad for snapping at her.

"I can smell it. It has a stronger smell than a small creature," Cairo answered bluntly. "We should go."

Cairo pawed at the ground and let out a little whimper jostling Faline out of her almost trance-like state. Nolan was standing perfectly still. His expression had changed from nervous, to completely frightened. He had never seen a person stand there and not speak or acknowledge that she had been spoken to. It was like Faline had disappeared from herself.

"Faline, are you all right?" Nolan asked again reaching out to touch her arm.

Faline flinched and moved back a little. "I think so. We need to keep moving." She turned on her heel and began walking again.

Nolan trotted up beside her looking troubled. "I tried asking you something and you didn't answer me. Are you spaced out or something? Are you sure you are all right?" he asked again grabbing her arm to look in her eyes.

Faline dropped her gaze to the ground trying to avoid eye contact. "Nolan," she hesitated not knowing if she should tell him what had just happened.

"What is it?" he asked with more concern than anything. "You can trust me, Faline. You chose me to come with you remember? I can't help if I don't understand." His eyes found hers and they stared at one another for a moment.

Faline decided that this was true and she had better tell him the truth. There was no sense in lying and what would happen if she was in one of those trances and she couldn't get out. She sighed and looked up at him as he slowly released her arm.

"I can talk to animals with my mind," Faline said sheepishly.

Nolan looked like he was going to pass out. He decided it would be best to keep walking while they talked as opposed to finding a much needed seat. "You can talk to animals?" he choked.

"Yes. A witch named Hildy came to me and told me that I would be able to control and talk to animals," Faline replied, her eyes flitting back and forth trying to gauge his reaction.

He just stood there staring at her not knowing what else to say. Trying to process what she had just told him he sat down on the ground with his hands in his lap.

"I understand that this is a lot to take in and I can't blame you if you want to leave," she began to say praying that he wasn't going to abandon her, but he held up his hand to quieten her turning his face to look up at her.

"I am not going to leave, Faline." he told her quietly. "Just give me a minute would you please?"

Faline stood there watching him as he sat unmoving on the ground. Neither of them spoke for several minutes which made Faline become a little impatient as she wanted to finish up and find a place to camp. She didn't want to upset him so she tried not to get very pushy, however the light was fading and they needed to move.

"Is Hildy the one who told you to go on this quest as well?" Nolan asked getting to his feet.

Faline gave a small nod and sighed. "Yes, she came to me in my sleep and told me it was time to go."

He took a second to dust his pants off a little and started to walk feeling Faline's urgency to move forward. "Does this sort of thing happen to you often?"

"It used to happen all the time!" she groaned. "I used to lay down trying to sleep with these big purple eyes just staring at me every night. Then one night I got mad and yelled at them in my head. That's when she began to talk to me. She had me meet her in the forest alone and after that she said she would only come to me when it was important."

Somewhat puzzled and maybe a little concerned for his friend's sanity, he just kept walking. "So you don't see her all the time?"

"No Nolan, I don't see her all the time because there is no need for me to." She glared at him a little.

He tossed his hands up defensively and laughed a bit. "All right, there is no need to get all testy about it."

"I'm not!" she yelled at him. "I just don't like it that you are questioning my story."

"I get it. However, I am a firm believer in things you can see. I have never seen Hildy nor a person with purple eyes, so please forgive me for finding it unusually hard to swallow." Nolan shot back.

"Ugh! There is no sense in the two of us fighting over this." she grimaced. "Just know that I am not crazy and we need to find a place to camp for the night and soon."

She picked up the pace and was a good distance away from Nolan before she realised he was so far behind. She turned and shouted for him to hurry up making him jog a little to catch up to her and Cairo. The pair were lucky enough to find a good spot to rest for the night before the hour was out and promptly began foraging for firewood and anything else they could find.

The stream where they stopped had become wider than it was at the start of their journey. For them this meant that it was probably deeper and they might find fish in the water. Nolan dug through his pack retrieving his fishing line and wrapped some around a long stick. Tying a hook to the other end he had fashioned himself a fine pole relatively quick. He went over to some of the rocks and lifted them up to look for worms or grubs. Finding a nice fat grub he jammed it onto the hook, walked over to the water and tossed it in. He looped the line around one of his fingers to feel for pulling and waited.

Faline oversaw building the fire tonight and was busy gathering some of the dead grass for a good fire starter. She brought it back over to their little wood pile and began clicking her flint rocks together shooting small sparks onto the dead grass. Once it began to catch she leaned in and began to blow gently on it to get the little flame to grow bigger and start catching the wood. She sat gazing proudly at the little fire she had built before going to get more wood to feed it. When she had re-emerged from the trees Nolan had come back with several little fish in his hand.

"They are not the biggest of fish but they will put food in our bellies." He smiled leaving the fish on the ground by the fire.

Cairo, catching a whiff of the fresh fish, licked her chops and started to drool a little. Faline shook her head laughing at her dog while rummaging for her knife to help Nolan prepare the fish. She had watched her father and grandfather do it and helped her mother a few times, so she figured it was time she learned to do it herself. Nolan smiled and handed her one of the fish and slowly showed her the proper way to do it. Cairo had no problem merrily eating all the pieces they cast aside anxiously waiting for the next one until they had finished.

"That about does it," Nolan said happily looking at their cleaned fish. "All that's left is to put them on a stick and roast 'em."

"Sounds good to me," Faline said grabbing her roasting stick of choice.

Unlike the rabbit the night before, fish did not take as long to cook. They took a second to dig a small hole in the ground next to the fire to place their sticks into and let them hang over the fire bracing the end with a rock so it didn't fall in. This gave them a chance to prepare some bread with jam and slice up an apple to go with the fish. All in all, the two of them had done very well as far as meals were concerned. Each of them hoped the return trip would be just as good.

Nolan pinched a piece of fish off to see how flaky the meat was and gave it a taste. "This is definitely done, Faline," he said smiling at her.

"Did you hear that Cairo? It is time to eat!" she chirped giving her furry friend a quick pat on the head.

Cairo let out a short "woof" and hopped around in a little circle to show her excitement for the upcoming meal. Nolan and Faline took their sticks off the fire and let them sit for a few minutes to allow the fish to cool off before trying to eat it. The two of them decided to enjoy the bread and apples while they waited for the fish to cool enough. Once they had finished they dug merrily into the fire-roasted fish that seemed to melt in their mouths. Faline gave the biggest of the fish to Cairo who lay on the ground and licked it for a minute before wolfing it down almost without chewing it. Faline gave her a scolding look that made Cairo shy away for a moment before letting her tongue loll out of her mouth as if apologising. Faline just laughed and continued eating her own dinner.

Sitting by the fire savouring the flavours of the fish, apples, bread and jam, Faline, Nolan and Cairo felt completely satisfied with themselves and their progress. The night was beautiful, the sounds coming from the forest were calming and gentle, and to them everything was perfect. They had all but forgotten the scare of the unknown presence from earlier in the day and sat full and warm by the soft glow of the small fire. The simple pleasure of the evening was soon interrupted by Cairo's head having whipped into the air her ears scanning the area like little radar detectors once again. Faline and Nolan were instantly on their feet straining their eyes in the now moonlit area they inhabited for the evening trying in vain to see what Cairo heard.

"What is it now?" Nolan tried not to shout, but he was more nervous now than he was earlier due to it being dark.

"I don't know Nolan," Faline whispered waving her hand at him to hush him up.

Cairo turned and looked at Faline pawing at the ground. "It's the same as before," she told her.

"The same thing from earlier is out there now?" Faline said aloud very alarmed.

Cairo turned and looked back towards the south. "Yes. I believe it is over there in the trees," Cairo said pointing her nose in the direction she was talking about.

"Nolan, we are being watched by the same thing from before," Faline told the now shaking boy.

Nolan who had been fumbling through his bag to find his hunting knife was holding it so tightly his knuckles had whitened. He merely nodded. "I heard you. You didn't talk to Cairo with your mind this time."

"Oh, well I guess that's good that she could hear and understand me anyway." Faline attempted to laugh but failed.

"It's not moving." Cairo told Faline.

"Hmm. I think maybe I have had enough of this tag along," Faline managed to croak. "I don't enjoy being spied on or hunted if that is what this thing is doing."

Nolan spun around and looked at her, his face twisted in panic. "Faline, don't go out there!"

"I'm not going to go out there, silly boy." Faline glared at him. "I'm going to make it come here," she said.

Nolan's face turned ashen and he about passed out. "Don't, Faline! Please! Just let it stay there," he begged.

"No. I've had it," she growled. "You there! Stop following me in the shadows and show yourself!" she bellowed into the darkness.

Faline stood as straight as an arrow, Cairo by her side. The grumbling in her chest grew more prominent as the leaves in the bushes nearby began to stir. Nolan remained a safe distance between Faline and the woods almost ashamed at his newfound cowardice. There the three of them remained silently waiting for the being in the forest to emerge. Slowly the twigs snapping on the ground became louder, the leaves on the bushes rustled more and then the branches began to part as a pair of glowing red eyes began to emerge from the darkness.

Faline and Nolan stood there trying not to breathe as they waited for the figure to emerge. The anticipation was killing them. Two long legs began to jut out from the bush line followed by a large horned head that appeared to be smiling at them. Nolan tried not to tremble as Faline's mouth began to hang open looking upon the beast that had been pursuing them as they travelled. As more of its body began to illuminate softly in the glow of the fire, Faline realised that the beast was not scary at all. It was merely a very large stag.

Nolan leaned forward and whispered in Faline's ear. "Why is there a big ole' buck following us around?"

Faline shrugged. "I don't know. If I knew we wouldn't be standing here right now."

Cairo had got all riled up and her fur was standing on end. She had softly made her way over between her master and the creature. Faline gently began stroking her fur to soothe and calm her down. She didn't want any unnecessary bloodshed. Cairo took the hint and let her growling turn to a low grumble deep in her belly.

"So who are you and what do you want?" Faline asked the animal very sternly.

The stag pawed the ground for a moment before bowing its giant antlered head. There was a brilliant flash of bright red light and a small breeze rustled some of the lower branches in the nearby trees before revealing a tall dark haired man with what appeared to be a crown of antlers on his head. He wore a scarlet silk shirt, black pants, black boots and a crimson cape flowed behind him in the soft breeze.

"Please do not be alarmed or afraid for that matter as I mean you no ill will," said the strange man who was smiling as he spoke.

Faline raised her eyebrow and stared at him. "Well, go on then, what do you want?"

"I was merely interested in watching you for a while, that's all. I never thought I'd be caught to be honest." He shrugged.

"Well, you are so now you can tell me who you are and why you're interested." Faline snapped at him.

The dark haired man leaned over and slapped Nolan on the shoulder. "Sassy little thing isn't she," he winked. "I am a warlock in Hildy's coven and I go by the name of Romulus. You can call me Rom for short if you like."

Faline just stood there staring at him not quite sure what to say. Nolan relaxed a bit having remembered that Faline said Hildy was a good person and there to help them. He came and stood next to Faline and stroked Cairo to help ease her mind. He thought maybe if the dog relaxed more, so would he.

"So you are associated with Hildy?" Faline asked.

Rom nodded and gave a little smile which gave Nolan the creeps.

"Why are you following me then? Hildy said I needed to ask to get help and I don't remember asking for any." Faline questioned him again.

Romulus pointed to one of the logs by the fire asking to sit. Faline shrugged and he took a seat warming his hands over the fire. "Running around all day and night can make a man's hands hurt sometimes," he chuckled. "They aren't always agreeable to being hooves."

Nolan was taken aback by this comment. He had never seen a witch up close nor did he, until now, truly believe that they existed. He found it was time to have a seat as well before his legs gave out.

"So you really are a warlock?" Nolan asked him intently.

Rom laughed. "Yes son, I really am a warlock."

"Can you do magic too then?" Nolan asked even more interested now than before having forgotten his fears.

Rom raised an eyebrow and smirked. The fire began to glow a brighter orange, then it turned scarlet and finally, Rom let it rest at blue. "How's that?"

Nolan's eyes were wide with excitement as he watched the small little fire show. Faline sighed and took a seat next to him on the log while Cairo lay in front of her at her feet.

"Okay, seriously, enough tricks. Tell me why you are out here," Faline said in a huff.

Rom raised his hands to calm her down before she got more upset. "Okay, Faline, relax. I was talking with Hildy and she told me all about you and your first quest. I wanted to see for myself if it was possible that the prophetic child was among us."

Faline sighed placing her hands on her knees. "So you basically just came out here to follow me around to see if I could hold up to all your expectations. Is that it?"

"Sort of I guess if you are trying to sum it all up." Rom shrugged. "I figured if I were to follow silently then I could also offer my aid if you needed it in a pinch as well."

Faline shook her head. "Hildy told me that I needed to ask for help, not that help was just going to follow me around."

"Well, sometimes things change and you can't prevent change my friend," Rom chuckled.

Nolan looked between the two before settling his gaze on Romulus asking quite matter-of-factly, "Are you intending to come along now that we know who you are and what your intentions are?"

Rom sat up straight and gave a wide grin. "Are you inviting me along on your adventure Nolan?"

Nolan stammered a bit and looked over at Faline hoping he hadn't just put his foot in it. "Um, well I..." he murmured.

Faline stood up and shushed them both. "Look," she said in an almost motherly tone, "if in fact you are hoping that now we will tell you that you can come then just say it. Stop beating about the bush!"

Romulus sat back and for a moment all was quiet. The silence was broken by him grasping his sides and letting out a bellowing laugh that seemed to shake the branches of the trees around them almost causing him to fall off his seat on the log.

"Girl, you are one sassy little whip I'll give you that," he said catching his breath. "I would love nothing more than to travel the rest of the way with you on your quest rather than skulk about in the shadows. I can even offer rides so you don't have to walk so much, there and home if you like."

Faline sat back down and folded her arms across her chest. "Fine then," she began "but no other aid unless we absolutely need or want it. Understood?" The tone in her voice was still very stern making Nolan cringe a little.

"You got it, Faline," Rom smiled with a wink. "It is after all your quest."

Faline nodded, her eyes fixed on his. "That's right it is and it is best to remember it."

Nolan sat there and stared at her for a minute. He had never seen her act this way before and he was uncertain how to feel about it. He was intrigued and a little unnerved at the same time. She was almost acting the way a princess would if they had been talking to their servants.

Faline stood up and brushed off some of the dirt and debris from the day giving a big stretch, then leaned down to stroke Cairo who had long since settled down and stopped her grumbling at their new found friend.

"I suggest that we all get some sleep now," she yawned. "Its been a long day and I am hoping to make it to the entrance of the cave in the next two days."

"Agreed," nodded Nolan. "We exerted an awful lot of energy running through the woods today instead of just keeping a nice pace like normal." He shot a sideward glance at Rom who gave a small smiling shrug as a kind of apology.

Nolan added another log to the fire to make sure they all stayed warm through the night as the others took their places on the ground next to it. Faline gave Rom her extra blanket to sleep on and made Nolan give him his to sleep under. Nolan had grown accustomed to using it as a pillow but handed it over once Faline gave him a look that could have made their pond boil over. Romulus thanked them both for their generosity and told them that it would be repaid fifty times over. Faline gave a gentle smile and curled up with Cairo on the ground.

It didn't take as long as it normally did for them all to fall asleep. The day had been long and it had been really the first time they had been pushed since they left the comforts of home. Faline watched the fire as it snapped and popped for a little while before her eyes closed allowing her mind to wander in the dark behind her eyes. Before long she was fast asleep and dreaming about the next part of her journey.

Chapter 12

Ride Like the Wind

The next morning the travellers awoke with some dark patches of clouds hiding the warmth of the sun. Cairo stretched her legs before sticking her nose in the air sniffing about and giving a few small whimpers. Faline reached out a hand and gently stroked her canine's fur easing her whining.

"I know Cairo," she grimaced staring up at the sky. "Let's just hope that it holds off until we can find some sort of shelter."

Cairo buried her head further into Faline's hand to prompt her to stroke her some more. Faline giggled and did as was requested.

"Silly dog," she cooed as she stood up giving her one last pat on the head.

Nolan and Rom stood up stretching away the remainder of sleep from their tired bones before Nolan kicked a little dirt on the last of the smouldering embers from the night's fire.

"Don't want to go setting any random forest fires now do we?" as he gestured at the small makeshift fire pit.

Rom shook his head. "No, we don't friend." He smiled at Nolan. "That is a very noble thing to do out here."

"It's the only decent and smart thing to do," said Nolan sincerely. "If it catches things will die and people we don't want to know our whereabouts will surely find us."

"Very true my boy, very true," Rom grinned. "On a different note, what's for breakfast? We can't start travelling without food in our bellies."

Faline sat down with her bag and started rummaging through it. "We have limited time given the look of the sky, so I suggest eating some of what we have in our bags and get going. We need to get to a place where we can shelter when the sky opens and look for food then."

"I agree with you there." Nolan nodded and began searching through his own bag.

Between the two of them they had pulled out the last four apples, a third of a loaf of bread, a couple of sausage links and the last bit of jam. Faline had pulled the smoked salmon out but thought better of eating that as well and stuffed it back into the bag for another time.

"Okay, so this is about it for food that we brought." Faline sighed placing the bits of food on the small blanket at her feet.

Each of them took an apple and ate it as slowly as they could savouring each bite before finally finishing them and moving on to the bread and jam. The bread had become tough from having aged in the bag over the last couple days, but the jam helped to soften it up a little making it easier to eat. The smoked sausage Nolan cut up and gave a little to everyone including Cairo who sat eagerly licking her chops waiting for her turn to eat. Faline had given her some bits of apple, but to Cairo nothing beat a good piece of sausage.

After finishing up the last bits of breakfast they rolled up their blankets and tucked them back into their bags. Faline had been watching the sky which had grown steadily darker as they ate and packed making her grow uneasy.

"Okay, is everyone ready to get moving? The rain isn't going to hold off forever." Faline groaned wishing she was already somewhere she wasn't going to get soaked.

Rom stood there staring at her smiling not saying a word. Faline glanced at him briefly before starting to walk towards the path motioning for the others to follow. Cairo hopped to her feet, her tongue lolling out at the side of her mouth and took her place by Faline's side. Nolan and Rom took a nice easy pace behind them and the party steadily began making their way west.

After about fifteen minutes or so of walking Faline could still feel Rom's eyes piercing the back of her head. She took a second to glance back at the two men following her and noticed that Rom was still smiling at her the same as he was before they left their little camp. She decided that it was time to figure out what it was that he might want, so she dropped back a little and took a place next to him as they walked.

"You've been smiling at me like that since before we left this morning. Is there something on your mind?" she asked quietly.

Rom chuckled a little before answering. "I'm sorry. I was unaware that it was against the law to smile at someone."

Nolan laughed under his breath but quickly stopped and looked straight ahead when he caught the fierce look on Faline's face as he did.

"No, it isn't but you aren't just smiling, it's like you know or want something and just haven't said anything," Faline retorted gruffly.

Rom just looked at her and calmly replied, "I was told that I am not to say or do anything without permission or having been asked first. I am just doing as instructed."

"Ugh!" Faline groaned stomping as she walked. "Fine. Please tell me what it is that you either know or want."

Laughing, Rom shrugged and agreed. "Since you asked so politely I suppose I can tell you." He cleared his throat and continued. "Last night after I emerged from the tree line I noticed that you had a shiny red amulet hanging around your neck."

Faline immediately reached for the stone dangling at her chest and clenched it in her fist having forgotten about it until just now.

"Yes, that would be the one," Rom smiled. "I am not going to take it if that's what you are concerned about right now. I just wanted to make mention that it was kind of glowing last night."

"Glowing? What do you mean glowing?" Faline's curiosity now peaked.

"If I am correct, and I believe that I am, that particular amulet is one Hildy gave you to help you out." Rom's smile becoming as wide as his face. "It kind of glows when it is trying to help you out or to let you know that there is something that you could use nearby."

Still clenching the amulet she pulled it out of her shirt to inspect it. Sure enough it still had a slight glow to it. "I wonder what it is trying to tell me then," she whispered.

Nolan stared at the stone and for a moment was held by its soft red glow. "Faline, I can smell the rain in the air now, it's going to be here soon."

Shaking herself out of her daze, Faline answered back quietly. "I know but I haven't seen anywhere we can go."

"If I may, Miss Faline," Rom began. "I know these woods pretty good and there is a pine-shrouded thicket a little ways south of here. It has kept me dry on many occasions."

Faline turned and looked towards the south noting all the thick brush and bushes that would make getting there very hard. "How long would that take us Romulus?"

"Not very long at all really," Rom smiled.

Nolan raised his eyebrow looking at all the obstacles barring their way. "How do you figure? There is no path and it will take forever to make one."

Rom laughed. "Leave it to me friends." He looked towards Faline and gave a small bow. "Faline, I am going to ask you to trust me no matter what."

She eyed him curiously for a second before nodding, not sure what to say now.

"Excellent. Now just relax and give me a minute or two." Rom laughed heartily and turned around spinning his crimson cloak around himself.

With his laugh still ringing in their ears a brilliant red light lit up the surrounding area making Nolan and Faline shield their eyes. The two of them had no idea what to expect after what they had encountered the night before. When they had reopened their eyes standing before them was a giant dark brown stag that just about matched the colour of Romulus's hair. It had enormous antlers that looked as if they had been growing atop his head for decades, and large piercing reddish coloured eyes.

The stag bowed to Faline pawing mightily at the ground and gesturing with his enormous head towards his back. Faline, still awestruck over what had just happened, stood there with Nolan and Cairo, none of whom were able to move. Again the giant stag pawed the ground and motioned with its giant head for her to get on his back. This time however a voice came into her head along with the movement.

"Faline, I am sure you can hear me if what Hildy says is true. I asked you to trust me. I truly am not here to hurt you," Rom told her softly. "I am in this form now to get you and your friends to a safe place before this storm hits."

"What about Nolan?" Faline asked aloud.

Nolan looked a little puzzled. "What about me?" he asked confused.

"Just a second Nolan," she said waving him off like a bothersome fly. "Rom, we cannot both ride on your back, it's too much."

Rom laughed. "Don't worry about that. Just get on and I will handle the rest. Cairo will have no problem keeping up with her four legs and magnificent speed either."

Faline nodded and looked over at Nolan. "I didn't mean to be rude a minute ago. I was just trying to get the information first since only I can hear Rom in my head while he's in his animal form."

Nolan, with his arms folded across his chest, simply sighed. "I guess I get it, but next time you could just say please wait or something."

Faline smiled. "Okay, Nolan. I will try and be more tactful."

"Thank you," he replied. "Now what's the plan? I have no interest in being in the wide open when the sky lets loose."

Faline did as she was told and hopped onto Rom's back and looked down at Nolan. "Um, Rom said he had you covered so I guess we wait a minute."

Once Faline was on his back Rom tipped back his head and let out one long very loud noise. It sounded like a mix between a donkey bray and a horse neigh to Faline and Nolan, but who were they to judge. Faline sitting atop Rom's back almost felt majestic as she waited for whatever he had called to come forth for Nolan. While they waited Rom told Faline it was best if she held onto his horns to make sure she didn't fall off once they really got going. Faline nodded and promised when he told her to do it she would hang on tightly.

A few moments later another very large stag emerged from the trees. This stag was not nearly as large as Rom and Faline guessed he was just your average male deer coming to do the job Rom had called him to do. Rom told her she was right. The stag knelt beside Nolan and let him climb onto his back. Rom told Faline to hang on, having her instruct Nolan to do the same. Both clenched their stags' horns as tightly as they possibly could.

"Okay, Rom, we're ready," Faline said as she gritted her teeth readying herself for the first bound.

With a chuckle and a snort Rom bolted south through the tree line, the other stag close behind and Cairo right on their heels. The trio of beasts ran through the forest as if it were a beaten down old path that had been trod upon for years. The brush that had tangled up in Nolan and Faline's clothes was nothing to the four-legged animals running through it as they crushed bits of it into the ground.

Faline and Nolan kept their heads tucked down near the antlers to ensure that they didn't get hit by any of the branches that were lashing by their faces. It was difficult she noticed to keep her eyes open while she was riding at this speed as they would begin to water as they went. Faline was persistent though and kept trying because she wanted to watch the world go by while she sped through the forest.

After a while Rom's voice crept back into her head. "We are almost there Faline and it's a lucky thing too, the rain is almost upon us."

"Thank you, Rom," Faline responded graciously. "I am, well we are very grateful for what you have done for us."

"You can thank me properly once we arrive, maybe with a nice meal and a fire," Rom replied.

"If there is still dry wood about then you have yourself a deal." Faline laughed.

Rom sped up at this point knowing she was right. They needed to get there in time to gather the wood before it got all wet or the night was going to be very damp and cold, possibly the next day as well depending on how long the rain stayed. Weaving this way and that through the thick trees and overgrown bushes, Rom, Cairo and the stag Nolan rode trampled carelessly over everything making their way to the thicket Rom knew about from his living in the forest. Faline peeked through a crack in one eye and noticed they were making their way towards a small opening and took a chance to fling her arms out to her sides letting the wind rush over her body.

"This must be what flying feels like," she smiled to herself with her eyes closed and arms spread wide.

Rom laughed. "Yes, it probably is, but if you don't grab back onto me you may fly right off. We are headed back into the thick of it in a second here."

Faline did as she was told and rode the rest of the way clenching tightly to Rom's antlers savouring the light airy feeling of her experience.

Rom's pace began to slow and the travelling party came to a nice easy walk after a minute or two. Rom stuck his large black nose in the air and gave a few sniffs about and turned a little to the right and continued to walk. Faline began to see a small somewhat hidden dirt path unfold under the overgrown bushes. Rom stopped and bowed down allowing Faline to get down and onto the ground. Nolan got down as well giving his stag a good pat on its front haunch. It looked towards Rom for a moment before Rom made a little cow type noise at it. Bowing its antlered head in acknowledgement, it ran back the way they had come. In another moment, a familiar crimson light lit the area surrounding the companions and Rom was no longer a stag, but once again a smiling man.

"We should gather wood while we walk the rest of the way to the thicket up ahead," Rom smiled.

Faline and Nolan nodded. "Thank you again Rom," Faline grinned. "Not only was that amazing, but you really saved our butts by getting us here so quickly."

"Yes, thank you so much." Nolan extended a hand which Rom graciously accepted. "That was a new experience for me. I've never ridden a deer before."

Rom laughed and shook his head. "Well they say there is a first time for everything. I'm glad the two of you enjoyed yourselves. Now let's get moving before we end up a bunch of drowned rats with no fire or food."

Again, Faline and Nolan nodded. "Lead the way and we will gather as you go. Are there berry bushes, fish, small animals or anything of note we can get here?" Faline asked.

Rom scratched his head as he walked. "Um well let's see. I think there might be some berries if the critters haven't eaten them already. I believe there is a small stream to the north of the thicket, but it's best we wait until we get there. And as far as small animals, yes you can probably find rabbits, squirrels and the like."

Faline sighed. "Okay, well I suppose it would be best if I took Cairo and hunted while you two get all the wood. You can both carry more than I can and I can rustle up more meat with Cairo at my side."

Nolan didn't put up a fight and agreed to do things her way. Rom raised his eyebrow and stared at her for a moment wondering if she was serious about going off alone.

Catching the concerned look spreading across his face Faline, shot him a knowing smile. "Rom, I am going to be fine." She patted Cairo on the head. "This girl right here will never let anything happen to me. We will get dinner and be able to find you with no problems."

Rom again raised an eyebrow. "Well, if you are certain about your thoughts on the situation I suppose I am not going to be the one that gets in your way."

Nolan for the first time in a while laughed aloud. "You have made a wise choice, Rom, a very wise choice. Arguing with Faline is like trying to drag an unruly bull out to pasture."

Faline threw her hands on her hips and shot him a look with the intent of saying something smart in her defence. She laughed instead reaching for her bow and waving for Cairo to make their way into the forest to hunt. Cairo, seeing Faline's bow in hand, happily bounded into the greenery and began sniffing about.

"Don't worry fellas, I'll be just fine and we won't stray too far from where you are. I'll make sure we can get to you quickly if something happens." Faline hollered over her shoulder as she bent some branches out of her way to follow her canine.

After she had disappeared into the thicket Rom looked over at Nolan who was making his way down the mangled path picking up nice pieces of wood along the way. Rom began scooping up bits of dry wood as well grumbling to himself under his breath. Nolan chuckled a bit before waiting a moment for him to get closer.

"Something bothering you Rom?" Nolan asked the still mumbling man.

Rom paused for a moment to look at him. "Is she always so, what's the word I am looking for here."

"Stubborn? Independent? Risky?" Nolan said, frankly.

"Well yes, I guess all of those things." Rom replied.

Nolan sighed. "Yes, she is. There is no point in telling her she can't do something, it just makes her want to do it even more. Everyone that knows her knows that. So we all just kind of let her do her own thing and make her own mistakes."

"I suppose that's one way to do it," Rom said with a little concern in his voice. "Aren't you worried that eventually she will get herself into some serious trouble?"

Nolan stopped and stared intently at Rom wondering what he was getting at. Rom's expression gave no inclination as to what his comment referred to, so now he had no choice but to ask.

"What are you trying to tell me here, Rom?" Nolan asked with a little tension in his voice. "Is there something that I should be concerned about or watching for to help protect her?"

Rom hung his head rubbing the back of his neck knowing that he shouldn't have said anything at all at this point. "Nolan, in the time that you will be by Faline's side every once in a while you are going to have to bite the bullet and tell her she is making stupid decisions. If you don't she may not make it to the end. She is going to need you to be an advisor of sorts through her journeying."

Nolan's eyes grew wide as he was not expecting all of this to come out of a walk to gather firewood. "So this is not the only time I am going to be adventuring with Faline?" Nolan choked.

Rom looked at him very seriously now. "No, Nolan it's not. You are going to be with her on pretty much all of them. You must learn to be braver and smarter. You were scared when I came around and I was friendly. This cowardice of yours must end. Leave the farm boy behind when you are out in the world and become the knight your father has been training you to become."

Nolan shook his head grasping tighter to the wood in his arms. "What if I can't? What if I choke and can't do it?" Nolan moaned.

Rom grabbed hold of Nolan's shoulder and made him look into his eyes. "You have to," he said sternly, his crimson eyes burning into Nolan's. "Her life may very well depend on it one day. When this is over go home and train harder with your father. Train like she does. Find the passion for it like you do your animals. You must because she will need you."

Rom let go of Nolan and began scooping up wood again leaving the boy almost trembling where he stood. Nolan was unable to move for a minute as everything he'd just been told was trying to engrain itself into the archives of his mind. He slowly took a deep breath and began scooping up more wood and walking in Rom's direction. By the time both had arms full of wood they had reached the entrance to the little thicket in the pine trees.

The thicket was just as Rom had remembered it was. It was small group of tightly knit pines with long soft needles surrounded by overgrown bushes that basically turned it into a green cave with a somewhat sticky pine needle floor. Rom and Nolan set their wood down and made a small opening in the front by twisting aside some of the branches, using Nolan's knife to cut away some of the prickly bush underneath. They made sure not to make the opening too large so that if the winds kicked up it didn't allow too much of it to get in bringing the rain with it.

Eyeing the entrance they had made themselves for a second Rom nodded his satisfaction with it and began retrieving his wood to take inside the thicket. "Let's get this wood inside before the rain falls shall we?"

Nolan bent down and grabbed an armful of wood and followed Rom into the thicket ducking his head under the still low hanging branches they had left to shelter them from the wind and rain. They each took two smaller bundles of wood inside and left them in a neat little pile off to one side. Nolan was pleasantly surprised that he could stand up inside the grove of trees and looked around him in the quickly fading light. It wasn't a bad little area, all three of them and Cairo would fit nicely inside without feeling too cramped or rolling into the fire while they slept. It seemed as if it would keep them warm with all the branches and bushes about to block the winds that were beginning to kick up, although he couldn't see how it was going to keep them completely dry once it really started to rain.

"Rom, how are we supposed to stay dry in here? I mean they are only trees after all and not a roof," he asked quietly not wanting to offend their new found friend.

Rom just chuckled. "Well, you are right there. It isn't a roof and it won't keep all the water from getting in, but it will keep a lot of the rain away which is all we can hope for in this situation."

"Okay, I was just curious, that's all." Nolan shrugged as he began to build their fire.

"It never hurts to ask questions, my friend otherwise you cannot learn new things." Rom gave him a pat on the back and made his way out of the opening in the thicket. "I'm going to go grab more wood before the rains hit. We don't know how long it will last or how long we will be here for."

"Good idea," Nolan agreed. "I will join you as soon as I get the fire started and stable."

Rom offered a small salute and turned towards the woods. Nolan sat there for a little while thinking about all that Rom had said to him while he brushed away the pine needles so they didn't set the whole place alight. He got the fire going, wondering how he could ever be the hero that Faline deserved. He was just a scraggly little farm boy with a passion for animals;

he was no hero. He had already shocked himself by agreeing to come along with her on this adventure, and it was not even a dangerous one. At least that is what she had told him. After several minutes he shook it off and got up. Looking about he realised it was dark out now and he was about to venture into the woods alone since Rom had long since left. He took a few minutes to organise their little camp and once he was satisfied with that he figured it was now or never.

"Well, now is a good a time as any to start manning up I guess," he mumbled to himself before taking one last deep breath and stepping through the opening in the thicket.

It was very dark outside and the wind was howling loudly through the trees like angry wolves hunting their prey. Nolan stood still waiting for his eyes to adjust to the darkness surrounding him until finally he could make out the shadows of the bushes and trees around him. Behind him he could barely make out the fire inside the thicket, but he reckoned this was a good thing. He looked up towards the sky wishing there was a moon to shine some light on things for him, but with the weather coming in the clouds were blocking it out letting it shine through every so often to remind the world it was still there.

"Okay, shake it off Nolan," he said to himself. "It is not going to get brighter outside and we need wood. Rom is right, if we get stuck in there for a day or two we won't last without firewood." With one last deep breath he slowly made his way towards the shadows of the trees.

He figured it best to stay near the little orange dot that marked the entrance to the thicket. You could never be too safe, he thought. So he crouched down along the tree line and slowly began feeling around for sticks and bits of wood gathering them into his arms as he went. After he had gathered all he could carry he got up and made his way back to the thicket. Halfway there he heard some branches off to his left begin to crack. Someone or something was coming. There was no denying that he was terrified, but he tried to remain calm and kept walking towards the safety of his fire. A moment later something grabbed him and he yelped loudly and dropped all his wood on the ground running now for the thicket.

"Nolan, stop you silly boy!" Faline shouted after him laughing. "I didn't mean to scare you."

"It's not funny, Faline!" Nolan replied angrily. "You can't just go creeping up on people in the dark."

"I wasn't trying to creep up on you, honest I wasn't. I mean I saw you look in my direction I thought you heard me coming." Faline shrugged.

"Well, I did hear something, but it's dark out, it could have been anything." Nolan said still upset.

"I really am sorry Nolan," Faline said politely. "Let me help you pick up this wood and get it inside."

"All right, that's a start of an apology at least." he said sarcastically.

Faline helped Nolan pick up the wood and get it into the thicket. She was impressed once she got inside and was able to look around. It was bigger than she had expected it to be and all the bushes along with the branches of the trees made a suitable wind blocker. The fire Nolan had already built warmed the area nicely. Cairo found herself a nice spot to lay down by the fire looking as if she was waiting for her dinner to be prepared. Faline having looked over at her furry friend laughed at the sight of her lying there like some queen waiting for her servants to wait on her.

"Oh, Cairo," she giggled softly "What am I to do with you?"

Cairo looking as if she was smiling at her loving master blinked her eyes softly and let out a soft whine to acknowledge having been spoken to. Again Faline giggled and set about preparing the food they had caught. She had brought back with her three good sized rabbits and a smaller squirrel all still speared on their arrows to make it easier to carry. Nolan had already retrieved his knife and took one of the rabbits to start skinning it. Faline smiled at him in thanks for his help readying the meat.

While the two of them were getting the meat ready to be cooked Rom had finally made his way back to the thicket. In his arms was a large bundle of wood and he had used part of his cloak as a makeshift basket to carry in something else. Faline and Nolan watched him unload his wares, making sure to be careful not to cut themselves as they prepared dinner.

Rom finished unpacking his goods on the ground and brushed his hands together. "Oh, well done Faline," he said as he saw all the fine rabbits they were preparing. "Three rabbits and a squirrel, huh?"

"Yep!" Faline chirped happily. "Cairo and I are no amateurs when it comes to hunting."

Rom was pleased. "You both did a very fine job. Nolan you did a fine job as well making sure we had a warm place to stay as well. It sure is neat and cosy in here."

They all took a good look around and noticed that Nolan had brushed away all the sticky pine needles under one of the far bushes, stacked the wood in a good sized pile and arranged everyone's sleeping spots for them.

"Well, there was no sense in waiting for everyone to get back making everyone do it, so I figured I might as well take care of it as I went." He shrugged. "Besides, all those pine needles could have caught fire and we wouldn't have a place to stay."

"Wow, Nolan that is very responsible of you." Faline smiled and gave him a gentle pat on the back. "Not to mention awesome!"

Rom laughed. "Yes, Nolan, very awesome. I didn't want to come back and rearrange a camp after wandering around in the dark trying to find food and wood."

Nolan's face got a little pink. "It wasn't much guys, really. I appreciate all you two did as much as just making a fire and moving some pine needles."

Faline laughed. "Okay, well that's all settled then. We all did a lot to help." She skewered her rabbit onto one of the sticks Nolan had fashioned for roasting. "Now let's cook some dinner, I'm starving."

They all nodded in agreement and even Cairo let out a little "woo-woo" to let them know she was very hungry as well. Rom showed them that he had managed to stumble upon and over to his dismay, a blackberry bush. The small animals and birds had not yet picked over the whole thing so he was able to grab a bunch of ripened berries and bring them back. This meant that along with rabbit and squirrel they had fresh berries to munch.

While dinner was cooking they ate some of the berries savouring the sweet yet tart flavour of the little blackish purple fruits. Faline had offered one to Cairo who sniffed it for a moment and decided that this was not a food for her. They all laughed and made mention of her being a food snob when she should just be eating whatever is offered to her when food is scarce.

The squirrel being smaller than the rabbits cooked a little faster so Faline took it away from the fire and allowed it to cool down. Cairo sat there drooling a little bit waiting for what she knew was her dinner to be ready to eat.

"Patience, Cairo" Faline told her softly. "You can have it in a minute."

Each of them turned the rabbits over a few more times allowing each section to become thoroughly cooked. Nolan took a small piece off the one in front of him and tasted it.

"This is probably the best thing I've had in days," he said rubbing his stomach and licking his lips. "They are done."

Faline took the squirrel off the stick and handed it gently to Cairo who eagerly took it from her hand. She tried not to be a big pig about eating it because she knew she'd get scolded, but she was so excited she just about inhaled it.

"CAIRO!" Faline yelped. "How on earth do you expect to digest an almost whole, partly chewed squirrel?"

Cairo hung her head still licking her lips and let out a small burp before lying down next to Faline on the ground by the fire.

Rom and Nolan were rolling on the ground laughing trying to make sure that they held onto their dinner. Faline looked over and shot them both a dirty look prompting the two of them to make an attempt at straightening out their faces.

"It's not funny you two!" she hollered at them. "She needs to learn to eat like a lady and not try to kill herself with her food."

"You are absolutely right, Faline," Rom said choking back his laughter. "Cairo, you need to eat properly. Stop making your poor master so upset over it."

Cairo let out a small huff and lay her head down in Faline's lap staring up at her with her huge brown eyes. Faline sighed knowing she couldn't stay angry when Cairo pulled the baby doll eyes out on her.

"All right, enough of this mess. Let's just finish dinner and get some sleep," she moaned.

"That sounds like a fabulous idea," Nolan said wiping a small tear from his eye from all the laughter. "Our dinner is going to get cold and the weather is getting worse."

"Yes, indeed. A good meal and some sleep before the wind and rain make it too noisy to fall asleep," Rom nodded. "Sounds like a grand idea to me. I'm starving and after all the running, exhausted."

They took their time eating dinner as they wanted to make sure they thoroughly enjoyed it. Faline as always shared hers with Cairo only giving her little bits at a time to make sure that she didn't choke. Cairo didn't mind her baby bites at all, anything was better than nothing in her opinion. The three of them diligently picked clean the bones of the rabbits giving the livers, kidneys and hearts to Cairo for extra protein, before throwing the remnants into the fire for disposal.

"That was an excellent meal after a long day of travel if I do say so myself." Rom smiled rubbing his stomach.

"Thank you Faline and Cairo of course, for making sure we had dinner tonight," Nolan added bowing slightly from where he sat.

Cairo gave a small yip and Faline simply smiled. "Okay, fellas, I suggest we try and get to sleep before the weather gets worse than it is."

They all looked up at the already swaying tree tops and fluttering branches that made up their dwelling. The wind was picking up rapidly now and the rain was coming down in bigger drops than before they had eaten.

"Hopefully, our little thicket stays true and we all manage to stay dry tonight." Nolan frowned listening to the rain pummel the ground outside of the opening they had fashioned out of the branches.

"I am sure we are going to be all right, and if push comes to shove I am sure we can figure something out." Rom winked at Faline as he lay down on his blanket by the fire.

Faline had barely caught Rom's gesture in the firelight as she too lay down on her blanket. Cairo wasted no time snuggling up to her as close as her furry body could get. Nolan had curled up on his blanket and bade everyone a good night before falling fast asleep. He never had any troubles sleeping anywhere Faline noticed, she was almost jealous of him as a result.

I wonder why Rom winked at me when he said we could figure something out," Faline thought to herself. I guess maybe he has another plan.

Faline sighed and lay there listening to the wind howl through the trees as the rain pelted the bushes and ground outside. She stroked Cairo's fur while she listened to the steadily growing storm outside, and after a short while the sounds became rhythmic and soothing allowing her to drift off to sleep.

Chapter 13

Waiting out the Storm

While the travelling party slept the storm outside had slowly picked up pace. The rain was coming down in buckets, the wind was howling and whipping through the trees making them shake and groan, not to mention the thunder and lightning that was having its own bit of raucous fun. All the creaks, groans, wind, driving rain and giant cracks of thunder jostled Faline out of her slumber in a panic.

She stared around the thicket trying to get a grasp on what was going on, Cairo was already sitting up panting by her side. It was still dark but that could be because of the storm so it was hard to judge what time it was. Looking over she noticed the fire was almost completely out. Only a few hot embers were left, the rest had been snuffed out by the rain that had managed to find its way through the canopy of pines they were sheltered in. She reached over and touched the ground feeling that it was damp to the touch. She decided that it would be best to wake the others as something needed to be done before they turned into soggy freezing heaps on the ground.

Walking over to where Nolan lay shifting uneasily on the ground she lay a hand on his shoulder. "Nolan, Nolan, get up. We have a small problem." She spoke gently but firmly.

Nolan sat up quickly looking this way and that. "What?! What is it? Did something try to get us?" he asked panicking.

"Nolan, calm down, nothing tried to get us." Faline rolled her eyes. "We are getting wet and the fire is almost out. The storm outside is breaking through the thicket."

Nolan was relieved that they were not in any danger. "Okay, so what are we going to do about it? We haven't got any where else to go and we can't wander around in this."

Faline was making her way over to Rom as Nolan spoke. "I don't know what we are going to do. I know that we are going to be in big trouble if we end up soaked and freezing."

She slowly bent down so as not to startle her sleeping friend and gently shook his arm. "Rom, we might need to move."

"Whazzat?" Rom said sleepily. "Move? Why?"

"Rom, it's kind of raining in here. Not too bad yet, but once the rain completely soaks the trees we are going to be in a waterfall." She groaned pointing up at the violently swaying trees.

Rom blinked up at the canopy trying to focus his still sleeping eyes on what she was pointing at. He then noticed along with the driving rain and whipping winds shoving the tree branches all over, there was a lot of thunder and lightning to boot. He rubbed his hands together before cupping them around his mouth and blowing into them for the heat.

"First things first," Rom said getting to his feet. "Nolan, we need you to get this fire back up before all the embers are gone. You'll never get anywhere with wet wood."

Nolan nodded and grabbed some of the drier wood from the bottom of the pile and started stoking the fire. He took more of the wood and placed it in a circle around the fire to dry it.

Faline looked to Rom for her instructions. He simply smiled at her and sat down. She didn't understand what he was doing. Why tell Nolan to do that and then just do nothing more?

"Well?" she asked. "Now what?"

"What do you mean?" Rom asked looking up at her.

"We can't just be satisfied with a new fire!" she shouted. "We are getting wet and it will make us all sick if we don't dry out. Who knows how long the storm will be here?"

"You are probably right. This is a huge storm and it could be here for days," Rom replied staring up at the canopy to watch the light show outside.

Faline threw her hands in the air and stomped around trying to figure out some way to stop the rain from getting in. She had no idea how they were going to pull it off. They didn't have anything to use as building materials really, and they didn't have anything to use as a better roof. She plopped herself on the ground next to the newly risen fire along with Nolan and Rom to try and warm her already chilled body and looked over at Rom.

"Rom, do you know how we can stop the rain from getting in or do we need to go somewhere else?" she asked quietly.

Sitting there staring into the fire and warming his hands Rom nodded. "As a matter of fact I do have an idea."

Faline and Nolan both sighed. "What is your plan?" Nolan asked, a little more confidence in his voice since their conversation the night before.

"Since we cannot move from here as there isn't anywhere else to go for miles, we need to make a roof." Rom's eyes glinted in the firelight.

Faline's mouth dropped and her heart sank. "What do you mean make a roof?! What on earth are we supposed to make a roof out of?"

Rom merely sat where he was watching her as she tried her best not to panic before he started to speak. "Faline, there are plenty of things to make a roof out of if you take the time to look around and imagine it."

She stared at him with wide eyes not believing what she was hearing. Her mind could not grasp what he was trying to imply and it was frustrating her no end.

"Rom, I am getting more wet by the second and the fire is not going to be able to keep me warm enough soon," Faline grimaced. "I am truly not in the mood to play guessing games so if you would kindly just get to the point."

"Okay, okay," Rom said trying his best not to laugh at her. "All I am saying is that with a little magical imagination we can make a nice sturdy roof over our heads."

Nolan groaned. "You mean to say that you could have made the canopy prevent water from coming in this whole time and you said nothing to us about it?"

"Well, Faline did say that I was not to interfere with your adventure unless she asked me to," Rom said, frankly. "In my defence, I was not asked to make a solid place to stay. I merely suggested where we could go." He finished by folding his hands into his lap waiting for their rebuttal.

Faline stomped her foot on the ground with a squish into what was once dirt now turning to mud. "Rom, you are really something you know that?"

Rom smiled and nodded his head politely. "Why thank you Faline. I will accept your compliment."

"So what now?" Nolan asked somewhat annoyed by recent events. "We are not getting any drier and the storm is not letting up."

"That is for sure." Faline agreed looking up at the canopy scowling at the black clouds over head. "All right, Rom, please help us to make this place a little more efficient for lack of a better word."

Rom winked at her and nodded. "Okay kiddies, pull up a seat and relax while I make some magic." He rubbed his hands together and moved them on his knees before closing his eyes.

"What's he going to do?" Nolan asked Faline with a look of concern on his face.

Faline shook her head and pulled up a chunk of wood to sit on. "I have no idea Nolan," she replied.

Cairo who had otherwise been quiet started to whimper a little, slowly creeping closer to Faline's legs. Faline looked over at her and placed a hand in her poor dog's soggy fur trying to comfort her the best she could.

"Shh, Cairo," she whispered now coddling her dog. "It's gonna be all right. We must trust that Rom knows what he's doing." Even though she was a little concerned herself, she figured she had better calm down her companions.

Not unlike the few times Romulus had done things before, an amazing crimson glow began to illuminate from his body. This time however it spread outward and up towards the tree tops enveloping everything that it encountered in its red light. It was almost as if the trees, branches and bushes were all being painted red then beginning to glow. Faline, Nolan and Cairo sat and watched as it spread all around them until it had reached every part of the thicket, all the way to the highest tree top.

Once the crimson light had covered everything it could, there came the sounds of things beginning to creak and groan. Branches began shaking, leaves were fluttering, bushes began to rustle and the trees seemed like they were moving. Faline moved a little closer to Nolan not entirely sure what was happening and not positive that she liked it.

"Faline..." Nolan began but was cut short by her hand coming up to hush him. Then she pointed at the branches.

"Look!" she whispered. "They are growing."

Nolan looked in the direction that Faline was pointing. Sure enough the now crimson glowing branches of the trees were growing longer and thicker moving towards one another like arms readying themselves for a warm embrace. The pine needles were weaving into one another like a giant basket as the branches intertwined. They looked around some more and noticed that the bushes were growing larger as well, their little leaves becoming bigger and all fanning outwards like a giant drape as the water rolled off them and away from the thicket like a little waterfall.

As they looked up towards the canopy, instead of being multiple branches jutting this way and that, it was like looking at one giant knotty needle-covered branch. Glancing around all the bushes had formed a green arc that was repelling the water out to the sides. It was as if a huge makeshift hut had just been built but no one had lifted a finger.

Rom took a deep breath which startled Faline and Nolan in their awestruck daze, and the crimson light that had enveloped every piece of their thicket, came away from everything and was slowly reabsorbed into his body. As the last of the light faded they took note that there was no more rain coming into the thicket. It was all they could hope for at this moment, just to be dry.

"Rom, thank you so much, this is amazing," Faline said happily.

Rom gave a weak smile. "You're welcome."

"You look a little tired Rom. Are you all right?" Nolan asked eyeing him curiously.

Rom nodded. "It takes a bit out of me to do what I just did, even for a skilled warlock. I will be just fine as soon as I eat a little and get some more sleep. Thank you for your concern, my friend."

Nolan grabbed his bag and felt around for a minute smiling and pulled out one last straggling apple. He gladly handed it to Romulus wishing there was more he could do for him after all Rom had just done for them. Rom graciously accepted Nolan's offering and enjoyed every bite of his apple.

While Rom and Nolan sat by the fire, Faline had found some lengthy dead branches that had fallen from the trees during the transformation of their thicket. She took them and started stuffing them into the mud near the fire as the two men watched her wondering what she was up to. It wasn't until she had them all in place and began hanging their wet belongings on them that they understood what she had been doing.

"Very intuitive of you Faline," Rom grinned, giving her a thumbs-up. "The blankets will be dry in no time hanging up like that."

"Exactly what I was thinking." Faline smiled as she hung the last blanket over the branch. "We can't very well be sitting inside on wet things. It would defeat the whole purpose of you making us a hut of sorts."

"Agreed," Nolan piped in. "What else can we dry on those?"

"Pretty much anything really," she said matter of factly. "I have them stuck in the ground pretty far so they should hold a good amount of weight."

"Awesome!" Nolan yelped happily as he began removing his boots.

Faline was immediately consumed with panic and she looked at him a little mortified. "What on earth are you doing?"

Slightly confused, Nolan continued taking his boots off. "I am removing my wet boots, Faline otherwise I will end up with some crazy foot fungus."

"I guess we don't want that to happen now, do we?" she said turning slightly red.

"No, we don't and if you were smart, you and Rom there, would take yours off as well and let them dry next to the fire." He laid them on the rocks around the fire with the opening of the boot facing the fire to let the heat inside.

Faline took a seat on her piece of wood so she could get her boots off without falling. Rom was already removing his and both he and Faline began placing their soggy footwear by the fire in the same fashion Nolan had placed his own. Faline felt the ground near the fire where she was sitting taking note that it was slowly becoming dry. This made her hopeful for their success in waiting out the storm without any of them becoming ill and not being able to carry on. She remembered that in her bag all she had left was the few pieces of smoked salmon that her mother had packed for her and knew that they were going to have to go out and gather food.

"Well," Faline began, taking note that her voice was shaking a little from the cold seeping into her skin, "we are going to have to venture out in this mess and get some things to eat at some point so we don't all starve. I suggest we take turns so that none of us are out there all the time giving us a chance to dry out in between."

"A fine suggestion, my dear," Romulus responded quietly. "If I may, I would appreciate taking the last run so that I can fully recover from my spell."

Faline nodded. "Of course, Rom. We can't have you running about in the rain feeling weak to start. I will go out first, then Nolan, then you."

Nolan sighed before giving his opinion on the matter. "Faline, you are soaked to the bone and shivering already. I think you and Cairo should stay here for a little while longer and let me go first. Besides, we are going to need some more wood brought in as well to begin drying it out and I can carry more than you, meaning no offence of course." His face was reddening as he finished speaking.

Faline merely rolled her eyes but knew he was right. She was in fact cold from having got so wet and the fire had yet to warm her. She was chilled to way to the bone and knew she needed to fix it before she became sick. She didn't want to let him be the first to go out, she felt obligated to be the one to take charge since it was her quest, but she was also proud of him for taking control for the first time in his life.

"Okay, Nolan, as you wish." Faline smiled at him as she placed her hands over the fire more to warm them.

Nolan had to look at her twice to make sure she wasn't joking before sitting a little more proudly knowing that he had finally done something noble and right for a change. Rom glanced over at him and chuckled a little. He had yet to see Nolan look so, well manly and it was somewhat amusing. The boyish ways Nolan had been accustomed to, were about to slowly start slipping away, and Romulus felt it was about time that they did.

"Very good then," Nolan said, his head held high. "I will give my boots a few more minutes to roast near the fire here and I will be off."

"Sounds like a fine plan, Nolan." Rom smiled leaning over and giving him a pat on the back.

"Thank you, Rom," Nolan grinned. "I just hope I can do well by the both of you."

"Oh Nolan, I am sure you are going to do just fine," Faline said encouragingly. "Besides, it might be pouring outside but at least it is daytime now."

"That's true," Nolan said forcing a smile this time. "I won't be in the pitch black at least."

Faline nodded. "This is very true, although with the weather outside it is still relatively dark. Make sure you keep a good eye out for things on the ground."

"Don't you worry about me," Nolan said smiling. "I am going to be just fine, you'll see."

Nolan flipped his boots around and felt inside one of them to see how dry they were. Satisfied with the feel, he began putting his mostly dry boots back onto his feet. He grimaced a little since the toes of them were still soggy but knew that once he started walking around outside it wouldn't matter anyway. Once his shoes were snug on his feet he got up and made his way over to the little hole in the thicket.

"Wish me luck," he said giving a small salute before exiting into the downpour.

"Want me to send Cairo with you?" Faline shouted after him as his last foot left the thicket.

Nolan poked his head back inside for a moment. "Thank you for the offer, but she will want to stay dry until you go out. I'll be fine." He turned and walked away pulling his jacket up over his head to shield him from the rain.

Faline, Rom and Cairo all sat snugly by the fire for some time with nothing to say or do. Faline had got up once to flip the blanket and other items around on her makeshift clothes lines to make sure that everything was able to get some heat and dry. Romulus merely sat and watched her, admiring her dedication and motherly attentiveness. Once she had finished she took her seat on the little piece of wood she had been using and picked up one of her boots. Feeling inside the way Nolan had she smiled and put it back onto her foot before grabbing the other one and doing the same.

"Rom?" Faline said softly. "Am I really destined to save the world?" She looked up at him with concern spread across her face.

"Faline, there are many scrolls telling the tale of a great warrior that is destined to save the world." Rom began in a tone that was serious but kind in the same token. "This warrior is supposed to have many great skills and have natural born abilities that no other man or woman shall possess. Some of these abilities are almost god-like in nature, some are honed, some are spiritual, and others will be divulged over time."

He felt around inside one of his boots that had been warming by the fire and with a satisfied look began putting them on his feet. Wiggling his toes inside his newly dried and warmed boots, Rom stood up and stretched.

"Faline, please don't put too much thought into it," Rom told her calmly. "It will add stress to a situation that doesn't require any now. This quest you are on is a simple task to find out if you are truly the one and only."

A puzzled Faline looked up at him. She stood and began pacing back and forth trying to figure out why on earth she was out here if she wasn't the one they needed her to be.

"What do you mean by that exactly?" she said, her face twisting into an angry scowl. "I thought Hildy said I was the one you all had been waiting for and that is why I am here doing this."

"She has been watching and waiting for hundreds of years, Faline. You are the first human being to have been born that fits the prophecy, so now we must make sure that you are The One." Rom glanced over at the pacing girl almost feeling sorry for her. He knew that there was nothing that was going to calm her down now.

"Well, that is just great!" she shouted tossing her hands in the air before pivoting about and staring at the dark haired man across from her. "I hope that after all this, after all I have done and gone through how far I have come and the excessive training I went through, that I don't disappoint you in the end."

She took a deep breath her bottom lip quivering, sat slowly on her log seat and buried her head into her hands. Romulus let her stay where she was in without saying another word. He didn't want to make the situation any worse than it was already. He was hoping that Nolan was going to return soon allowing Faline to go out with Cairo to hunt. She needed now more than ever to feel like she was worth more than she thought.

Almost as if Rom had willed it to happen there was some crackling of branches and a few huffs before Nolan came through the hole in the thicket. He was soaking wet and his arms were loaded with dripping muddy wood.

"Um, maybe a little help please." Nolan gasped trying to hang onto the slippery pieces of wood in his arms.

Faline and Rom hurried over to grab some of the slipping wood from Nolan's wet shivering arms. Nolan walked over towards the fire and began assembling his remaining pieces around the edge of the fire to start drying them out.

"Want us to do the same with these Nolan or do you think they will be dry enough by the time we need them?" Faline asked.

"I think that we will be all right," Nolan said trying not to let his teeth chatter while he spoke. "Once the fire gets hot enough it will burn the remnants of water out of those pieces."

Faline set hers out in a row giving them the chance to air dry more than they would if they had been piled up. Rom did the same with his before going over to help Nolan arrange his around the fire. Once again Nolan had taken his boots off and lay them inward towards the flames to dry them out after hanging his light jacket over Faline's clothes rack. He then sat as close to the fire as humanly possible without catching on fire himself.

Faline had finished laying her wood out, brushed her hands off on the sides of her pants and immediately went for her bow.

"I am not wasting any more time here. Cairo and I are going to head out now." She spoke rather quickly and didn't give either of them the chance to tell her otherwise. She whistled for Cairo and was out of the entrance to the thicket in a mere matter of seconds.

Nolan looked over at Rom who sat saying nothing as he warmed his hands over the fire. He wanted to ask Rom what had just happened but thought that maybe the explanation would just come out. After several minutes of staring toward the opening of the thicket completely confused Nolan realised Rom wasn't going to say anything.

"Rom, is Faline all right? I mean she seemed kinda, I don't know, upset or something." Nolan almost choked out the words trying not to make an awkward situation.

Rom just sighed still warming his hands flipping them over periodically to even the heat. "She is going to be fine, Nolan. I told her some things that she had inquired about and now she is trying to process them."

Nolan scratched his head looking even more perplexed. "I don't understand what else she could possibly need to know or what could bother her like that after knowing all that she does."

"It's quite simple really," Rom shrugged. "I left her with reasonable doubt. I told her what she needed to hear to make her realise that she still must work for what she is to become. That's all."

"Oh, I suppose that makes sense. Guess I'll just let her have her space for a bit then," Nolan replied quietly. "Last thing I want to do is make her angry.."

Rom laughed. "No, we don't want to do that. We are just going to keep the fire good and hot until she gets back with lunch and hopefully dinner. Then I will go out and get some things if I can find anything that is. If nothing else I will grab more wood. It is still a two day journey from here and we can keep this thicket the way it is for the way back."

Nolan sat up a little a smile spreading across his face. "That sounds great to me. Thank you so much Rom for everything you have done already."

"No problem, my friend. It's my pleasure." He leaned over and gave Nolan a pat on the shoulder.

Having been out in the rain for a bit now, Faline was already getting a slight chill. Cairo was soaked but still sniffing around trying to find some game to hunt. Crouching slightly as she walked trying to keep her footsteps shallow, Faline gripped her bow extra tight as it was getting slack from the rain, holding it straight out waiting for her opportunity to shoot.

"Come on. Cairo. You can do it," she mumbled softly under her breath as she strained her eyes through the downpour to see what was around her.

Cairo's fur on the back of her neck was beginning to prickle out telling Faline that something was near. She crept slowly to where Cairo had stopped and waited there for her to make her move. Faline knelt in the muddy grass to steady herself taking aim at nothing but air as Cairo began to creep forward.

Sneaking slowly up into the trees towards the thick patches of bushes, Cairo, nose sniffing about this way and that, turned her towards one bush that began to rustle slightly as she came nearer. Faline watched carefully at what Cairo was doing and took aim at the bush she was drawing closer to getting ready to make her shot, or hopefully shots. She had stuck a few arrows in the ground next to her feet to make it easy for her to grab and fire. Waiting for the chance to shoot always seemed to take forever and seeing that it was pouring outside it felt like it was taking even longer.

Cairo crouched down and Faline steadied her bow readying her shot as Cairo pounced into the bush. With a small creep forward and a little swish of her bushy tail Cairo leapt forward into the bush sending branches spraying water all about as pheasant flew into the air in a panic. Faline wasted no time aiming her bow and arrow upwards firing one arrow after another until all five arrows she had pulled were spent.

Faline slowly stood up and called out to Cairo who was sniffing around in the bushes. "All right Cairo, let's get our birds and get back and dry up, shall we?"

Cairo let out a happy woof and started rustling through the bushes looking for the food that Faline had shot down. Faline let out a small sigh of relief when Cairo came bounding out with a big fat bird hanging from her mouth. She had never gone hunting in weather like this and was afraid that she had spent most of her time squinting due to the rain that she had missed. The noise from the water hitting the ground and the leaves around her made it hard for her to hear her shots hit their mark.

Grabbing the flopping dead fowl from her dog's mouth in one hand, she yanked out the arrow that was jammed it in the mucky ground for a quick cleaning before placing it back into her quiver. She reached down and gave Cairo a nice pat on the head and smiled at her.

"What would I do without you, my friend?" she mused as she ruffled her dog's sloppy wet fur.

Cairo gave her a nudge in the thigh with her head before prancing proudly back into the thick of the bushes. She came back out a few moments later with another limp bird dangling from her mouth. To Faline's amazement this one was even bigger and fatter than the first. She took it from Cairo following the same procedure as before and again thanked her faithful companion for her efforts.

"I cannot believe I managed to hit two birds in this slop. I can barely see with all this water pouring down my face." She smiled proudly to herself as she tied the two birds' legs together for easy carrying.

Cairo gave out a woof and went bounding back in again. Faline was in shock and could not fathom there being a third bird. She thought for a moment remembering that she had in fact shot five arrows but thought it impossible that there were five birds or that she would have hit five had that been the case.

She shook her head. "Impossible. I know I am one of the best archers in my family, but…." she shook her head again. "Impossible."

Cairo came prancing out of the woods with another bird, this one smaller than the others and to Faline's shock not completely dead. It was writhing and twitching in Cairo's mouth as the dog almost danced to her master's feet utterly proud that she had found another one of Faline's targets.

"Oh, Cairo," Faline gasped as she watched the bird suffering. "The poor thing isn't dead. I feel terrible that I didn't hit it right."

A soft voice she had known to be Cairo's came into her mind as she gently placed the bird on the ground. "It isn't your fault, Faline. You know had the weather been more cooperative you'd have made your mark perfectly."

Faline looked over at Cairo who just sat there staring at her waiting for the job to be finished. "I guess you're right." She gave her a weak little smile. "I suppose I should end its suffering so we can get going."

Faline squatted down next to the flailing bird and held its head with the tip of her boot. She grabbed hold of its body and gave it a quick hard twist snapping its neck allowing the bird to become still at last. Still holding it down she yanked her arrow out and cleaned it off a little in the wet grass where they sat.

"Well, now that's finished, are there any more out there Cairo?" Faline asked half heartedly still pitying the bird she now held in her hand.

Cairo sat looking up at her before standing and shaking some of the water from herself. "I don't believe so but I will go check." With that she ran back into the woods to sniff around.

Faline spent the time she waited tying all the birds she had together and wiping rain out of her eyes from time to time. While standing there watching for Cairo to return she noticed that not only was she soaked to the bone, but due to all the rain the temperature outside was much colder than she was used to and she was beginning to tremble from being idle for so long.

Cairo came back after a little bit holding one of Faline's stray arrows in her mouth but unfortunately no bird to go with it. She sat and waited for Faline to take her arrow and put it away.

"Guess we are all done out here then." Faline gave Cairo another quick pat before starting to walk back. "Let's go get warm and dry now, huh?"

Cairo gave a big woof and quickly set pace alongside Faline. Walking back Faline felt proud of her accomplishments for the day; three decent sized birds to eat and she had been gone only for an hour or two at the most. She tried to wrap her head around what Rom had said earlier and figured that he just meant that she needed to make sure she was always ready for anything that life threw at her. At least that was how she felt comfortable justifying it.

Coming to the entrance of the thicket Faline felt it best to let go the troubles she had been carrying. She had managed to work them out in her head and they seemed to make sense now. With that she took a nice deep breath and made her way through holding her trophies high above her head with a radiant smile spread across her face. Rom and Nolan were off their seats in a heartbeat, Nolan grabbing a blanket to drape over her and Rom grabbing the dangling dead birds from her hand.

"Wow, Faline!" Rom grinned as he took the birds. "Once again you have proven to be a mighty hunter."

"I couldn't have said it better myself." Nolan agreed wrapping the blanket tightly around Faline's body to try and warm her up as they walked to the fireside.

"Thanks guys, that really means a lot to me," Faline managed to say through chattering teeth.

"Well, while Nolan gets you all warmed up and cleans these fine feathered meals, I will make my trip out into the horrendous weather and see what I can scrounge up," Rom said standing up straight and puffing out his chest.

Faline laughed. "Okay, Rom. Be careful out there. The rain has made the ground very soggy in some spots and slick in others."

Rom nodded. "Noted, dear girl. I will mind myself while I am out and return with something to contribute." With that having been said Rom was out of the hole in the thicket.

Nolan made sure that Faline was snug and warm by the fire before thinking about anything else. "You're sure you are comfy and getting warmer then?" he asked her in a tone that was almost as if he was parenting her.

Faline rolled her eyes. "Yes, Nolan, I am sure I am getting warmer. In fact if I were any closer to the fire I may catch on fire myself," she chuckled.

"I just want to make sure you don't get sick is all." Nolan sighed before turning his attention to the birds.

Cairo had her head nestled in Faline's lap happy to be drying out herself and let out a sigh. "My sentiments exactly my friend," she giggled as she gave Cairo a pat on the head. "We are fine Nolan. We appreciate your concern and promise to tell you if we need anything. Cross my heart."

Nolan glanced sidelong at her before tending to the birds again. "I will take that. These are some mighty fine pheasant Faline, big ones too. What do you suppose Romulus is after?"

Faline shrugged sniffling a little. "I am flattered, thank you. As far as Rom, I am not sure really. He did say there was a stream, but that was back where we were. Being that he is a deer in his other form I would bet he can smell things we can't."

Nolan looked at her with some curiosity. "Like what? I mean deer eat lots of things that people don't."

"That's just it," Faline said casually. "He knows about all sorts of vegetation that can be consumed that we would otherwise be clueless about. We are probably going to have a world of knowledge bestowed upon us today. We should be grateful about it as well."

Nolan nodded and set the first pheasant aside and started on one of the bigger ones. Feather by feather he pulled each one out and set it on the ground. Normally he'd have just skinned it to avoid having to yank them out as it was a tedious and tough process, but due to the weather being wet and cold he figured the fats from the skin would serve them all well.

"Well hopefully it's nothing too gross," Nolan teased.

"I am sure Rom will keep that in mind while he is out there," Faline laughed.

"I hope so. I don't want these beautiful birds being ruined by some weird smelling slimy fungus or something." Nolan chuckled as he started slicing the centres of the birds to remove the innards for Cairo.

Faline smiled as she watched him work. "Surely he will bring back something somewhat eye appealing and edible Nolan. Stop fretting, you silly thing."

Nolan raised his hands in defeat. "All right. I am sure Rom knows what he is doing out there. I will mind my business and wait."

"There's a good boy," Faline giggled as she stroked Cairo's warm dry head. "All we can do is sit and wait being thankful that we are not getting soaked at the moment."

Nolan nodded as he kept cleaning the pheasant. Cairo was anxiously waiting for her first portion of the meal to come her way knowing that it was going to be any time now. Nolan got up bringing her all the little goodies from inside the birds, and she promptly sat up and graciously devoured them all making Nolan wince a little at the sight.

"I am thankful that I am not your dog," he grimaced. "That just doesn't look very tasty at all uncooked."

Faline ran her hand down Cairo's now mostly dry back. "I am sure being an animal she doesn't mind at all and is very happy to have been given this meal. In fact, looking at her face she says thank you."

Nolan studied Cairo's face for a minute or two and realised that Faline was right. Cairo did in fact look as if she were smiling at him, it was strange that he could see and or feel that. All he could do at that point was smile back at the furry beast sitting before him licking the last bits of entrails from her chops.

Nolan shuddered. "You're welcome, Cairo." he told her. "I am happy to serve you." He gave her a little bow.

Cairo gave a small yip before lying back down next to Faline and softly placing her head back into her lap. Faline couldn't help but laugh at the two of them.

As the time drew on Rom finally made it back coming through the entrance with his cloak gripped in one hand as a makeshift bag and naturally completely soaked.

"Well I have managed to grab a few things while I was out." He beamed as he walked over to join Faline and Cairo by the fire.

"Warm up a little and fill us in," Nolan said as he stuck the pheasants on sticks and placed them over the fire to roast.

Rom sat down draping his cloak on the ground beside him. Taking his boots off he turned them in towards the fire to dry. "Well I sniffed out some goodies while I was out there. Took a little doing as the rain throws me off some, but I managed to find some mushrooms, berries, and a few wild pears." He grinned.

Nolan's face lit up with excitement. "Pears!" he shouted. "I love pears!"

Rom and Faline both laughed hysterically at Nolan's outburst. "Well," Rom began, "let's get cooking and fill up these bellies shall we?"

"Big fat dinner here we come," Nolan grinned rubbing his belly.

Again, Rom and Faline couldn't help but laugh at him and his insatiable stomach.

Nolan tended the pheasant carefully turning them periodically to ensure they were roasted evenly, while Rom and Faline finished drying out. Rom did a little mild preparing of his brought food, skewering the mushrooms on long skinny sticks to roast, with a little help from Faline who cut up the pears. Faline went and grabbed some bark to use as plates and set them by the fire to dry as they waited for the food to cook. All they could do now was keep warm, dry and wait.

Chapter 14

A Tale of Three Kings

As the companions sat anxiously awaiting the final preparations of their meal, they sat comfortably by the fireside listening to the rain beating on the outside of the fortress Rom had made of their quaint little thicket. Cairo's big head still nestled in Faline's lap content for the time being with the bits of bird that Nolan had fed her a little while earlier, while Faline finally dried up enough so that she was no longer shivering. Nolan sat turning the sticks so that each pheasant got enough heat, and Rom was happy not to be soaked to the bone at last.

Rom broke the silence with a small clearing of his throat which instantly drew everyone's attention. Even Cairo popped her head up from its resting place to see what he could want.

"What is it Rom?" said Faline now very concerned wishing him to say what was on his mind.

"How would the two of you like a story with your meal, you know like a bedtime story of sorts but for big kids?" He laughed so the two of them were less likely to be offended.

Nolan just chuckled. "I enjoy a good tale to be honest. Sure Rom I would love to hear what you have to say," he said poking at the biggest pheasant before turning it again.

Faline flipped her blanket inside out so the part that had been on her wet body could get some of the heat and dry her up the rest of the way. "I gotta say that it has been a long time since anyone has told me a bedtime story, so I am definitely intrigued by the idea of it."

"Excellent." Rom grinned as he rubbed his hands together. "It's quite a large one so you are all in for a real treat. Lots of action and adventure too." His face lit up as he prepared his thoughts.

"Oh, very nice. It is a guy story." Faline joked as she gently stroked Cairo's head.

"It has princesses in it too," Rom winked. "Oh yes, and maybe a unicorn or two."

"Oh?" Faline raised her eyebrow with some curiosity. "Unicorns you say? After having met you and Hildy I suppose anything is possible. All right Rom, let's hear your epic adventure story."

"Yes, let's get started." Rom agreed. "My story is about three kings, one in the east, one in the west, and one in the north. It didn't begin that way of course. Several thousand years ago there was only one in the north who unfortunately had three sons. Once the king died the two younger brothers were dissatisfied with the idea of the older one being able to sit on the throne and not either of them. So they both took some of the army and left, one in each direction. This is when the wars began as each brother was desperately fighting for grand supremacy over the land. The world began to fall into ruin as the armies marched nonstop for decades laying waste to villages, tearing down forests to keep their barracks maintained and stocked, and let's not forget all the great beasts that were dragged into battle as steeds, whipped and beaten into submission from birth until all they knew was to serve the man that rode them."

Faline's eyes widened in terror as well as anger at the very thought of animals being brutalised. "What kind of animals could they possibly have to do that to? Horses can be trained so easily with the right hand behind them."

Rom clapped his hands together and set them in his lap. "Well, let's see, the northern king and his men found it was their right to breed and raise lions. Lions were considered a noble animal and the king being a noble man, it was fitting. So lions were caged, bred and the cubs were taken and trained to do as the men wished. The eastern king knowing of his brother's lions decided that he needed something better. So he sought the aid of some of the magical folk and asked where to find some unicorns. At first they declined to help him until he offered this ridiculous amount of gold and they took it in exchange for information on where to find them and what they would need to do to get them to come out. After gathering his information the eastern king sent an army out to search the forests for the unicorns that dwelled inside making sure they knew to tread lightly; unicorns are not keen on being found or captured. Small girls were sent along with the men as a distraction, being sent out ahead while the men hid in the bushes waiting for the beasts to come out and see the innocents."

"So it's true then," Faline said quietly. "You need to be pure of heart in order for a unicorn to show itself to you."

"In a sense," Rom answered. "Even a child can already have been corrupted. The girls that were taken were carefully screened and hand chosen by the king's mage. Back then witches and wizards worked for the kings helping them with whatever they needed in order to preserve their covens. So the children would be brought forth and the mage would read the child's aura to see if they were pure enough for the unicorn to want to show themselves to them."

Nolan took a minute to take the pheasants from the fire and dish them out to everyone. Rom and Faline added pears and mushrooms to their bark plates making a nice looking meal for all. It was well earned and all of them were watering at the mouth waiting to start eating the delicious looking meal in front of them.

Nolan swallowed his bite of pheasant and wiped his mouth on his sleeve. "I am having a hard time believing that people like you would help someone with their dirty work."

Rom sighed. "Well to be honest Nolan not every witch and wizard throughout time has been a good one. There have been many of us who have sold their soul to the dark and didn't care who got hurt as long as their power was greater than any others. So helping a king procure and break a beast of ultimate light was just showing their true nature really. Some were only aiding the kings to make sure that the covens they belonged to and assisted didn't become added to the list of people the kings hunted and destroyed."

Nolan looked towards Faline who was handing Cairo a piece of meat and smiled. "I understand wanting to protect the people you care about."

"Yes and for most of them this is all it was, just for a select few was it about more power," Rom added." Now the king in the west being the baby of the family, was the most power hungry. He had always been pushed around by his brothers and was not going to be outdone as far as animals went. So he sent his armies out deep into the forests and mountains. They scoured every cave and cavern they came across looking for eggs."

"Eggs?" Faline said raising an eyebrow. "I cannot imagine this is going to be good at all." She stuffed a mushroom into her mouth and waited for Rom to go on.

Rom laughed. "No, it wasn't. The eggs they were searching for were those of dragons."

"Dragons!" Nolan shrieked. "Are you kidding me?"

"Sorry my boy, I'm afraid not." Rom replied as casual as could be.

Nolan and Faline just sat there with their jaws hanging open slightly not knowing what to say. It was the most insane thing they had ever heard of anyone doing, purposely hunting dragon nests to steal their eggs. It was like signing your own death warrant.

Rom continued. "So off they went. The strongest of the king's men were sent to seek out dragons. They all knew the danger and yet they went anyway because the pay off was worth the risk. Those that brought back an egg were very well compensated. If you brought back two or more, well you were granted the title of a Lord with a large estate and plenty of gold to get you started. Any man breathing took on the task of egg hunting, and the king was able to get his hands on quite a few. Hatching them was time consuming as they needed to be heated in fire to keep them as warm as a dragon mom would. Some of the eggs were already mature so they didn't take very long, others were just laid so they took upwards to a month to hatch, which meant constant maintenance of the fire beneath it. Egg hatching was time consuming and they used a lot of their lumber resources making the king to send people out to gather more daily, but in the long run he felt it was completely worth it. Not a soul on earth was going to be able to stand against his army of dragons."

"That just doesn't seem right or fair really," said Faline mumbling through a mouthful of meat. "I mean what could possibly stand up against a dragon?"

"Dragons although large and able to breathe fire through their enormous dagger-filled mouths are not invincible. They have their weak spots, it is just a matter of getting to them. Unicorns can penetrate a dragon hide with their horns, where witches and wizards can use magic to soften the hide and get their weapons in their skin among a few other tricks we may have up our sleeves. Men, well men need to shoot an arrow directly into an open eye piercing the brain or they can get their hands on a diamond steel blade and pierce the heart. A sword blade forged with diamonds mixed with the steel is the only blade that can pierce dragon hide. These are very hard to get as they are expensive and they take forever to make."

The group took a minute to let Rom's story sink in a bit and ate some of their food. Faline's brow was wrinkled up in thought as she sat sucking on a bit of bone ensuring she got all the meat off. She reached down and snatched a bit of pear and munched it slowly thinking about these diamond steel swords Rom was still wondering if it was at all possible for any of them to exist after all this time.

"Rom?" Faline said swallowing the last bit of her pear. "The diamond steel sword you mentioned. Are there any still in existence or did they all get lost along the way?"

Rom looked over at her and just winked. Faline sat upright and stared at him a little funny not sure what that meant exactly, but she had a sinking suspicion she was going to find out.

Rom took a moment to finish chewing his mouthful of food before continuing. "So there they all were, three kings all with their own personal armies of man, beasts and magi. The battles that ensued over the years were devastating to everyone and everything. The western king with his dragons raged across the lands pillaging every village that was not part of his kingdom before having the great beasts ignite anything in their path burning it to ash on the ground. It didn't matter if the things being lit were living or stationary "BURN IT ALL!" you could hear the king shouting from his steed. He just sat back and watched as his great army did as they were told and massacred the people and destroyed the land."

Nolan was completely distraught and looked as if he might be sick. "What happened to all the people? They all died. I mean that is absurd."

Rom shook his head. "Some managed to get away, but mostly people were burned alive by dragons' fire which to be honest is a quick death, or they were killed by the soldiers."

After looking down at his food a few more times, Nolan set it aside. "That is the most terrible thing I have ever heard. I mean seriously, was all that necessary?"

"For people trying like hell to take everything for themselves? Yes, it was an absolute must in their book," Rom replied. "The kings didn't care who got hurt, just as long as they were the ones winning. The eastern and northern kings fared well for themselves considering they were not dragon riders.

When battling against the king of the west they usually had a lot of casualties, man and beast alike. None of them had any troubles however ransacking any of the poor villages that cropped up along their way."

"So they all did that then?" Faline asked a little troubled. "They all ran around butchering people and wiping out little villages for their own selfish purpose?"

"Unfortunately, yes they did. It was quite the sight when they came blazing in too. The masters of the unicorns generally had them all adorned in some golden armour to protect their heads and flanks, dazzling gold reins hung from the armour on their heads, and their saddles were black and gold with a few jewels scattered about them just for extra added lustre. The lion riders also had golden armour on their steeds. It was an interesting helmet type thing that split down the middle to come out and over the nose, some allowing the ears to poke out. When you took the helmet off it sort of looked a little like an elongated triangle with a round top to protect the skull and a strap at the base to keep it on. They also had big brown leather saddles to sit in with golden stirrups. Nothing fancy there. For some odd reason they opted to give them shin guards, I couldn't tell you why as I can't imagine what they thought was going to be attacking their legs."

"Maybe it was to guard against the unicorns or any other horses they had in the enemy armies. If they tried to stomp at them then they would be protected," Nolan chimed in.

"That's pretty quick thinking," Faline said smiling at him. "That seems like it could have been the reason. I would surely want my steed to be protected from any dangers I could think of."

"I am sure you are right, Nolan," Rom said scratching his head. "I don't know why I hadn't thought of that."

"I'm sure you would have over time," Nolan grinned.

"My boy, I have been pondering this stuff for, well longer than you have been alive," Rom chuckled. "Now the dragons having natural armour didn't need much as far as that went, but the king decided that he would fancy them up anyway and gave them all these shining silver saddles with flames embroidered on the sides, and they also had some fancy helmets with horns fashioned in the middle for extra damage. When the kings and their armies met on the battlefield it was an all-out assault. Men and beasts were screaming, howling and roaring in every direction. Heads were rolling this way and that, blood was being splattered from all the swords and horns, staining all the lustrous gold and silver plated armour a nice red hue. No matter how hard any of them tried there was never a final victor. There was just death, destruction and anger throughout the kingdoms."

Faline, having finished all the small portions of her meal, was slowly working through her pheasant now making sure to share with Cairo who sat wagging her tail eagerly awaiting her next bite. "If there was never any victor then why did they keep at it? Why didn't they just make peace with each other and try to work together instead of against one another?"

"That is something that still has yet to be answered," Rom politely answered. "To this day even though the great battles have long since ended and the beasts they captured and forced to ride with them into war have vanished, the kings still refuse to cooperate with one another. There are still three of them, and there has never been peace really."

"What do you mean by the beasts having vanished?" Nolan asked curiously. "I get how a unicorn or a lion can just go about its business and live its life, but how can a dragon hide?"

Rom laughed. "You would be surprised at how well dragons can hide," he told him. "As a matter of fact, they hide so well you may have even passed by a few and never knew you did."

Again, Nolan's mouth dropped. "Are you kidding? I thought dragons ate people or anything that got too close for that matter," he said completely unnerved at the very thought that he may have been that close to a dragon.

"Dragons are curious creatures more so than they are vicious. They are also very old and very wise. When the blue moon or the blood moon comes about they lay their eggs. This is when they become aggressive but only because they are protecting the babies that had once been stolen from them. I can't say that I blame them really. Dragons as well as the unicorns have been around longer than any of us and they remember everything. They are not going to easily forget that it was man who stole them, broke their will and spirit, drove them into bloodthirsty battles for power, and got them all slain until they were near extinction. Unlike the lions that were captured, unicorns and dragons cannot have litters of babies, they can only have one at a time allowing them to remain a sacred animal." Rom finished before eating some more of his supper.

"When you put it that way I feel a little better about it now." Nolan responded grabbing his plate of food before Cairo came and ate it. "I'm just happy I didn't end up as a dragon snack."

Faline laughed. "Oh Nolan, you really are something else." She stripped away a bit of meat for Cairo and gave it to her before looking back at Rom. "Okay, so we have the kings of old who spent centuries destroying one another and their surrounding kingdoms with great animals that were trained to do so." She paused and Rom nodded. "Did the animals get tired of being forced to participate? You said dragons were smart, I'm now wondering just how smart they really were. What about the unicorns and lions? They had to have some intelligence as well." Faline stared at him waiting for his response.

"Dragons, having grown weary of having their young snatched from their nests, simply stopped producing eggs. The dragons that were captured, well those poor beasts were rode into battle until the breath left their bodies. The unicorns took to cloaking themselves with their magic, therefore only the innocent could find and see them. This made it very hard to capture them even when they took the children into the forests. The lions took to living high in the mountains making it difficult for man to get at them. It was much easier for them to scale the mountain walls than it was for any of them." Rom paused for a bite to eat and take a sip of water.

"I'm glad that the armies had a hard time gathering animals to abuse," Nolan said grinning. "It serves them right for mistreating them anyway. It still confuses me as to why the animals went along with it."

Having finished his food and taking another drink to wash it down, Rom continued. "I told you that the animals raised by the kingdoms were loyal until the bitter end. They all were. It didn't matter what type of beast rode along with you. Back in those days animals did not look at man as an enemy or a threat to their way of life, they were a friend and ally. They were raised from birth to know that you fed and cared for them and that their sole duty was to make sure they served and protected you. If you fell during battle they went to a master whose beast had also fallen to create a new team. It wasn't until the last beast, hand raised by each kingdom, had fallen that they finally gave up and stuck with horses instead as they were much easier to raise and breed. Dragons, unicorns and lions after about a century became a thing of the past."

Faline shook her head. "Well, gee it only took a hundred years for that to be over with. I cannot believe it took that long for those animals to smarten up. Cairo wouldn't let me abuse her like that, would you, girl?"

Cairo looked up at Faline adoringly as she gobbled up the last of her pheasant. Faline couldn't help but giggle at her furry friend as she licked her chops and eyed her master for another bit of her meal. She graciously accepted the scratch under the chin in lieu of more food for the moment.

"So what are we looking at now? I mean the kings of old are long since gone. I assume the ones that are here these days aren't as bad. Are they?" Faline inquired as she took another piece of her pheasant and put it into her mouth.

Rom looked at her and sighed. "I wish I could say that everything was peachy and the sun was shining everywhere with rainbows lining the sky. I cannot do that however."

He reached over into his cloak and grabbed some of the berries he had found and stuffed a few into his mouth. "Let's see there is Silas Monokeros who rules the east and his people adore him. He governs his land very fairly and treats people the way they should be treated. He has a lovely wife named Marina who is a very soft, gentle and sadly a frail little thing. They have one daughter named Christine. Now Christine, unlike her very gentle, kind hearted parents who always find a way to avoid trouble, seems to have a knack for getting herself into trouble, and one of those ways is with her mouth. She has no problems telling people exactly how she feels, whenever she feels like it."

"Sounds like someone else I know." Nolan chuckled as he looked over at Faline.

She whipped her head around and thought about saying something to him, then just to spite him she kept her mouth shut and simply smiled at him.

Rom simply laughed and carried on. "Then we have Martin Leocor in the north. He has a good heart, strong will but a nasty temper when he finds things are not as they should be, especially when one of his cousins tries to wipe out various sections of his kingdom. He does not take very kindly to people ambushing his lands. He has a wife named Chloe who unlike Silas's very gentle wife, is very snobbish and well, rude really. She feels like she and Martin are above all things and acts that way. I have never seen anyone look down on people as much as she does, and she gets a great amount of pleasure flaunting her rich life around. Chloe is always dressed to impress and jewelled to the high heavens. The two of them had a son by the name of Darius. Poor Darius is not like his parents at all. He can generally be found in the library reading everything he can get his hands on and is jam packed full of knowledge. Unlike his crazy parents, Darius is a very quiet boy, polite and well mannered. He swears he is adopted and is waiting for his chance to get out of there."

"Well, if he is that unhappy why doesn't he just run away?" Nolan inquired.

"When you live in a castle surrounded by hundreds of guards at any given moment, one cannot simply just run away. It would have to be a well executed plan and carried out to a tee," Rom told him before grabbing some more berries.

Rom took his cloak after stuffing his mouth full of the sweet berries and then walked over to Faline and then to Nolan offering them both some of the little ripened fruits. They both graciously took a small handful and thanked Rom before eating them slowly enough to savour each one's delicious flavour.

"So that brings us to the last king right?" Faline asked as she shoved another berry into her mouth.

"Yes it does, but this is not a king that you are going to find easy to handle," Rom said hanging his head.

Faline, now intrigued, raised an eyebrow. "How so?"

Rom looked over at Nolan who only knew bits about his family tree, and most of it his father didn't talk about. Nolan sighed as he knew the truth about his lineage was about to be revealed and just hoped that Faline did not think any less of him after she found out.

She looked between the two with a puzzled look on her face. "Well, go ahead and tell me then. I'm a big girl and can handle it."

Rom took a deep breath and continued. "Finally the last king, the most horrendous man you can ever imagine resides and rules in the west. His name is Balthazar Drakona."

With that said, Faline was about to spit out the mouthful of berries she had just eaten. She whipped her head around and stared at Nolan with a look on her face that was a mixture of confusion and contempt. He tried to avoid making eye contact but it was too late, she had already got hold of him. All he could do was sit there with a pathetic look of "I'm sorry" across his face.

She turned her attention back to Rom and glared at him. "Well, isn't this a pleasant surprise? I'm travelling with the kin to one of the nastiest people to roam the earth." She folded her arms across her chest in a huff.

Nolan hung his head and stared into the fire. He was hoping she wouldn't think of him a bad person after knowing him for who he was after all this time, but she was only looking at it one way, by his bloodline.

"Anyway," Rom spoke up to break her train of thought, "Balthazar is a nasty man as I said. There is nothing he won't do to get his hands on more territory. He feels that he should be the one to have it all and will stop at nothing to get it. His wife Elizabeth died during the birth of their only son which only helped to fuel his rage. Elizabeth, before she died, was the only one who could calm him down or make him see things in a different way. Once she passed he became almost mad and swore to take everything. Their son Tobias paid a heavy price for his mother's passing. Balthazar worked him hard pledging an oath that he would make him the strongest man in the world, and that no man alive would be able to defeat him. As soon as Tobias could walk a sword was thrust into his hands and his training had begun. Every day all day the boy trained with one weapon or another, on foot, on horse, swinging from the towers with ropes tied to his waist, until he never missed a shot or a heart. There was no love there between father and son. Tobias was looked at like a trophy, not anything more."

Faline gave a small huff. "You want me to feel sorry for them? Is that what you are doing now?"

"Just be patient, Faline and let me finish my story," Rom told her as politely as he could.

Cairo who was sleeping on the dry ground next to the fire opened her eye to look up at Faline briefly, stretched her legs with a small whine, licked her lips and went back to sleep. Faline crawled onto the ground with Cairo resting her back on her furry friend's warm side.

"Fine then. Please carry on with your tale," she told Rom gruffly.

"As you wish." Rom winked at her hoping she'd smile. Getting no such reaction, he carried on.

"After years of day in, day out, training, studying, and learning how to do some miscellaneous things by walking around the castle grounds watching the men work on a regular basis, Tobias decided that this was not a life he wanted. He was lacking something but was unsure what it was. One day when he was about seventeen, he was walking around outside the castle walls as he often did while his father was off slaughtering the innocent, and he happened upon a field of berries. He stopped to grab a snack and came out of the field with a whole lot more. In the field ways was a young girl with long flowing red hair and a tattered grey dress. Tobias, not fearing any man or beast, walked further in to go and speak to her. She was a little timid at first as she knew who he was, but after some conversation and some berry eating she realised he was nothing like his father."

"Oh, great! Now we have a love story on our hands," Faline said rolling her eyes. "Why is this relevant?"

"Shush, Faline and you'll see," Rom said abruptly. "The day grew late and the two were somewhat disappointed it was over. Tobias made arrangements to meet the girl in the forest west of the field every day if he could. She promised to be there every day without fail. He took her hand gently and kissed it before wishing her a good evening and returned to the castle. To his surprise his father was there at the giant dinner table surrounded by servants and great plates of various foods. Tobias sat near to his father to eat dinner and discuss the outcome of the battle he had just returned home from. Balthazar being a proud man told him that naturally he had won and not only that, he had also arranged for Tobias to marry Christine from the eastern kingdom. Tobias began to protest, but Balthazar would hear nothing of it. He told him that it would be a few years before it could happen as the princess was ten years younger than he, so he had time to stew it over meaning Tobias had time to accept his fate in the matter."

"What in blazes would make the king in the east give that man anything?" Faline choked out angrily.

Rom clapped his hands together. "Well, Balthazar made the arrangement to "merge" the kingdoms, meaning that he would just have an easier time taking that one over. His son would be the next king once Silas died and he would have one less kingdom to fight. Naturally he wouldn't wait for Silas to have a natural death, I assume. He'd probably have waited for the marriage to settle in for a bit of time and then send someone in to assassinate him."

"Seriously! What a sick man. Yes, let's arrange a marriage for my son and then kill his father-in-law so that I can rule so much more land. Sounds like an awesome plan." Faline grimaced as she gave a thumbs up.

Rom sighed and went on. "Tobias didn't have any intentions of marrying this unknown child. He had already fallen in love with a beautiful girl he had met earlier that day. He dared not tell his father about her as it would just enrage him. So Tobias spent all his free time sneaking around with this red haired beauty in secret and before you knew it she was pregnant. They found a little priest and paid for his silence to wed them. Tobias did everything for her that he could possibly do. She never went without, but still maintained her modest means of living so as not to give them away. She lived in a little hut that Tobias had built for her in the deepest part of their secret place in the forest by the field so she could live in peace, clearing out a bunch of the trees within to let in the light and allow her to grow some food and raise some animals. He was informed by a raven one night that she was to give birth to their child and snuck away from the castle to be by her side. In the little hut was her mother who also had skills as a midwife and was in shock when Tobias came bursting through the door. Tobias grabbed Dania's hand and waited, and a few agonising hours later their son was born. He was a bright eyed, red haired little boy, who would come to be known as Nolan."

Nolan perked up a little as he had never heard any of this before. Neither his mother nor his father had ever told him of their courtship or his birth. He was glad finally to hear the story and saddened by it as well. He knew only what his parents had told him, he was of noble birth but needed to be hidden and left as a simple farmer in order to maintain his safety, as well as his mother's. His father came around quite often to make sure that everything on their little farm was still running smoothly and to watch him grow. Nolan knew growing up that he was not to talk about his father and that if anyone inquired he was to say he was killed fighting for the king in one of his wars. It wasn't until the king's army came swooping through the forest hunting him and his mother that he truly understood the brutal reality of the situation.

Faline, catching the uneasy saddened look on Nolan's face, felt her heart sink a little for him. "Nolan, are you all right?" she asked him quietly.

He flinched at the sound of her voice snapping him back into reality. "What? Oh, yes I'm all right thank you." He managed to force a smile even though he was still envisioning the large troop of armoured men ransacking the forest before they found him and his mother in their small field.

Faline studied his face for a bit before returning her focus on Rom. "Please continue."

Faline was sure that this story was to become a grim one soon. She recalled after a bit that when Tobias and Nolan had first arrived at her family's quiet little valley home, that Tobias had made mention of Nolan's mother having been killed before Tobias could save her.

Rom nodded. "Everything for Tobias, Dania and Nolan was going beautifully for several years until the time came for Tobias to man up and marry the princess Christine. When Tobias refused and refused to give a good reason as to why, Balthazar became enraged. He threatened to throw him out and hunt him down like a wild animal if he didn't tell him what was going on. Tobias stood firm and said nothing. The king decided to send spies out and discover the secret that his son possessed. It didn't take very long for these men to gather the information Balthazar needed. Once he had figured out what was going on the king was so angry he vowed to stop at nothing until this woman and her child were found and destroyed. Tobias tried to stop him, screaming that Dania was a good woman and that her place in society shouldn't mean anything. Balthazar did not care to hear what Tobias had to say."

Rom paused briefly for a sip of water before continuing. "Tobias, knowing that the love of his life was now in danger, grabbed his horse and took off. Balthazar had already sent troops out by the thousands to scour the countryside to find this peasant woman and her son, to wipe away the blemish Tobias had left on the family name. By the time Tobias had made it to the forest, fires had already been lit burning the timber all around him. The animals from the farm were racing away to escape from the flames and trying not to be slaughtered, Nolan was dashing towards his mother on his little brown pony as she was running towards her son from the fields, her red hair flailing behind her as she ran. Panic was written on her face. She was waving violently at him to turn around and go back but he paid her no heed and kept going for her. He thought if he could get her onto his pony they could both get away."

Tears began to well up in Nolan's eyes now. He remembered this part of the story all too well and it still hurt to think about it even after all this time. His attempts to hide his thoughts failed when he glanced out of the corner of his tear-filled eye at Faline who was now staring at him with a look of sadness and concern.

"Tobias pushed his horse as hard as he could, running as fast as its four legs could take them. Unfortunately, the king's men were already surrounding his beloved Dania and all he could do was snatch his son from his pony and ride him out of there." He gestured to Nolan who was all but sobbing now. "The last thing either of them saw as they raced out of the meadow and in through the forest was Balthazar's men slaughtering their wife and mother with daggers leaving her in a limp heap in the middle of the now burning fields."

Faline wiped a tear from her own eye. "Rom, that is terrible. I mean that is really a terrible thing to do just because you don't feel someone is worthy of you." She scooted over next to Nolan and wrapped an arm about his shoulders. "I am so sorry, Nolan, I really am."

"It's not something anyone could have done anything about really." Nolan sniffed as he tried to force a small smile. "I thank you for your sympathy just the same."

Faline still holding onto Nolan looked back at Rom who sat quietly watching the two of them waiting to finish. "What happened after that Rom?" Faline asked trying to hold back her anger.

"Well, Balthazar in his rage not only sent his men to kill Nolan and Dania, but he also made it very clear that Tobias was not to return home unless he was prepared to face the consequences of his actions and potentially be killed himself. Balthazar is not a man to be trifled with and he is not the forgiving type." Rom made sure to put emphasis on that last bit. "He has had men out looking for Tobias and his son but no one has ever been able to come back with either one of them. This is only angering the king even more and fuelling his fire so to speak. He will try and find a way to get to them both no matter the cost."

Nolan had collected himself by now and looked up at Rom. "What do you mean by that?"

Rom sighed. "Well, if you remember the beginning of my story, the king in the west used dragons to fight their battles along with men and witches. I would wager that Balthazar has probably got some of his men searching for the dragons by now, as well as trying to buy off some of the magi to aid him in conquering everything he can."

Faline got to her feet and stomped her foot so hard it sprayed dirt into the fire. "That will not do!" she shouted. "I will not let that tyrant take anything else from anyone!"

Rom put his hands up trying to get her to relax a bit, pointing to Cairo who was now on her feet at full attention after being startled out of her sleep by Faline's outburst. "Calm down a minute and listen Faline," he said gently. "There is a way as well as hope."

"Well, spit it out then," she grumbled as she sat down in a huff before stroking Cairo's coat.

Rom shook his head and sighed. "You are so quick to get upset and need to learn to control your emotions or you will never succeed. Now we need to get you back on your quest and find what your destiny holds."

Faline threw her hands up in frustration. "You told me the other day that you weren't sure if I was the one of prophecy, which is why you were following me. This was my test to find out for sure. So why am I going to bank on finding this item?"

"I have to have faith that you will succeed, Faline," Rom said quietly. "We all do. If we don't have faith in something then Balthazar has already won and everything else is pointless. We will get you where you need to go, and you will go in search of what is inside. Hopefully, you will be able to claim it or them depending on what is there and we can move on. If not, then Hildy and the rest of us need to look elsewhere. Let's just hope that you can do what we need."

"What's in the cave, Rom?" Faline asked curiously hoping that he would give her some clue.

Rom winked at her instead. "That, my dear, I cannot tell you."

"Well why on earth not? You have already told me so much more than that," Faline whined at him.

"I can't tell you because honestly I don't know for sure," Rom shrugged. "For every champion it has been different. Given the way the world has been and what has been going on throughout the centuries who knows what is going to be in there. The only person that will know for sure, is you." He smiled at her.

Faline sat for a minute and moaned. "I have no clue, what I am looking for?" she sighed. "Ugh! This is almost as aggravating as trying to shoot an apple off a tree with a blindfold on."

"Listen." Rom sat quietly for a minute. "The weather is beginning to let up. Hopefully by morning it will be clear enough to travel and we can get moving again. We have spent far too long in here. Balthazar will not have let his men rest because of the weather. We need to move."

"Agreed," nodded Nolan, who up until then had sat quietly. "I say we go even bad weather or not. It's only a day and a half to the cave from here if I have my calculations right. If Rom and his friend are willing to lend us some extra legs we can get there much faster."

Rom laughed and slapped his knee. "Well done, Nolan my boy! Well done."

Faline just gawked at the both. "I'm glad the two of you are so amused. What did he do that was so great anyway?" she grumbled.

"Well, very simply he asked for assistance," Rom replied plainly. "I said you just needed to ask, and you told me not to offer my help unless you specifically requested it. So here we are, and I would love to help the both of you get there as soon as possible."

"Okay then. Since we all have full bellies and have had a bedtime story suitable for nightmares, let's get some sleep and get a move once day breaks," Faline said as she stood and snatched her now dry blanket.

Rom stood and stretched. "That sounds like an amazing plan." He reached over and grabbed his cloak to spread on the ground by the fire and lay down. "We will get a good night's rest and set out as soon as we are all up."

Nolan simply nodded, spreading his own blanket on the ground before lying on it. Faline walked over and grabbed a few pieces of wood to set on the fire to keep them warm through the night and lay down. Cairo instantly snuggled up as close as she possibly could once Faline's body had touched the ground.

Faline lay there trapped inside her thoughts for a long while wondering what could possibly be contained inside the cave that could be that important. Visions began appearing in her mind as she lay with her eyes closed listening to the rain spatter on the thicket, images of dragons, lions, unicorns and men all tearing each other apart in bloody battles. Soon the soft rhythm of the rain put her to sleep and she began to dream of the story Rom had told.

In the depths of her mind she could see a faint glimmer of light in the distance beyond all the battling. It was an object of some sort but she wasn't quite sure what. She struggled to get through the mess of bodies and beasts to get to it, avoiding the flames, swords and blood flying all over making sure to keep her eyes on the light. As she got closer she realised it was a sword stuck in the body of a dead dragon. She kept walking forward until she was close enough to try and reach out and grab it.

Chapter 15

Fire on the Mountain

Faline was woken from her slumber by Rom calling her name and a slobbery tongue licking the side of her face. Cairo sat over her panting and whining waiting for her to open her eyes, which she finally did slowly not wanting to get dog slobber in her eye.

"Okay, Cairo," Faline groaned. "I'm awake even though you all woke me before I could get it."

Rom eyed her curiously. "What were you trying to get, Faline?"

Nolan laughed while he was packing his bag. "Probably a big fat fish, or a nice pan of fried eggs."

"It's not always about food, Nolan." Faline yawned. "If you must know I was dreaming about Rom's story, only there was a sword there. The most magnificent sword I have ever laid eyes on and I tried to touch it. That's when I got drooled on," she chuckled as she scratched Cairo's head.

This caught Rom's attention immediately. "What did the sword look like? Where was it?"

Faline studied him briefly wondering why he was so interested. "What's the big deal? It was just a sword and in your story there were millions of them weren't there?"

"Yes, there were. I was just wondering if this one was, well, special," Rom said. "Some have the power to discover what items they require before they have them or even know that they exist. It is a gift that only certain people possess, and I believe now that you have it."

"So this sword that she saw in her dream is something that is real and she is supposed to go and find it now?" Nolan asked as he shoved his blanket into his bag.

"This isn't always the case, but for Faline she has many gifts that have been showing up and this may be the newest one. So yes, I believe that she intended to find the sword in her dream," Rom answered politely.

Faline was slowly packing her bag still deep in thought. "Rom, what is this new gift exactly? I mean I know I have the ability to talk to animals, Cairo showed me that. I know of no others."

Rom laughed. "This gift, my dear, is the gift of premonition. You saw a sword you do not yet have."

"Right. I don't have it, it was in a dream," Faline said half heartedly.

"You don't have it, yet," Rom responded quickly. "Premonition shows the future. It's not always one hundred percent accurate, nor does it always show exact detail, but it does let us know the gist of things." Rom grabbed his cloak and shook it a few times to get the dirt off before swinging it around himself and closing the clasp about his neck.

"Well, time's wasting and the longer we stay here the closer Balthazar gets to finding what we need first," Rom said flatly.

Nolan grabbed his stomach. "Too bad we didn't have anything to munch before we leave. It's a pity to travel on an empty stomach."

Faline rummaged through her bag until her hand found what she was looking for. She pulled out the few pieces of smoked fish she had been saving for a moment like this and passed them out to everyone. There was just enough for each of them and even one for Cairo.

"Okay, now that we have had a little nibble let's get outside and see what the weather is really doing." Faline looked up at the canopy and nodded. "It seems like it has let up quite a lot, but we won't know for sure until we are out there."

Taking one last look around the little thicket that had protected them from the storm, they all felt satisfied that nothing was being left behind and they made their way out of the hole into the cool air outside. The storm had let up quite a lot since they first barricaded themselves into the thicket. There was just a fine mist coming down from the still somewhat darkened sky. The ground was muddy and wet and debris had been washed in from all over, making the path they had used to get here seem invisible. In the sky behind all the dark grey masses of clouds still lingering in the air, the sun was trying to make its way through. It was a sight for sore eyes knowing that eventually the air would warm up and the ground would dry.

"Well, if nothing else all the lakes and streams that had been coming to a shallow end, will certainly have filled up making it easier for us to catch some fish," said a smiling Nolan.

Faline perked up a little at the thought of being able to gather some fresh food later that day and smiled at Nolan for his thoughts on the matter. She hoisted the other strap from her bag onto her shoulder and turned to Rom.

"How long do you think it will take us to get to the cave from here if we are riding?" she asked as she made a slight adjustment to her pack.

Rom looked around at the wet, sticky, sloppy ground trying to survey the area and the weather. "Well, if my friend and I don't get out feet stuck too far into the ground with your extra weight on our backs, then I would imagine that we could make it by dark."

Faline grimaced at the thought of making it into some foreign cave when there would be no light to shine on her except for torches that they made, especially when there was the prospect of something living in there. She had a feeling that she just might find that sword inside the cave as she was able to just about touch it in her dream, but she was also a bit scared of a possible guardian. Nothing that great is going to just be sitting around waiting for anyone to just come and take it.

"Okay, Rom let's call one of your friends to give Nolan a ride and get ourselves moving," Faline instructed. "It is still very early in the morning judging by the height of the sun hiding back there, so we should be able to stop once or twice to try and get something in our stomachs."

"All right!" Rom clapped his hands together and gave them a little rub to warm them up a bit. "I love the positive energy today despite the still kinda gloomy weather. Let's get Nolan a ride."

With that Rom tipped back his head, cleared his throat and made the odd sound from before to summon the other deer from the forest. All they could do was wait, and as they did so Nolan retrieved his twine and cut a nice piece off, gathered some of the smaller bits of sticks and twigs into a nice burly bundle and tied them together before tying them to his pack.

"Never know when you might need little bits like this for fire starter or whatever," he said as he finished lashing it to his pack.

Faline took note and did the same grabbing up a bunch of small bits and lashing them to her own bag. She sat squat on the ground patting Cairo for a bit as they waited for the other deer to arrive, which Cairo enjoyed immensely. Rom was busy kneeling over by a tree digging in the soft earth randomly pulling objects from the ground.

"What is all that?" Nolan inquired as he walked over to investigate.

"These here are edible roots. They are called skirret. Fairly sweet, with a hint of carrot flavour and a little pepper taste towards the end." Rom pulled a big bundle of dirty roots from the ground where he was digging. "You can sometimes stumble upon these out in the wild, they look like mini cow parsley with froths of tiny white fragrant flowers on top. They get to be about two feet high and attract bugs, especially these guys." He picked up a lacewing off one of the petals of the white flowers that grew on top of the root.

Nolan eyed the bunch of dirty elongated roots hanging in Rom's hand. "These are something you are going to offer us to eat?"

Rom laughed and started wiping them off as best he could. "Yes, Nolan, they are quite sweet as I mentioned. Just think of it as eating a healthy piece of candy."

Nolan scrunched up his face. "I don't think I know what that is."

Rom was shocked, his eyes bulging from his head and he nearly had to sit down. "You have never had a piece of candy? Oh, you poor boy. We will fix that at some point in our time together." Rom smiled at him and gave him a pat on the back.

Just then a giant fourteen-pronged stag waltzed into the clearing where they all stood and dropped a knee to give a shallow bow to Rom, who in turn gave a slight bow back. Rom grabbed hold of his horned crown and looked at Faline.

"Are you ready to go then?" he asked with a small sly grin.

Faline gave her bag one final tug to make sure it was tight to her body. "Yep, I sure am. I can't wait to get to where we need to go. The anticipation is almost killing me."

Rom nodded. "Okay, then let's get out of here and shake a deer tail, shall we?"

With a laugh and a flash of brilliant crimson light Rom was once again the great giant stag he was when he rode her to the thicket. Rom dropped his front knees to the ground to give Faline the chance to get onto his back with ease and the other stag did the same for Nolan. Cairo gave a big yip and pranced around Rom waiting for her chance to get in a good run. She had been cooped up for far too long as far as she was concerned and needed to get some exercise.

Inside Faline's head Rom's voice came loud and clear. "Hang on good and tight now Faline. The weather we have been having has made things a little more difficult than they were on the way here."

Faline smiled. "No problem. I will make sure not to let go."

"Good girl," Rom chuckled just before turning and nodding at the other stag.

Nolan grabbed hold of his stag's antlers as tightly as he could and within a second of his doing so, both deer took off at a full run down the debris-filled path until they found a clear spot to make their way through into the thick forest. They ran northwest through the trees, weaving in and out of them like a basket weaver. They leapt over fallen logs, trampled little bushes and plants scaring all the little critters out from hiding so they didn't get crushed by the giant hooves of the deer. Several times Faline and Nolan found themselves ducking to avoid a low hanging branch and being knocked off the back of their rides. Cairo was having the time of her life rampaging through the forest, slinging mud out from under her paws, her tongue lolling out to the side as she ran.

They ran at a fast steady pace for over an hour before Faline heard Rom in her head again. "There should be a river up here somewhere. Would you care to stop and try to fish and fill up your water pouches?"

Faline thought a moment not sure whether to go on or stop. "How far is the next place, we could maybe find something like that?"

"I believe the river runs on for quite a long way, it may even be the one that stems from the mountain itself. So we could go for another little while if you aren't ready."

"Okay, Rom, why don't we go on for a bit more if you and your friend are all right to keep going. Just keep close to the river in case it begins to end so we don't lose our opportunity," she replied.

"You got it," Rom laughed as he picked up the pace. "We are gonna go a little faster now if we are sticking to the river bank. It will be easier to run along there rather than trying to make it through the thick of the forest."

"Sounds good to me, Rom. Maybe we will get there faster too." She smiled at the thought of maybe reaching their destination a little ahead of schedule and not making it there when it was dark.

Rom and the other stag bolted through the trees until they found the river which went a little more north than Faline had expected. She just hoped that it was the river that ran from the mountain and that it would take them straight there. The only problem with running along the river bank was all the rain they had experienced. It was slippery and very muddy. A few times Rom's back legs tried to give in to the mud and slide into the river. How he managed to keep them from falling to the ground was beyond Faline, she was just grateful he stayed on all four feet. The other stag had experienced the same type of difficulty in several spots and grunted as he tried to keep himself upright.

After about another hour of slipping, sliding and sticking in the muck Rom spoke to Faline again. "We are getting tired Faline and need to rest for a bit. Running through the forest where there is moss and tree bark padding the ground is one thing, trying to maintain balance on a sloped river bank is another."

"All right, Rom, let's stop at the next grassy patch you find and we will make a little fire and catch some lunch." Faline decided that was the best way to do it. The grass would give them somewhere sort of dry to sit and relax for a few minutes. There would be things around for the other stag to eat, they could fish for some lunch and make a small fire.

"Sounds great to me," Rom replied gratefully. "I will inform the other stag that we will be stopping soon. He will be very grateful."

It took them about another twenty minutes or so to find a good spot to sit and relax. Everyone was excited to have been able to stop for a while. The stag went off to go and munch some of the tender bushes and grasses inside the forest, Nolan started making a small fire while Rom and Faline took the fishing stuff and water pouches down to the river to gather what food and water they could. Cairo bounded down ahead of them panting the whole way before burying her face in the water to grab a good drink herself.

"Cairo, please be careful," Faline laughed. "The last thing I need is for you to get all muddy and or scare away all the fish."

Faline shook her head chuckling as she and Rom walked the rest of the way down to the edge of the water. She set the fishing stuff down before looking for a sturdy piece of wood to tie the line to. Rom was already squatted down by the river filling the pouches up in a nice rocky bed of clean water. Once she had finished making her pole she joined him and flung her line into the water.

"We should have some pretty decent luck since we had all that rain the last few days," said Rom as he found a dry spot to have a seat.

Faline sighed. "I hope you're right. The last thing I want to do is sit here for hours and not catch anything." She turned and looked about and saw a good sized log waiting to be sat on. "Nolan is usually the one who fishes, not me. I am more of the go out and shoot it type."

"I guess this is your chance to make it a two way deal then yeah?" Rom replied softly.

Faline shrugged as she watched her line for a bite.. Cairo having been satiated for the time being came strolling back towards them water dripping from her snout as she walked. She took a lap around the pair before finding her select spot by Faline's side and lay down. Rom lay back in the bit of grass he had found to sit upon and watched the clouds roll by while Faline sat waiting for the fish to bite. The two of them sat there for quite some time before Faline's frustration got the better of her and she yanked the line from the water.

"This is absolutely ridiculous!" she shouted glaring down at the empty hook.

Rom sat up and stared at her quite amused. "It seems to me that you may be lacking something as far as fishing requirements go," he said quietly.

Faline shot him an angry look. "Oh yeah, Mr. Smart Guy! What would that be exactly?"

"Well," Rom began as he grabbed the pole and took the hook in his other hand "you need bait to catch fish, my friend."

Faline threw her hands in the air and stomped about. "How are you going to just lay there this whole time and not say anything about that until now?"

"You didn't ask for my help, and when you were making your pole I assumed that you knew what you were doing," Rom answered politely.

"Well okay then let's dig up some bait and get some lunch and get the hell out of here." she grumbled angrily. "I would like to get to the cave before dark if at all possible."

Rom gawked at her not sure what to make of this new kind of temper tantrum. "Yes, ma'am," he said as he got to his feet and went to look for grubs.

They spent some time lifting rocks, rolling rotting bits of log, digging under clumps of soggy leaves, and finally had about a dozen or so grubs and worms to stick on the hook for fishing. Faline took the biggest, juiciest one and crammed it onto the hook and tossed the line back into the water before taking her seat back on her little log. It took all of ten minutes before she could feel the tension in the line and she gave it a little snap.

"A bite!" she exclaimed happily. "I've got a fish!" She was so happy once she pulled the rest of the line in and on the hook was a fat flopping fish.

"Good job, Faline," Rom said as he helped her get the fish off the hook and into the little net pouch she had for holding them. "Now we need to catch some more, get us a nice meal and maybe a little extra. That was just one grub."

"Yes, yes," she smiled from ear to ear. "Let's use all the bait and see how many we can get!"

Faline was in her glory. She was an excellent hunter, there was no doubt about that, but fishing was not her forte. This was going to be a great achievement. Cairo too was very happy that her girl had caught a big fat fish. She sat and watched it flop around in the net, twisting her head this way and that every time the fish twitched, until finally the fish stopped moving.

Rom and Faline sat at the river until all the bait had been used up managing to catch seven fish. Faline said some of the fish had bigger brains and managed to eat the bait off around the hook. She was not concerned though as they had enough for everyone to have their own and a few extra for later. They took their fish and went back to where Nolan had been waiting. Nolan had already built a nice fire, gathered some extra wood to keep it hot long enough to cook, and to their surprise somewhere along the way he had found an apple tree.

"Wow Nolan, you did all this while we were down there?" Faline smiled at him as she lay the fish on the ground near the fire.

Nolan smiled at her from where he sat sharpening roasting sticks. "Yeah, I figured while I had some extra time I would walk about some and see what was around."

Rom was impressed. "Good job, Nolan. This is a fine fire and the apples are a fantastic find."

"Well to be honest it was your friend who led me to the apples. I was out gathering wood for the fire while he was walking about eating grass, next thing I knew he had his nose in the air sniffing about. So I figured maybe I'd follow him and see where he went. Next thing you know we are standing about five feet away from a single apple tree." Nolan laughed and stuck the sharpened stick into the ground on an angle over the fire.

Rom chuckled and gave Nolan a pat on the back. "It was still ingenious of you to have followed him my friend. Enough about that though, let's get these fish cleaned and cooked so we can eat and be on our way."

Faline was already pulling the fish from the bag as she looked at Nolan for approval. "I would have been done sooner I think, but I forgot I needed bait." she glanced sideways as she told him to hide her embarrassment.

Nolan did his very best not to laugh, instead he took one of the fish and slit it open to begin cleaning it. "These are great fish and sometimes I am a little hasty when it comes to fishing and forget the bait myself."

Faline let out a small sigh of relief. "Thanks for not laughing at me."

Nolan finished scooping the innards out of the fish in his hand and smiled at her. "No problem."

It didn't take very long for Nolan to have all the fish skinned and gutted, free of all the miscellaneous junk they didn't want to consume before spearing them on the sticks he had placed over the fire. The smell of the cooking fish had everyone salivating in minutes, including Cairo who sat as close as she could without singeing her fur.

While they waited for the fish, Faline thought she would cut up the apples to kill some time. She took out her knife and started cutting them into wedges. Nolan went with Rom to grab some slabs of tree bark to use as plates, and since the rain had made everything so damp it made it very easy to slip some off the older trees. They set them down in a row at Faline's feet so she could place the apples on them. She had the wedges cut rather small and thin and arranged them neatly around the outside of the plate.

"My mother used to cut our food into smaller pieces sometimes," she said quietly. "She said that when there was less food to eat, cutting it into smaller pieces made it appear to be more. I don't know why, but it always made us feel like we ate more than we did."

"Maybe when you have more little bites instead of less big ones, your mouth gets too tired to eat," Nolan joked.

Rom shook his head. "Oh, Nolan whatever will we do with you," he laughed. "Honestly, the reason behind that is because it takes you longer to eat it, so your stomach has the chance to begin digesting the food and recognising that it doesn't need any more."

Nolan looked at Rom and rolled his eyes. "Okay, smarty pants," he sighed and rotated the sticks for the fish to cook on the other side for a bit.

"Oh for Pete's sake! I hope you don't intend to squabble over this bit of nonsense now?" Faline glanced warily between the two of them.

The two men looked between each other and then shifted their gaze back towards her. They shook their heads and went about their own business. A few minutes more and a couple of tender pokes to their white fleshy ribs, and Nolan announced that the fish were ready to eat. He pulled each stick out of the ground individually as Faline picked up plates for them to go on and passed them out. Once everyone had one they sat around the fire and prepared to eat, the last plate being lowered to the ground for Cairo who wagged her tail happily as her lunch was delivered.

Before Nolan began eating his food he took the other three fish and speared them on the sticks to cook over the fire. They ate silently, the only sound to be heard was the fire crackling or a random forest animal chattering in the distance. Lunch was a treat due to Nolan having come across the apples. They had run out of apples, and they all loved their sweet taste.

As the last bites were being taken and the plates tossed into the fire to burn, they took the carcass from each of their fish and gave them to an eagerly waiting Cairo. She just couldn't get enough and tried her best not to drool as she waited. Faline shook her head and giggled a little as she handed her fish remnants to Cairo as well. She stood up and stretched for a minute before packing the remainder of the apples into her bag.

"Nolan, how long until the fish are finished?" she asked curiously.

Nolan flipped the fish over and gave her a quick smile. "Just a few more minutes."

Taking a sip of her water she turned and headed for the river grabbing the others' water pouches as well. "Okay, great. I'm going to the river to refill the water pouches and then we should be able to get a move on."

Rom nodded. "Sounds like a great plan, my dear. We should make it there just about by dark if not sooner if we head out shortly."

Faline looked to the sky and smiled. "That is what I wanted to hear." With that she turned around and walked down towards the river.

Nolan took another look at the white flaking fish and pulled them away from the fire. "She sure is anxious to get to that cave now, huh?"

Again Rom nodded. "Yes, she is."

Nolan looked up at him as he stowed the fish in some cloth before placing it in his bag. "Do you know why she is trying to hurry us up all of a sudden?"

"She obviously senses something there and wants to get to it," Rom said glancing over at Nolan. "Either that or she just wants to get there and establish a place to sleep for the night before it gets too dark to see."

As Nolan pondered on that for a moment, Faline returned with their water and handed them back. to their owners. She looked over at Nolan who was spacing out trying to decide what Faline was up to, and turned her focus again to Rom.

"Okay, water is filled, looks like the fish is finished, so now all we have to do is snuff out this fire and get out of here," Faline said looking completely satisfied with how things were turning out.

Rom and Nolan looked at each other and chuckled. Faline rolled her eyes and turned her back towards them as they both faced the fire and readied themselves for putting it out the fire "man style". She was not interested in watching or knowing that this was going on, so she started to walk back towards the river with Cairo.

"I'll be waiting for you two manly fire extinguishers by the river." Again she rolled her eyes and walked down the small slope towards the water.

A few minutes later Rom and Nolan emerged from the edge of the forest near where Faline and Cairo waited. She had been watching a pair of geese play on top of the water and was half tempted to reach for her bow and shoot them. She opted not to however and sat watching them instead, enjoying their playful game of tag across the water.

"All right then, are we ready to get to that mountain?" Rom smiled as he rubbed his hands together eagerly.

Faline nodded. "I sure am." She turned and looked at Nolan who was adjusting the straps on his bag. "Are you all set over there?"

"Just about," he answered as he pulled his strap a little tighter. "I just want to make sure I don't lose my bag. On the ride here I realised I hadn't fastened them tightly enough and it was sliding. Our dinner is in here." He grimaced at the thought of losing what little food they had stowed for the night.

"Let's not forget that I have the skirret from Rom and the remaining apples in mine, and I am sure if push came to shove we would find some more when we arrive at our destination," Faline replied with a gentle laugh.

Nolan just looked at her with a blank expression. He had no interest in having to forage for food again tonight, so he would make sure that the fish and his bag stayed secure on his back. They had been lucky in his opinion to always come up with decent meals while they had been travelling, and he was too nervous that their luck would run out.

The last strap being tightened to his liking, Nolan smiled. "All right, I am ready to go now."

"Well it's about time," Faline mused. "Let's get this show on the road.

Rom nodded, letting out one of his famous laughs before emitting his crimson light and turning himself once again into his giant magnificent stag self. What really got Faline about him being the stag was that his fur coat was the dark brown almost black colour of his hair. The antlers on his head were huge, but what was interesting was that his eyes did not stay brown, they instead turned crimson and almost seemed to glow.

Rom bowed down and allowed Faline to get onto his back before braying for his companion to return for Nolan. It didn't take long for him to return as he didn't go far, knowing his services were still needed. The great stag knelt to let Nolan sit on his back before standing back up and pawing the ground as he was ready to go. Rom pawed the ground as well which was Faline and Nolan's cue to grab hold and hang on tight.

Once he felt Faline's grip tighten, Rom whipped his head back and took off like a shot, the other stag and Cairo hot on his heels. Even though she knew the stag she was riding was now her friend in an animal body, she loved knowing that she was able to ride some of the way. The wind blowing through her hair was simply fantastic. It still made her feel as if she were flying when she closed her eyes. Nolan, too, enjoyed being able to ride instead of walking. This made the voyage go faster and it saved the wear on their bodies.

For the first hour or so Rom had set a hard fast pace, the other stag and Cairo did their best to keep up and not let him get too far ahead. Rom was an amazingly fast runner when he was in his deer form, and his stamina was outstanding. After making up a lot of ground, Rom changed his pace and slowed down to a nice laid back gallop for a while giving the other runners a chance to catch up and catch their breath a little.

They made one pit stop to relax for a few minutes and give everyone a nice refreshing drink of cool water before setting off again. Rom started after their brief rest in the same easy gallop knowing that Faline was anxious to get to the mountain.

Faline sat atop Rom's back watching the river get wider and the sky start to grow dim. She was very curious as to how far away they were now. "How long until we are there?" she asked Rom with her mind's voice.

"We are close now," he replied softly. "Just watch for the tree line. It won't be too much longer."

"Sounds great," Faline smiled.

They rode on down the side of the river carefully avoiding the slick decline on their left so they didn't slide down into the water. The gaps in between the trees to Faline's right were getting noticeably larger than they were about an hour ago. She was excited and nervous as to what was coming up ahead. Some of her nervousness was due to the sky overhead becoming darker by the minute. Rom began to slow down just as Faline was grimacing at the dimming sky which prompted her to shift her gaze forward.

Up ahead was the end of the forest, at least this portion of it. She could see the vast stone walls that made up Mt. Diamanti looming in the distance like a giant black and brown fortress. Rom stopped when he made it out of the trees and let Faline get down, the other stag following suit.

Once Nolan's feet hit the ground he turned and thanked the stag for allowing him to ride on his back. He reached into his bag and pulled out the apple he had saved for it as thanks for its help, which the stag graciously took and ate before giving Nolan a bow of the head.

"My friend there says thank you for the apple." Rom's voice came from nowhere and startled both Faline and Nolan.

"I didn't realise you had changed back already," Faline gasped. "You startled us."

Rom chuckled. "My apologies, I didn't mean to."

"It's all right, Rom, and it is I who needed to thank your friend. The apple was the only thing I could think to do for him." Nolan smiled and gave the deer a gentle pat on the back before he bowed again to Nolan and then to Rom before taking his leave.

"He was grateful to have been of some use. Forest animals don't get to do very much as far as services to man any more, not since the great wars anyway." Rom shrugged.

"Let's hope that we don't have any more of these great wars," Nolan sighed. "Far too much death for my liking."

Faline was standing watching as the sun hit the horizon lighting up the sky with reds and purples. It was very pretty to look at with the mountain there as well, but it also meant that night was drawing dangerously near and they hadn't made it up the mountain yet.

"Okay, so let's see if we can make it up the mountain before we lose all the rest of the light," Faline said casually as she shifted her bag on her back.

"I don't think we are going to make it all the way up there before we lose the light, my dear," Rom sighed. "I think it would be best to make a camp here by the river before it gets too dark to find some firewood."

Faline stared at the mountain. She was so close to being up in the cave looking for whatever she was here to find, and now she was stuck down here on the edge of the forest due to daylight having begun to fade away. She was irritated and it was showing all over her face.

"Faline, it is going to be all right," Nolan said as he walked up to stand beside her. "We will get a good night's rest and travel up to the cave at first light. It will be better that way you'll see."

Faline flung her arms in the air and spun around to help them find firewood. "Fine!" she half shouted. "We will just build a fire, eat some food and sleep. The same things we have done for the last several days." She stomped off and began picking up hunks of wood.

Nolan and Rom looked at each other and shook their heads. They knew it was best to say nothing at all when she was in one of her moods. Instead they grabbed some wood from the ground as well and began making their fire. The weather having been as bad as it was recently playing in their favour as it dropped a lot of dead branches to the ground making fire building a snap.

Once the fire was built they pulled out the food they had stored away and had some supper while they enjoyed the warm, crackling fire. After their meal was done Nolan helped get everyone with their blankets beside the fire. Faline took hers placing it on the front side of the fire so she had a clear view of the mountain. She lay there staring at the enormous mountain with its blackish brown walls, cracks, and dips, wondering what kind of secrets were buried inside the depths of it.

Nolan and Rom had all but gone silent with a little whisper of conversation here and there as Faline stared at the giant piece of earth she and her companions were going to have to climb in the morning. The sun had all but faded leaving a little bit of itself behind on the horizon. Little crackles of the fire mixed with the rustling of leaves in the gentle breeze that blew at times was a peaceful soothing mix, until Faline jumped to her feet pointing to the mountainside.

"Did you see that!" she cried, her hands shaking. "Tell me one of you two saw that."

Faline's reaction startled Rom and Nolan having startled them both looked at her with confusion. "I'm sorry, Faline," Rom began quietly, "calm down and tell us what happened."

"I cannot believe neither of you saw what I did." She stomped her foot on the ground. "There was fire! Fire came from the mountain, Rom!" She pointed up at the mountain top. "I know that's what I saw! It's dark enough out now for me to be mistaken. It was a flash of fire and then it was gone."

Rom and Nolan stood there staring at her. Nolan's face had gone ashen and he felt sick to his stomach. Rom was now very curious as to Faline's haste to get here. He was hoping that the king's army hadn't reached the mountain before they did, and that the fire was not manmade. He stood watching the place on top of the mountain Faline had pointed to in hopes that he could see what she had witnessed. There it was a single small blast of fire before it had disappeared. Rom's mouth fell open. Could she have possibly stumbled across one of the dragons that hide here still?

Chapter 16

Into the Cave

Standing perfectly still on the edge of the forest Faline, Nolan, Rom and Cairo waited for more flashes to come from the top of the mountain. After about an hour Rom went back and sat on his blanket next to the fire. Faline, Nolan and Cairo joined him after a few more minutes, Faline still watching the now black shadowed mountain as she took her seat.

"What was that Rom?" Nolan asked quietly. "I mean could the king's army have made that fire?"

Rom shook his head. "No, that was not any kind of fire that a man could make I'm afraid."

Nolan looked back towards the mountain, his face twisted in fear. "I am not so sure we should be going up there."

"We have to," Faline uttered calmly. "We have to go to the cave and get whatever it is that Hildy sent me here for."

Rom nodded in agreement. "She's right, Nolan. She was sent here for a reason unknown to either of us. If she leaves now we won't get the chance to see if she is who we think she is."

"Well, that's just great," Nolan grumbled. "And what do you mean unknown to both of us? Hildy didn't tell you what Faline was being sent for?"

"No, she didn't," Rom replied yawning. "Hildy knew I would try to help her get here faster, and I did. It was best I didn't know."

"Fantastic," Nolan mumbled as he lay down on his blanket. "Well then I suggest we all get some sleep. At least then if the end of our journey finds us all burned to a crisp, we can at least be well rested for it."

Faline lay staring at the dark mountain that was now just a large shadow against the night time sky. Cairo snuggled in close to her as Faline reached out to stroke her fur, calming her furry friend into a soft slumber. She wanted so badly to be in the cave already; wanted to know what was waiting in its depths for her. She closed her eyes and tried to fall asleep. Visions of the sword she had tried to reach out and grab came to the forefront of her mind as she lay there. Dragons spouting fire at men in the distance, and then Rom's voice came through.

"Remember what Hildy told you, Faline. This is not a quest that is going to be the end of you. This is just a challenge, a challenge to see if you have what it takes to be the saviour we have been waiting for."

Faline wrapped her arms around Cairo and squeezed in closer to her friend, Rom's words still echoing in her mind. She was still uncertain as to what her dreams were trying to tell her, but it comforted her to be reminded that Hildy wouldn't have sent her somewhere to get killed, at least not yet.

The next morning as the sun was rising behind the looming mountain, Faline woke with the sound of birds chirping all around her. It was a pleasant way to wake up, she thought. If there was any real danger waiting nearby, the animals would remain silent. Rom and Nolan were also beginning to stir, stretching away the last remnants of sleep. The fire they slept near had died down to a smouldering pile of ash and bits of debris that had eluded the lick of the flames. Faline sat up and stared out toward their destination, happy and scared that they had made it, as well as anxious to get moving.

Rom softly broke the silence as he began to speak. "I suggest having some food before we head out. Maybe some extra of whatever we can find to take along with us just in case."

Faline stretched as she stood trying to shake the sleep off. "Yes, we probably should do that." She looked around where they sat. "I suppose it is back to the river for some fish, it's easier to clean and cook and we can get moving faster."

Nolan grabbed his bag and pulled out his fishing supplies. "I'll go this time, Faline. You two can scavenge the forest. Maybe there will be something tasty in there."

Rom nodded. "Sounds good to me, but I suggest everyone going in a straight line and heading back after a bit. No one will get lost that way."

Faline nodded. "All right, let's get moving so we can get to that cave."

The three of them broke off in separate directions, Nolan towards the river, Rom and Faline took two different lines into the trees, Cairo sticking close to Faline's heels. Faline looked around at everything, studying each plant and tree for things to be eaten. Cairo wanted her to hunt as she kept whining in different spots telling her there was game nearby.

"Not today my friend," Faline whispered to her companion. "We will get more chances to hunt on the way home. For now let's just get what we can and finish this journey."

Cairo whined in defeat but did as she was instructed staying close to her girl to make sure she could protect her if need be. Faline was getting ready to give up and turn around after feeling like she had walked forever, when she spotted a large berry bush to her left. She bent down and picked up a small stone and threw it toward the bush. When nothing moved or ran out, she walked over to it and began picking some of the berries.

"Blackberries, Cairo, we got lucky," she said gently.

She put her bag on the ground and pulled out one of the pieces of cloth that had held her food when she left home, laid it on the ground and began placing handfuls of berries on it. When the cloth was full she pulled each of the opposite sets of corners together and tied them at the top, making a small pouch out of the cloth and placing softly into her bag. She stood there for a minute before deciding to grab the other cloth and set it onto the ground.

Looking down at Cairo she whispered, "Just in case." Smiling, she filled the other cloth with berries and tucked it away as well. She turned and started walking back to their camp site.

When Faline had made it back Rom and Nolan were already there, Nolan was busy cleaning the fish he had caught while Rom was rebuilding the fire. They looked up at her and smiled as she neared where they sat. Rom patted the ground next to him asking her to sit. Faline took off her bag placing it next to her on the ground and sat next to Rom taking little sticks and adding them to the slowly growing fire.

"Happy to see you, Faline," Rom smiled. "Did you manage to find anything while you were out there?"

Faline grinned as she grabbed her bag and set it in her lap. "As a matter of fact I did," she replied merrily as she snatched the little makeshift cloth bags filled with berries from inside her bag.

Nolan looked over at her little bags of berries and smiled. "Nice find, Faline. They will go nicely with these big fat fish I got for us."

She gave him two thumbs-up in approval. "Awesome job, Nolan! It looks as if you caught quite a few of them too. I will go get some sticks and spear them off to roast the fish."

She got back up and went to rummage through the fallen timber near the trees. Rom decided that since he had the fire all ready to go he would help her find the sticks, grabbing a few extra pieces of wood along the way. After finding five decent sized sticks the two of them returned to their seats and began shearing the ends of them with their hunting knives before sticking them into the ground near the fire.

Nolan finished gutting and scaling the fish handing each one to Rom and Faline to spear onto their sticks, taking the last one and spearing it himself. He smiled at his work as they began cooking over the fire, then sat back down to start cleaning the other six he had caught. Faline was seriously impressed that he had so many, and that they were so large. She knew that these fish would make them meals a few times before they ran out of food again.

"This is the best we have done yet, be proud Nolan. We will be okay for the next little while if we use them sparingly." She gave Nolan a pat on the back as he sat cleaning them.

Cairo sat close to Nolan as he was gutting the fish, hoping that he was going to give her the insides. Nolan just looked at the wagging fur ball next to him and rolled his eyes. He knew what she wanted and thought it was disgusting but he gave the innards to her anyway, figuring this would save them a fish.

Faline laughed as Nolan wrinkled up his nose while Cairo licked at the innards of the fish before almost swallowing them whole. Rom didn't find it appealing any more but knew that this was a good way to feed the dog and save them their meal. Nolan pulled the already cooked fish from the flames of the fire, while Faline and Rom replaced them with the others.

"Guess I should have found another stick, huh?" Faline asked Nolan as she placed the last fish onto its spear.

"Not necessary," Nolan replied going to where Faline stood. "Just turn this one sideways and then you can place two on the same stick. That's why

I leave the bones in, cooking them becomes less of a hassle as they stay held together."

Faline smiled as she turned the fish sideways and slid the other on the stick above it. They sat down and each took an already cooked fish and a few berries. They ate their breakfast under the small canopy of trees, while the sun rose into its full power over the mountain, and the rest of their food cooked slowly over the now dwindling fire. Each of them made sure to give their fish remnants to Cairo so she could fill a little more of her belly with much needed protein for their journey.

Once the other fish had finished cooking, Nolan gave them a minute to cool before wrapping them up and placing them into his bag for their travel. Faline looked up towards the sky noting that from where the sun sat it was probably drawing close to noon.

"We need to get going guys," she said as she grabbed the rest of the berries and stuffed them in her own bag. "The light isn't going to hang around forever, and I don't know how long it's going to take us to get up there."

Rom and Nolan stood up and kicked some dirt onto the small fire Rom had built to smother it out. The fire out, the food cooked and packed, they slung their bags over their shoulders and made their way out of the trees toward the mountain. Rom glanced this way and that trying to decide the best route to take, Faline was beside him doing the same. She noted that there was something that looked like an old path beside the river that led up the side of the mountain.

"From what I see," she started, still scanning the area, "we should follow the river. It looks as if there was a path there once, and the cave is up at the top to the right of it."

Nolan squinted ahead trying to see this cave she said she saw. Seeing nothing of the sort he asked softly, "How do you know where the cave is? I can't see it up there where you suggest it is."

"I don't know for sure that it's there to be honest. It's just a gut feeling I have and where I saw the fire come from last night," she replied.

Rom started walking down the slight slope in the forest's edge leading towards the river below. "I say that she probably knows more than we do, and I am going to bet that the cave is there."

Faline smiled and followed along behind Rom. "Come on, Nolan." she chuckled. "We are going to get this over with and head home, maybe even tomorrow if we hurry it up."

Nolan smiled and sighed with relief. "All right let's go see what's in that cave and get our butts back home."

As they all walked beside the gently flowing water, Faline made sure to make mental notes of everything that she saw around her. She was constantly surveying the area for food sources and wild life. Water was not going to be a problem due to the shining gurgling river bed they followed, so she was able to focus on other things. Every now and then some pheasant would come flapping out from a bush they walked past, Faline tried not to grab her bow and start collecting food. Cairo whimpered every time the birds flew away wanting so badly to help her girl hunt. Faline gave Cairo a small pat on the head and reassured her that they would get their chance.

Faline looked up towards the mountain noting that the sun was no longer behind it. It was at its highest point in the sky now which meant it was past noon. She turned and looked back to where they had started attempting to figure out how far they had come since they began walking. She sighed when the forest didn't seem all that far away.

"Rom," Faline said quietly. "Why does it seem like we are moving in slow motion? We haven't come very far in the time we have been walking."

Rom laughed a bit before answering. "Faline, you are in too much of a rush. Look around you and take in the scenery. We are not exactly walking on even ground, and because we are heading up hill now it takes a little longer than walking a straight path."

Faline groaned. "I just am so anxious to get there."

Nolan giggled. "We are aware of your desire to reach your destination. Trust me."

"Quiet back there." Faline joked. "I hope we make it before dark if nothing else."

"I am sure we will make it before the light gives out, my dear," Rom reassured her.

Faline took a deep breath and kept on walking. The ground beneath her feet was just as Rom said, sloping upward and uneven with its bumps and twists from little stones jutting out of the ground, then there were also roots growing over the half mangled path making it just a little harder to walk on it quickly.

They paused briefly to get a drink from the river which was cool and refreshing. Rom said that due to the grit and stone in the water from the mountain, the water was well filtered and much cleaner making it more suitable to drink. Finishing their brief rest they continued up the side of the mountain, which was becoming less and less green, turning into more of the black, brown rock Faline had seen when she stood at the edge of the forest.

"Rom, does Mt. Diamanti mean something? Or is it just some random name?" Nolan inquired as he tried to keep up with his other companions.

Rom stopped and scratched his head in thought. "Yes, I believe it does, most great mountains do mean something."

Nolan waited to see if Rom was going to add more to that. When he didn't he was a little distraught. "Well, what is it then?" he asked.

"The meaning of the name is eluding me as of now, but I am sure I will remember at some point," Rom laughed.

Nolan rolled his eyes and watched the ground turn from bits of grass to plain old rock. He paused a moment to look behind them. They had come quite a long way from where they began their morning munching fish and berries. He looked ahead noticing that there were bits of the path that had been completely buried under fallen rock.

"It looks like our way has been blocked off in several spots up ahead," Nolan commented as he trotted a little to catch up to Rom and Faline.

Faline shifted her gaze from the ground at her feet to what was coming ahead. She grimaced at the fallen rocks and small boulders that had fallen across the already mangled path. It was not going to stop her though. She was making it to the cave if it killed her.

"Don't worry, Nolan we will be all right. It's just a little extra climbing that's all." She laughed trying to conceal her hidden angst about the way there possibly becoming too hard to climb.

Rom looked back at the two younger people, watching their faces wrinkle up at the thought of not making it after they worked so hard and come so far. "I will lead the way up. If the two of you do as I do, you'll be just fine."

Faline turned to look at Nolan. His face said it all. They were both a little nervous about trying to scale the rocks on an already bumpy surface, but the thought about them giving way and sending them racing for their lives back down the mountain, did not sound at all appealing.

As Rom moved forward coming closer to the first obstacle, he gave it a little nudge with his foot before trying to get over it. It looked easier than it was going to be, Faline was sure of that. One or two very large rocks with a few dozen smaller ones tucked in around it. Even the smallest of missteps would break the hold the small ones had on the big ones keeping them in place, and there they go, rolling down the hill after a band of screaming travellers running for their lives.

Faline and Nolan studied Rom's steps as he carefully manoeuvred around the rocks and boulders, safely making his way to the other side. Cairo with her big furry paws had no trouble making it over the rock pile and waited patiently beyond the rocks, giving a small yip at Faline to hurry her along.

Faline took a deep breath and placed one of her feet gently on the rocks as she grabbed hold of one of the boulders to steady herself. "This is it," she mumbled. "Time to be brave and get over this."

Nolan stood behind her his arms extended and ready in case she fell backwards. "It's all right, Faline, I'm right behind you."

Faline carefully looked back at him shooting a weak smile his way. "Thanks, Nolan."

Nolan waited until she was safe on the other side before trying to climb over himself. He figured one at a time was best so that their combined weight didn't upset the mound. He began making his way up and over the rocks slowly. Before he knew it he was back on the slightly disturbed path that they had been following.

"That was the easy one I'm afraid," Rom stated as he pointed further towards the top at the very rocky buried path.

Nolan looked to where Rom was pointing and groaned. "Oh, you have got to be kidding. There is no way we are walking over all those rocks without disturbing at least one of them."

"As long as we don't shift them around too much it should hold," Rom said studying the formation. "We need to get closer so I can really know what we are up against."

"Okay, then let's get going," Faline said hesitantly. "I want to get up there and the sun is already starting to go down."

Rom nodded and began to walk forward up the little winding rocky path forged in the stone wall of the ever sloping mountain. It was getting harder to walk the higher they climbed with all the little rocks rolling out from under their feet. Each of them slipped a little once or twice as they made their way to the next obstruction. With each step they took closing the gap between them and the giant pile of rocks, the path became more unstable. Little rocks were jutting out of the ground everywhere making it impossible to move at anything but a snail's pace. Faline had to grab onto Rom at one point to keep herself upright and avoid face planting in the middle of him and Nolan.

"Sorry, Rom," she muttered as she steadied herself.

"No worries," Rom replied as he helped her get back her footing.

"I suggest keeping closer together," Rom said quietly. "Don't yell out and don't move too fast, either of those things is going to loosen up all this little stuff and create a small rockslide."

Faline and Nolan merely nodded scooting closer to where Rom stood. They carefully walked across the slightly shifting stones trying not to make them move, but it was near impossible with as many as there were. Nolan watched as Cairo made her way to the top with ease, her wide padded paws making it an easy trek. He wished they all had her big furry feet to get them up there.

"It makes me sick to watch Cairo get up there so easily to be perfectly honest," Nolan mumbled as he tried not to lose his balance while one of the small rocks shifted under his feet.

"I guess being a dog has its perks sometimes," Faline chuckled looking up at Cairo who sat wagging her tail while she waited.

Rom laughed as he trod his way up to the most dangerous parts of the rock-filled portion of the incline. He stopped for a minute to see where the best spots were to place their feet. Once he was satisfied in his desired path, he slowly moved forward grabbing onto the bigger boulders that were scattered about. He paused for a minute and reached a hand back to help Faline get to where he was, and then to Nolan as he scaled his way up and through.

It was a long process it seemed getting through the mass off fallen stone, but they were almost where Cairo sat marking the end of the cluttered path. Faline and Rom seemed to move a little easier than Nolan, which made him feel like an infant being tended to by his mother as he needed more assistance from Rom than Faline did. Nearing the end Rom helped Faline get between the last two enormous boulders and safely to the ground that lay several inches beneath the stones they had walked over.

It was like a rocky stair that need not be disturbed. Rom hopped down beside her, grabbing onto the left boulder to steady himself, before reaching his hand to Nolan to help him through. Nolan grabbed hold of Rom's hand and stopped moving when his foot slipped, causing it to become stuck in between two of the larger chunks of rock that lay there.

"What do I do now?" he asked trying not to panic. "My foot is caught and I am afraid of trying to wrench it loose and causing everything to shift."

"Put your hand there on the boulder then slowly step your free foot backward a little." Rom instructed. "Then you can try and wiggle it out once you have steadied yourself there."

Nolan looked up at him, took a deep breath and did as he was told. He slowly moved one foot back to try and get steadier footing. He took his hand off the rock and slowly stood up. He leaned over a little and began wiggling his foot a bit to try and release it from where it had been caught without making everything around it move. It was the scariest thing he had done thus far, even scarier than wandering alone in the dark outside the thicket during the storm.

Several agonising minutes went by before Faline spoke to him, her voice shaking a little. "How ya doing Nolan?"

"I don't know that this is going to work to be frank," he answered beginning to get upset.

There were two giant boulders blocking his view of Faline, Rom and Cairo, and not being able to see them was making him feel more scared than anything. He just wanted his foot to be free so he could slide through the gap in the rocks and be with his friends. Was that too much to ask? he wondered.

"All right Nolan, we are going to reach our hands through, once you see them grab on tight," Rom told him.

Nolan didn't like the sound of it but agreed to do as Rom said. Rom had whispered something to Faline that Nolan could not hear and it was making him nervous. Just then Rom and Faline each had an arm in the gap of the rocks. Nolan leaned forward and reached for them, grabbing on as tightly as he could without hurting either of them.

Rom's voice came again from the other side of the stones. "Get ready, Nolan. Faline, one, two, three!"

Faline and Rom both yanked Nolan's arms pulling his foot free and partly out through the boulders. Once they had his arms out each of them grabbed hold with their free hand and yanked him the rest of the way through as the rocks beneath Nolan's feet gave way, shifting everything else around them sending the rock mound barrelling down the slope in a loud, dusty, thundering roll.

They all stood there and watched as the giant rock slide smothered everything on its way down the mountain, including the smaller barrier that they had passed over an hour or so ago. Nolan's face was pale thinking about how he could have been wrapped up in that slide, being smashed to bloody bits as all the rocks rolled over his little body. He turned to Rom and Faline who watched as the last of the rocks came to a standstill at the base of the mountain.

"Thank you both so much," he gasped. "I would have been crushed if it weren't for you."

Rom wiped the sweat from his forehead and smiled at him. "No problem. Besides, I'd expect that you'd have done the same for me."

Faline pulled the straps of her bag tight and gave it a small adjustment as it had slid down her back some pulling Nolan loose. "Okay, now that the excitement is over, let's get up into that cave."

She turned around and began walking higher up the mountain, Cairo, Rom and Nolan staying close behind her. The sun was beginning to drop laying shadows on the ground where they walked making it hard to discern between what was a small stone, and what was a shadow mimicking a stone.

Faline had misjudged her step a few times thinking she was avoiding a rock, but when she placed her foot back on the ground she found a rock almost falling. Rom and Nolan were not doing much better walking behind her as her shadow was causing even more problems for them.

"Walking this in these darkening conditions is becoming a nuisance," Nolan grumbled as he tripped over another hidden stone.

"Stop griping, Nolan. We are almost there, just hold on a bit longer." Faline said realising that she had almost scolded him. "I'm sorry. I didn't mean to be rude about it."

"It's all right, Faline." he replied. "I need to buck up and stop whining."

Rom had a hard time controlling his laughter at this point. Chuckling, he told them, "You two are like peas and carrots. One is sweet and mushy, the other has a sweet strong crunch to it."

Faline laughed. "I suppose Nolan is the peas in this analogy and I the carrot."

Nolan's face grew red, not so much from anger but embarrassment. "I have been getting better as we have been travelling. Can't I at least be a fresh pea that has a nice snap to it?" he jested trying to defend himself.

Faline and Rom couldn't take it and burst into laughter. They laughed so hard and loud that it echoed off the walls of the mountain, tears running down their faces.

"Nolan, you are definitely becoming a more snappy sort of pea," Rom laughed hysterically.

Faline's laughter came to a slow giggle and then she came to a dead halt, standing there looking around trying to see something that they could not. Cairo was standing next to her, the fur on her back was standing up straight, and she was growling in her low grumble that let everyone know something was not right.

"Faline, what is it?" Nolan whispered.

"Shhhh." She put her finger to her lips and continued to scan the area. "Can't you smell it?"

The small breeze that was blowing on top of the mountain had shifted away from them, carrying away whatever smell she thought was there. She held up her hand and had them wait. Soon enough the wind circled back around bringing the smell with it.

Nolan covered his mouth and nose with his hand. "Ugh, what is that?" he choked trying not to let it get up his nose.

"That would be the smell of death and," Rom took a couple deep breaths smelling the air around him like a dog, "the other part is coal or ash, a fire residue of some sort."

"Let's go, but quietly no talking." Faline gestured with a wave of her hand for them to follow as she drew her bow and readied an arrow.

Rom and Nolan took out their hunting knives not sure what it was they were about to encounter as they crept around the bend to the entrance of the cave. The final curve began to show them what they smelled. There were dozens of dead men and animals alike, partly burned and rotting on the stony path. Some of them had been there much longer than the others, their flesh having been rotted clean to the bone as maggots crawled around in the still lingering fleshy parts.

Faline looked around at all of them covering her mouth; the closer they came to the cave, the more pungent the smell. It was completely nauseating and very hard for any of them to tolerate. None of them were accustomed to such things, and it was making Nolan especially sick to his stomach.

"What on earth did all of this?" he groaned through his fingers not daring to take his hand away.

Rom knew but was hesitant to say anything. Faline turned and stared at him studying his face for any clues as to what he knew. She figured out in an instant that he knew something. She was also positive that he was going to tell them.

"Rom, I can see by the look on your face that you know what is up here, so what is it?" she asked sternly.

Rom shifted his gaze away from her prodding eyes. "Faline, I'm afraid you already know what is here. I have watched you figure it all out as we have been travelling. My story, your dream, the fire on the mountain, think about it," he answered softly.

She stood for a minute rummaging through her brain, sorting through all the things Rom had just mentioned. Then the wheels turned to the right spot and it hit her. "There is a dragon here," She said, her eyes growing wide.

Nolan looked as if he might pass out but stayed on his feet despite being completely terrified. "A dragon you say? Are we in danger here or are you supposed to do something with this dragon and that's why we are here?" he asked her as calmly as he could.

"Honestly, I am not sure." Faline's face had become sombre and she was deep in thought. "I thought for sure that when I had that dream about the sword that I was coming here to get that. There were dragons in that dream, but I figured that was just my mind rehashing Rom's story." She tilted her head to one side and thought for a moment. "Maybe the dragon holds the sword and I have to get it to give it to me."

Nolan was scared for her now and was growing a little irritated. "How in the hell are you supposed to get a sword away from a dragon exactly?" he said angrily.

"I don't know," Faline answered. "But I am going to have to try." That being said she began making her way past the dead things littering the ground towards the mouth of the cave.

Rom looked at Nolan and shrugged, as he followed Faline through the maze of death trying not to inhale too deep. Nolan and Cairo were tailing the end of the line, Cairo especially since she found it fascinating to sniff everything she could as she went. Before long they were standing in front of the mouth of a large dark cave that was emitting a strong foul odour. It smelled like the death they were currently surrounded by, but it also smelled of something else, something odd.

"Okay, let's get the stuff out for making some torches and get in there. Better make a few of them so we don't have them burn out without back-ups," Faline instructed.

Nolan and Faline placed their bags on the ground and began pulling out the lines, lamp oil and flint. Nolan got up and looked around a bit for some wood to wrap the linens around; the pickings for timber up here were scarce not like it was down below.

"I don't know how we are going to make torches, Faline. There isn't any wood here," Nolan called to her.

Faline turned and began looking around trying to find something to use to make the torches. Nolan was right. There wasn't much as far as wood, just rotting bodies. There were a few pieces of wood up there that other travellers had used for torches themselves, but they weren't very long and they wouldn't last if they started to burn.

"You two hurry up and gather all the old torches lying around in case we need to make a fire," Faline told Nolan and Rom pointing at all the used bits on the ground. "I will come up with something for our lights."

Rom and Nolan nodded as they hurried up and began gathering all the torch fragments they could get their hands on. Some of them needed to be pried out of the hands of dead men, which made Nolan very uneasy. Faline walked around through the masses looking over each one carefully, some of the men and animals were fresher than others, some of them had been there for quite some time. She figured she would find some of the older ones and use bits of bone to wrap the linen on.

"Bone will not burn like wood will," she said to Cairo as she bent over to grab a femur from some poor dead soldier. "This will do just fine, now to find a few more oldies but goodies," she giggled to herself.

The bones Faline grabbed were picked clean by the scavenger animals and flies, making it much easier for her to tolerate handling them. They had also been there for so long that there really wasn't any chance for any decaying substance to be left behind anyway. Faline found five good bones and took them back to the bags laying them in a row on the ground. She took the linen and began wrapping the tops of each bone thoroughly before soaking the linen with the oil, turning the bone in her hand as she gently poured the oil to make sure she covered the whole piece. Once she had finished, Faline went to help Rom and Nolan finish gathering the wood pieces for the fire.

"How are we doing over here fellas?" she chuckled as she saw the look of disgust on Nolan's face while he pried open a dead man's hand to get his torch.

"Oh, this is the most fun I've ever had in my life," Nolan grumbled as he rolled his eyes before placing the bit of wood next to him with the others.

Rom laughed as he picked up a few more of his own bits. "Faline, I don't think messing with the dead is Nolan's cup of tea."

"No probably not, but when you see what I did you will be happier for it," Faline mused as she picked up a few pieces herself.

"I think we have plenty for a nice little fire now," Rom said as he picked up his bundle and got to his feet. "I suggest making all this into a pile right inside the entrance and start heading in."

Faline smiled and helped Nolan pick up his bunch. "I agree with that. Let's get going."

When they made it back to the mouth of the cave Nolan looked down at Faline's torches, He was mortified. Rom laughed as he placed his wood inside the cave and came back for Nolan's who was unable to do anything but stare at the bone torches Faline had constructed.

"You expect me to walk around with someone's, what is that? A leg? An arm? You want me to carry a piece of someone and light it on fire? Are you mad?" Nolan said disgusted.

Rom just laughed and shook his head. "I think what Faline did here was very clever, and very bold."

"Thank you, Rom," Faline said grinning ear to ear. "Besides, unlike wood, bone will not start on fire so the torch won't go out unless the linen burns away. All we must do is make sure the linens stay fresh."

Nolan wrinkled his nose. "Well all right, but I'm still not very happy about any of this really."

"You don't have to be. You can stay here and wait for Rom, Cairo and I to get back if you like," Faline smirked.

"Very funny, Faline," Nolan replied. "I am definitely going with you."

"Well all right then, let's get these torches lit and get in there," Faline said without hesitation.

Rom grabbed the matches and Faline's bone torches, handing one to everyone, then he struck his flint with his hunting knife and lit all of them. The three torches made quite a bit of light, which made them all very happy as it was very dark in there. Rom held each of their torches as they placed their bags back onto their backs, handed the torches back, and they began walking down into the dark.

As they walked they noticed that there was a shimmer on the walls from the lights of their torches, it was beautiful to watch it sparkle as the fire light danced off it. Looking around they also noticed that in little clumps there were bats suspended from the ceiling, their droppings on the ground underneath them.

"That explains some of the newer yucky smell," Nolan griped. "Bat poop."

Faline and Rom chuckled a little. "Be careful walking through here," Rom warned. "Just like outside there could be dips, rocks, or even chasms that we cannot see because of the dark."

"Got it!" Faline and Nolan answered as they slowed their walk. Faline held her torch straight out in front of them, Nolan had his out to the side and Rom's was straight up in the air. The three of them with their torches outstretched, made a makeshift circle of light around them allowing them to see just a little more than they otherwise would have.

Faline could feel a warm heavy feeling beginning to grow in her chest. She couldn't quite put her finger on it, but then she remembered the amulet. She pulled it out from inside her shirt and in the dark of the cave she could see that the beautiful red stone was almost glowing.

"We have to be getting close," Faline told Rom and Nolan as she slipped the amulet back inside her shirt.

"How do you know?" Rom asked curiously.

"I am not sure really, I just feel like we are," Faline replied still scanning the surrounding area.

They walked on for a little while longer before Cairo nudged Faline's thigh with her nose, the hair on the back of her neck beginning to stand up as she started to grumble.

"Stop!" Faline whispered as she put up her free hand to halt her companions.

"What is it Faline?" Rom whispered back.

"I'm not sure, but whatever it is it has Cairo on edge and I can feel it up there," Faline said quietly.

All of them stood there in silence as they waited for whatever Faline felt was there to either emerge or make a sound. For quite some time they heard nothing other than bat wings shuffling in the distance behind them. Then they heard something moving, it sounded as if it were slithering and walking along the floor of the cave. The steps it made were heavy, which told them the thing in the darkness was extremely big, the slithering however threw them off. The movement came to a stop and there was nothing.

"Hello?" Faline's voice echoed off the walls of the cave startling Nolan, Rom and Cairo.

The thing in the dark snorted blowing a big cloud of cave dust up and out toward where they stood, forcing them to shield their eyes. Nolan almost dropped his torch and Cairo was at the ready, waiting to charge into battle. Fear enveloped the travelling companions as they stood and waited, ready to run.

Chapter 17

The Keeper

The cloud of dust that had blown around their faces had finally begun to settle, leaving the three of them coughing as they had inhaled a bit of it. Faline was wiping it away from her face, her eyes watering as she blinked away the debris that had got in. Rom and Nolan were in the same shape as she was, using their sleeves to try and get some of the dirt off their faces, holding their torches out as they scanned the area for any signs of what had made the dust spew out at them in such a fashion.

A long, low growl came from within the depths of the cave, followed by more slithering of the unknown thing in the dark. Faline held her torch out in front of her taking a few more steps forward, trying to inch slowly closer to the source without upsetting it.

"Excuse me, but could you please not eat us," she whispered her plea into the dark in the hopes that whatever it was would understand her.

To Faline's amazement the thing in the dark did understand her, in fact it laughed. Its laugh was deep, harsh and loud, loud enough it seemed to shake the walls of the cave. Then to stop them all dead in their tracks and make Rom, Nolan and Faline almost pee their pants, it spoke.

"Dear girl, I do not intend to eat you or your friends," the voice said in a deep almost feminine tone.

It almost seemed human, but they all knew that whatever was there was not a man or woman. Its voice was too loud, deep, and almost contained a small hiss. Then there was the fact that when it walked its steps were hard and thundering, and something slithered when it moved.

Faline took another step closer trying to get a look at the creature hiding in the dark. "Can I ask what you are intending then?"

The voice answered back plainly. "You may, but I may not answer that question just yet."

Rom sighed. He was not really in the mood for playing games at this point. "What are you?" he asked without hesitation.

The creature laughed shaking the ground where they stood. "You know perfectly well what I am wizard, stop playing games and come closer so I can have a look at all of you."

Nolan, grasping for his last small shred of courage finally mustered up the will to speak. "If I may, it's kind of hard to manoeuvre in here with such limited light. None of us are very keen on falling into a hole really."

With a particularly eerie chuckle and a deep breath, the being in the dark sprayed forth a large fountain of fire which ignited a pile of some unknown substance to the right of its extraordinarily large body. Faline and her friends looked on in awe as the pile ignited into a huge roaring inferno and standing next to it was an enormous black winged dragon. It had brilliant green serpent like eyes, two gleaming white rows of razor sharp teeth that seemed to be smiling at them, four feet filled with spears for claws, two wings as big as houses on its back with talons on the ends, spikes all along its spine down to the tip of its tail and two giant black horns on its head. It was the most fantastic thing that any of them had ever seen. Cairo, on the other hand, was not impressed, standing in between the dragon and her girl growling to prevent any unwanted attacks.

"Your canine amuses me in its attempt to protect you from me," the enormous dragon sneered.

Faline reached down stroking Cairo's head. "She is the best protector a girl could ask for," she replied smiling at her dog.

"Is she now?" The dragon questioned. "What if you were meant to have something bigger and better than her?"

"I doubt that is even possible," Faline retorted. "I would not trade her for my life. Cairo will be with me until she is no longer among the land of the living."

"I didn't mean any offence, Faline, the dragon said bowing its head. "I only meant that there are things waiting for you."

Faline looked up at the dragon her curiosity now peaked. "How do you know my name? And speaking of names, what can we call you?" she asked as politely as she could.

The dragon laughed spewing a small cloud of smoke as it did. "My name is Ditri. As far as how I know who you are, well it should be obvious since you were sent here specifically were you not?"

Faline knew she was right, she was sent to the cave in search of god knows what by Hildy. "So you know why I am here when I do not. Why are you here exactly?"

Ditri lay on the floor, her giant tail slowly swishing back and forth watching the people that stood before her. "I am here because I am the keeper of the item inside this cave. My job is to make sure that it goes to the one that was chosen and is not stolen by someone unworthy of its greatness. That is why I had to lay waste to all those outside and in this cave," she replied as if it bored her to say it aloud. "You are here because Hildy sent you to come and make a claim to the item I possess, potentially getting more than you bargained for."

Faline motioned towards the floor of the cave not taking her eyes off Ditri, who lay there almost motionless except for the slow swishing of her tail. "Do you mind if we all sit? It has been an awful long day and we are tired," Faline asked figuring it was only polite.

"Be my guest. It is a mostly free country, and as I said I am not going to eat you. If I were intending on doing so I'd have done it already without the polite conversation." Ditri mused as she watched them all cautiously sit on the floor of the cave in front of her.

"Don't like to get to know your food?" Nolan joked without thinking about the potential consequence of his joke.

"Not at all. My mother taught me not to play with my food, didn't yours?" Ditri joked back grinning at him with her large, fanged grin.

Nolan just sat there his cheeks burning as red as the fire Ditri had started from embarrassment, almost sorry that he had spoken at all. Faline had taken her bag off her back and set it on the ground next to her taking the apples out of it passing them around to Rom and Nolan. She offered one to Ditri who politely declined. Faline shrugged and bit into her own apple thinking about what she was going to ask Ditri next. There was a plethora of things she wanted to ask her but figured she should stick to the things that mattered most.

Swallowing her bite she looked up at the dragon, watching her intently, and asked, "So can I have it?"

Ditri looked at her a little bewildered. "Have what exactly?"

"The sword I keep dreaming about, or is that just some grand illusion my mind has created from the story Rom told me?" Faline said without hesitation.

Rom was floored and sat staring at her in disbelief. "Faline, the story I told was not just any story, it was based on facts and things that happened centuries ago. A sword from then that is still in existence? That is almost as unbelievable as sitting here with Ditri. No offence, madam dragon." He bowed his head slightly at Ditri in hopes that she didn't become irate at his minor disbelief of their current situation.

"None taken, although you being a magi should make it more obvious that there are still so many unknown possibilities out there for her than she may be aware of." Ditri began as softly as a dragon could. "Dragons are not any rarer than you are Romulus. Swords however, that's another story."

Faline sighed and hung her head. "Then it was just a dream, something my mind was tricking me into believing. I have to say that this is depressing news."

Ditri chuckled. "Now don't get all worked up so quickly, child. You came here for a purpose and I intend to divulge that purpose soon enough. Then you can get a good rest and head on home."

"Well, that's excellent news," Nolan smiled and nudged Faline in the arm a little.

Faline shifted a little on the ground straightening her legs out in front of her allowing them to stretch out. "All right then let's get things going so I can get home to my family, and my bed." She smiled thinking of the small wooden bed back home.

Ditri nodded and took her tail swiping it along the ground behind where she lay, the tip of it eventually bringing forth an elongated gilded wooden chest. "Now, before you can have what is inside you must understand that it may not choose you to have it."

"But I thought you had to be the one to choose who it went to?" Faline huffed, now worried that she wouldn't be good enough for the contents of the box.

Ditri sneered showing half of her large dagger like teeth. "Yes, I am the one who decides initially, then it is up to the box. The box decides whether the one who places their hands upon it is born of prophecy and therefore chosen."

Nolan looked over at Faline, whose face had otherwise lost all its enthusiasm. "It's going to be all right, Faline." He placed a hand softly onto her shoulder. "We all have faith in you. Look at how far you have come already, and this is just the beginning. Don't let a silly chest stop you."

She smiled at him and perked up a bit. "Okay Ditri, what is it that I have to do to get the item inside?"

"It's very simple really," Ditri said plainly. "All you need to do is put your hands on either side of the chest. If it glows gold it is going to open and the thing inside is destined to be yours. If not, well then I was wrong and I am going to have to eat you," Ditri laughed.

"I hope that's a joke," Nolan grumbled under his breath as he got to his feet, a little scared that she might not be joking.

"Relax, boy." Ditri grinned. "I said from the beginning that I was not going to eat you, and I am going to stay true to my word. Now Faline if you would kindly come over here and place your hands on the chest we can see what your inner soul is truly made of."

Faline sat for a moment drawing her knees up under her chin staring at the old dusty chest that was glistening in the firelight. She wondered if all the travelling and the little hardships they had endured to get here were going to be for nothing. What if she wasn't what they had expected her to be? How could a box possibly be the teller of all her inner secrets that even she did not yet know she possessed? Questions were flooding her mind like a water spigot that had been kicked open by a mule, and she was suddenly overwhelmed wanting to run back home, forgetting about everything that had happened here and just trying to live a normal life like she had been before Hildy came along.

Rom's voice came quietly into her mind like a soft cloud passing along the sky above. "Faline, this is only a small test of your will to achieve greater things, that's all. Don't let it suck you in and consume you. It is going to be all right as soon as you do what needs to be done."

Faline closed her eyes thinking about home and all her family that were waiting for her there. It was a calming thought that allowed her to relax a bit. The face of her father,, Jonas sitting by the fire with his pipe after dinner, and her mother's soothing voice reading her bedtime stories at night.

Opening her eyes and looking around she saw everyone watching her, waiting for her to make her move for the chest and see what it would grant her. Faline took a deep breath slowly getting to her feet, taking a few steps forward until she was standing before the chest.

She knelt in front of the chest and gave one last look around at her friends. "Here goes nothing," she said quietly before she placed each of her hands on either side of the elongated dusty chest.

They all sat there waiting for what felt like an eternity for the chest to hopefully do something, Faline's hands were beginning to sweat while everyone stared at her with bated breath. She felt like a failure because the chest didn't open right away and she was tempted to pull her hands away.

Sensing Faline's discomfort with the situation Ditri spoke softly to her. "My dear, please keep in mind that it takes time to achieve the greatest of things."

Faline nodded and held fast on the sides of the chest, sweating and trembling now, but not moving other than the outward motion of her chest as she breathed. She stared at the chest now trying to will it open with her mind, telling it that she had what it takes to be the bearer of the gift it held. Faline explained that she had worked so hard to be here, trained every day with Tobias, and that there might be a lot of people depending on her success. She needed to be successful. She felt it in her bones that she had to be the one to help the people now.

She sighed and looked at Rom who just smiled at her. She looked over at Nolan who gave her two thumbs up and a small nod. She looked over at Cairo who lay there wagging her tail, tongue lolling out the side of her mouth pleased to be acknowledged by her girl.

Faline looked back at the chest "Please," she muttered softly under her breath. "Help me help them."

Just then the chest began to glow, so softly at first that with the light of the fire it was barely noticeable. The golden glowing light began to get stronger and before long the light of the chest was so bright it took Faline everything she had not to pull her hands away to shield her eyes as everyone else had done. There were two very loud clicks that reverberated off the walls of the cave and the lid of the chest popped free. Faline sat there with her hands still firmly planted on either side of the chest not daring to pull them away even after the golden light began to fade, looking to Ditri for further instruction.

Ditri looked highly impressed and nodded at Faline. "It's all right, Faline. You can take your hands away now and lift the lid. You have been granted the gift inside, now claim it."

Rom, Nolan and Cairo came over to huddle around Faline and her chest waiting for her to open the lid and see what was inside. Rom's eyes were wide with excitement looking like a small child on his birthday. Nolan was just as excited but was a little better at containing himself giving Faline a soft pat on the back to congratulate her on a job well done.

Faline looked between the two of them smiling at them both before leaning over and giving Cairo a pat on the head. "Well, I didn't think I had it in me to be honest, but now that I have it let's see what it is once and for all."

Still kneeling on the floor Faline moved her hands to the front of the chest grasping the two latches on the front between her shaking fingers. Her heart was beating so hard now she thought it might explode from her chest at any given moment, until slowly she began lifting the lid on the wooden chest to reveal the contents inside.

Staring inside Faline sat back on her knees placing her hands in her lap not believing what she saw in front of her. She was right, there was a sword waiting here for her, but it was far more brilliant than she could have ever imagined it to be.

It started at the hilt with a golden, thick maned, roaring lion's head as its pommel, tightly woven gold lacing down its grip. The cross guard was also made of gold bejewelled with emeralds and rubies, a golden rain guard, bringing her to the blade. The blade was just as superior as the rest of the sword. She assumed that due to its sparkling luminescent sheen it had to be the last blade forged from diamonds. It was miraculous and the way that it sparkled made it so that she couldn't take her eyes off it. The scabbard was equally beautiful considering it was just a container for the blade and served no purpose really. It was criss-crossed in black and gold, the locket and chape at the ends were both golden as well.

Ditri broke the elongated silence almost laughing at all of them. "Well, are you going to take it out of there, or do you plan on just staring at it for the rest of eternity?"

"Yeah, Faline, let's get a real good look at that thing," Nolan said excitedly. "I have seen a lot of swords in my day being around my dad, but this one takes the cake."

"Oh right," Faline said almost shaking herself out of a small stupor. "I will take it out and see how it feels."

Faline reached in and took the sword in her hand lifting it out of the dusty wooden chest. It felt like the most natural thing she had done since she left the comforts of her home. It felt light and cool in her hand. She gave it a few swings through the air listening to the sound the air made coming off the fuller in the middle of the blade. It made a beautiful sound as it flowed through the air, almost as if it were singing.

"Faline you have really lucked out here," Rom said beaming from ear to ear. "We all knew you were the one, and this proves it. You are the child of prophecy, you are the one destined to save us all."

"Good lord, Rom," Nolan groaned. "What a way to try and spoil the moment with a ton of pressure there."

"He's right though, boy." Ditri chimed in. "She is the one destined to set things right. Either that or she will be the one to destroy us all."

Nolan went pale. "Can the two of you just let her enjoy her moment in the sun for a bit before you start slamming her with a bunch of crap?" he shouted. "Christ."

Rom's eyes grew wide as he watched Nolan finally become a man, and in his opinion it was about time. "Good for you, Nolan," he chuckled. "All right we will wait until she is done playing and then it's back to business."

"Fair enough," Nolan agreed as he walked over to check out Faline's new weapon. He tried to hold it but to him it seemed like a tree trunk. It was weird since she seemed to have no problem wielding it.

"Don't let it bother you, boy," Ditri said casually. "Only the chosen one can hold it with ease."

Handing the sword back to Faline Nolan smiled at her. "I always knew you had it in you.."

Placing the sword into its scabbard and giving it a place with her other things she hugged Nolan. "Thank you my friend for coming all this way with me. It means a lot to me that I have such good friends."

Nolan's face was again as red as the fire burning behind him and his heart beat a mile a minute. "It was nothing really." he managed to stammer. "I'd have been a fool to let you go alone."

She released him from her bear hug and turned back to Ditri and Rom. Faline supposed it was time to wrap things up. "What happens now? I mean, I came here to make sure I was the one, and I assume that has been proven now that I have done all that I needed to," Faline said waiting for anyone to argue these facts.

Ditri nodded. "Yes, Faline, you have proven yourself to be a worthy candidate for the tasks ahead. Collecting the sword was just the first part of a very long road ahead of you though."

Rom sighed and took a seat next to the still roaring fire inside the cave. "She's right, Faline. Being the child of prophecy has its perks." He began motioning toward the sword gleaming in the firelight. "However, it's also going to have a lot of bits where you are not going to enjoy it so much."

"Thus far I have been doing all right with everything." Faline smiled as she sat across from him. "The only thing I haven't cared for really is being caught in the rain for two days. That stunk like rotting meat."

Nolan wrinkled his nose looking towards the front of the cave, remembering the dead strewn about the ground out there and the smell they carried with them. "What an analogy, Faline. Couldn't you have thought of something else?"

Faline giggled at him. "Nolan, you are going to have to get used to dead things if you are going to continue to hang around with me I think."

He looked at her, an expression of fear and disgust spreading on his face. "I am not sure that is true. No one said anything about any dead things other than the food we eat."

Rom laughed hysterically now. "And there it is!" he bellowed. "Right back to Nolan's stomach. Quick, let's get this poor boy something to eat so he can digest the things we are about to tell you Faline, along with his dinner."

"Right," Faline answered reaching behind her for her bag. "Nolan, I'm pretty sure that the fish are in your bag."

"Oh yeah, I do have them. Hang on a sec." He walked over and retrieved his bag from the wall and came back to sit with Rom and Faline.

Between the two of them they had berries and fish ready and available for dinner. Once again Faline offered to share her food with Ditri, who respectfully declined.

"Go ahead and eat your food, sweet girl," Ditri smiled. "I appreciate your generosity, but one fish would not do me any good." She laughed a little before he motioned to her right side. "I have half of a cow waiting over there for me when I am ready."

Nolan shuddered. "Well, that's kinda gross."

"Maybe to you, but to me it's delicious and filling," Ditri said leaning in towards Nolan's face.

Nolan leaned back a little as Ditri's fanged face was far too close to his own. "To each his own or her own I should say," he said quietly as he ate some of his dinner.

Faline sat quietly eating her fish while Rom and Ditri chatted about history and how they were going to try and avoid making the same mistakes in the future. They both knew that Faline was going to need all the help she could get, but getting the help was going to be tough. All the creatures and magi left roaming about were not going to be persuaded too easily.

"I can only assume that you two are talking about me," Faline said eyeing the two of them.

Ditri smiled. "Yes, Faline, we are. We were talking about gathering you some help for the rest of your journey."

"I thought this was my journey?" Faline said hesitantly. "All I have to do now is get back home, and that shouldn't be too tough."

Rom looked at her expression which was now very serious. "Faline, this was just the beginning. You are going to head on home, but you won't stay there for very long."

"Oh," she sighed. "I was kind of hoping to be with my family for a while."

"You will be able to stay until the time has come for you to really begin," Ditri replied.

"How am I going to know when that is?" Faline asked before stuffing some berries into her mouth.

"Hildy will come and get you just like last time," Rom answered. "You will have more time to train with your new sword and get a good feel for it. Meanwhile Ditri and I are going to try and gather you an army."

Nolan almost choked on his bite of fish. "An army?" he sputtered. "An army built from what men? The kings have all the manpower these days and the village folk where we live are no fighters."

Ditri laughed and stretched out her legs as if she were a cat, her giant talons gripping the cave floor like a piece of paper shredding it on the way back to a sitting position. "It will not be an army made of men necessarily. We know of certain people, and beasts that will be more than willing to fight alongside of the prophetic child. Some of them will have to be talked into it a bit, but that was to be expected since the last wars of man they fought in led to a lot of their kind dying."

"So after I make my way back home, you two are going to go and get people and animals to fight with me in a war that is inevitably going to take place somewhere in the future?" Faline inquired as she handed the rest of her fish to an eagerly waiting Cairo.

"This would be correct," Ditri responded.

"Why are the two of you doing all of this? Shouldn't I be trying to form my own army? And what is it that you hope I'm to accomplish?" Faline asked, a sense of irritation in her voice.

Rom took the blanket Nolan was now handing him and lay it down on the floor, taking his boots off and stretching his legs. "Yes, I agree that you should have a hand in forming your own army when it is an appropriate time. There will be battles you must fight, some of them big, some small, and one that is going to be the largest we have seen for centuries. We are helping you in the hope that the prophecy will come to fruition and you will change things back to the way they were, one big kingdom of happy people instead of three segregated kingdoms of warring people."

Nolan chuckled. "No pressure there."

Faline reached over and slapped him on the arm. "Well, all right then. I am now potentially the maker or breaker of everyone's hopes and dreams."

"It will all be okay. Just listen to what your gut instinct tell you as you go along. You were born to do great things, so your inner self is going to keep you headed down the right path," Ditri said calmly.

"You mean my dreams?" Faline asked. "They seem so real sometimes, and other times I seem to space out while I am awake and see things."

Ditri smiled. "Yes, those are visions you are having. It is one of your many gifts and they should never be shrugged off. Always pay close attention to them, just as you did with the sword you now possess."

Faline turned and looked at her new possession smiling. "I will keep that in mind."

"Now as far as your army, there are beasts we can get to help you and others that are going to need to see you for themselves. That means you will have to travel to where they hide themselves and call them out," Ditri said before she yawned.

"I don't suppose you want to elaborate on that?" Faline asked watching Ditri as she twisted her head a little allowing it to crack some of the bones in her neck.

"Rom will most assuredly gather up as many magi as he can, whereas I can get the dragon dens to co-operate. Rom may be able to get the unicorns to join you, but like the trolls, lions, fairies and elves, they have been scarred by the last wars and may be unwilling to join in anything right away," Ditri replied.

"Trolls? Fairies? Unicorns? I am just so, I'm not sure what I am right now," Nolan said shaking his head in disbelief.

"You are a silly boy," Ditri said glaring at him. "If you have not figured anything out by now, then you aren't going to. Sitting here with a dragon and a wizard isn't enough to make you believe in all of this, huh?"

"No, that's not what I'm saying at all." Nolan stammered trying to defend himself. "I just, it's a lot to take in, that's all."

"Well finish it up then and get it together," Ditri grumbled. "If not you are useless past this point."

Nolan hung his head as he lay a blanket down for himself and took Faline's to get it ready for her as well. He knew that Faline understood where he was coming from even if the others didn't. Just because they had been around all this for so long, he and Faline were rookies as far as war and creating armies, was concerned especially those consisting of creatures out of fairy tales.

"Don't be so hard on him," Faline protested. "He will be all right after he gets over the fact that our bedtime stories were not just stories. It's a lot for anyone to handle really, and we are doing the best we can."

Rom smiled at her and stretched out on his blanket. "Well, I say if there are no more questions, it is time for some sleep. We still must get you three back home."

Faline nodded. "Just so I am clear, between the three of us an army of all sorts is going to be created so I can battle the kings and take over therefore making the kingdom a whole again?"

"Yes, that about sums it up," Rom said quietly.

"Is there going to be a lot of death?" Faline whispered.

"With any war comes death somewhere along the way," Rom answered. "It is unavoidable, trust me."

"Okay," she sighed as she lay down beside Cairo. "I guess we will have to try and limit the amount on our own side then."

Rom smiled. "We will do our best, Faline. Now get some sleep."

Faline yawned and snuggled close to her furry companion. "No problem, I'm pooped. Good night everyone."

"Good night, Faline." Nolan forced through a yawn.

"Good night little saviour." Rom chuckled as he rolled over and curled up next to the fire.

Faline smiled while stroking Cairo's fur, feeling completely content to be where she was, surrounded by friends, a warm fire, a somewhat full belly and a new sword that was going to help her along the way. She grabbed the sword from its resting place beside her bag running her fingers over the beautifully crafted lion's head and watched the light of the fire dance off the emeralds and rubies that lay on the cross guard.

"Its name is Lion Heart," Ditri whispered so as not to disturb Faline's slumbering friends.

"What's that?" Faline asked as she rolled to look over at Ditri.

"The sword, the sword's name is Lion Heart." Ditri repeated. "It was forged for the original king of the north from the diamonds that used to be plentiful in this very mountain. The northern kingdom bears a red lion on their banner, hence its name being Lion Heart and most of the jewels on it being rubies."

"Fascinating," Faline said softly as she studied the sword in her hands. "Are there still diamonds here or did they all get mined out?"

"No, child," Ditri laughed quietly. "Mt. Diamanti hasn't had gemstones left in it for hundreds of years. It should really be called Mt. Barren these days as there is nothing left to it really except for the fresh water that flows through it to the river from the natural spring underneath. That happened by accident while the kings peons were mining for the last of the diamonds here. Instead of finding gems, they found water. They had dug so deep into the belly of this place."

"Honestly, digging all the way through a mountain is a pretty great accomplishment in my own opinion," Faline responded smiling. "I couldn't dig through a mountain."

"Regardless, they still ruined this wonder of nature with their greed," Ditri grumbled. "I just wanted to fill you in on some of its history before you got some sleep."

"Thank you, Ditri, I enjoy learning all that I can," Faline smiled up at her.

"I hope you gather as much knowledge as possible, my friend. Battle skills are all well and good, but knowledge is a powerful weapon. Know everything you possibly can about the people you are going up against, it will help you more than you will ever know," Ditri told her quietly. "Now get some sleep. The next several days you will venture home, once you get there talk to Tobias. He can fill you in on the kings when you are ready."

"All right, I will make sure to do that. Rest well Ditri," Faline said as she set Lion Heart back on the ground with her bag as she curled up once more with Cairo.

Unlike most nights Faline found sleep came with ease being in the cave with the fire keeping her warm, and her friends being all around her. As she slept her mind wandered off to her little valley home, the little wooden houses bustling with all the people that lived there. They seemed to be sort of panicked, scrambling about this way and that. Faline noticed that some of the animals were loose as Adam and Enid Platter were running down the dirt road chasing after some of their pigs, while Jeb and Agnes Fritz were running in another direction after their sheep. What was going on? Faline wondered.

Lilly and Graham along with a few others from the far end of the valley came high tailing it in towards Faline's house, where she saw standing in front of it was her mother, father, grandfather and Margo. They were all shouting and pointing, at who or what they were saying, Faline couldn't tell just yet. She did however need to know.

As the visions played out in her mind she finally saw what the people were all so upset about: there were men coming in from all directions and she assumed they were the cause of the animals being set loose. These were no ordinary men, these were men sent by the king. All of them were dressed in armour as black as the midnight sky, with a golden dragon embossed on the breast plate. They each carried a large gold sword and a black shield with the same golden dragon embossed on it. They were ransacking each of the houses that they came to, searching for something or someone becoming more furious each time they came out empty handed.

Faline watched in horror as they made it to her front door shoving her mother out of the way and onto the ground. Drake lashed out at the man who pushed her only to get a sword hilt to the face as punishment for raising a hand to a knight. They left them both there on the ground as they walked to Tobias' house, which to Faline's surprise looked completely vacant. She watched as the king's guard smashed everything they laid their hands on doors, windows, tables, chairs, just everything. It was so terrible what these men were doing.

They surrounded one of the Platters' little pigs and killed it before stuffing it into a bag and latching it to one of their horses. The men dressed in the black armour looked as if they were laughing as the people from Faline's quiet village were scared and upset. They took some torches from their saddle bags and set them alight. As the men began walking towards the houses, torches in hand, Faline sat up still half asleep, screaming.

"NO!" she cried. "Not this, not now!"

Rom, Nolan, Ditri and Cairo were all at full alert by her sudden outburst looking all around trying to figure out what was happening and why.

"Faline!" Rom walked over and knelt by her side. "Faline, wake up!"

She blinked a few times and stared at him, her face ashen. "Rom, I have to go home."

"What happened?" Rom asked now worried about her.

Faline took a minute to collect her thoughts and explained to all of them what she had just dreamt about. Nolan looked as if he were going to be sick not knowing where his father was in all this mess. It bothered them all that he wasn't there.

"The army belonged to Balthazar, he was probably looking for Tobias and Nolan," Rom said quietly. "I agree that you two need to get on home and figure out what is going on but take care that they may come back and try to finish the job."

"Not to mention that we might stumble across some of them on the way home." Nolan muttered.

"I'm not worried about any of that. I am worried that they burned the village down!" Faline shouted angrily. "I am leaving, with or without any of you!"

With that Faline grabbed her bag, her new sword, scratched Cairo on the head and began walking towards the entrance. She turned around long enough to thank Ditri for her hospitality and was gone, leaving Rom and a slack jawed Nolan standing there, not believing she would leave them behind. They looked at one another and raced to catch up to her in the dark to make their way back home. None of them knew what they were going to see when they got there; they would find out soon enough.

Acknowledgements

I began writing this book as I sat at my laptop playing a little game one random morning. Characters began flooding my head, along with villages, armies and creatures. When I told my husband I was writing a book it took him until I was starting chapter two to realise that, yes, I was really writing a book. He has been super supportive along with my daughter both of whom have given my time and space to be creative and write this book. To both of you, thank you for believing in me, I love you. An extra thanks to my husband for taking the extra time to proofread for me and give me your feedback. Every little bit helps, even when it seems to take forever because you have an impatient wife.

To my mother who has always been supportive of everything I have done throughout my life, even when she didn't like it. When I told her I was writing a book, she couldn't have been happier for me and is patiently waiting for the first signed copy. She has always told me I could do or be anything I wanted. I thought that was just a thing moms said until I started writing. Mom, you have been the biggest inspiration in my life. Your courage and dedication to everything you tackle in life is astounding and it makes me proud to be yours. Thank you for being my mom and giving me all you have. I love you to the moon and back.

My dad, who had the spectacular response of, "Oh you are writing a book? Cool." This is what you receive from a biker dad just for the record. I have a great dad and find that I wouldn't have him any other way than sitting atop a Harley and riding into the sunset. He is not the mushy type, but he is a great dad. Throughout my life he has taught me a great deal of things, like how to landscape, and wield a chainsaw to properly take down a tree. Coolest dad ever! I love you dad.

To my Grandma Jane who told me once that I was going to write something some day and share it with the world. She is no longer with me and I didn't make this a reality until many years after she left. I did however make it happen, and she said I would. She was one of my biggest role models as I grew up. Her vocabulary, grammar, the way she was able to communicate with people, it was all so amazing. She rarely cursed and said, "People who need to swear to get their point across lack the vocabulary to hold an intelligent conversation." She was and is an amazing woman. Thank you Gram for always believing that I was something better than I thought I was. I hope I am making you proud. I love you.

To one of my buddies who took the time to read the whole thing and give me an honest opinion, Ryan, I thank you. You were supportive and truthful and it helped me a lot. You told me to take the ideas I had and run with them. Here they are in a big book. You have a story too, take it back out, re-read it, and finish it up. You are just as creative as I am and I have all the faith in the world that you can find a way to make it into an awesome book. I look forward to reading it in the future.

To the rest of my family and friends who have been with me through the writing of this book, thank you for your love and support. It means a lot to have people around that care about you and what you are doing. I appreciate all of you.

Printed in the USA
CPSIA information can be obtained
at www.ICGtesting.com
CBHW030416070824
12782CB00030B/441